A CLAIM OF FORTUNE

SHIFTER CITY FATED MATES
BOOK 3

JAYMIN EVE

Jaymin Eve
A Claim of Fortune: Shifter City Fated Mates #3
Copyright © Jaymin Eve 2025

All rights reserved
First published in 2025
Eve, Jaymin
A Claim of Fortune: Shifter City Fated Mates #3

Cover and art: Tamara Kokic
Editing: Ocean's Edge Editing
Proofing: Jaymin Eve's Badass Team

CONTENT WARNING

Your mental health is important to me! If you need any specific information about what might be included, please contact me at jaymineve@gmail.com

Triggers include:

- Death of a parent
- Discussion of suicide
- Abuse by a parent
- Past trauma/flashbacks
- Panic attacks
- Scenes of sexual nature with dominant alpha males.
- Violence
- Stalking
- Kidnapping
- Graphic death
- Blood and Gore
- Therapy and healing in unconventional ways

STAY UP TO DATE

You can keep up to date with my releases by following me on Instagram, joining my Facebook group The Nerd Herd, or subscribing to my newsletter.

This is where you'll get all updates and information about my worlds and publishing schedule.

CATCH UP ON THE WORLD

A CURSE OF FATE

Emmeline is a wolf shifter in a world where all packs live in cities, with multiple alphas, betas, deltas, and rarer: omegas. These designations form quintets, packs of five, and are governed by alpha councils. Emme is an omega, just like her mom, who was killed by a pack of alphas when Emme was fourteen. This was the catalyst for her to run from the cities and the alphas who controlled them. She swore she would never end up like her mom.

Fast forward over a decade and Emme has been moving between human cities, avoiding the five major pack cities at all costs, and keeping her head down. An unfortunate series of events finds her in the path of an alpha with tracking capabilities. She runs again, but he tracks her and drags her to Golden Claw, the largest of the five pack cities.

Here, she faces the Alpha Council, charged as being a rogue—a shifter without a pack city affiliation. But when they discover she's an omega, they are less inclined to give her the usual sentence of death.

When one of the most powerful alphas scents Emme as his true mate, it's Emme's worst nightmare, as she believes that if she bonds with an alpha she'll be killed the same way her mom was. Her mom's pack was a scent match too, and they still murdered her.

When she finds out that this alpha is one of four alphas in her scent match, she believes her life is over. Quintets are usually made up of one alpha and a mix of delta and betas. Her pack, though, consists of four alpha males, making it strong, and *dangerous*, especially for an omega.

Just like her mom's.

Emme has no choice but to reject the alphas, which receives mixed reactions from the four.

Hunter, the entitled alpha, doesn't give up when he sets his mind to something, and he's determined to win her into the pack by whatever means necessary. He convinces her to move into their pack house for a while, save up some money, and not worry. He also promises not to bond her without her explicitly begging for it. Hunter is an obsessive and possessive alpha stalker, with a goal of keeping his pack safe, and as strong as it can be. Also… hand tattoo. That is all.

Kellan, the golden retriever alpha, comes in with his sweet and kind soul (though don't underestimate his ability to rip another shifter's head from his shoulders if he looks the wrong way at Emme). Kellan would follow her through this life and into the next no hesitation. Emme, who has been alone her whole life, is won over by Kellan's sweet and unconditional obsession with her.

Slade is a scary dragon shifter. Cold and clinical, he has an observational interest in Emme. She certainly intrigues him. He keeps an eye on her through security cameras, and is as intense a stalker as Hunter, just in a less forceful way. For now.

Finley, a bear shifter, doesn't take her rejection well. It triggers his childhood trauma where he was rejected and hurt by his family. He decides she is toxic to them all, and he's determined not to have her in their lives.

Once she's in the pack house, bonds start to form between Emme, Kellan, and Hunter, despite her best efforts to reject them. As an omega, who can stand outside of normal pack dominance, she is desired amongst alphas, and her pack is determined to keep her safe.

During one attempted kidnapping by a guard on the Reeves pack security team, she fights back long enough for Hunter and Kellan to arrive and destroy the shifter, which seals another portion of their relationship. Emme grows even closer to those two.

While investigating the attempted kidnapping to find the source—the guard was a hired hit— the end of *A Curse of Fate* finds Emme and Slade on motorcycles, heading to an interrogation. On the way, they're blown up by a rocket, and an injured Emme is thrown into the back of a van before she blacks out. When she wakes again, she's in a basement cell, bars blocking her exit. Slade is across from her, in another cell, restrained by magical bands.

When her kidnapper steps into the room, she freaks out because it's the entitled alpha of her mom's old pack. They've been searching for her, and when she showed up on the pack register for Golden City, they took their opportunity to track her down.
    This is where *A Twist of Luck* begins.

CATCH UP ON THE WORLD

A TWIST OF LUCK

Book two starts with Emme and Slade as prisoners in Silver City, where they were taken and held by Blaine and his alpha pack. The Rogers pack (Blaine's pack) uses magic to keep them contained. Meanwhile, back in Golden Claw, the Reeves pack (Emme's pack) are hunting down anyone involved for information to find out where their kidnapped pack members are. They get a lead they're in Silver City and jump on their plane to head straight there.

In Silver City, the kidnappers underestimate Slade's power, and he busts through his cell to comfort Emme during a panic attack, which is triggered by being held captive again by Blaine and his pack, as they destroyed her mother and tormented her growing up.

After Slade scares away everyone in the house, they head upstairs to discover the house is magically locked down, and it'll take the dragon shifter hours to smash them out. Thankfully, by the time he breaks through, the rest of the Reeves pack have shown up with their own witch in their ranks. To fight magic, you need magic.

They decide to regroup and head back to Golden Claw, since Blaine and his pack have vanished, but on the way to their plane they're ambushed by a witch. She tries to hit Emme with a knockout spell but Kellan gets in between them. He's taken down by a spell that can only be lifted by the witch who cast it, and unfortunately, she's dead via Sladdy—I mean Slade, the dragon baddie.

They rush an unconscious and possibly dying Kellan back to Golden Claw and demand their ally witch (Jewels) figure out how to save him. With time running out, they do everything they can to keep Kellan's energy flowing strongly, including *almost* naked pack huddles.

Eventually, Jewels and her coven come up with a solution, but they're afraid Kellan is too weak to fight, even with the counterspell. With no other option, they give him the spell, and in the end he's so weak that he can't survive, and Emme makes the choice to bond with him in the hopes she might be able to share some of her energy.

Which works!

She gives him the strength to fight the spell. This is one of her greatest fears in bonding to alphas, as she feels this is what destroyed her mother, but she notices no changes with Kellan, and he doesn't try to take any more of her wolf essence.

After this, everything is going fine, as they deal with the Alpha Council and what the future plans for Blaine and his pack are. Silver City puts up roadblocks to hunt the Rogers pack, and it's all red tape and paperwork getting in the way.

Toward the end of the book, Emme bonds with Hunter (her entitled alpha) in a lovely *Hunter and Prey* scenario, through the forests of Golden Claw. She makes this decision because she loves him and trusts him completely. He's done nothing but support and care for her almost since the first moment he dragged her into their lives.

Bonding is still an experiment at this stage, as Emme still doesn't know what will happen if she bonds all four alphas, but she's willing to try. Her life was empty without them, and they've shown time and time again that they're nothing like her mom's pack.

She also grows closer to Slade (dragon shifter, aka scary motherfucker) as he attempts to teach her how to defend herself, which leads into a prank war. During one of these pranks, where Emme turns off the cameras momentarily, she gets herself into a bit of trouble.

She opens a book in her room about omegas and packs. A book brought to her by Chelsea from the Thenguard pack. A book she hasn't touched since that attack at the guard house (in book 1), but which she hoped might give her answers to her designation as an omega in a pack of alphas.

The book is spelled, and has been waiting there all this time for her to open it. As soon as she flips the page, the spell is enacted and she's under Chelsea's control. It binds the two omegas together, and she has to follow Chelsea's actions.

Chelsea takes her far from Golden Claw and deposits her in an old house, right into the clutches of the very alpha who's been trying to kidnap her all along. It's not the alpha she expected. Blaine is still there of course, but he has a boss (or father, more accurately) running the show.
　　Who also happens to be Hunter's father.

He is the big bad alpha behind everything. He has been kidnapping omegas and experimenting on them for years. It was him who orchestrated Blaine and his pack into her mother's life, and got them to drain her mother until she chose to end her life.
　　And now he wants Emme.

Hunter's father calls a familiar-looking shifter into the old house. If it weren't for the scar on his face and shorter hair, the shifter stalking toward her would exactly resemble Slade Riverson.

This darker, scarier version of *her* dragon bites and forcibly claims her under his alpha's command, and with the last of Chelsea's control still flooding her system, she's forced to bite him back and seal the bond forever.
　　This is where *A Claim of Fortune* begins.

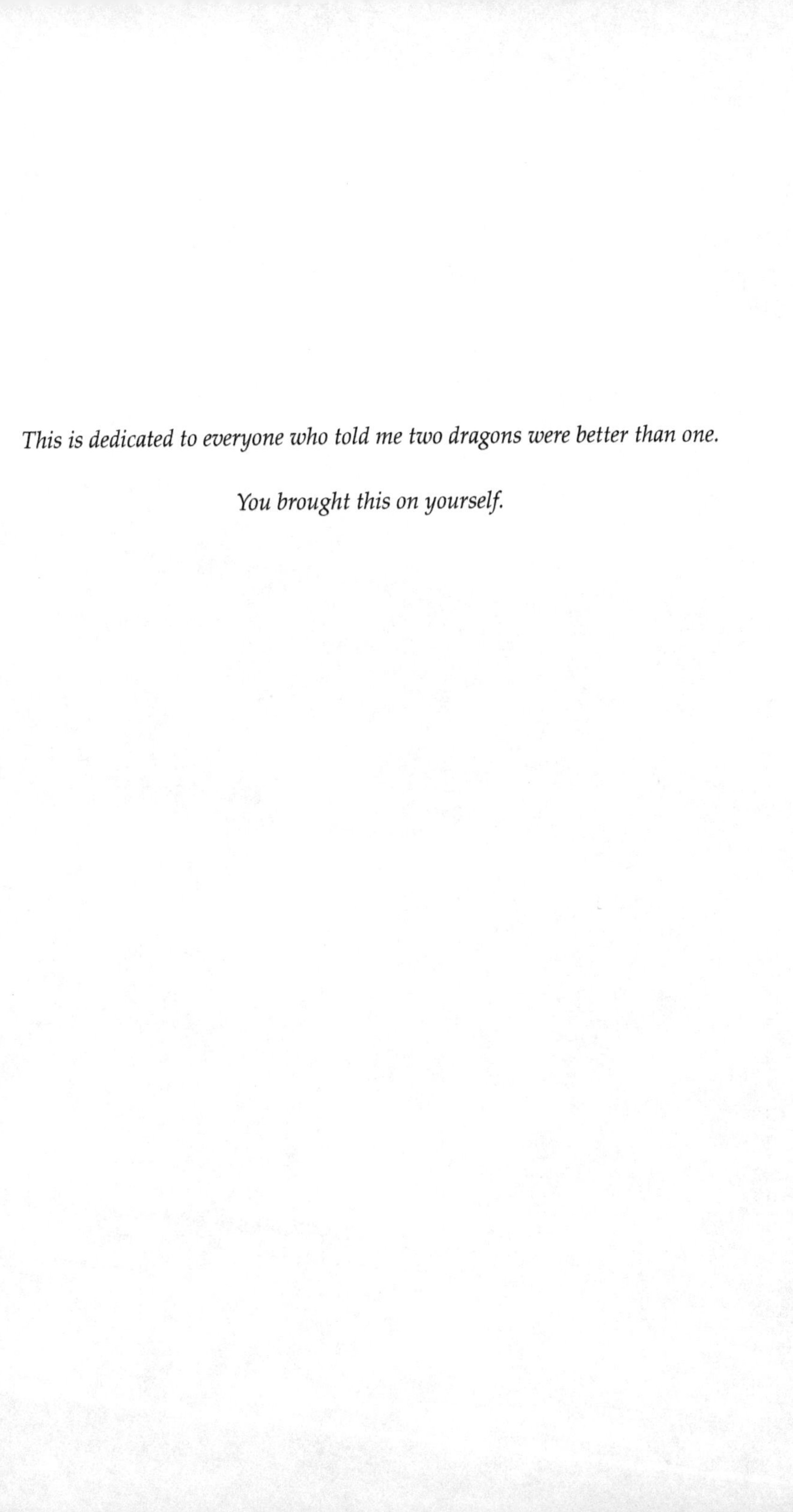

This is dedicated to everyone who told me two dragons were better than one.

You brought this on yourself.

CHAPTER 1

FINLEY

It was a fairly obvious statement to say that you couldn't choose your family, but in the shifter world, it wasn't technically true. You couldn't choose the family you were born into, and I sure as fuck didn't want to exist in the same universe as my mother, let alone be part of her den, but you could choose your future pack. The quintet you would spend most of your adult life with.

Unless of course you were part of a scent match.

Then fate chose for you…

Lucky for fate, I loved the brothers I'd found in the Reeves pack, and while I'd always miss and mourn Tommy, the younger brother I'd failed to protect, the reality was that we'd never really been that close. Thanks to our mom's instabilities.

My pack and Kenzo had saved my sanity, and were the only reason I existed today.

At almost twenty-seven, I felt like I was a thousand years old and broken beyond repair.

Even with my hands buried deep in an engine, the scent of oil and diesel filling the air, it was all bittersweet. I'd hated my father for at least eighty percent of the time I'd known him, but the other twenty percent there'd been moments when he acted like a parent. It was during a few of these *moments of clarity* that he taught me how to take cars apart and then put them back together. A hobby I still found soothing.

Or I should say a hobby I *usually* found soothing, just not today.

Today, my bear was in a frenzy, and I had no fucking clue what was riling him so hard. It had been a long time since he'd raged with this intensity—not since the day my world imploded and I'd destroyed my last immediate family member. After *she'd* slaughtered Dad and Tommy.

Rubbing at the back of my neck, black grease slicked across my skin.

My tension continued to rise. I pulled out my phone, leaving more black marks as I slid it open and checked messages. I didn't have the intense instincts of the wolves, but when my danger radar kicked in, it was rarely wrong.

I checked the message thread in the family chat to find just one from Hunter asking Emme if everything was okay. No doubt in response to the camera system scrambling for a few minutes earlier. We all got the alert, and we all knew it was Emme fucking with Slade.

At this point, I was invested in their prank war, not that I'd ever admit it out loud. Not even if someone was skinning my fucking balls with a rusty knife.

Emme, of course, hadn't responded to Hunter, and for once I didn't call her a *selfish bitch* in my head. She never had her phone, and it reminded me of how I was when I first found my pack. Growing up, we hadn't been allowed phones. Mother didn't want us easily accessible to anyone other than her, and I had no one to call anyway—except Kenzo and his family, who lived nearby.

It took me years to remember to take a phone with me, which was a trauma response to my upbringing. Emme was the same. We both had more *traumas* than I could fucking count, and many of them were similar. Except for her ability to sleep. I could almost hate her for that one alone.

I hadn't slept well in years… except for that night we pack huddled, where my fight or flight response calmed. I was going to call that one *exhaustion and stress over almost losing Kellan* getting the best of me.

When I found nothing on my phone to alert me to my bear's unease, I was about to pocket it, when a message came through from Kellan.

> Kel: Brother, look at the bike! She's going to lose her
> mind. This is perfect for our pretty mate.

I clicked the attached image and had to admit that Kellan had outdone himself. The motorcycle was still her favorite make and model, a *Ducati Panigale V4R*, but this time it was sleek and black, with just splashes of the pink. There was a wolf head painted in pink flames across the tank, the tail morphing into the pink seat. There was also a matching helmet and jacket in the picture.

After almost losing Kellan to magic, I was on my best behavior when it came to *Emmeline*, and with that in mind, I shot back the most positive text I could manage.

> Fin: She's going to love it, bro. You did good.

> Kel: This is part one of her birthday present. Now I'm
> just waiting for part two to arrive.

Wait… it was her birthday? My fingers moved before I thought it through, and when I hit send, I had to shake my fucking head at how pathetic I was to even care.

> Fin: When's her birthday?

I shouldn't want to know more about the omega, when she hadn't wanted to know us. Sure, she might end up staying, and I was working hard on acting less like an asshole, but that was as far as it went. Birthdays were personal.

> Kel: The 12th, Fin!! Only a couple more days. You
> better figure out what to get her because you need
> an apology present too. DO NOT COMBINE THEM.
> *Shocked emoji face* *Crying emoji face* *Begging
> hands emoji*

A derisive snort escaped me.

> Fin: Never gonna happen, Kellan. You need to keep the dreams and happily ever afters on your side.

> Kel: *Laughing face emoji* *Laughing face emoji*

> Kel: Good one, Grouchy. You might fool everyone else in the world, but not me. I see you. I fucking see you.

My chest ached again, and even when I palmed it with the heel of my hand, it refused to ease up.

> Fin: Stop stirring where you shouldn't. Some trauma is meant to rest. For all of our sanity.

Kellan took more than a few minutes to respond.

> Kel: I won't ever let you rest in your darkness. I promised you that long ago, and now… you're just going to have to trust me. Emme is the salvation you never knew was yours. She's our fucking salvation, brother.

A million angry rebuttals and responses flooded my brain, but I slipped the phone into my pocket before I voiced—*or texted*—even one of them. The problem with salvation was it could also be your downfall. I didn't have any more downfalls in me. The next would be *my last*.

Slowing my breathing, I forced the tendrils of scattered thoughts and pain deeper inside and tried to focus on the engine. But there was no settling tonight. More than the stirring messages from Kellan, my bear continued huffing and puffing inside like he was channeling the Big Bad Wolf. *Wrong fucking fairytale, friend.*

Goldilocks was more our style, but then again, the pinkish gold of Emme's hair hit a little too close to home with that human fairy tale.

After returning my tools neatly to their respective shelves and drawers—the need to take care of my items was heavily ingrained after years of having nothing to my name—I trudged upstairs to shower and change. It was almost dinner, and part of the message Emme hadn't read in our group chat was Hunter reminding everyone that we would be eating together.

He'd also tagged on a brief note about the Alpha Council convening again tomorrow to discuss plans for the Rogers pack, and vote on them being barred from Golden Claw, using their scents panels as identification. Most shifters had blood and scent panels taken when they first revealed their beasts, and that information was logged with the national register. It was how we found our scent matches and missing family. But it could also be used to control our travel and entry to the cities.

Emme would definitely be interested in any plan that kept Blaine and his pack away from her—whenever she remembered to check her messages.

As I walked past her room, I heard the chime of her phone and paused for the telltale sounds of her steps moving toward it, but there was only an echoing silence. Her scent was very faint too, and when my bear stirred again, I was compelled by forces beyond me to lift my hand and knock on her door. I never sought out the omega without reason, but the unease inside was all instinct.

There was no response to my knock, and I couldn't hear or sense her anywhere else in the house. Florence was cleaning Kellan's room, Gerald was in the kitchen, but the omega who was, in general, an annoyingly strong beacon for me, didn't appear to be anywhere close by.

With a growl, I hit the handle to slam open her door and stormed into her room. Her scent was stronger in here, but there was no sign of Emme.

Where the hell did she go?

I'd seen her return to her room earlier after pranking Slade, and… *shit*, her scent hadn't taunted me as per usual. She'd clearly masked it, which made sense with her prank, but now I couldn't track her.

Prowling through her room I checked the bathroom too, giving no fucks if she was naked or in the bath. This omega was trouble, and now I was worried she was *in trouble* again.

My bear roared, and for once I didn't fight my mate bond instinct. I let myself rage over our missing mate. There was no doubt in my mind that Emme had either run away or been taken again, right out from under us.

She promised not to run without telling us first. She'd made that promise, and while I wasn't sure I trusted her enough to keep it, for now, I decided to give her the benefit of the doubt.

Until I reached her desk and found a neatly penned note, every word precise and perfectly spelled.

Dear Alphas, I can't do this anymore. I don't trust you all not to force the bonds, and I need to forge a life away from the risk of being part of a completed quintet. If you care for me, you won't come after me. This was never meant to be. Emmeline.

My roar was loud, rattling windows and sending all birds in the vicinity of our pack house screeching into the sky. At first, pure rage was the driving force, and then sorrow as I fell to my knees, clutching the evidence of her betrayal.

For many minutes I mourned a loss that shouldn't have hurt this much; I hadn't let myself get close enough to feel the bond.

Somehow, I still did though.

Somehow, she'd still burrowed her way into my chest and into my fucking bear's soul, and now we had to figure out how to deal with it.

Ripping out my phone, I shot off a text in the group chat with my brothers.

Fin: She's gone.

Hunter rang almost immediately, even as the others shot back messages. "What do you mean?" he rumbled, spitting out each word.

"I mean, she's not in the fucking house and she left a goodbye note."

Props to Hunter for even understanding me through the growls of my distraught bear.

"There's no way," he said, voice shaking. "Our bond is stable. Her emotions are very calm, almost clinical—"

When he broke off, I pressed the phone harder to my ear, desperate to hear his next words.

"She's too subdued," he murmured in a raw whisper. "If she was running, she'd be sad and panicked. She'd be hurting and screaming for her mates. She can't leave us without pain now, but it's as if she's not even *feeling anything.*"

I straightened, letting the note fall to the desk as a sliver of logic pushed through my panicked mind. "The note is also very neat and spelled completely correctly," I said quickly. "And she signed it as Emmeline… She never calls herself that. This has to be fake, right?"

Or I was just a stupid, hopeful bastard desperately attempting to keep my sanity intact.

Hunter growled so loudly my ear ached. "I'll be home in ten."

The phone went dead and I was left with a dozen frantic messages from Kellan. Slade called me right after, having no doubt listened to my exchange with Hunter through our security cameras.

"She scrambled the cameras to prank me," he growled down the line, and I could feel the heat of his rage, even over the phone. "I didn't watch the footage. I wanted to experience it all— *FUCK!*"

If my eardrum wasn't already busted from Hunter, Slade had finished the job.

"I saw her not long ago," I managed to get out. "She can't have gone far. I'm going to head out and search for clues, but just know it's going to be harder to track her scent. She used the blocking spray as part of her prank."

I was front row and center to Slade's heavy breathing until he uttered in a tone so flat it was chilling: "When I get my hands on whoever touched our omega, they will pray for death."

With that, he was gone as well, and I threw my phone on the bed. I'd be shifting to track her as my bear's nose could detect even the smallest scent fluctuation. If I got on the right path, eventually that spray would wear off, and I'd be able to hunt her down.

Giving her room another once-over for clues, I noticed her window was slightly ajar, and a sniff along the sill produced a minute trace of her scent. Without another thought, I ditched my clothes and shifted to my bear, launching through the window. With the glass and shutters shattering around me, I landed heavily on the ground below, Florence's shriek following the rumble of the house.

I was out of control, lost to the rage of my beast, unable to do more than track our prey.

There was no time to lose, and waiting for the others would cost another ten minutes at least, allowing whoever had Emme to get too much distance on us.

I was the best chance of closing that gap.

The dusting of snow from the previous day had already melted, leaving the ground muddy, which helped me track Emme's steps across our estate. At the back perimeter, a fence lay on the ground, looking like it had been blasted inward.

There was the faintest scent of sulfur coating the area, and my hackles raised at the way magic was screwing with our lives once again. Those with magic were at the advantage, which had me in a full blown rage.

Beyond our territory, Emme's footprints joined a set of boots, which were small like hers, and I finally picked up a faint scent. Only it wasn't Emme's.

Unsure if this other shifter was involved, or if they'd been here recently for another reason, I followed the tracks until I reached a clearing filled with the distinct odor of burning oil. An older-model vehicle with an engine in need of repair, which was unusual for Golden Claw.

Resisting the urge to bellow, I followed the burning oil all the way to the front gate, finding security standing in the shadows. One stepped forward as I approached, before backing up just as quickly when he realized I was not only in bear form—I was in enraged bear form.

For a long second, my bear wouldn't let me change back, but when I reminded him that we wouldn't get the information if I couldn't ask questions, he released his hold.

Even in my human skin, I could scent that same shifter who'd been behind our house, and I swore her low citrus tones intermingled with Emme's sweetness. *Chelsea.*

Could the other omega be involved somehow? As far as I knew, the two of them weren't really friends, and didn't hang out. I wasn't sure Emme had even contacted her since the day she'd dropped those books off. But her scent was definitely here, and I would be finding out why.

"Did you let two omegas leave Golden Claw?" I snapped at the closest guard, who I was fairly sure was an enforcer, though his name eluded me in my current state.

The wolf shifter didn't even flinch. "Nope," he spat out, eyes hard. "No one has been out of here in hours."

I sensed the lie, but his balls of steel wouldn't save him today. Lashing out with my hand, long claws topped my fingertips, and I cut through his chest.

His wolf's howl rang out through the night, and I withdrew slightly to give him a shot at the truth. One last fucking chance.

"Let's try this again," I rumbled quickly, aware that with every second wasted here, Emme was getting farther away. "How fucking long ago did you let Chelsea of the Thenguard pack steal my mate? What car were they in? What direction did they drive?" There was a chance that Chelsea was also a victim of whoever took Emme, but until I heard differently, I had her pegged as the instigator.

He swallowed roughly, face pale as blood seeped out from behind his hand. "I-I don't know what you're ta-talking about."

I took one step forward, and he choked before backing away. "Wait! She didn't tell me anything. I was paid to look the other way and not sound an alarm. They took off east. It was an old piece-of-shit car. I don't know the make."

He was dead before he hit the ground, and I fought the urge to tear into his body until nothing but blood and entrails remained. Weak-willed shifters had no place in Golden Claw, especially not when they got my pack hurt.

The other guard stood trembling nearby, clutching his Taser which would do very little against me. I'd been preparing myself to withstand the voltage of our technology for years, determined that nothing would ever render me weak or incapacitated again. "Alert the council and the rest of Reeves Pack. Tell them Omega Chelsea of Thenguard Pack has stolen Omega Emmeline of Reeves Pack. I'm going after them in bear form and won't have a phone."

I waited for his shaky nod, and when he reached for his radio I knew he'd do as I asked. Not that it would hurt to add a little extra incentive. I closed in on him: "And if I find out you had anything to do with this, or you didn't pass on the correct message, I will make his death look like a pleasure cruise."

The other guard shook his head so violently that it had to hurt. "I only started my shift a few minutes ago. Owens and Carter were on before that, but Carter is still patrolling. There's usually only one of us here at the gate."

That lined up with what I knew of patrols, so I shifted back into my bear form and left him to pass on my message, hand trembling as he held the radio.

My bear was bigger and far more brutal than most shifters of my kind. I'd learned to be meaner and grouchier, which would hopefully be to my advantage when I caught up to Chelsea and Emme.

Bonded or not, Emmeline Anders was my scent match, and no fucker was stealing her out from under me. Not while I was alive.

CHAPTER 2

EMME

There were too many unfinished parts of my life for it all to end now.

Too many unknowns.

Too many questions.

They kept running over and over in my mind, holding me in a near catatonic state.

Like, I'd never asked Kellan why he read romances, or when he figured out he loved being surrounded by plants. I had no idea who taught Finley to tinker with cars, or if he played hockey when he was younger, and if so, how he managed to get his horrible family to support a relatively expensive sport. I didn't have a clue what Hunter's first invention was, or how he'd created a billion-dollar company under the control of his cruel, ruthless father. Slade was as much a mystery to me today as he ever had been, and I had so many questions for the dragon: When did he learn to hack? How did it feel to fly? Was there fire burning in his dragon's gut moments before it spewed from his mouth? What were his dragon's thoughts like?

For many years I'd had no one in my life. No one to be curious about or ask questions, and then for a brief moment I'd had what felt like *everything*, before it was cruelly taken from me.

I'd been stolen from my pack and forced into the arms of my mother's murderers.

Bonded against my will.

Since then, my mind remained locked down in a state of shock with the world moving around me, but I couldn't open my eyes. I couldn't deal with what had happened in any way other than to retreat into myself completely. I felt the presence of the dragon in the new bite, a ragged, unstable connection. Whatever he'd tried to do, it hadn't worked as well as they hoped.

But it was there. *It was a bond.* We were joined forever through this tenuous connection.

In my broken state, no one touched me, and I was left with the tingling bite and the reminder that life would never be the same again. A true quintet couldn't form when one of the parties was bonded outside the pack. A quintet was five, and I'd brought in a sixth.

A scary, evil dragon who looked like Slade, but even at his coldest, cruelest moments, Slade would never have *forced me* into this bond.

"She needs to eat and drink fluids. We need her at full strength and health, or she'll be less than useless to us."

The slivers of my brain not locked down recognized the voice—Hunter's father. No doubt the alpha had a name, but I had no idea what it was. He'd forever be the devil in my eyes, the evilest shifter in existence, who'd been influencing my life, *in the most negative ways,* since before I was born.

I might not know everything, but I knew of his omega experiments, which included pushing my mother all the way to her suicidal death. This alpha was the reason I'd had to wade through darkness and pain for most of my life. I was sure of it.

"The bitch won't starve herself. She has other mates to worry about."

Blaine *fucking* Rogers. The entitled alpha of my mom's former pack, and Hunter's alleged brother. Apparently, he was still here as well, which had me cringing, seething, and mentally screaming.

"It's been a fucking week—"

Hunter's sperm donor was cut off by a low rumbling growl. The first sound the dragon shifter had made in *a week?* I caught another hint of his maple sweet scent, and I refused to comprehend what that meant.

"The dragon wants us to leave," Blaine scoffed. "If you kill her, dragon, I'll be unhappy. Don't make me unhappy—you know that never ends well. Just get her to eat and drink."

The dragon's response was another guttural rumble, and I almost sighed in relief when the heavy, malicious essence of Hunter's father and *brother* left the room. I had no idea where I was being held now. They'd moved me multiple times in the first few days, and I'd tried to keep up with where we were, but eventually I'd lost myself to the darkness. And here I'd stayed.

Now, though, I was alone with an unhinged shifter, and while he probably wouldn't kill me due to our bond, there was nothing to stop him from hurting me badly.

I'd been fighting against my own destruction for so long that the very thought should have me springing to my feet and battling with everything left inside me.

But my wolf never stirred. She hadn't stirred in days.

I could only assume the forced bonding and distance from my pack had sent her into a depressed hibernation. *Where is our fight or flight?* I demanded, but my weak question was ignored.

The wolf wasn't going to help me here, which meant I had to use other strengths to keep myself safe.

Open your eyes, Emme. Open your fucking eyes.

Rough hands lifted me from where I'd curled in on myself, the hard floor my current companion. I was surprised when he placed me on a bed, the sheets smooth but slightly musty, as if no one had been in here for quite some time.

When the dragon dragged a thick blanket over me, a tiny sliver of the tension that had been holding my muscles in a cramped position for hours eased.

Painful tingles erupted through my limbs, and my neck ached from more than the new, forced mark. My bites from Hunter and Kellan were throbbing too. The physical distance between us was hurting our beasts, and I would continue to wither away in their absence. We hadn't been bonded long enough to withstand the separation, as our beasts screamed out for the connection.

Although my version of screaming appeared to be fading into an abyss.

I felt them out there, but the tethers that bound us were too strained to ease my pain.

As the pressure built in my head, it grew harder to fight the agony. My parched lips parted, cracking on the edges, and I was about to scream when I felt the gentlest tug against my scalp. It took me a few seconds... maybe even an entire minute, to figure out what was happening.

The dragon was brushing my hair.

His touch was hesitant at first, and a little heavy-handed as he tried to pull through my tangled mane, but eventually he figured it out. He settled into a soothing, rhythmic motion that left my scalp tingling, and with each stroke of the brush, my body relaxed deeper into the bed. The ice in my limbs didn't abate, but the relentless screams in my head eased as I focused on the feeling of him and the brush. I wasn't sure I'd ever had my hair brushed before. From what I remembered, when I was young Mom had kept my hair shorn close to my head, and then when I was old enough to care for it myself, I was always the one to brush it. Always.

The heat of the dragon burned into my skin, even though no parts of us touched. He exuded even more heat than Slade, and I wondered if that meant anything. Or was the fire burning in their essence an individual dragon trait?

With each stroke through my now smooth hair, he brought my consciousness closer to the surface, until a raspy sound emerged from my throat. He paused, and left my side for a moment. I tensed when he returned, waiting for what he would do next, flinching when a few drops of water landed on my lips. My thirst roared to life, and I greedily licked them up, my stomach cramped and aching. He continued to sprinkle the water until my mouth was no longer parched.

He started brushing my hair again, and it was the oddest sensation to feel so relaxed and calm in the face of such danger. "What's your name?" The question slipped out as a rusty scrape—those few drops of water weren't enough after a week without fluids.

His movement stilled, leaving the brush against the nape of my neck. When he didn't answer, I wondered if he could talk—I couldn't recall hearing him utter a word in my presence. Was it possible there was a shifter out there less talkative than Slade?

Impressive.

The brush moved again, sending my eyes fluttering until they almost opened.

"*He* calls me dragon, *it*, or creature."

His voice was a low rasp, and weirdly, he had a similar accent to Slade's. *Another dragon trait?* It took me a second to move past the fact that he'd answered to focus on *what* he'd said in that answer. *Dragon, it, or creature.*

As much as I wished it wouldn't, my heart hurt at the significance of what he'd just said. That bastard of an alpha had never given him a name. Debased him until he understood that he was nothing more than a tool to be used.

The part of me that heavily blamed the dragon shifter for his part in raping me of my free will and mate bond eased a fraction with this knowledge. I'd heard humans say that when a dog bit someone, it was, in a lot of cases, the owner's fault—not the animal's. Abuse and lack of training could turn any animal feral.

Was that what had happened here?

Slade at least always had Hunter, along with a fucking name and identity. This shifter, it appeared, had had nothing and no one. Hidden away from society and used as a weapon.

It was this thought that allowed me to finally force my eyes open, the darkness releasing its hold. Instinct had me reaching over my shoulder and grasping his hand.

He stopped moving as I weakly gripped him, the brush once again motionless against my scalp. There was no other reaction from him except for the fire burning under his skin, scorching into my palm.

Tension wrapped around us both, and when he started to rumble, I found a sense of self-preservation and released my hold. In the same second, I scooted away, spinning on the bed, more present in my own body than I had been in days.

The dragon sat on a chair beside the bed, his onyx eyes locked on me as if there was nothing else in the room. We were in a bedroom, dimly lit, and there was a chill in the air now that I'd moved from his natural heat. Even as I backed away, my gaze remained drawn to him in a way I couldn't fight.

Goddess, he looked so much like Slade—a harder, darker version.

"You need to let me go," I whispered.

His cold expression didn't ease. If anything, those granite-like features grew hard enough to give diamonds a run for strength in molecular structure. His focus flicked down for a beat, to the bite he'd left on my shoulder, right beside Hunter's mark.

"Mine," he rasped, sending tingles down my spine and leaving goosebumps all over my skin.

He didn't say that in the same way Hunter did.

My entitled alpha wasn't shy about his claim over me either, but he made it clear that while I was his, he was also mine. A mutual bond.

This dragon believed me to be his possession, and I wondered if that was the only sort of claiming and *love* he'd witnessed in his life. It reminded me again of Slade telling me *I'm a dragon, Snow. I ferociously guard what is mine, and right now, you are my possession. I own you. I watch over you. There's no part of you that is kept from any part of me.*

The main difference though, was that Slade's actions didn't fully back his words. While he wasn't the most outwardly caring and demonstrative of shifters, he protected me and respected my wishes not to bond. He'd promised to teach me to defend myself, helped with my reading, and taken part in a fucking prank war. He'd shown that I was more than a possession to him, even if he wasn't ready to admit it.

This dragon had done nothing of the sort.

There was not one playful bone in his body, and if Slade thought himself a monster, the shifter before me could quite possibly be one.

My gaze fell on the brush in his hand, and I ignored that memory, refusing to soften toward him because of one gentle touch. I couldn't forget what he'd done and why I was in this position.

The dragon's gaze was unwavering. The only flaws on him were a jagged scar that spanned from his left ear to the corner of his lip, and the bite I'd been forced to leave on his throat. With omega magic controlling my actions, I hadn't been able to choose where I bit him. My *claim* had landed on the left side of his throat, just under his scar and ear.

If anything, these "flaws" only added to his dangerously attractive appeal. It was unfortunate that he was a literal weapon of destruction for an evil alpha, and the reason I would never have a future with my pack. Not as a completed quintet anyway.

CHAPTER 3

EMME

When the dragon stood, his movements were far too graceful for a male so large.

I scooted off the bed and pressed myself to the wall.

There was no indication that he was going to immediately kill me, and as we were newly bonded, our beasts would suffer greatly if one of us was to die. But now that I was upright, functioning and focused, I was determined to be more careful in his presence.

My breathing eased when he opened the bathroom door and entered. This place was nothing like the house Chelsea, the omega who kidnapped me, had brought me to. This bedroom was much nicer, with its worn beige carpet, dusty white walls, and antique queen bed in the center of the room.

Through the open door of the bathroom, it appeared plain and generic, with small white tiles and basic amenities. While *the dragon* was occupied, I headed straight for the other closed door, unsurprised to find it locked. Leaning back, I kicked as hard as I could, pain ricocheting up my bare foot and into my calf. I'd been dragged out of the house in sweatpants and bare feet, which still bore the evidence of my forced walk through the mud outside my pack's property.

Far too silently, the dragon appeared at my side like magic, and thrust a glass of water at me. "Drink."

Holy goddess, he was huge, and his darkly captivating presence elevated him beyond his almost seven feet height. The heat and power radiating off him was unlike anything I'd ever experienced before, and the scent was stronger. *Annoyingly,* it took my breath away. *Stupid mate bond.*

"Trying to drug me?" I drawled, letting my irritation spill out. He hadn't drugged me before of course, unless it was super slow-acting, but I'd also been all but comatose. Now, I was up and ready to fight. "There's really no need. I'm apparently trapped here. A fucking prisoner once again."

When he frowned, it pulled at the scar near his full lips, and I resisted the urge to reach out and trace my fingers along the rough surface. I hadn't met many shifters with scars like mine. Most of them healed minor injuries with ease. It took a certain weapon, and a certain level of injury inflicted at a young age, to leave a mark like ours.

Not that having anything in common meant I would be forgiving him. Like I'd told Finley, we all had our traumas, but that didn't give us an excuse to act like an asshole.

"Drink," he commanded again, thrusting the glass hard enough to spill liquid over the sides.

Ignoring him, I stepped around his towering form and beelined into the bathroom, slamming the door behind me. Thirst hit hard when the sink came into view, the white basin pockmarked from age and lack of care. Dipping my head under the faucet, I let the water run for a second before I drank from the stream. It took a long time to quench my thirst, and when I was satisfied, feeling full and sloshy, my bladder took over complaining to remind me I hadn't peed in days.

If I wasn't a shifter, I'd probably have a nice kidney or bladder infection, but thankfully, even with my wolf diminished, I retained enough healing abilities to keep that at bay.

When I was finished with the toilet, I flushed and washed my hands, staring into the mirror over the sink. Thanks to the dragon, my hair was smooth and shiny, while the rest of me looked like a bag of crap. My light pink sweats were marked with streaks of mud, and my face was so pale that the dark circles under my eyes stood out starkly, along with the spattering of freckles across my nose.

The icy blue of my eyes was dull, and I could see the pain I felt deep in my essence spilling out in my gaze. It was the agony of mate bonds stretched far too thin. The irony of it all was the dragon's presence would be helping me cope, as he was *technically* a mate now too.

Mate. My wolf was sluggish, and I debated shifting to try and rouse a stronger reaction from her.

He's not our mate, I snarled back, pissed off and exhausted, as my lungs filled with a sweet scent that I couldn't purge. *Someone open a fucking window!* Only it appeared that there were none in this bathroom, or the bedroom I'd fled from.

Where had they brought me to?

Why had I let myself fall apart to the point where I hadn't been aware of my surroundings?

The fact that I'd shut down so thoroughly after the initial attack was disgraceful. In that vulnerable state, it was only sheer luck I hadn't been hurt or abused far worse. Hunter's father had already shown he had no morals, and he'd do whatever it took to achieve his end goal.

I'd almost made it too easy for him.

I jumped at the slam of a hand against the door. "You cannot escape from there."

That was probably the longest sentence I'd heard this asshole mutter, and it just made me all the angrier. "I know that," I shouted back, enjoying the release of potent fury bubbling inside me. "There's not even a window in here."

That locked door out there was the only possible exit, and I was far too weak to bust through it or the tiled walls. And there was no guarantee there'd be freedom on the other side of these walls anyway. No windows often meant you were in the middle of the house, or in a sub-sub-basement.

I fought against the urge to scream. I had no skills to beat a dragon, not even if my wolf were at full strength, which meant my best bet was to play along as the nice, compliant captive, and try to stay alive long enough for help to arrive.

Or even better, if the opportunity arose to escape, knock this fucker out and save myself.

Sucking in a deep breath, I splashed water on my face, wishing desperately for a shower. There wasn't a chance on this tainted Earth that I'd get naked around that dragon though, so I headed for the door.

When I pulled it open, he loomed on the other side, and as I tilted my head up to meet his gaze with all the false bravado I could muster,

I swore I caught a hint of panic, before his expression was once again dark and impassive.

Locked in his gaze, I regretted my decision to meet his stare. It was terrifying being this close to the dark aura he exuded, and the unhinged edge to his actions sent trickles of fear down my spine.

Fear I decided to cover with bright, inane conversation. "I can't keep calling you dragon or asshole in my head." Ah, whoops. *Staying alive, Emme,* I reminded myself. *Your goal is to stay alive.*

Thankfully his only response was a low rumble, and I hurried on airily. "What do you think about Jason as a possible name?"

Another rumble, and this one held a note of menace. "Okay, okay. Not Jason. What about Richard?" And I'd silently call him dick for funsies. Last name *head.*

The dragon's fists clenched at his sides, and it took absolutely every ounce of my inner fortitude not to step away. "Yeah, you don't really look like a Richard. Okay…" I tapped my chin, as if this was one of life's great questions requiring all my focus. "Samuel?"

The growl was slower this time, as if he didn't hate that name, which told me I was on the right track. "Shaun? Michael? Dominic? Talon?"

As the name for a dragon's claw spilled from my lips, his gaze intensified, and if I'd been a regular shifter, I'd have been swooning or blushing. Alas, this shifter hated his guts for stealing a piece of my soul from me. But I hadn't missed his reaction to that last name.

"Talon," I repeated slowly, letting it roll off my tongue. "You like that name?"

When he nodded, I almost passed out from shock. "Okay, Talon it is."

He rubbed a hand across his face, and I almost lost my resolve to hate him when I saw the confusion tugging at his features. I'd surprised him… and for a brief moment in time, he wore an air of vulnerability.

When he stepped back from where he'd holed me up in the bathroom doorway, I sidled into the room and took a seat on the bed. With the return of silence between us, I found my pulse racing and my hands clammy. "What happens now?' I babbled, desperate to break the quiet intensity. "You've brought me here for a reason… or at least your evil master has. What's the reason?"

Talon kept me locked in his unblinking gaze. "We must complete our bond."

As terrifying as that statement was, I appreciated his honesty. Maybe it wouldn't be as hard as I thought to get all the information I needed from him. "Complete the bond? As in… we're supposed to have sex?" I shook my head. "I will never let you touch me like that. Not ever. Our souls and beasts are bonded from the bite. Why do you need more?"

Talon's growl was deep enough to shatter windows—if there'd been any in this room of course. "I don't want to have to *take* your omega powers… I want you to give them to me."

My breath hitched, and while I'd known stealing my powers was the end goal for this forced bonding, it still took me by surprise. "He wants me to boost your powers and turn your beast into an even greater weapon." As I voiced the horror out loud, I wondered if Talon understood the full ramifications of what they planned to do. Did he know I could lose my wolf?

Talon didn't confirm it, but he also didn't deny it.

I shook my head. "I will never give you one iota of my power. You'll have to kill me first." I hadn't even realized I'd leapt to my feet on the bed until I was meeting his hostile stare. "I won't comply with you raping my energy. You've already taken too much from me."

Like my quintet, and my free will, and my sense of safety.

All of which was unforgiveable.

"You have no choice."

He was probably right, but I sure as shit wasn't about to make it easy for him.

"When will Hunter's father return?"

Talon took a step towards me, and I shuffled back on the bed, keeping him in my line of sight. "Alpha Fletcher Davenport will return via helicopter in two days. He expects the task to be completed. If we fail, there'll be consequences."

A matter-of-fact statement, and now I had the name of the asshole haunting my existence: Fletcher Davenport. I'd been expecting something more along the lines of *Evil Motherfucker*, but I supposed Fletcher would do.

"Why do you comply with him?" I asked, genuinely curious. "He treats you like an object, a weapon he owns and can do whatever he wants with. You didn't even have a name, Talon. He doesn't give a single shit about you."

When he tilted his head to the side, observing me animalistically, it reminded me so much of Slade that I almost lost my composure.

"He is my family," he said in a low, strangely soft voice.

Which was wrong on so many levels. "Family don't call you *it*. I promise. You deserve better than that poor excuse of an alpha. Just kill him and find your freedom."

I had no idea what would happen to me if Talon *found his freedom*, but at least Fletcher would no longer have this extremely powerful weapon under his control. We could save a lot of lives just by removing this one player from his board.

Now all I needed was the dragon to be in on the plan.

CHAPTER 4

HUNTER

A week. An endless, agonizing week had passed in our search for Emme.

"How can there be no trace of her?" Kellan snarled, his phone pressed to his ear as I floored the Range Rover, on another endless chase which would probably lead nowhere. Once again.

We'd followed leads. We'd killed and destroyed and broken our council down to pieces, but in the end, no matter how much blood we'd spilled, no one in Golden Claw knew where she was, including my former best friend, Sorenson. He was involved in this somehow, and had disappeared the same night as Emme.

"We're in Silver City." Kellan rested his head on his hand, exhaustion and pain dragging his features. "It's the only lead we've got at the moment. Find us something else. Now. You're the best tracker in the business. You're the fucking one who found her in Florida in the first place. How could you have lost her scent?"

I pressed my foot harder to the gas, swinging around a corner to follow the navigation system directions. We'd received a tip that the Rogers pack were holed up deep in the industrial area of Silver City. We'd staked out their compound earlier today but there'd been no sign of life, so this was our last hope. It might have been quicker if we had Slade's help, but his dragon had taken control, sending him hunting after Emme in his beast form. Finley was the same.

Leaving Kellan and I in a struggle to remain semi-coherent.

We were barely fucking holding on, but the pain of our strained bond and missing mate was enough to keep our beasts subdued. I hoped our more animalistic brothers were having better luck at tracking our mate.

My growls filled the car as my wolf mourned and cried out for her, the clawed end of my hands digging into the steering wheel. Kellan hung up a second later with a huff. "Fucking useless," he muttered as he leaned forward and peered out the windshield, taking in the large lots of land.

The secret Rogers Pack property was surrounded by warehouses, all of them behind large chain-link fences. It was late afternoon, the sun already setting, and while it would be safer to wait for the cover of night, I knew we wouldn't.

Our mate was out there, in the hands of whoever took her, doing whatever they wanted with her, and it was only the tendrils of our bond that even told me she was still alive. When she'd first been taken, I'd felt nothing but a cool calmness from her, and then there'd been this sharp slash of pain, and then... nothing. They'd taken her too far for me to *feel* her as I should.

Our bonds were too new, and we were all suffering.

"Fuck," Kellan groaned, palming his chest and rubbing briskly. "My wolf is getting worse. We're restless and broken without her. I don't know how much longer I can do this. It's only the sense through the bond that she's still alive that's keeping me functioning at all. That, and the need to fucking gut whoever took her." His breaths heaved in and out in a rasp, and the car filled with the scent of his beast. "We missed her damn birthday. The first one she could have had with us, being actually celebrated..." His voice rose dramatically. "...and she's out there having goddess knows what done to her."

Without taking my eyes from the road, I grasped his shoulder and used my alpha influence to soothe his wolf. It offered a few seconds' reprieve at best, as the ache of our missing mate wouldn't ease until she was back in our arms. "We will find her," I muttered, the statement bitter on my tongue. "We won't stop until she's back with us, and there will be a hundred birthdays to celebrate." And those responsible for touching her would be dead at her feet.

Tearing them apart with my own hands was the bare minimum I'd require to let the matter rest.

When we reached the eastern border of their property, I slowed the vehicle, searching for a place off the main road to stash the car. Which ended up being a pocket of forest.

"We go on foot from here," I said, retrieving my gun from the center console and sliding it into my jacket pocket. We weren't outfitted as thoroughly as last time, but we'd managed to bring ShiftLar protective gear, guns, and Taser S. The weapons were our backup. We might be fueled by fury and adrenaline, but we'd also had no sleep and were working with very limited intel. They could have an army inside. Not that I gave a single fuck. Army or not, we were going to hurt these bastards.

We should have taken them out weeks ago, but we'd waited for the council to do their jobs, which had gotten my mate stolen from me again. This time I'd show no mercy.

I stashed the keys under the tire, in case I had to shift, and then headed through the forest toward the fence. Kellan followed silently, and I kept my senses on high alert for alarms or security. There was no scent of magic in the air, which hopefully meant we wouldn't be dealing with witches too.

"Jewels said she'd take out the witch who helped kidnap Slade and Emme," I said softly. "Hopefully that's why there's no magic tainting the air."

Kellan snorted. "That witch does nothing for free. If she had taken them out, we'd have heard from her in the form of an invoice."

He wasn't wrong. "I've already paid her a hundred mil to do it right and leave no loose ends. We don't exchange favors with her any longer. Not with any fucking witch."

"Good," he muttered, before shutting up as the chain-link fence came into view.

It was at least nine feet high, with barbed wire circling the top, and I scaled it quickly, throwing myself over the cutting barbs. My jacket sleeve caught briefly, but then I passed, landing lightly on the other side. Kellan was right behind me, both of us melting into the shadows of trees and shrubbery.

Our target was a large silver warehouse a hundred yards away, and I jabbed my fingers to the right, telling Kellan to circle around from the other side. He shot me a quick nod, his expression grim as he took off silently. Through our pack bond, we all felt untethered. Hanging on by the fucking edge of our sanity.

As I headed for the side of the building, I picked up a dozen voices inside, making us vastly outnumbered. Which was the only reason I didn't bust in through the front door in my wolf form, ready to tear them apart.

I had to stay alive for Emme, and the rest of my pack, which meant taking them by surprise.

Scaling a tree near the back quadrant, I climbed until I was level with a slightly ajar window on the second floor. I'd have to jump six or more feet, but I'd make it easily enough.

Hoping Kellan was in place on the opposite side, I leapt for the window, and while the ledge was narrow, I landed cleanly, gripping the edge of the frame to keep myself steady. The glass lifted soundlessly, as shadows washed over me from the sun descending behind me.

When I peered inside, I found a platform storage level, which was a lucky break. Sliding inside, I carefully dropped to the wooden floor, my boots leaving marks in the dust, on what appeared to be a rarely used area. The platform extended out over the main level, and I used the stacked boxes to keep my cover.

The scent of drugs and ammunition was strong enough to mask my scent, and I wasn't surprised by the contents of the boxes. This pack was clearly rich. They had a portfolio of properties, and Slade hadn't been able to find any legitimate business activities outside of their roles on the Alpha Council, which didn't pay enough for their lifestyle.

Silently skirting around the boxes, I peered over the edge to take in the scene below, only to find there were more than just shifters present. They had humans.

Five human women were bound to chairs in the middle of the giant warehouse.

Fuck. Whipping out my phone, I shot off a quick message to Kellan.

> Hunter: They have humans with them. We need to be careful.

Kellan's reply came back almost immediately.

> Kellan: If we can save them, we will, but this is about Emme. I don't give a fuck about humans.

I didn't give a fuck about humans either, but I also knew that their deaths would bring the councils down on us.

Hunter: Worst case scenario, we blame it all on the Rogers pack. The councils can hunt them down.

Kellan: Agreed. Now, let's take these fuckers out.

I switched out my phone for my gun and screwed on the silencer, preparing to take a few out before we were noticed. Hit the strong ones, and the weak would scatter.

The Rogers pack would be last though, as we needed at least one of them breathing. One of them had to know where Emme was. Our little omega might be alive, but she felt weak through our bond, and I truly feared that by the time we found her, it might be too late.

And if it was too late to save her, it was too late to save all of us.

CHAPTER 5

SLADE

*H*unt. *Kill. Destroy.*

I'd lost control of the beast, our mind a blur of rage that had leveled cities to the ground. The humans that were scorched were collateral damage, their media explaining it away as out-of-control forest fires.

If our mate wasn't back with us soon, a forest fire would be the least of their concern.

Someone had stolen her out from under me. Nothing would save these shifters from death, and I could be very creative in *how* I killed my prey. If she bore even so much as a papercut or had any sort of mental strain from this event, they'd know the sort of pain that would drive a beast crazy in six seconds.

I'd been scouring the state for days, following my senses. I'd found the old shack where she'd originally been, just the faintest hint of chocolate and honey left behind. That had been the first *forest fire* but not the last.

They'd moved her to another two locations, and I'd lost the trail when it was tainted with witch magic, designed to confuse and send me in a dozen different directions. I'd probably have more luck on the ground, but I couldn't get my beast to release me.

As I crossed another city, staying high in the clouds, a twinge ran through my bond. Flames spilled from my lips as I felt the buzz from Hunter and our connection. The last I heard they'd been heading for Silver City to try and track the Rogers pack.

Hunt. Kill. Destroy.

An iota of clarity eased through my beast's cold, deadly intent and we changed directions to follow the call of our pack. If that twinge through the bond was any indication, Hunter had stumbled on to a location that might lead to our mate.

I moved even higher, well above the clouds, and powered my way across the country. Even as exhausted as I was, the stores of my energy felt endless, as if I could have crossed the world for my mate. Eventually my body would demand rest and sustenance, but we'd make it to Silver City first.

With fury and fire fueling me, time passed in weird increments as I mentally mulled over everything that had happened. Before Emme was taken, I'd only been missing a few pieces of the puzzle, but apparently they were important pieces.

I hadn't seen the betrayal by Chelsea coming. When that message arrived from Finley, Hunter had shaken his head as if he couldn't believe it, but we'd scented her outside our house and found the fucking books in Emme's room, tainted in magic. It was undeniable.

We were betrayed by one of our own.

The Thenguard pack had disappeared by the time we'd stormed their house—okay, *that* was the first forest fire—and then their offices. We had no time to track them now, but they were on the list after we got our mate back. Hopefully, if my instincts were correct, we'd find them all in the same place.

As I closed in on Hunter and Kellan, my beast settled in the connection of pack, which was all that kept us from descending into darkness. Hunter had been keeping my more murderous side at bay for most of his life. My bond with him surged again, and with it came a sense of pain and fatigue. Along with the knowledge that my brothers were under attack.

Hunt. Kill. Destroy.

My dragon slammed to the forefront once more, and I didn't fight him as his instinct in battle far surpassed mine. We were a few miles from Hunter and Kellan now, their scents stronger on the air, and I started to glide down. I could fly higher than commercial airliners, where it was so cold that ice formed on my wings and scales, and if it weren't for dragon fire I would freeze. Our energy also helped to hide us from radars and human eyes, blending our scales into our environment.

Dragons could manipulate energy and matter around us, and it was mostly an instinctive skill my beast controlled. He didn't always share the secrets of our powers, and I had long ago learned to accept that it just was. Especially when it was useful.

Warehouses came into view as I dipped lower, night falling on the horizon, as shadows caressed my bulky form. Roars, shouts and the scent of blood hit me as I landed on the roof, claws digging in and tearing through the metal, until I created a large enough gap to descend into the chaos.

Hunter and Kellan stood in the center of a large warehouse, back-to-back, slashing their way through dozens of shifters. They had the main group fairly under control, but then doors opened near the back of the warehouse and a dozen more alphas appeared—many of them powered by magic.

The fact that they had access to such strong spells was concerning in more ways than one. Ever since the last war, shifters and witches had been at odds, and this was the first time in years we'd had so many attacks that involved magic.

Jewels better be working to sort out that rogue witch and figure out which coven was behind it all.

Diving down, I let the swirls of molten lava rise from my core, spewing through and incinerating the newcomers. None were the Rogers pack, who were the only ones we needed alive.

Ideally Blaine, the entitled alpha, as he'd been at the old shack where Emme was first taken and would have the most information. I hadn't scented the rest of his pack there, and I wondered if they weren't ranked much higher than the mid-level muscle we took out tonight.

As my flames raged through the shifters, Hunter threw his head back and bestowed a strained smile on me. "Thought you were hunting in Washington," he called.

My dragon roared loud enough to rattle windows and burst eardrums, and any of the assholes who'd missed my initial entrance were now very aware that death stalked them.

Hunter shook his head. "Good to see you too, brother. Can you help us round up the Rogers pack and get some fucking answers? Just try not to kill the humans."

Not a problem, brother. Not that I'd noticed any humans, and I didn't care about them either way.

He nodded as if he'd heard me, though we'd never been able to truly communicate mentally. Even if it did come close at times.

My prediction was that if we formed a completed quintet, there'd be changes in our bond, including the ability to communicate mentally. Especially in our beast forms. A prediction that could never come to pass if I didn't find the center and core of our quintet.

Our heart. My Snow.

Spreading my wings as wide as I could in this enclosed space, I focused on each of the shifters, searching for familiar faces and scents. There was no sign—or scent—of Blaine, but I found the next best shifter: Donnie. The second strongest and only other one on the Alpha Council.

Landing heavily, I crushed a few shifters, and my dragon was about to eat one until I reminded him that we didn't eat trash. He shook off his front paw then, as if it was tainted, and carried on.

As we stomped forward, my tail swung and clipped two other shifters, sending them flying into a wall. Kellan whooped, shaking his head as he ran a hand through his blond hair, streaking it with blood and dirt. "Bro, that was fucking awesome. I love being a wolf, but shooting fire and crushing dickheads under your bulk is peak alpha-ing. Fucking peak. You know I'm right."

A smoky snort of amusement escaped my beast. Who'd have thought there'd be two shifters in the world who could break through my dragon's unhinged, unpredictable personality. Hunter kept me sane, but Emme and Kellan kept me humanized.

Finley was just as broken as me, but he was another reminder of why I could never lose control.

There were too many shifters I cared about in the firing line.

When my beast reached Donnie, my claw closed around his gut, squeezing tight enough for a few pig-like squeals to burst from the pathetic fuck. I'd almost killed him last time, and there was a sense of satisfaction in my beast that we'd finally get to finish the job.

"Yeah, you're fucked now," Kellan called cheerfully, and I noted how blown out his pupils were as he bounced around. "You might want to keep squealing like a pig, and spill whatever dark secrets Blaine has if you don't want to suffer horribly. Painfully. Immensely. You'll—"

"Tell us where our fucking omega is!" Hunter snapped, his patience having run out completely.

He wasn't the only one. I squeezed tighter, letting the tips of my claws prick into Donnie's side. With a little more pressure, they'd slide through his body like a hot knife through butter. It took a lot of skill to injure without instantly killing, and I hoped he appreciated the skill my dragon was demonstrating here.

The scent of urine filled the air as Donnie lost control of himself, and my claws *almost* slipped and tore his head off. This weak-willed, sad excuse for an alpha was on my last nerve.

"Where did they take Emme?" Hunter growled once more as he moved beside my leg, taking care not to brush me, even though the touch aversion was rarely triggered in this form.

When there was still no response, my claws dug a little deeper—I'd hit important parts soon, and alpha healing was near humanly slow against a dragon attack.

"They're in Texas," a voice roared from nearby.

My grip eased up and Donnie grunted as I swung my head to find another one of their pack on the ground, nursing injuries from where I'd stomped on him earlier. "I don't know where," he continued, expression pained as he held his gut, "but we were commanded to fly out in a few days to start congregating in larger numbers. For war."

Hunter tilted his head and met my gaze, one of the few strong enough to peer right into the depths of the dragon's eyes. *A few days.* That meant that whatever Blaine had planned was happening soon. What did it have to do with Emme though? How did she play into this plan?

She'd been the target all along, through both kidnappings, and while Emme had told us it was for the same reason they hurt her mother, she never told us *what* that reason was.

We returned our focus to Donnie and Hunter said, "Slade won't kill you if you tell us everything." I'd have laughed at that absolute fucking lie, but a dragon didn't have the vocal cords for such a sound. "You might be broken, but you have a chance to survive."

I allowed another delicate slide of my claws, and I was piercing organs now.

Donnie cried out, choking on his next breath. "Marfa, Texas. They're in an underground bunker."

He'd broken so easily it was almost sad, but with a useless piece of shit as his entitled alpha, what else could we expect.

"What are they planning on doing with her?" Kellan stepped

forward, kicking another shifter in the head on his way through. It took a lot for Golden to lose his shit, but when he did, he was a terror.

Donnie coughed a few times, spatters of blood visible in the phlegm. Definitely hit a vital organ. "Exactly what we did with her fucking mother."

He gave us the same answer as Emme, and while I had my guesses of what that meant, guesses weren't truth. A truth we needed to hear from our omega. She'd told Hunter the night they bonded that she was ready to explain everything to us, but then she'd been taken almost straight after.

"What did you do to her mother?" Kellan's hand was around Donnie's throat in the next breath, and now the pathetic fuck had claws in his jugular too.

This was the Kellan who'd killed a dozen humans when he'd stumbled into a gang initiation in a nearby town, and found a group of men brutally raping women. We didn't usually involve ourselves in human business, but none of us would walk away from that. He'd made sure none of them walked away from anything ever again.

Donnie's chuckle was weak, and Kellan flexed his fingers to allow him to speak. "Of course she wouldn't have told you. She wouldn't want you to know the very power in your hands. Literally. When you bond with an omega, they can power your alpha essence. You siphon their power, draining them day by day. Eventually the essence fades, and she'll be left as nothing more than a husk, while you feel powerful enough to take on the world. Emmeline's mother was an experiment while we waited for the daughter to be old enough. When the bitch tapped out, we planned to make a move on Emmeline, but she disappeared before we could." Another strangled cough, and I knew he was going to bleed out soon.

"Tapped out?" Hunter asked, his tone deceptively calm, though his beast was raging.

Donnie's grin was manic. "She killed herself right in front of her daughter, and we made the pup cut her down."

Kellan stepped back as though he was disgusted, releasing the shifter and wiping his hand on his pants. "Oh, our pretty mate should never have gone through that," he murmured, his face falling. "Everything makes so much fucking sense now."

Of all the scenarios I'd considered, I'd never expected one of them would be an omega powering an alpha until they lost their essence completely. Was that the reason there were so few omegas left in the shifter world? And if so, why the fuck would Chelsea help them?

"Whatever the reason," Hunter snarled, his face wreathed in dark shadows, "our priority is to get our mate back. We'll deal with the rest of them later."

I waited for his command, determined not to pre-emptively kill again and make the situation worse. No matter how desperately I wanted to end this fuck's life.

"Finish him and torch the place." Hunter gave me the nod of approval as he turned and marched toward the women bound on chairs. "Kellan and I will get the humans out, and then we're going after our mate."

"Wait, you said I'd live," Donnie bellowed, and Hunter's dark laughter was the soundtrack to his final breath.

I tightened my hold, severing him right down his middle.

Once Kellan and Hunter finished their task, flames tore from my mouth to destroy everyone else in the warehouse, and then I took to the sky. Following my brothers to their vehicle.

We were finally on track to get our mate back, and this time I'd never let her go again.

CHAPTER 6

EMME

Talon stared at me for so long that I almost forgot I'd suggested he destroy Fletcher Davenport and rid the world of his evil. Not a single word passed his lips, no matter what I said or what questions I asked.

Eventually, I just babbled about whatever topic came to mind. I'd done this before with Slade, and it had about the same effect: none.

In the middle of explaining, *in great detail*, every step of taking apart an old Hemi engine, I found that I was only making myself more depressed. Cars were one of the few positive memories I had of my childhood, when I'd escaped by sneaking into the garage below. It was also a connection I held with the Reeves pack, who were into anything with an engine, and had a garage full of incredible vehicles and bikes.

With my eyes burning, I slumped against the bed, hoping I could stay awake. No doubt this asshole planned on taking my power by force if I didn't give it to him, and I wouldn't want to make that task any easier by being unconscious.

The silence stretched on as I stared at the ceiling and he stared at me, the only sound the gurgling of my very empty stomach. During my time with the Reeves pack, I'd grown used to multiple meals being provided for me. Multiple *delicious* meals, which my pack would watch me consume, ensuring I ate first before they touched a single item…

I squeezed my eyes shut at the pain of missing them, before a knock at the door had me lurching into a sitting position and scrambling back against the headboard. Talon didn't flinch at the intrusion, as if he'd anticipated this visitor. When the dragon crossed to the door, he pulled out a chain from around his neck, and I noted the key at the end—the key I'd need to get out of here.

Once he unlocked it, he cracked the door an inch. There was a murmur of a low, male voice from the other side, and it wasn't familiar. Talon didn't reply or acknowledge the other shifter as he opened the door a fraction more to accept a tray. The scent of food hit me so hard I almost groaned, and it momentarily made me feel queasy.

I'd spent a lot of my life hungry, scrounging around to feed myself, and somehow in my short time with Reeves Pack, I'd gotten spoiled enough to crumble under a little hardship and hunger.

In the middle of more hushed words from whoever was outside this room, Talon shut the door in his face, and if I wasn't determined to hate him with the heat of a thousand fireballs, I'd have laughed. He was worse than Slade with manners, and that was saying something. They legitimately had zero fucks to give about what other shifters thought or felt about them. Which made sense once you knew they were the apex predators. The rest of us had to care to stay alive.

Talon approached the bed in his usual rapid stride, and I'd already started to note mannerisms about this shifter. For starters, he was either moving with determination or completely still—there was no in between for him. No nervous pacing or fidgeting. He gave the impression that when he was called to action, he moved at rapid, intense speeds, while the rest of the time he was left to sit and wait.

He placed the tray on the bed, and I tried my absolute best not to even look at the offerings. My stomach screamed at me, and I spoke to it the same way I would my beast. *No! We're not eating drugged food, so they have us at their mercy. You're not that hungry.*

As I remained in a tense huddle at the head of the bed, Talon released a smoky huff and reached out to lift the bread roll and take a bite. He placed it back on the tray and proceeded to do the same with each of the small dishes. Unfortunately, despite my best efforts, I noticed it was rice, chicken, and a bread roll. No vegetables.

"It's not drugged." Truth rang out in that statement, and I got the sense that like Slade, he didn't really lie.

Eyeing the tray, I knew there was still a risk. A dragon was so much stronger than me, and any drug in here could have been administered to him for years until he was all but immune. Still, I was shaky and struggling to stay awake. Food would fuel me… and maybe my beast.

She remained too weak for my liking. Hurt and hiding away.

I had to help her in whatever way I could.

Grabbing a bread roll, I took a bite to find it slightly stale, but who really cared when you were hungry. Swallowing roughly, I moved on to the chicken and rice, which held faint flavors of garlic, lemon, and paprika, but otherwise remained fairly bland. Talon didn't touch anything on the tray again, watching me in that intense, unwavering stare of his. Which bothered me less than it should have.

My pack had been warming me up to the obsessive nature of alphas for weeks now, and I was starting to crave their *stares and touches and need for me.* It wasn't one sided either. Except in this case, Talon and I were enemies.

Nothing more.

When my stomach protested, I pushed away what was left on the tray, and Talon moved into action, eating everything in a neat, systematic motion. A surge of worry that I hadn't left enough food for him hit me—I hadn't realized we'd be made to share.

Was food a way they controlled him too? Surely, they fed their soldiers and pack members as much as they needed? A shifter of Slade's size couldn't survive on a few bites of bread, rice, and chicken. *Why hadn't he said anything?* He'd just sat there and watched me force food into my mouth. Was the instinct to feed your mate ingrained into all alphas?

No… no, it absolutely wasn't. Blaine and his pack of pricks had never let anyone eat first.

Where did Talon learn it, then?

"Sorry I didn't leave more," I found myself saying, and then immediately regretted it. He'd forcibly bonded me, and here I was going all *Stockholm Syndrome* worrying about my captor.

Idiot.

Talon grunted, showcasing another alpha instinct. "Tell me more about cars."

I blinked at him, trying not to squirm under his stare. "You weren't bored?"

He shook his head without hesitation. "No."

Okay, then. With nothing better to do, and in the hopes of keeping him calm while I figured out an escape plan, I launched into another story. "When I was twelve, I snuck down into the garage later than usual. It had been a really hard day with my mom and her pack. They were home more than usual, and they hurt her right in front of me. Of course, when I tried to intervene, Blaine slapped my face. The bruise healed up fast enough, of course, but I was feeling a little sore and sorry for myself as I escaped, only to find one of the owner's clients had brought in a Mclaren F1. It was just sitting there, the orange shining so brightly that it briefly blinded me."

Talon leaned closer, and I swore that he was hanging on my every word.

"You need to understand, they only made them for a few years, and they were so rare. It was a literal multi-million-dollar car just sitting there in this old garage. Mack was one of the best mechanics in the state, but still... that was beyond.

"He didn't let me touch it of course, and I didn't really know about the car at the time, but once he explained how rare and precious it was, a sliver of hope bloomed inside me. Hope that maybe better days were coming." A sad laugh escaped me. "It's ridiculous that a car gave me hope, but even at twelve I knew it was special and felt the awe in its presence. Thinking about the shimmer of orange, with the sunlight hitting it just right until it glowed, kept me sane through a lot of bad days."

Talon's expression was unreadable, but deep in the icy darkness of his eyes there was the slightest flicker of a flame. "What happened to the car? Did you take the engine apart?"

He had finished the food now, the tray empty and the plates and bowls neatly arranged from smallest to largest across the surface.

I shook my head. "Nothing happened. They were having a small issue, but Mack was able to fix it up in an hour, and then we said our goodbyes to the beauty. He didn't even let me breathe on it, let alone take the engine apart."

"Do you drive?"

My eyebrows drew together as I considered if that was a serious question or not. He didn't show any indication it wasn't, so I answered. "Yes. I have my license for cars and motorcycles."

Talon considered that, and I wasn't sure if it meant anything more to him other than learning a new fact about me. I couldn't get a read on this dragon.

"Do you drive?" I returned the question his way.

With a hooded gaze he shook his head. "Dragons fly."

My mind flashed right to the memory of Slade squished into his Lambo or soaring on his bike. "I'm sure nothing compares to flying, but fast cars and bikes are a close second. Or as close as those of us without wings will ever get."

I hadn't realized that I was leaning toward him until he straightened with the tray and I almost fell onto the bed. "I will take you flying and you can tell me which is better."

My heart pattered hard in my chest, and I forced myself not to soften. *No.* Just no. I'd already Stockholm'd myself into a relationship with four assholes. There was no room for a fifth. Even if the other four turned out to be the best alphas I'd ever met. Including the surly ones.

Talon was part of the *bad guys*, ready to destroy the fabric of our world and send us back to the Dark Ages. He might be a victim here as well, but while he refused to change his path and loyalty, I had to treat him as the enemy.

With the conversation over, Talon got up with the tray and opened the door to return it. I caught a glimpse of a dark hallway, and a mildewy scent filtered in from outside, disappearing when he closed and locked the door once more.

When he settled into his seat, ready for another few hours of staring at my face, I asked, "What are Fletcher's plans? Once you forcibly steal my energy and are all powered up, what will he have you do?"

There was no evasion in his stare or tone as he replied, "I don't know. He doesn't tell me the plan. He just sends me out to ensure it happens."

"You're the muscle, not the brains," I snarked meanly.

Talon shrugged, unconcerned by my little dig. No doubt that was the least of the insults he'd heard in his life. "I am whatever he wants me to be. But yes, mostly a weapon."

"You can't let him do this," I whispered, swallowing roughly. "He's already destroyed too many lives. So many omegas taken and hurt through his experiments. I know he said there weren't enough of them to truly experiment on, but that doesn't mean he didn't hurt the ones that were around. And they were innocent. You understand that, right? They didn't deserve what happened to them, and I don't deserve it either."

For the first time, I caught a flicker of unease in his expression. Pushing forward, I hurried to try and chip away at his icy exterior. "Do you know what will happen to me if you drain all of my essence?"

More silence.

"My wolf will fade. My wolf will fade and I'll be a shell of a shifter, unable to touch or call my beast. In the end, I'll wish for death... and maybe even seek it out."

Mom hadn't been able to take the echoing silence in her head any longer or the weakness in her veins. She'd chosen to end it all, and I'd been the one to cut her down from the rope that stole her last breath.

Talon surged to his feet suddenly, and at first I thought I'd gotten through to him, only to hear another knock on the door, one he clearly hadn't been expecting.

When he crossed to the solid door, he placed his hand against it, as if to sense who was on the other side. There was a beat as he reached for the chain again, pulling it from his shirt, and when he clicked the lock open, the door burst inward. I'd have thought it would catch the dragon by surprise except he was too fast, jumping out of the way of the bear who surged into the room, a dead shifter speared on his massive claws.

I was on my feet now too, and a gasp escaped me.

I'd only seen this bear one other time, but I knew his huge, menacing presence immediately.

Finley Thornton had come for me.

CHAPTER 7

EMME

There was a brief pause from Talon as he assessed the situation. At no point did his expression change. The steady thrumming of his heartbeat remained even too.

Finley, on the other hand, was a raging inferno of fired-up shifter.

His bear threw his head back again, roared into the ceiling, and tossed the body of the shifter aside. When the deafening sound of his rage faded, the bear's inscrutable deep black eyes locked in on me. His gaze ran over me more than once, taking in every inch from the dirt on my bare toes to the top of my smooth hair.

When the bear sidled forward, Talon snapped into action, launching himself between us. "Wait," I called, almost reaching out to touch Talon, before I remembered he was the enemy. A powerful, dangerous, possibly sociopathic enemy. "It's Finley. One of my pack. Don't hurt him."

Talon's head swung around and he shot me a dark stare. *Uh*, okay. Was it really *that* of all freaking things that finally upset him?

He'd managed to ignore the bites under my clothes, but Finley standing here in this room, had apparently broken through his iron will and composure. His expression was now wreathed in darkness as his full lips thinned and pulled at the scar on his face. His heartrate didn't change much, but it was stronger than it had been before. "I'm your pack," he rumbled, and hell if that didn't set Finley off as well.

The bear didn't have the ability to express himself with words, but he launched forward, those blood-tinged claws outreached. Talon reacted like the giant beast moved in slow motion, swatting him out of the way and into the wall. A near ton of bear slammed into the panels, shaking the room, and Talon didn't even break a sweat.

"Leave now or I'll kill you." Like Slade, this dragon didn't fuck around with pleasantries, and I wasn't going to pretend that was an empty threat. Talon was Fletcher's most lethal soldier, trained to obey and kill on demand. A true assassin.

Finley was already back on his hind legs, standing near nine or ten feet tall as the shadows of the room danced around him. This time when he launched, he anticipated the slap from Talon and dodged the dragon's hand. The two of them clashed like a boulder slamming into a rock wall. It was loud, and I barely refrained from clasping my hands over my ears, caught up in watching their deadly dance.

No matter what happened, I would not let Talon kill one of my mates. I had to protect Finley, and not with my strength—a mere pittance compared to these two—but with my intelligence. With the knowledge that Talon needed me, and not just because we were bonded. I was the key component to his alpha's plan.

Finley roared as the dragon tore a large tuft of fur from his chest, leaving a bloody welt behind. Talon hadn't shifted any part of his body, as it appeared he didn't need to be in dragon form to win this fight. Scary, powerful bastard.

Before he could hurt Finley again, I threw myself between them, and for the first time didn't avoid the bear like he had a shifter disease. With my arms held wide, I backed into Finley's huge form. I'd expected, when I put this plan into action, that he'd step back with me, and we'd put some distance between us and Talon. Instead, I found myself plastered against his raging, heaving form, snatched up in two huge bear paws.

Talon let out a huff, the scent of ash filtering through the room. He didn't follow as Finley dragged me against his massive chest, my feet dangling a few feet off the floor. The warmth of the bear was soothing against my back, and even in this form, he still smelled of vanilla and cherries, mixed decently with sweat and dirt.

The sweet scent overpowered the rest though, and I hated the way I still craved this male when he didn't want me. The irony of being stuck here, between one pack mate who hated me, and one who had forcibly bonded me... that was fucked up. Part of me wished I could just destroy them both and walk my ass out of here, alive and strong in my own right. Unfortunately, an omega couldn't play in the world of alphas like that. At least not without more training than I had.

"If you release her," Talon murmured slowly. "I will let you leave with your life."

Finley snorted; the sound of derision almost cute coming from a bear. He continued to back away slowly, with Talon matching each step so they remained the same eight feet apart. "You cannot leave," he ordered, the dragon's dominance washing over me and Finley.

Panic surged to the forefront of all my convoluted emotions as I was reminded of one miscalculation. *Dominance.* It never factored for me, as it didn't work on omegas. But it worked on alphas. It worked on any who were weaker, and while shifters rarely used it these days —no need to start fights that could come back to bite you on the ass— it remained a solid option in battle.

And Talon knew it. "Return her to me," he said, releasing an even stronger wave of dominance.

Finley's paws shook, and I clutched one of them with both hands. "You are strong enough to resist," I whispered to him. "Fight him, Fin. Fight him. Call on the strength of the rest of your brothers."

He tried his best, but in the end the dragon was stronger. Maybe if we'd all been bonded in a complete quintet, Finley would have stood a chance, but there was no way to know for sure.

His staggered steps moved us closer to Talon, who remained still and patient, as if he wanted to draw out the humiliation of the bear being forced to *return me to him*. "Release me," I said to Finley, and while his paws flexed against my skin, he couldn't free me to any but Talon.

Glaring at the dragon, I snarled, "I will fight you. If you hurt Finley in any way, I will never stop fighting until one of us is dead. I don't care if it's you or me, but it will end in blood."

Talon tilted his head, giving Slade vibes, and I hated how much the bastard reminded me of my pack mate. "If he returns what is mine, then he is free to leave."

The spark of anger that had been simmering since I woke and found myself once again at the mercy of my mom's old pack and their *alpha,* flared to life in an inferno of fury. "I'm not yours," I shot back, heat building in my center. "Not yours. Not now or ever."

Talon's gaze landed on my covered neck, and the mark tingled at the reminder. We were no more than two feet apart now, Finley's ability to fight extending only so far as in how slow he moved. "You are mine. Always."

The dragon shocked me with that simple statement, and my stomach flipped in a way that I didn't like or understand. My wolf even piped her head up, and I wanted to scream at her for abandoning me when I needed her the most, only to return at that fucking declaration.

Still, her return was enough to have that ember of energy in my chest flaring harder, emboldened by the beast within me. My torso ached at the sensation of my essence pulsing.

When Finley finally reached Talon, the dragon reached for me, and as his fingers connected to my chest, I lifted my legs and kicked him. The energy surged with that strike, and it was as if I suddenly developed super strength, knocking him back at least a dozen feet, until he almost hit the far wall.

My fingers and toes buzzed as if I'd hit him with a damn spell, but since that wasn't possible, I decided it had to be pure adrenaline.

Talon wasn't rattled as he straightened, his focus on me, like nothing else in the world existed. "You're one powerful omega," he said softly. "You will be our greatest weapon."

"Not a fucking chance," I snarled back, but it was all fake bravado. My wolf had sunk back into my essence, and I'd have panicked that she was fully gone this time, but I felt a flicker of her deep down.

When a bout of exhaustion hit me, I deflated in Finley's hold, wishing that this day was over.

I just wanted to be home with my pack.

"I can't let you leave," Talon said, and it might have been my lack of focus, but he almost sounded torn by this statement. "I am willing to negotiate, though. What would it take for you to stay and work with us?"

A choked laugh was my initial response. He had to be kidding. "A lobotomy," I said with a shake of my head. "What could you possibly offer that would get me to sign up with the evil fuck who killed my mom and a bunch of other omegas? A shifter who wants to destroy the pack cities and turn the clock all the way back to the Stone Age? All I want is to wipe Fletcher from the face of this planet."

His eyebrows drew together, and there was a moment where a

flash of what looked like vulnerability crossed his features. "I can offer you a true pack and the promise that you won't ever be alone again. You will have a powerful mate, and we can rule at our alpha's side. We will be his most trusted weapons. Together."

The stupid stomach flip returned, and Finley growled behind me, no doubt expecting I was so disloyal that I'd just run off into the sunset with this delusional asshat. "Your plan has one flaw," I said, my voice softer than I would have liked.

Talon's eyebrows drew even tighter, as if a flaw would never dare to sully his presence.

"Without my other bonded mates, I will fade away, and so will my power. I'll be useless to you. My wolf is already broken and mourning, buried so deep in my essence I can barely feel her. You and I alone…" I pointed my finger between us. "…can never be. I've already gifted parts of myself to other mates. Mates. I. Love. There will never just be *you and I*."

Of everything that had happened since Finley busted into this room, this was the first time the dragon completely lost control. Ash and maple filled the room, until I was sweating and panting against the dense air. Whatever dominance he held over Finley broke as he lost control, and the bear moved again, racing for the exit.

We made it into the hallway, and while Finley moved fast on two legs, it was an awkward gait. "Let me down," I hissed, tapping his arm. "I can run, and you'll fight easier without me in your arms."

The walls around us shook as flecks of plasterboard and stone fell from above, and there was still no sign of a window. Finley shocked me by dropping me to my feet, and after ensuring I was in front, his snout nudged me to start moving.

I sprinted down the hall as the building shook harder. I couldn't figure out what Talon was doing until I heard the roar and glanced over my shoulder to find a dragon tearing through the hall, destroying the structure around us as he moved.

When we reached the end of the hall, there was the option to go left and right, and both ways looked exactly the same. Finley nudged me toward the right and I took off again, my body fatigued but my will to get out of here alive and strong.

Not that I was sure what would happen when we made it into the open.

The open skies were a dragon's domain, and through the broken tendrils of our bond, Talon felt slightly unhinged.

He had lost it at my last statement, and I wasn't sure he'd even stop for me now.

CHAPTER 8

EMME

We had been underground—in a bunker that was completely buried except for one doorway, that we ran up a single set of metal stairs to reach.

That was why there'd been no windows, and if I hadn't had Finley's bear nudging me in the right direction, I'd never have made it out of the labyrinth of halls and rooms.

Two dead guards were sprawled near the exit, puddles of blood congealed around their torn throats. It didn't bother me. These traitors made the decision to work for evil itself, and *death via bear* was the consequences of their actions.

As dry, frigid air hit me, I noticed that the bunker appeared to be buried in the middle of what looked like desert. The late-afternoon light showcased the rocky and arid terrain, with large cliffs visible off in the distance. There wasn't any snow on the ground, which was great news for my bare feet. The rocks would be bad enough, and I didn't want to add frostbite to the mix.

I mean, I'd have literally run over burning coals or through an icy tundra to get the hell out of here and back to my pack, but it was much nicer if I didn't have to.

We sprinted as the ground shook, Finley falling on all fours to move faster. My fitness in my human form was woeful at best, and I was filled with an urge to shift, but my wolf remained buried deep, and I didn't have time to coax her out.

Finley noticed fairly quickly that not only was I slowing, I also breathed like an asthmatic human. In my defense, he was really barreling along, and I doubted many could keep up in their bipedal form. He slowed to my pace, and as I turned to apologize, he swept his head around and hit my side. With a shriek, I was lifted and tossed onto his back, landing awkwardly as I scrabbled not to fall. I caught myself on his fur, and he didn't give me a chance to get comfortable. He took off rapidly again.

At first it felt weird riding on the back of a bear, but I quickly stopped caring and slumped forward into his fur, my legs hanging awkwardly on either side. I had to keep them a little tucked to not hit anything—not that Finley appeared to notice or care in his race for our safety and freedom.

The ground still shook behind us, and energy in the air crackled against my skin. It reminded me that a dragon was busting through that underground bunker, and he was going to hunt us down like prey.

Finley and I both understood how it felt to be prey, though for him it was only when he was younger. I'd been prey for most of my existence, and even with my alphas and pack, it remained the case.

Slade had tried to warn me that I needed to be stronger in all ways if I wanted to survive. Fitness, fighting ability, weapons. My skills were lacking, and it was never more obvious than today when I had to be *carried by a freaking bear* because I couldn't keep up.

Today would be the last time I was this pathetic and vulnerable.

Yeah, I'd always be smaller and weaker than alphas, but that didn't mean I couldn't train to be the very best version of myself.

The vibrations picked up, and so did Finley's pace. How long he could keep this up with my additional weight was a concern, but so far he wasn't faltering. I didn't know a lot about bears, but I got the sense that they were fast over short distances and not designed to sprint for miles.

Where are you? I called for my wolf, and the faintest hint of her essence touched my fingers. *We need to shift.* Her desolate cry was my reply, and my frustration reared up strongly.

I mourned our missing mates too, and the fact that we'd been forcibly mated to a beast didn't help either, but we couldn't just give up. *Please. Find your strength.*

When I got nothing more than a listless huff, I decided to let her be.

She might have the wild spirit of a wolf, but she was also an omega. We weren't designed to live without our mates.

We were the heart of the pack, and when the tethers to our bonded ones—which also included Talon now—stretched thin, it crushed our spirit.

Only the human side could fight, and I would, with everything I had.

Like that surge of heat and strength back in the bunker. I had no idea what it was or where it came from, but it was power I hoped to find again.

Ahead of us, a parcel of trees rose up to break the endless desert landscape. This random patch of forest was bordered on one side by a rocky cliff that might also offer shelter from a dragon's sight. Finley beelined for the trees, and we both knew our only hope was to find somewhere to hide and regroup.

There was no outrunning Talon, not once he got clear of the bunker —his size would only slow him down until he was out in the open. And despite our bond feeling ragged and not quite complete, he would be able to track me. The tugging of his beast was in my chest, along with the feeling of my wolf wanting to return to her mate. Forcibly bonded or not, this was the nature of the connection.

The rapidly disappearing sun didn't cast much light in the woods, and without my wolf's active presence, I was left squinting into the semi-darkness. Finley shifted directions constantly, bringing us deeper into the wooded area. It was too sparse under here to hide properly, and with the trees thinning from winter, we would be easily spotted by a flying beast.

Beneath me, Finley was slowing, his gait rougher than it had been earlier. Just as I was about to suggest that I walk myself again, he took a sharp right turn and almost unseated me from my perch. He sniffed the air as he ran, and I panicked it was Talon.

Tilting my head back, there was no sign of anything in the darkening sky, and the tugging was no stronger than before. Finley picked up the pace, and I had to duck my head under some very low hanging branches as he barged into a new section of woodland.

Ahead of us, I spotted a rock wall that must have been part of those cliffs I'd seen before. Finley headed straight for them, still sniffing.

This couldn't be about Talon's presence.

He wasn't running away from a scent—he was searching for it.

It took a few more minutes before a black spot on the wall came into view, stark against the white and gray of the rocks. That spot grew until eventually we met the entrance of a cave, which was so small I had to slide off the bear for us to fit.

Finley wouldn't let me enter at first, sniffing thoroughly before he nudged me into the darkness. Without my wolf, I was walking blind, so I murmured, "Just as an FYI, I can't tell if I'm about to stumble into a hole or a rock wall. My wolf's hiding. She's been like this pretty much since I was forcibly bonded, leaving my senses not much stronger than human."

His menacing growls at my back were so deep that my pulse raced in a natural fear response. Logically, I knew Finley wasn't going to attack me, but that sound was guttural and terrifying.

Forcing my tone to remain even, I said, "Just—just tell me if I'm going to hit a wall. Tap me on the back with your nose or something."

He grunted and nudged me in what I hoped was an acknowledgement.

As we walked, the pounding of my heart settled, and I kept my hands out in front as an added security. The walls were close on either side, forcing Finley to have to squish his way through, his hot breath and cherry-vanilla scent strong behind me.

When we'd been walking for what felt like five minutes, the oppressive feeling of the walls on either side of me lessened, and I caught wafts of fresh, cool air. There were a few rays of natural light filtering in from fissures above, which turned this larger cavern into a landscape of shadows. But it wouldn't last much longer, as the sun was almost set.

When Finley nudged me, I stopped immediately, both hands still out in front. "Is there a wall?" I asked, and he nudged me again. Which meant… what? "Can you shift back now. I think we need to discuss our options before an angry dragon tears this cave apart."

Instead of the whirl of shifter energy to suggest he was changing, all I got was another nudge. With a sigh, I said, "Okay, let's say one nudge for yes and two for no. Do you want me to stop here?"

One nudge.

"Okay, is it because there's a wall in front of me."

Two nudges.

No wall. "Then you must think this is a good place to stop and regroup?"

One nudge.

Excellent. "But you don't want to change back?"

Two nudges, which gave me a moment's pause. This was followed by a less menacing rumble than before, which brought with it an odd thought. Unsure how he'd react to my next question, I hesitantly said, "Can you change back?"

Two nudges.

Oh, fuck. Finley had lost control of his bear, and the beast wasn't about to loosen his hold.

He was stuck in his bear form.

CHAPTER 9

EMME

We were working on limited time before the dragon tracked our steps—he had a direct link to me after all, and I could feel him out there, circling above the woods.

He was probably hoping I'd be forced out, with thirst and hunger already a factor. First, though, I had to figure out how to get Finley out of his furry suit and back into the lumbersnack version.

The natural light was gone now, and I sank against the closest wall, with Finley remaining on my right side. There was electricity in the air when he was this close… a prickling awareness over my skin and seeping deep into my essence. It existed with all of my pack, but it always felt more intense with Finley. I could never tell if it was due to the anger and pain reverberating around inside him, or something more.

Right now, his energy pulsed strongly, and I could only assume his inability to shift back was linked to an overload of emotions. "Has this happened to you in the past?"

We didn't know much about each other, through his choice, which was highly inconvenient now that I had to have this conversation with a bear.

One nudge.

"Did you manage to shift back on your own?"

Two nudges.

Fuck, that meant it wasn't going to be as easy as I'd hoped.

"Okay, that's fine," I said, forcing positivity into my voice. "We can figure this out. Whatever triggered you into your bear form might be what we need to reverse it."

A wash of his musky-sweet scent was my response as he shuffled closer. Instinct had me reaching out to run my hand over where I thought his shoulders would be, only I misjudged in the darkness, and collided with his hard chest.

When Finley grunted, I winced, remembering that he'd lost a chunk of hair and skin during the fight. It should have healed by now, though, and that hadn't really sounded like pain… more surprised.

Gentling my touch, I stroked his fur. "You just need to relax, Finley," I whispered, attempting to keep my voice soothing. "We're safe for the minute. *I'm safe*. Was it my disappearance that had your bear so agitated?"

A gust of air surrounded me as he exhaled, and then *one nudge*.

"Understandable," I continued in the same tone. "You probably thought I ran. I left a note saying goodbye, but I promise I was forced to write it. It was shitty timing right after I told you I would let you know if I ever had to run. You no doubt assumed that stupid note was my way of *letting you know*, and you thought the worst of me."

His two nudges were a little rougher than the last ones.

"No?" I said, blinking through my shock. *No?* "You mean to tell me that Finley Thornton didn't immediately assume the worst of me?"

There wasn't any yes or no response to this question, which told me that there'd been a moment he'd thought the worst of me. But it clearly hadn't lasted. He'd been tracking me for days, which meant he couldn't have believed the note. That was huge progress for us.

"I understand, big guy," I continued, forcing myself to focus on what was happening right here in this cave. "Your bear is protecting you, and I'm here to tell you both that it's going to be okay. You're strong enough to deal with what's happening. You've been through way worse than this and that didn't break you. You hear me. That didn't fucking break you, and neither will this. Now shift back."

My hand lifted as his huge chest expanded with a rumble, but that was as far as it went.

Well, fuck. "It was worth a try," I said with a sad chuckle. "Maybe we should get some rest. What do you think? It's been a long few days and sleep would help. I'll take the first watch."

Another snort and grunt, and I knew he was going to fight me.

He nudged me twice, and then when I said nothing, he did it again. "I get it," I huffed, pushing his snout away from my arm. "Fine, I'll let you take the first shift if you promise to let me watch after, so you can rest. You're the strongest one here, so it's safer for *both of us* if you're rested too." There was a pause and then he nudged me once to approve my plan.

With a sigh, I leaned back against the rough, rocky surface, exhaustion crushing me. Finley moved even closer, his fur keeping me warm from the damp, icy air of the cave.

As hard as I tried not to, I couldn't help but slump into Finley's side, his muscled bulk slightly softer than the wall. The beat of his heart and scent were soothing, and my eyes closed against my will. Not even the tugging ache of Talon in my chest could keep me awake, and I drifted off surrounded by cherry and vanilla, with the very real sense that this might be my one and only time to ever sleep next to this alpha.

I had no idea what woke me, but it was likely the sweltering heat of being surrounded by a bear, his soft fur cradling my head. I'd slept so heavily that I was disoriented for the first few seconds of consciousness, before reality crashed in once more.

Pushing myself up, I wiped a hand over my face, taking note that the cave was still pitch black, with no tendrils of light making it through the fracture points.

The sun hadn't risen yet.

Finley stirred at my side, as if he hadn't moved a muscle since I'd crashed on him and needed to stretch his limbs out.

"Sorry," I murmured, voice husky. "I didn't mean to use you as a pillow."

The gentlest of rumble was his response, and I wiggled a few inches to also move my body, lifting my ass to get the blood flowing.

"I'm glad there were no issues," I continued, just as softly.

Finley nudged me once, and I took that to mean he agreed with my statement and not *yes* there were issues.

"Okay, well big guy, it's your turn for some sleep. I've got it."

The rumble this time was much stronger, but he didn't nudge me.

He slumped down to the floor, and I knew it was stupid, but I found myself stroking his back. One slow glide, followed by another, and to my surprise his breathing deepened until he had to be asleep. Slade had told me that Finley didn't sleep well, which meant he was absolutely exhausted.

As I sat there, fighting my own fatigue, I couldn't stop touching him. My frustration was with the other version of Finley, not his bear, who had stepped up to protect us both.

After about an hour, I shifted to get blood into my butt once more, and the bear stirred. A few hurried strokes got him right back into sleep though, and I spent the next hour trying to draw on my wolf. It was as if she also slept so deeply that she couldn't be roused, and while I felt her essence, it was muted.

The thought that Finley's bear was protecting him had me wondering if my wolf might not be doing the same for me. Was her hidden essence keeping me from fracturing under the separation from Hunter and Kellan? I had no experience with mate separation pain in new bonds, but the fact that I was functioning at all surprised me.

I did expect that the mate still out there, *circling above*, was unfortunately helping. The *tug tug tug* in my chest wouldn't abate, no matter how hard I shoved it aside.

Around the time the sun started to rise, tendrils of light filtering through the cave, Finley stirred. Knowing this might be the last moments of peace with him, I slid my hands into his fur and breathed him in. "I'm sorry, mate," I whispered, my voice breaking. "I know we'll most likely never be more than antagonistic pack mates, and I accept that, but I wish I could take away your pain. You didn't deserve what happened to you."

Neither of us did.

A tingle of magic caressed my skin, and I jerked back as the change washed over him. It was a smooth transition, and I was left staring at a big body no longer covered in fur.

Finley was all smooth, light-brown skin, long limbs, and heavy muscles.

I swallowed roughly as I noticed his beard and hair were longer and more disheveled than usual, which only added to his visual appeal. Stupidly sexy asshole.

His head snapped up as if he'd finally remembered that I was here, and I was locked in his gaze, the heat of his blazing eyes turning them burnt gold. They were accompanied by a furious expression, and as I'd expected, the peace between us was about to end.

Violently.

CHAPTER 10

EMME

"What the fuck are you doing, Emmeline?"

Nice opening line, asshole. It was almost a relief to have this version of Finley back, as I'd been softening toward his furry side.

"What *the fuck* does it look like I'm doing?" I shot back. "Keeping an eye out while you slept. Just like I said I would."

Finley pushed himself up, his powerful arm muscles drawing my gaze briefly before I looked away. His packaging was pretty, but inside he was broken and abrasive. Regrettably, it was hard to miss that he was as stacked as the other alphas. Less defined, with more of the *big boy* bulk.

Stupid appealing fucker.

It was also hard not to look for his tattoos, as I'd been intrigued to know what the artist himself had chosen for his own skin, but…

No! Finley was a prick, and I was done with his shit.

My wolf didn't even stir to fight me on that statement, which at least distracted me from the naked alpha. If I didn't get her back soon, I would be in real danger of ending up like my mom anyway. The day my mom stopped feeling her beast's energy within her, she took one of the ropes from Blaine's collection—he liked to tie me and her down, for different reasons, thank the goddess—and hung herself from the streetlight out the front of our apartment.

I'd found her.

Along with the note she left to explain how she was too empty to go on living. I'd run the same day, leaving with that final memory of her and a newfound fear that I would end up the same way.

"—you can't just disappear. We're under fucking attack."

Finley's shouts broke through my trauma, and I groaned, rubbing at my temples. "Could you just shut up for a few minutes. I might not have a father, but I don't need you to step in and take the role."

His chest shook as he grumbled. "Did you just tell me to shut up? Do you need a reminder that I rescued you, Ice Queen. How about a little gratitude?"

I pushed to my feet, refusing to have this argument sitting down. "While I'm grateful that you tracked me down, and you're going to have to explain how you managed that, I'm not grateful enough to continue to be *your fucking punching bag.*"

His eyes blazed into me, but I was on a roll, as everything I wanted to say to him for weeks poured out. "Listen up, Finley Thornton. I've told you this before and I'm about to repeat it again: don't take your past traumas and bad attitude out on me. I don't deserve it, and I will not accept it any longer."

In one graceful leap, he was on his feet, towering over me. "You don't deserve it?"

As he stepped closer, I caught a glimpse of a line of text near his hip, and another on his ribcage, but I couldn't make out the words. "I don't deserve it," I confirmed with force, and his eyes darkened.

There might have only been a couple of feet of physical distance between us, but our emotions were a million miles apart. "You could have been my salvation," Finley choked out, a note of sorrow underlining his anger. "Instead, you broke me just as badly as the other shifters in my life who were supposed to love me."

That direct hit burned deep in my chest, and I reacted defensively. "You will never find salvation until you can get over your own shit," I said, a red haze tingeing my mind. "I know you're a victim, but you can't play that role forever. You can't *use* that trauma forever to excuse away your own shitty behavior."

I sucked in a deep breath and tried to lower my voice as we were still being hunted by a dragon. "I have my own trauma, Finley. I have my own tragic past and shattered heart. I have my own scars that will forever mark and change me. I'm no one's salvation. I'm barely surviving as it is, let alone capable of taking responsibility for another shifter. You have to deal with your trauma. You have to find strength in yourself before you look for it in someone else."

This speech wasn't just for him either.

My new plan moving forward was to make myself stronger so I could stop relying on alphas to fight my battles. They could help, of course, but I wanted to *save myself* on occasion too.

"You never took responsibility for your rejection," he said with a scoff, crossing his arms over his chest, redefining how broad and thick his shoulders were.

His jabs were as sharp as always, and my laughter was brittle. "The irony of what you just said is next-level."

When he smirked, that red hovering on the edge of my vision turned molten, and I knew whatever was about to come out of his mouth next would tip me right over the edge. "My actions have been completely justified. You needed to understand the consequences of your actions, and the rest of our pack are too pussy whipped to do more than accept your treatment of them. Fuck, you've all but stolen Kellan from me and the team."

The angrier Finley got, the more irrational his attacks became, like a toddler lashing out in confusion and pain. But he wasn't a toddler, and I wasn't taking it any longer.

"Hey, Finley…" I said, my lips curving into a smile.

His eyes narrowed at my sudden change of tone. "What?"

I grabbed both of his shoulders, and as he went to lower his arms toward me, I slammed my knee right into his balls. Our faces were close enough that I saw his eyes widen, and a flash of pain creased the corners of his lips. When I stepped away, he crumpled to the ground, gasping for air.

I crouched until I was closer. "How's that for a consequence of your action?"

He replied with a gasping grunt, and despite the tendrils of guilt I felt at causing him pain, I wasn't sorry I'd hit him. "I won't be your punching bag any longer," I murmured, my voice breaking. "I won't be your anything any longer. We're done."

There was a fissuring in the air between us, and a second later my wolf rose strongly. At first, I thought it was in response to my fight with Finley, but then I felt them out there.

Kellan and Hunter.

They're here.

Finley groaned from the ground. "Pack is here," he huffed out. "Not sure I can walk though."

Tempted to kick him again—in the side this time, I wasn't a monster—I stared down at him. "I'm walking out of here now. I don't care if you follow or not. I don't have time or energy for you any longer, and if you *EVER* speak to me that way again, I will cut your balls off and feed them to my wolf. She'll gobble them right up, and neither of us will lose a wink of sleep over it. I. Am. Done."

I repeated it with force, and Finley's features, already blanched from the nut shot, went starkly white. His eyes were wide and shimmering in unspent emotions, and I got the sense he was pleading with me not to go. Which I flat-out ignored.

Spinning on one foot, I strode through the mouth of the cave without a single glance behind me.

Finley had gone too far this time, and while he might not have deserved what happened to him in the past, he absolutely deserved my knee in his balls.

When the bright morning light hit my face, I picked up the pace and ignored the frosty bite of the crisp air. Righteous anger was fueling my blood, so I'd be fine. In the harsh light of day, the forest looked even more desolate, and I hurried through it, ignoring the new attack against my bare feet.

It could be worse; I could be Finley who was bare-ass naked. I doubted he'd risk shifting back to his bear and getting stuck, especially since I wouldn't be helping him again.

Next time, he was on his own.

With the tugging of my mates growing stronger in my chest, my wolf's presence came back in heavy waves. The ground trembled as I moved, and when a crash shook the sky above, I picked up the pace until I sprinted. The chill of the air faded under an assault of fire from above, and I was fairly sure I knew what I'd find in the skies when I stepped out from the trees.

It took every scrap of my scattered focus not to trip over the gnarled roots and exposed brush, and even when my hair caught on branches, I didn't stop. Another crash had me stumbling, as near deafening roars shattered the air around us.

· · ·

My face was hot, and I had no doubts it was tinged pink from the unnatural heat. Every breath I drew in scorched my lungs, and I was afraid that by the time I found my pack, it'd be too late to stop what was happening out there.

This was one for the history books. The first of its kind.

An honest to goddess dragon battle, and I had no idea how I was going to stop them from killing each other—and the rest of us in the process.

CHAPTER 11

SLADE

e'd made quick progress across the country to Texas, and as badly as I wished to be in my dragon form, shielded from the heavier emotions of losing my omega, I refused to tire myself out before we arrived.

I had no idea what to expect or how hard they'd be to find; none of my searches brought up any property owned by Blaine or his pack in Marfa, Texas. Wherever they were holding Emme was completely off grid, with no registered electricity or plumbing connected.

We'd be tracking them the old-fashioned way, helped along hopefully by the tangible connection between Hunter, Kellan, and Emme. A connection I didn't have yet, maybe *ever*, and for once I was grateful not to be suffering with my brothers. I needed to keep my head clear while in enemy territory.

During our flight, Hunter had taken to staring pensively out the window, his hands steepled in front of him. His face was expressionless but his eyes blazed gold—he was on the edge. I'd never seen him this close to losing it, and a complete loss of control would have him making mistakes.

Mistakes that could hurt Emme.

Hence why I was determined to remain as calm as possible, despite the rage building in my gut.

Kellan had taken to pacing up and down the plane, his hand rubbing in circular motions across his chest. Sorrow, pain, and desperation bled from them both, and I couldn't begin to fathom how hard it was to have bonded and then lost her, when I was struggling not to shift and all but disintegrate this fucking plane.

Emme had burrowed under my skin so flawlessly that I never saw it coming. She'd been a curiosity when she first appeared on the scene, and I'd had no idea if I would embrace or destroy the interloper to our pack life. That curiosity soon turned into obsession as I found myself stalking her every step, following digitally, along with in real life.

Everything about her took me by surprise, from the way her eyes lit up and she'd throw her head back to laugh when she was truly happy, to the concentration on her face when she was attempting to decipher words. She had no idea how strong she was, but I saw it. I saw it every damn day.

Fuck, I knew her face better than my own, with all her tanned skin and freckles—that I could map in my sleep—along with the icy blue of her eyes and strawberry hint in her hair.

I knew her… and I'd still fucking lost her.

The memories of our prank war were some of the best I had in my life, but I couldn't let it happen again. I'd been amused when she shut down the cameras, and I hadn't overridden them so I could experience her prank without any prior knowledge.

My selfish needs had gotten her kidnapped and hurt.

I had no idea yet what my choice fully cost her, but I would find out soon enough. I just hoped I could live with the consequences of my actions. One thing I did know for sure was that it would never happen again.

Our mate might have thought she was under surveillance before, but that was nothing on how closely I'd watch her now. Every step. Every breath. Every fucking second, she was mine.

The pilot's voice came through the speaker advising us that we were about to land, and to take our seats. Kellan ignored him completely, growling and grumbling as he stomped up and down the aisle. Hunter continued to scowl into the dark sky, the morning sun not yet breaking through on the horizon.

We were heading for a private airfield that we'd paid a fuck-ton to use, keeping our names and organization out of all paperwork. We wouldn't risk Emme by giving those bastards advance notice of our arrival.

Hunter pulled to his feet and grabbed the tactical gear we always had stored on our plane. He handed Kellan an armored vest and weapons, before he donned his own. I didn't bother. Most likely I'd be in my dragon form for this battle, and it was better not to weigh myself down with gear that'd only get destroyed.

"There's a car waiting here for us," Hunter said, his voice rasping from lack of use. "And an ATV in Marfa. If she's in an underground bunker, I doubt they're keeping her in the town itself, and I want to be prepared for anything. Including isolated and rugged terrain."

"I'll be in dragon form," I said flatly. "I can track her better that way. You will follow my lead."

It wasn't that I generally toned down my dominance around Hunter, but I never pushed it either. He was the entitled alpha by my choice; we all accepted the hierarchy with no need to challenge it, but today I was too furious and worried to keep my essence contained.

Hunter, thankfully, just nodded, also too pissed off to fight me when we had other assholes to deal with.

The plane touched down smoothly, none of us in our seats as ordered, and by the time we came to a halt, Kellan had already released the door and was preparing to disembark.

"Fuel up and plan to take off at short notice," Hunter advised the pilot and copilot as we headed down the stairs. I immediately spotted a black Mercedes Maybach S680 sitting off the side of the runway, waiting as Hunter had promised.

We'd never owned one of these, and frankly I didn't give a shit about cars today, but at least I knew it was fast and somewhat discreet. Hunter got into the driver's side, and Kellan slid into the back so I could take the passenger seat. I was our greatest defense if we were attacked, which made this the best formation.

"Get there fast," I growled, my beast sending flames through my center until the car filled with the scent of smoke and the heat of dragon fire.

"My fucking pleasure," Hunter murmured, putting his foot down so hard we were thrown back in our seats.

The speed helped to calm me. I maintained it was the second best feeling to flying.

The airfield was a fair distance from Marfa, but the car handled the roads well and got us into the city in record time. Once we reached the main street, Hunter navigated through a series of backroads until he reached an old mechanic's yard. The metal gates opened after Hunter keyed in a code, and I knew this facility was human-owned.

Humans liked money, which came in handy when we needed their assistance. They all had a price, and generally, we could afford it.

Hunter parked the vehicle behind a mound of old engine parts, then we relocated to the ATV. It was a newer model, one of those rugged off-roading versions that would be fast and capable over any terrain. It didn't appear to be registered for road use, but that wouldn't matter.

If everything went to plan, we'd be out of town before anyone here noticed.

"You shifting now?" Kellan asked.

I nodded, already calculating in advance. "Yeah, we're still in early sunrise and this area is isolated. I'll be able to get high enough to blend before anyone notices. You two follow as closely as you can, and signal if you feel her through your bonds."

I ditched my clothes, leaving them in the back seat of the Mercedes. The shift was seamless, and my beast wanted to roar at finally having his freedom to hunt our mate again. For the sake of remaining undetected though, we kept that roar internal.

Spreading my heavy wings and pumping them until my body lifted was as easy as walking. As I soared into the chilly morning air, the fires in my gut burned hotter and brighter. I traveled in shadows as the sun rose, and pushed my essence to the surface until the shimmer of my scales reflected the light. If any humans looked up, I'd appear as nothing more than a sunbeam.

In this form, my senses were strong, and while I couldn't scent Emme, there was a tugging in my center that led me away from the town toward an uninhabited section of land.

I flew for a while, changing directions as I followed the tug. I'd always felt a pull toward the omega, but this calling felt different. It reminded me of the time I was hit with an urge to return to the volcano and search for more of my kind—a search that had ended in disappointment. I refused to believe today would yield the same results.

When I got closer to whatever was drawing me, my beast took over, moving frantically as if he was afraid we'd be too late. Trusting in his instinct, I let the human side of my mind fade under the ferality of the dragon. Our kind was ancient and wise, and I trusted him to act right when it came to our mate. At least when it came to saving her.

That pull in my chest deepened, and I smelled a rich sweetness on the air for the first time. Only it wasn't Emme's chocolate and honey, it was different. Deeper and tied to the land, with a very mild undercurrent of the same smokiness of my scent.

My beast roared suddenly, and to my fucking surprise, there was a roar in return.

A dragon roar.

I'd know that sound anywhere. My wings moved faster as I raced across the countryside, leaving my brothers behind for the first time.

I had to get to whatever waited out there.

I had to know who had called me.

A dragon appeared on the horizon, roughly the same size and dimensions as me, but his scales were an inky black, with just a shimmer of green, like an oil slick across water. My beast roared again, and he returned it once more, this time with a hint of rage underlying the sound.

Emme was here too, I felt her in my gut, but the tugging had been for this shifter. *A dragon.*

Who, in my center, I knew was part of my clan.

My family line.

The same that had called to me when I was younger. He hadn't been there when I arrived that time. But he was here today, and he had something to do with my omega.

The darker dragon raced towards me, and I wasn't sure what he intended to do, until he struck out with his tail, aiming right for a vulnerable section of my throat. I dodged and rolled to the side, shaking off confusion and pain as I registered that, kin or not, we were about to fight.

Spinning into another evasive maneuver, I came up from below him, my fangs out as I bellowed fire and sliced with my claws into his side. The fire would do nothing, but while we were vulnerable to very few weapons in this form, dragon claws cut through our scales.

Ignoring the gouges now dripping blood from his side, he attacked with force, swiping across my right front leg. I pulled away in time for it to only end up a minor scratch, but it was a close call.

He was well trained too.

As we moved closer again, clashing mid-air, I locked my gaze on his dark eyes, noticing that they held the same hint of green as his scales. It was almost as if he had inverted colors to mine, and I wondered if his green went darker or lighter depending on his beast's mood.

Wait. I shouldn't be wondering about him at all. He'd attacked me, and was clearly part of whomever took Emme. Which meant he was the enemy.

An enemy who had to die.

Even if it did feel like I would be cutting out my own heart in the process.

For my mate, I'd do that, and worse.

I'd cut out every fucking heart in this world and let her bathe in the blood.

CHAPTER 12

EMME

In the moments between hiding in the forest and emerging into the open, the sun came out in force, bringing with it an extra chill to the air. When I stepped out under its rays, I tried to anticipate what I would see, but my expectations couldn't even touch the reality.

The sky was awash in intense orange and red flames as two dragons circled each other, huge wings flapping and casting shadows as they dipped and dived, roaring their rage into the world. Slade's dragon was immediately familiar to me, the early morning light reflecting off his predominantly green scales, which really highlighted his difference to the other dragon.

Talon. His beast was so black it appeared devoid of light, like he bore a layer of darkness around his scales. As the pair moved, I thought I caught a tinge of green on Talon's hide, but it might have been Slade's reflection when they clashed.

Other than the colors, the pair were identical.

Same size, same head shape, same neck, boning, and tail.

Identical.

I couldn't quite wrap my head around how this was possible, but clearly Fletcher had found one more dragon egg, or he'd figured out how to clone Slade without his knowledge.

I had no idea what role Blaine played in all of it, but he was another secret family member in Fletcher's life.

More flames spewed from Slade's mouth, and even at the distance the heat scorched my exposed skin. It was a nice deterrent against the frosty breezes, but also a touch too intense for comfort.

When my mate bites tingled again—all three of them—I knew the others were closing in.

I hated that to my wolf, and in my shifter essence, Talon was as equal a mate as the other two. Our bond might feel less complete, but it was no less important to our shifter side.

My wolf surged up as if she agreed, and I almost lost control and shifted. *Where have you been?* I mentally cried, my hands shaking as I clenched my fists.

Mates.

That was the only reply I received, and I hoped she was confirming my thoughts from earlier. She'd retreated to protect us from the pain of the strained mate bonds. Now they were here, she was strengthening and giving me my shifter side back.

Looking around, I waited for Hunter and Kellan to appear, racking my brain for a solution to the battle above us. Unlike when Talon and Finley fought, I wasn't in a position to jump between them. Not only could I not fly, I wouldn't survive even one hit from a dragon.

But I had to do something.

"EMMELINE!"

Speaking of the fucking bear... His shout crashed into me, but I didn't turn or acknowledge him. From the moment we met, there'd been a crack between us, and while I'd accepted the fracture had been put there through my actions, it was Finley's *reactions* that kept chipping away until we now had a chasm the size of the Grand Canyon between us.

A chasm that was too large to ever fill, and I would not indulge in his attitude any longer.

We had so much other shit to deal with that Finley's trauma was no longer on my list.

"Emme!" he growled again, closer to my side. "Emmeline Anders, can you hear me?"

His voice deepened, but I found it easy to ignore in the face of the dragon battle above. Neither of the magnificent beasts were gaining an inch, but at least they didn't appear badly injured yet.

"Emme." A softer inflection from Finley, and I shivered as his heat and scent mixed with mine. "Please."

This whispered plea had my throat tightening, and there was a telltale burn behind my eyes, but I didn't break. No one could bring me to tears faster than this bear, and the fucking pain in his voice was my undoing.

I knew if I turned to meet his beautiful eyes, I'd lose my resolve, and nothing would ever change between us. Finley had shown me his softer side before—a brief trickle of warmth and care—only to then tear it away in a brutal and devastating fashion.

I had to protect myself and my mental health, which, let's be real, was held together by gum and string at this point. I'd been forcibly bonded by one shifter already this week, and that was my maximum tolerance of asshole, bully behavior.

Finley fell silent, but I could feel his gaze on the side of my face, while mine remained firmly on the sky. In truth, I was freaking out over their fight, and barely resisting the urge to scream at both dragons to get their asses down here and resolve this like adults. Only we weren't *adults* in the sense that humans used that word. We were shifters, with beasts in our souls, and beasts fought when cornered, hurt, or afraid.

"How is this possible?" Finley asked, pain still lingering in the deeper recesses of his voice, even as he attempted to sound conversational. "How was there another dragon in our world all along and no one ever knew? And he looked just like Slade, right? I didn't imagine that in my bear rage. He was the near spitting image of our mate."

Our mate. So inclusive for an asshole who'd made an artform out of disassociating himself from me and my place in this pack. Ignoring him was harder when I wanted to discuss this with him, but the chasm between us kept me silent.

"We were panicked when you disappeared on us, Emme," he continued, "and I'm sorry I handled that so poorly back there. When my bear takes hold, I lose control of my reason. I *become* the bear completely, and he was terrified that we'd lost you. If it wasn't for the soothing nature of your omega side, there's no way I could have shifted back. Last time it took Kenz weeks to coax me from the beast. When we're terrified or raging, we react poorly, which led to me placing blame in the wrong place." He turned fully to face me, and *fucking hell this was hard.* "But none of us believed you'd left of your own volition."

I was desperate to ask him everything that had happened after I was taken, from who discovered it, to how long it took them to come after me. But the answers made no difference to where we were right now, so I remained strong and silent.

Finley's chuckle was unexpected. "How did we know you didn't choose to run, I hear you ask? Well, firstly, you signed the note as Emmeline. You would have used Emme, even if you were leaving us. Secondly, you told me you wouldn't leave without discussing it, and I know you well enough that a brief note wouldn't count as a 'discussion.'"

My breath shuddered out of me as I took a step away from him, wishing I had wings to escape into the sky too. Finley was hurting me again, only this time it was with his gentleness, and it felt like too little and too late.

Still, there was no denying that I was crumbling and so was he, until eventually we'd both just be broken fragments on the floor, swept up in the wind, the pieces of our souls scattered across the universe.

Desperate for a distraction, I snapped my head to the left as soon as I heard the faint rumble of an engine, finding an ATV popping into view off on the horizon. My wolf perked up too and she strained against my hold as the vehicle got closer, until we could see the two, huge alphas inside the open cab. *Hunter and Kellan.*

I was running in the next breath, with a naked bear-shifter keeping pace by my side. Finley stayed with me every step of the way.

"You're doing so well," he encouraged when I started to puff out a mile in, and it hadn't escaped my notice that the smug bastard wasn't even breathing heavily.

Shift. My wolf piped up and I found myself tearing up at her exasperation over my lack of endurance. I would never take her presence for granted again.

Can't be naked at the moment, I reminded her, and she huffed a few times but didn't argue.

The ATV flew across the landscape, jumping over rocks and anything in its way, as both alphas hung out the open-door cavities. As they closed in, I saw that Hunter was behind the wheel, and when he brought the vehicle to a halt, he leapt out in a flash, Kellan right behind him.

They reached me together, the three of us collapsing as they swept me into their arms.

I had no idea who was where as limbs surrounded me, but it didn't matter. It was a big ol' love pile, and I soaked up every second of it as I clung to them, the tears I'd been holding on to for days soaking their shirts.

There were no other shifters in the world I'd fall apart with so thoroughly, and not only know they'd hold the pieces but would also put me back together. It was a level of trust I'd never expected to have, and the fact that it had come into my life the way it did told me that fate wasn't my enemy. Not anymore.

When I finally pulled away, Kellan's face was damp too, and Hunter's eyes flared with gold as he examined my face and body, as if searching for injuries. My new bite was covered by my shirt, and I didn't have the heart to tell him during our happy reunion.

I mean, happy if you discounted the dragon battle above our heads.

Hopefully *someone* had a solution to that.

CHAPTER 13

EMME

Kellan and Hunter started talking at the same time.

"Pretty mate, we've spent the last week tearing our way across America searching for you," Golden wailed. "Can you never leave my side again. Please. My sanity depends on it." His blue eyes bore into me as he held on.

Hunter's voice was all growl: "You're going to be the fucking death of me, Emmeline. And the death of anyone who touched you when you were away from us."

I mentally frolicked in a happy place at their declarations, leaning into my mates. "I'm so fucking relieved to see you. I've been dying a million deaths without you and our bond. Did your beasts retreat into your essence as well?"

Hunter slid his hands up to grip my cheeks, forcing me to focus on him as I attempted to look at both of them equally. I'd just missed their perfect faces so much. "Your beast retreated?" he demanded, and I nodded around his grip.

"Yeah, I was almost human. No extra senses and no ability to shift. I knew she wasn't completely gone, but she was close enough that it genuinely worried me I'd lose her."

Hunter's expression never changed, but his growl ripped through the morning air, as loud as the dragons fighting above us.

"As concerning as that was," Finley piped up, from where he stood behind us, too damn close for my liking, "we have a slightly more pressing issue. As you've probably noticed, Slade is not the last of his kind. I found Emme with the other dragon in an underground bunker. It was nearly impossible to track her there, as the walls were lined and magically blocked, keeping her scent hidden. It was only when I followed a shifter getting supplies in town that I got on the right track."

He paused, and I didn't turn or acknowledge him, not even as he added, "Emme was locked in a room with the dragon."

Kellan added to Hunter's menacing growl, his eyes nearing an intense violet in color. "What did he do to you, Emme?" he asked slowly, as if he barely got the words out. "Did he hurt you in any way?"

It was a loaded question, considering the pulsing bite on my neck. "He didn't rape or beat me," I said quickly, offering what little reassurance I could. "There's so much I need to tell you, including how I was taken and who was responsible for that, but first we need to deal with the dragon fight before Slade gets hurt."

Or Talon.

Not that I'd mention that out loud until I'd shared all the information, including the fact that our pack was now irrevocably tied to another dragon.

Hunter didn't release my face, his wolf's gaze locked onto me. I silently pleaded with him to give me time, and that I'd tell him everything when our pack was no longer in immediate danger. With a heavy exhale, he leaned forward and pressed his lips to mine. A brief touch, no more than a slide of his tongue across mine, and then he released his hold.

Kellan stepped into that space, and his kiss was more passionate as he ran his hands through my hair and pulled me close. His tongue demanded entry, and I gladly obeyed, losing all focus. We needed this reassurance that we were together, alive, and our beasts were all safe.

"We felt your pain," he whispered when he pulled away, still cupping the back of my neck. He looked exhausted, and I'd bet good money that none of them had properly slept since I was taken. "Hours after you were stolen away, there was a rush of pain, and then you faded from our bond. We knew you weren't dead, but our connection was being blocked."

I nodded harshly. "Yeah, they teamed up with the Termaine witches to block us." And break our quintet. Fletcher had revealed his continued involvement with that coven right after my forced bonding, to really drive home that there was no hope in waiting for my pack to rescue me.

Hunter gaze narrowed on me. "Termaine... you mean the ones from—"

"Yep, that powerful line who were front and center of the last war. Apparently, they weren't all killed off, and they've been planning this for a long time. They're involved in my kidnapping, the death of my mother, and a lot of other shit."

The confusion remained on all their faces as Hunter asked, "What are they trying to achieve? Last time they had an alpha at the helm, but are you saying they're working alone now?"

Swallowing roughly, I wished I didn't have to reveal this part, though I doubted he'd be surprised. "Yeah, they still have an alpha, and he wants the same result as last time. The end of quintets and cities, and the return of packs with a single alpha."

"I will fucking kill Blaine, that piece of shit," Kellan burst out, grinding his boots into the dirt.

Squeezing my eyes briefly closed, I shook my head. "It's not just Blaine. He's involved, but there's a stronger alpha at the helm." Hunter met my gaze, and I saw the resignation on his expression right before I said, "It's Fletcher Davenport."

Hunter nodded, having guessed it in the seconds before my reveal. "There's more too. Blaine called him... Father."

There was a flicker of gold in the darkest recesses of Hunter's storm cloud eyes as he said, "I don't know or care about that part, but I wished I was surprised about Fletcher's involvement. That fuck has always been obsessed with omegas, which was why I was determined to never allow him near you."

Swallowing hard, I whispered, "I think he's killed omegas in the past. I believe he's been taking them for years, secretly, and experimenting on them. He implied that there weren't enough to experiment on, but in the same breath told me that my mom's death was his doing. If we investigated his life, I bet we'd find others."

There was a surge of Hunter's rage through our bond. "Did he touch you?"

"No," I hurriedly said. "Not really. He has others to take care of his dirty work."

Unintentionally, my gaze lifted to Talon, and as I stretched, the neckline of my sweatshirt slipped, and Kellan's howl was my first indication that he'd caught sight of my new bite.

As his broken, furious cry filled the air, it caught even the dragon's attentions, and Slade dropped into a dive, heading straight for us.

Talon right behind him.

I didn't see what happened next as Kellan wrapped his hands around my biceps and lifted me off the ground. I focused on his paler-than-usual face, hoping this wasn't the moment my pack was destroyed beyond repair. "Emme," he choked out. "Baby. What did they do to you?"

I brushed my hand down his cheek in an attempt to calm his raging beast, as Hunter pressed in closer to my side, no doubt wondering what he'd missed.

Finley's expression was sad as he met mine, and he nodded as if to say he had my back.

"Fletcher has had that dragon under his control for years," I said, as calmy as I could. "When they first took me, he forced the dragon to bite me, and since I was being controlled by magic, I had no choice but to bite him back." As their devastated expressions wavered before my tear-filled gaze, I pushed on. "We're bonded. Me and Talon. Which means you can't kill him, at least not until we figure out if the bond can be broken."

Hunter's expression shattered as he reached out, as if to tear me from Kellan's shaky hold, only he never got the chance. The thump of Slade's dragon slamming into the ground distracted us all, as he raced on all fours in our direction. Talon right on his tail.

"Put me down," I whispered, wriggling against Kellan. "Come on, Golden Boy, you need to pull it together. We're all still here and able to fight. Don't give up yet."

That snapped him out of his daze, and when my feet touched the ground, I turned to run for Slade, only to have Hunter stepping in my path. I ducked to avoid his hold, which was impossible when the damn alpha had arms longer than my body.

"We can't let them kill each other," I shouted, fighting his hold. "I'm the only one who can stop it."

"Not a fucking chance!" Finley snarled, taking both of us by surprise—Hunter's eyebrows drew together as he attempted to process the bear protecting me. "You will not risk yourself by getting between two fire-breathing dragons. They can take care of themselves. You cannot."

Goddess, I needed proper fight training so they'd stop seeing me as this vulnerable little cupcake. "You saw Talon in the bunker," I said with a snap. "He's protective. He considers me to be part of his clan, or his possession… whatever concept dragons use. He's not going to kill me, especially not when we're newly bonded, which would possibly kill him as well."

Finley's stubborn expression didn't soften, and Hunter's hold only tightened.

Yeah, we were all shocked.

"Baby," Kellan breathed, still sounding so devastated, it felt like that word stabbed through my heart. "We can't lose you. Not even to save Slade."

I couldn't see him around Hunter's hold, but he'd hear me just fine. "It's going to be okay, Golden. After living through almost losing you, I'm not willing to accept any of us not surviving and having our happily-ever-afters. There's a way to fix this, I'm sure of it, and if not… well, we'll be the first sextet or whatever the hell you call a pack of six. Even if Talon has to stay locked in the basement for the rest of eternity. He was raised in isolation by Fletcher Davenport, so I have no idea if he's redeemable or not, but for now he's part of our pack."

There was a choked growl from Hunter, reminding me he was raised by the same male. "You're one of the best alphas I've ever known," I said, meaning every word. "Slade too. Which means there's a chance for Talon, and I'm willing to bet on that chance." I shot him my most pleading stare. "Now I just need you to bet on me. Please, Alpha."

As Hunter contemplated my request, his breaths even and deep, Finley pushed closer to me. "They're heading right for us." His body swelled like he wanted to shift, though he didn't make the final change. "What do you want to do?"

Even though I was angry at him, I wanted to assure him that if he shifted and couldn't get back, I wouldn't leave him to deal with it alone.

We would always be a pack, even if that was all we ever had.

CHAPTER 14

EMME

"You can shift," I said softly, and though I wasn't looking at him, he knew that statement was for him.

"It's too big of a risk," he said. "The bear is useful in a physical fight but not against dragons. To win this, we'll need words and negotiations."

Hunter broke in with a rasp. "You said no rape, outside of the violation of the bite, so the bond isn't completely sealed… We will find a way to break it, little omega. Whatever it takes."

The forced bonding *was* a violation, which was why I'd initially assumed my wolf had retreated from the trauma. Now, though, it appeared likely that her withdrawal was to protect me from the repercussions of new mate bonds and distance.

The violation was my human side's trauma, and once I was safely back home, I'd let myself feel the full extent of the pain. Until then, we were in crisis mode.

The ground thundered as the dragons raced towards us, and there was an innate fear that came when facing terrifying beasts, even from those of us in their pack. Dragons were mystical creatures, and their sheer size alone had me near peeing my pants.

Ancient energy sparked between their giant bodies, but there were no more flames. Talon's wings remained slightly aloft as he ran, their darkness standing out starkly against the sunlight. While Slade's green glowed brightly in comparison.

They were both beyond breathtaking.

"I know we're supposed to be terrified right now," Kellan murmured as he moved to stand beside Finley, "but have you ever seen anything this spectacular before? It'd be a shame if they fried our asses before we got to brag about watching two dragons run across the desert."

Hunter grunted, and Finley released a strangled laugh. "Too soon, bro," the bear said, "You can't joke about our impending death until *after* it has passed. At this stage, we're still right in the line of fire."

Kellan's laughter was lighter. "Nah, Slade would never fry us. Or at least not Emme… not that any of us will be using her as a human shield. Fuck no. She needs to get behind us right this instant." Getting behind them would not help. I needed to be out in front.

Struggling once more against Hunter's hold, I racked my brain for the self-defense moves Slade had been trying to teach me to use against a larger opponent. There'd been a step where I dropped my weight into my attacker and then twisted to break his hold…

"I don't like that look on her face," Finley said, drawing everyone's attention to me. "She's plotting."

Wrinkling my nose, I let my annoyance spill free. "Kellan, can you please remind Finley that he doesn't know me well enough to make comments like that."

Finley just laughed, the arrogant bear completely untroubled by my comment. "I know you, Ice Queen. I know you better than you think."

Kellan cleared his throat, and when I looked his way, his expression was calmly amused.

"You should also ask Finley about his balls," I suggested with a smirk, and before I could continue, Kellan's chuckle cut me off.

We were probably about to be stampeded to death by dragons, but of course now was the right time for laughter.

"My balls are also fine," Finley replied in his chilled-out rumble. "If you glance down, you'll see for yourself. It'd take more than your impressive right knee to keep me down for long. I'm… used to pain."

My anger deflated, cutting off my next passive-aggressive reply, and I returned my focus to the dragons. Slade was still a touch in front of Talon and would reach us first—within the next minute.

"I need you guys to trust me," I said, hoping they would accept what my role really was in this pack. "Trust that neither of those dragons would hurt me, and I'm literally the only one who can defuse the situation. We don't have much time. I'm sure Fletcher has figured out his guards are dead in the bunker, and he'll come with his entire army. We're not strong here, away from Golden Claw, and I'm determined that we beat that bastard."

Fletcher Davenport was a powerful alpha, and I had no doubt magic fueled his strength, which was another reason we needed to return home. Return and regroup.

With both dragons.

"I can't let you go to them," Hunter groaned, sounding torn. "I trust in you and your strengths, little omega. You're literally the heart of our pack, and no one's opinion matters more to me, but my wolf is feral and refuses to release control. He has to protect you. Even from yourself."

Finley shuffled closer, and when he met my gaze I waited for him to chime in and agree again. A small smile tilted his lips, and then he… *winked* as he lowered one shoulder and charged at Hunter, taking the alpha by surprise and breaking his hold on me.

What the fuck? Apparently somewhere along the line, I'd convinced him to let me try this my way.

Kellan got caught in the tackle too, and all three alphas went down in a tangle of limbs as Finley shouted, "Run, Emme."

I'd been knocked to the side, and it took a few steps to right myself, as I took off at a sprint toward the dragons. I headed for Slade first, his green beast skidding to a halt before we collided.

The brawling of the other alphas was loud behind us, but I ignored it all to stare into the dragon's unflinching green gaze, assessing his current temperament. When Slade lowered his head, his nostrils flared as he sniffed my body. When he reached my cold and dirty feet, a puff of heat encased them, and they were much warmer when he was done.

"Slade, are you okay?" I asked, running my gaze over him too, taking in the scratches marring his scales. "Did Talon hurt you?"

A clear and derisive rumble escaped the beast, and I backtracked. "I mean, I know you're the most ferocious of beasts to walk this world, but I doubt you expected to encounter another dragon today. That must have been confronting."

He shook his huge head, before it swung up as a rumble shook his thick chest. Talon had stopped about ten feet away. His beast was watching me in the same intense way his other form did in the bunker.

This close, I noticed he had quite a lot of green pigment bisecting his dark eyes, and shimmering over his midnight scales. I found myself moving toward him, as if to bridge the distance between us all. Before I could take another step, though, a long neck snaked around me, dragging me back. Which had Talon roaring and shooting flames into the sky.

The fact that he didn't try to hurt any of us was a good sign, reiterating my belief that we had to give this dragon a chance to show us who he truly was. And it had to happen before Fletcher or Blaine returned.

"You need to trust me," I said to Slade, repeating my words from before. "There's only one way we can *all* move forward, and it's going to require Talon come with us. *Whether he likes it or not.*"

Slade's body rumbled, shaking me and the ground, and then to my astonishment, he unfurled his hold around me. When I took a step forward, he followed, but didn't stop me again.

Holy shit. The two alphas I'd never expected to have my back had come through so completely that my poor heart was thundering in my chest. Kellan, Hunter, and Finley continued to grapple behind us, with the bear giving me this chance to calm the situation.

He'd dropped the first shovel of dirt in the chasm between us, and only time would tell if there'd be more.

Talon calmed as I moved closer, and I forced myself not to fidget. "Hey," I said softly, "fighting won't solve this issue. You're mated into this pack, and with that, you're going to have to work with us. Fletcher might have promised that I'd come to you without baggage, but he was wrong. I'm already part of a quintet. One I've claimed."

Visible steam emerged from Talon's nostrils, and his head lowered, which had Slade's hackles rising. "Enough!" I snapped, fueled by false bravado. Which they'd clearly know from the race of my pulse and sweat coating my skin. "Talon, I need you to change back so we can talk. Will you do that for me? I promise that Slade won't attack you in his dragon form." I turned to meet the greener dragon's gaze. "Right?"

Slade's beast blew out a stream of smoke as he nodded.

In the distance, the sound of a helicopter filtered through to us, which meant our time was almost up. "Please. Do this for me," I pleaded with Talon. "Show me that there's more between us than a forced bond."

This new information set off Slade's beast, who roared so loudly my ears ached, but Talon didn't react to the rage. If anything, he tilted his head in a gesture that spoke of curiosity, but before I could figure out why, a flash of electrical energy caressed my skin, and the black dragon disappeared.

Leaving the man behind.

CHAPTER 15

EMME

I'd seen Slade naked once, and shirtless a couple of other times, but there was no getting used to the sort of body that came along with massive, ripped dragon shifters.

There were obvious differences between Slade and Talon at first glance, from the lack of tattoos and piercings to Talon's shorter hair and facial scar. But they were also so similar it was scary.

Hunter would be freaking out at the sight if he wasn't currently busy trying to crush Finley into the dirt.

"Talon," I called, gesturing him closer, all the while hoping my plan would work.

With that helicopter on the horizon, there was no time for a plan B.

Without pause, he did exactly as I hoped, and headed right for me, his focus flickering between me and Slade, who was pressed in close behind me.

"Back up," I hissed at the dragon.

Talon's steps slowed, but before he could retreat, I dashed forward and lifted my arms as if to hug him. His eyes widened, but he didn't step away or try to avoid my touch as my arms closed around his shoulders. I pressed against his naked length, annoyed when my skin tingled and wolf howled.

She wanted to be close to *all* of her mates, including Talon. I hadn't felt this possessiveness from her in the bunker, as she'd been hiding from me then. But now her interest was strong and obvious. Talon's scent grew stronger too, and I picked up hints of smoky ash in his maple, just like with Slade's marshmallow.

No, I internally cried as my beast cozied up to his curious dragon. *I don't care that he smells good. We need to subdue him until we can figure out how to fix this.*

Ignoring the whimpers of my wolf, I whispered in his ear, "You're my mate, Talon. I won't let them hurt you."

His huge chest rumbled as his arms moved to close around me, which I couldn't let happen. If he pulled my feet from the ground, I'd lose the leverage I needed to get him into position.

"But I don't trust you," I added in a breathless rush, sliding my hands farther along his shoulders, and yanking him toward me.

I fell back with all my weight, and while he clearly hadn't expected the maneuver, he didn't completely lose his balance as I'd hoped. Luckily, he still stumbled close enough that Slade's dragon could swing his head, cracking his hard skull into the side of his doppelganger, knocking the other shifter off his feet and out cold. If the way he slumped to the ground was any indication.

A flicker of guilt washed through me, even though Talon deserved that and far worse after what he'd done to me. Hunter, who'd finished with Finley by now, reached my side and helped me up from where I'd fallen.

"We need to get out of here," he said, after checking me over quickly. "Reinforcements are on their way, and there are too many of them for us to take on today. Especially not when this bastard wakes up and joins in on their side. Slade, you fly him out of here. We'll meet you at the plane."

No one argued, and I wasn't surprised to find myself hoisted in my entitled alpha's arms as he raced across the desert, dirt flying around us as he headed for the ATV. He slid into the passenger side, keeping me against his chest, while Kellan dove into the driver's seat and Finley leapt onto the back, clutching the roof bars as we took off.

"Will Slade be okay?" I shouted, the sound of the helicopter echoing through the valley

"He'll be fine. He's faster than any chopper," Hunter replied, his grip tightening on me as Kellan did a near ninety-degree turn, zooming in the opposite direction of the helicopter.

Slade came into view above us, Talon gripped in his... talons. *Ironically.*

It didn't look like a comfortable hold, with one giant claw wrapped around his right arm, and the other on his right ankle, but Talon's comfort was no doubt low on Slade's list of worries, especially with Fletcher on his tail.

I slumped into Hunter and he wrapped his arms tighter around me, both of us bracing our feet against the floor as Kellan demonstrated impressive driving abilities. Not only was he going as fast as this vehicle could move, it was over rugged terrain that shifted from sand to rock constantly.

"We left our plane on a private strip out of the main town," Kellan said as he jumped a small mound, landing heavily and almost unseating me. "We have to switch out vehicles first though."

"Fucking excellent," Finley muttered from behind us. "Don't worry about me, I'll just be back here with my balls flapping in the breeze."

Kellan didn't miss a beat. "At least it's cold. I bet that's helping minimize the flapping."

Finley growled, and even Hunter cracked a brief smile. I forced myself not to laugh, or turn around, to add visual to the commentary.

"If we put a bit of distance between us," Kellan continued, airily, "we can switch out as drivers, Fin. Give your balls a rest… and you too, since I'm sure you haven't had much sleep since Emme was taken."

"Which was… over a week ago now?" I asked, wanting to confirm what I'd learned in the bunker.

"Yes," Hunter murmured, burying his face in my hair. "You've been gone for eight of the longest fucking days of our lives. We're lucky that we tracked Blaine's pack, otherwise we wouldn't have found you here so quickly."

"And where is *here* exactly?"

"Texas," Finley called. "I've been tracking you from the moment I found your note. My bear form has the strongest senses, and he kept up with your trail until you were taken from the old shack. From there, they put you on a private plane, but thankfully once I dispatched a few security personnel, I found the flight plan for Texas. My bear hitched a ride on the back of a truck, which was why it took so long to get here. I hoped I wasn't going to be too late, especially since I couldn't shift back again and warn the others. Though apparently you had it all under control."

I was absolutely blown away by the effort that they'd all put into tracking me, and for Finley especially. It was another shovel of dirt into the chasm. His actions over the past week had very aptly demonstrated that he wasn't indifferent to me. And… he mustn't hate me.

You didn't work that hard for someone you hated.

"We went the route of tracking the Rogers pack," Hunter continued, "searching out their holdings in Silver City. It was obvious those fuckers had their hand in this."

"We didn't get Blaine though." Kellan sighed, hands tense on the wheel. "But the rest are dead. They won't bother you ever again."

The relief I felt to know that most of that pack had been wiped from this world almost took me out. "Blaine was in the bunker when I woke up," I said, the memories filtering back in. "That's why he wasn't with his pack. He's still out there with Fletcher, and the Termaine witches, and they're all dangerous."

"So are we," Hunter rumbled, his hands firming along my thighs, as if he was afraid to loosen his hold and have me slip away again.

"I honestly wasn't sure if you'd all believe the note or not," I said, voicing the fear I'd felt since the moment magic held that pen in my hand. "At first, I was confident that you and Kel would know through our bond I was being controlled, until I realized the magic locking me down blocked my fears and emotions."

"None of us believed the note," Hunter said firmly, leaving no room for doubt. "We knew you were taken by Chelsea from the start. Was Sorenson or anyone else involved? Who betrayed us?"

Holy crap… they knew about Chelsea too.

I'd been dreading having to break the news of that pack's betrayal, not that I was sure Sorenson was involved, but it was still his pack. His responsibility.

"It was only ever Chelsea that I saw," I said as Kellan took another sharp right, the helicopter's whomp finally getting quieter. "She waited outside our compound for days on the off chance I'd open those fucking books. She had a spell hidden in the pages, and it bonded me to her energy so I had to follow her lead. She was the one who penned the note for you all. She delivered me into Fletcher and Talon's hands." I had another thought. "Oh, and she bribed a security guard to look the other way when we left Golden Claw. He'd be worth investigating."

Finley grunted. "He's dead. No need to worry about him."

I blinked, but after seeing what he did to Fletcher's guards, I wasn't shocked by that admission.

"What did Fletcher say about Talon?" Hunter asked in a careful tone, and I wasn't surprised by the hint of curiosity I heard buried deep. No doubt he had a lot of questions about this shifter who was the spitting image of his brother.

"Not much. Fletcher treats him like a weapon under his control, but he has to be Slade's twin or brother or… do you think all dragons look alike?"

"There's no way to know," Finley said with a huff. "We've never seen another outside of Slade."

Kellan nodded as he flexed his hands on the wheel. "Talon has to know if they're related, right? We can ask him when we're safe and he's no longer unconscious. I'm sure Hunter's father told him something about his origins."

Hunter swore under his breath. "He's no father of mine. I've cut all ties with that bastard, and he will die at my hands sooner rather than later. Slade might not have thought his death was worth pursuing before, but I can guarantee he won't feel that way now. The second he touched our mate was the second his life ended."

I slid my hands up Hunter's arms and clutched him closer. "I'm scared for you guys to go up against him. He's strong and has magic at his disposal. Magic from an ancient line of power-hungry witches. It's not a good combo."

Hunter didn't even flinch. "He has no idea how powerful and dangerous I can be too. I've held back over the years for multiple reasons, but that's finished now. Slade will have my back, and between the two of us, he doesn't stand a chance. Especially when Talon is now our prisoner."

"The four of us," Finley shot back, leaning down until his scent hit me. "We're all in this together."

I liked the sound of that. "Five of us," I said with force.

I was determined to stand alongside the others in this final fight. I might not ever be as strong as they were, but I was going to train, and hopefully one day soon I'd take them all by surprise.

Especially those who'd underestimated me all along.

CHAPTER 16

KELLAN

There wasn't time to enjoy the dash across the desert in the awesome ATV. Not with an asshole in a helicopter dogging our steps the entire way. I took the longest possible route back into Marfa in the hopes of losing him, and by the time we switched to the Mercedes, there was no sign of Fletcher.

Hunter took over driving, and Emme fell asleep in my lap in the back seat.

"We might need to look into acquiring one of these when we're back home," I said, running my hands over the supple leather. "It's like a supercar but understated. Blending in when needed but also giving us the speed to get the fuck out of here."

Finley shifted in the passenger seat and got distracted by our mate, his gaze resting on her beautiful face. His expression was tinged with longing, and I wondered what had happened between my Shortcake and Fin before we'd showed up. The tension had been hard to miss.

"Understated isn't usually your style," he finally said, managing to tear his eyes from her to meet mine.

With a shrug, I brushed my hands through her soft hair, my wolf settled now we had her in our arms. "I'm evolving," I decided, feeling that truth settle in my bones. I brushed my hand down Emme's cheek but she didn't stir, and I hoped like hell that the dark bruises marring the delicate skin beneath her eyes were lessened by the time she woke.

As my hand skimmed her shoulder, I fought the urge to reveal the new bite. Another glimpse might send me over the edge of my sanity, but at the same time I was drawn to see it again. "I don't care if there's a sixth in our pack," I said. It changed nothing for me. "I mean, don't get me wrong, I'd love if we could just kill him and fix the issue. But with the risk to Emme, I say we just accept that we're now a sextet and move on with life."

As furious as I was that she'd been forced into a bonding, it didn't lessen our connection or my love for Emmeline Anders one tiny bit. *She was everything.* A fact that had only been reiterated in the days I'd been without her.

Hunter grunted in what sounded like an agreement as Finley asked, "Do we have record of anyone bonding into a pack of more than five? What happens to the perfect magic of a quintet?"

Hunter strangled the wheel and huffed. "There're no rules stopping packs from having more than five, but it has been shown to dilute the power of the pack. Hence why a quintet became the norm. I don't personally know packs with more, so I can't say what changed for them."

Emme stirred under my touch, her breathing rapid, and when she whimpered I stroked my fingers down her cheek until she settled once more. "I wouldn't care if we lost all of our power and turned into humans," I murmured, unable to stop from leaning down and pressing my lips against her skin. "Emme is all I want. Power is nothing without her, and we're already rich enough to live like fucking kings in the human world."

Hunter nodded, as I knew he would. "Emme is the priority here. A loss of power would only be an issue if it stopped us from protecting her. Once we eliminate the threats against us, I don't care if we're human either. But first we need to deal with the pressing issue of Fletcher and his fucking pet dragon. I can't even think about the fact that he sank his teeth into her against her will, while magic controlled her body, because I'm two seconds from flipping out and tearing the world apart."

Finley's bear rumbled loudly before he got it together. "You should have seen the way he claimed her in that room. His possessiveness rivaled all three of you fuckers, and she was desperate to get away from him."

My vision blacked out briefly, and it was only when Emme tensed under my touch that I forced myself to calm. Part of me wished I was the one carting Slade's evil-twin across the skies so I could drop his ass into a huge hole and bury him there. It was the least he deserved.

"What are we going to do about Chelsea and Sorenson?" I rumbled, changing the subject to another one that was equally as awful.

Heat rose in the car as Hunter snarled. "I want to speak with Sorenson, but as far as I'm concerned, he's responsible for what his pack does. Chelsea's actions have forever hurt and scarred Emme, and for that, they all need to die."

I hadn't been concerned that Hunter's loyalty to one of his oldest friends would win out over Emme, and I was right there with him, ready to make them all pay for their part in this.

Finley dropped his head back, exhaustion pulling at his lips. "We needed to kill them anyway, just as a warning to every other pack. Touching our mate means instant death. No excuses. No trial."

"Agreed," I said, feeling positively chipper about that whole arrangement.

Emme didn't stir again until we reached the airfield, and I was relieved to find no sign of Fletcher in the vicinity. He hadn't tracked us this far, and our plane, which was ready and fueled, as ordered by Hunter earlier, was the only one on the runway. Whatever Hunter had done to hide our path here had worked, and once we got back home, we'd have a chance to regroup and plan for our next move.

Golden Claw was our territory, and as Fletcher Davenport no longer sat on the council, and was out of the city most of the time, he held very little power there. I'd only met him a few times, and his presence always left my wolf uneasy and on edge. Even back then I'd seen the darkness lurking below his surface, and I took Hunter's warnings to stay away from him seriously.

Slade hadn't arrived by the time I carried a drowsy Emme inside and secured her in the bedroom, while Hunter and Finley did a visual check over the plane.

"He's almost here," Hunter called as I leaned out through the open door for an update on their progress. "I can feel him approaching."

My brothers and I were bonded through an official Golden Claw ceremony, which tied the essence of our beasts together. It wasn't as strong as the bite exchanged with Emme, but once she bonded all of us, we'd be in a stronger and completed quin—sextet. *Whatever.* We'd be complete.

Hunter and Slade held a more powerful connection already, thanks to a blood bond from their youth.

"Okay good," I grumbled. "I'm so fucking ready to get out of here. We need to take our girl home and support her through the fallout from what happened here. Then we have some assholes to hunt down."

Hunter's expression tightened, and it wasn't often he looked tired, but today his aura was dark. As our entitled alpha, he took on everything as *his responsibility* and blamed himself for any missteps. "She felt relatively stable when we found her, but you think there's a fallout coming?"

Yeah, I did. "I don't believe the full ramifications of what happened has hit her yet. She's been in fight and survival mode, but when she's home and safe, she'll have to deal with what was stolen from her." And what she gained, in the form of another mate, who might be a psychopath.

Hunter and Finley were silent, until the bear muttered, "She told me she was done. She told me that she wouldn't be my punching bag any longer, and I felt this... crack between us. Like, I finally broke a connection that I might not be able to repair."

Panic and pain hit me first, and I almost took a swing at him, so angry that he'd finally pushed her too far. "I warned you about that, dickhead. Now, you'd better fucking fix it," I snarled. "I don't care what it takes. If you don't want to be the one we kill so she gets her perfect quintet, fix what you broke." I loved Finley. He was my brother through and through. But I had a line, and I drew it at Emme.

"I will," he assured me, and there was nothing but determination and grit in his drawn features. "I fucked up badly by falling into my anger and pain... no, not falling, relishing. I crawled in and didn't come out, but I'm ready to move forward. I'm ready to change. I will show her that I am worthy. No matter what it takes."

It was a breakthrough we'd all been waiting for. I just hoped it wouldn't be too late.

Only time would tell.

"We will support you through this," Hunter assured him, his hand landing on Finley's shoulder. "Whatever it takes for both of you to move forward in life."

Finley looked like he wanted to cry, and I felt like an asshole for being so furious with him. Our broken brother did need support, and I'd dreamed of him being a proper member of our quintet for far too long to give up now. "Fuck," I said, wiping a hand over my face. "I'm here for you as well, Fin. You know that. Whatever it takes."

The whoosh of wings broke the tension, and we let that conversation go for now. Finley and I would need to debrief again soon, but we had bigger issues to deal with today.

When Slade was close, he dropped the unconscious shifter from a decent height, before coming into land beside him. He shifted back fast as he said, "I had to stop a few times along the way and knock him out again. The last was a decent blow and should hold for an hour or so."

Hunter's low bark of laughter was filled with satisfaction as he hauled the huge male over his shoulders. "I'll get him strapped into his seat. You do your check of the plane."

Slade nodded as he ran a hand through his hair, and headed around to do his own safety check. He didn't bother to get dressed first, as our pilots, Carl and Eugene, were shifters and knew our ways.

I stepped aside as Hunter dropped Talon into a chair, and then I helped him chain the fucker down as best we could. If he was anything like Slade, nothing we had here would truly keep him contained, but we could just keep knocking him out whenever he started to stir.

Sounded like a fun fucking game of whack-a-mole.

Once he was strapped down, Hunter stepped back. "He's Slade's fucking twin," he said, staring. "How did Fletcher do this? How did he manage to keep him hidden from us for all these years? The fact that he has other children out there doesn't surprise me, but a hidden dragon… that's harder to believe."

I grunted, wondering if there were other mythical creatures hidden in our world too. Just wandering around, in giant-ass bodies. "Ever since Emme came into our lives, all I've had are questions. Hopefully we can finally get some answers, and that they'll help us deal with the threats always lingering in the background."

Hunter nodded, his expression harder. More resolute. "Yeah, that's the gameplan moving forward. We get our answers and take out our enemies." He shot Talon one last, disgusted glare, and then headed farther into the plane. "I need to check on Emme. My wolf is raging, and we don't like her out of sight."

He strode off before I could assure him that I felt the exact same way. After days without Emme, I was filled with restless energy, and no matter what it took, we couldn't let her ever be taken from us again.

While I kept an eye on the dragon, Finley wandered into the main cabin, dressed in just a pair of sports shorts. "We're almost ready for takeoff," he said when he reached my side. "Slade's done with his final checks—"

Slade stomped into the cabin cutting him off, and we watched as the now dressed shifter secured the main door behind him. He radiated annoyance and anger as he tapped on the cockpit door to let the pilots know we were good to go.

When he reached us, he eyed the chains and ropes strapping down Talon, and his expression didn't shift. "Get ready for takeoff," he said, his voice calm. Too calm.

Our brother wasn't okay—he was very fucking far from okay.

As if he'd heard that comment, Hunter stepped out of the bedroom, his gaze meeting Slade's down the aisle. It was a charged stare, a silent communication between the pair.

As the engines grew louder, and the pilots got the plane moving, I headed for the bedroom. Emme opened her eyes as I slid in beside her, wrapping her up in my arms. "Are we safe?" she whispered, and the break in her voice shredded my heart.

"We're safe, baby," I whispered, barely restraining myself from squeezing her until I could feel her bones imprinting on mine. I was so fucking gone over her. If I could have crawled under her skin, I would have. "No matter what it takes, we'll make sure you're safe."

Emme pressed her face into my chest, and I took a second to breathe her in, and I found my beast calming under her presence. "Whatever it takes," I repeated, determined that this would be the last time she suffered at the hands of another. "We will destroy them all and live happily ever after."

I felt her smiling against me. "I love you, Golden. Wake me when we get home." She pressed her lips to my shirt in a brief kiss and then promptly fell asleep again, her exhaustion too great to fight.

"I love you too, Shortcake," I whispered, my throat tight as darker emotions raged below my calm surface.

I managed to keep it together all the way back to Golden Claw, and when the familiar city came into view, Emme was awake to see it, snuggled in my arms.

For the first time, she released a true sigh of relief, and her old spark shone in her eyes. "Home," she murmured.

"Yep, sweet mate. We're finally home."

And here we would stay, until we figured out a way to eliminate Fletcher and his evil from the world. Permanently.

CHAPTER 17

FINLEY

We'd been back in Golden Claw for a week.

A week of confusion, council meetings, and plans for what we needed to do next. A week of Slade losing his shit and crushing everyone under the might of his dominance. But it didn't make a difference. The traitors were missing or dead, Fletcher and his band of fuckheads had gone to ground, and the only one he could take his fury out on now was Talon. Who was resolutely not giving up his code of silence.

All of us were fraying at the edges, and unless something drastically changed soon, the Reeves pack were on a downward spiral to destruction.

Ironic, considering I was probably in the best mental space of the last few months.

I'd suffered a huge wakeup call out in that desert with Emme and had decided to stop denying my true feelings for her. I was just as fucking obsessed with that omega as the rest of my pack, and I was determined to finally deal with my trauma and past.

So it didn't destroy my future.

Over the last week, I'd made it to three training sessions with Coach Connor, the defensive line assistant coach, and two with Coach Gerrado, who'd been quiet since we returned. There wasn't much he could say when our mate had been kidnapped, *again*, but I got the sense he wasn't happy.

"Take as much time as your pack needs to deal with this," he'd told Kellan and me when we returned, but I knew I wasn't the only one wondering how much longer we'd be able to make hockey work with our pack dramas.

The thought of losing hockey should have sent me into a spiral, but with my new mental clarity, I was mostly indifferent about it. My priorities had changed, and it was clear that someday soon, there'd be a point that hockey didn't fit in my life. For the first time, that didn't feel like the end of the world.

After finishing my gym session for the morning, I found Kellan perched in the doorway of the kitchen, staring at Emme. "She hasn't stopped baking," he grumbled as we watched her pull a tray of cookies from the oven. "I mean, the cookies, tarts, and mini-cakes are the second-most delicious thing I've had in my mouth, right after our omega, but my heart breaks watching her hurting like this. Why doesn't she cry? It's like she's channeling all of her demons into baking."

Kellan didn't understand; he'd grown up in a stable, loving environment. In his house, you talked through your problems, and everyone jumped in to figure out a solution. That wasn't how it worked for Emme and me. Even Slade and Hunter had each other, but we'd had no one. Not really.

My brother was too young when he was murdered, and Kenzo had been dealing with his family, leaving me to handle everything on my own. Or with my beast. Hence why my bear took control at times, in his own bid to protect me.

"Compartmentalizing and staying busy is a way to cope and deal," I told him, keeping my voice low so the omega locked in my gaze wouldn't hear. Not that she appeared to be mentally present, her eyes vacant as she moved about in a well-rehearsed routine.

"She's not dealing," Kellan muttered. "My Shortcake is absolutely not fucking dealing."

I couldn't deny his statement. Our mate was pale, the dark circles under her eyes standing out prominently. Even with Hunter and Kellan on either side of her at night, she cried out with nightmares that we all heard, and brought our own dark thoughts to the surface.

"I can count every damn freckle from here," Kellan added, releasing a ragged sigh. "I love her freckles, but they shouldn't be visible from outer space. She's too pale."

"I love her freckles too," I murmured, proud that I could finally admit the truth. "Though, I agree. Seeing them stand out so starkly isn't my favorite, but if she's anything like me, she needs to work through this in her own way. It won't last forever."

Kellan side-eyed me, his expression drawn in pissed-off lines. "Yours has lasted forever, asshole. You're still over here angry at the world."

I opened my mouth to argue because *fuck this smug fuck*—I'd done the best I could under the circumstances. Before I let that thought escape, I breathed in and out a few times and owned my trauma. I *had* to start owning it. "You're right."

He almost jerked his head off his shoulders as he blinked at me.

Containing my smile, I continued: "But I'm determined to grow and heal from my past. For Emme, I would walk through every one of my demons and change a whole fucking lot more than my attitude."

That statement was the first to keep his desperate gaze from our mate. He stared at me for many long seconds, and I didn't try and hide my determination. I could *and would* do this.

"Thank the fucking goddess," he breathed, his face crumpling for the briefest of seconds before he got himself under control. "What are you planning on doing?"

I rubbed a hand over my face, my beard in desperate need of a trim. It wasn't a priority at the moment, and I wondered if Emme cared about my shaggy caveshifter vibe. "When Emme was taken, the panic I felt made it very clear that no matter how hard I pushed her away, I was already connected to her. She was already one of the singularly most important shifters in existence to me, and I'd been hurting her all this time because *I hurt*. I pushed her away because *I was afraid of losing her*. It was fucked up, and has taken me far too long to piece together."

Kellan's scoff as he furrowed his brows was completely unnecessary. "We all knew it was fear driving your anger, and that you'd flip your shit if she ever did actually leave."

"Yeah, well, as my dad liked to *lovingly* say, *You're one dumb motherfucker, Finley Thornton.* Turned out that was one of the few accurate statements he ever made."

Kellan was quick to anger again, this time in my defense. "Absolutely the hell not. He was an asshole, and despite your momentary lapses in sanity, you're far from dumb. Your dickhead of a father is one of the reasons you're afraid to be hurt again. He was the dumb motherfucker."

The inner waves of gratitude for my pack, who had my back no matter what I threw their way, were stronger than ever. "Thanks, bro. But yeah, when Emme was taken, and I found her with that bite on her neck, I mentally lost it and lashed out… blaming her again. Knee-jerk reaction, and I regret it so badly." Kellan's fists clenched at my revelation, and if he took a swing at me I'd have welcomed it at this point.

"If it makes you feel any better, she kneed me so hard in the balls I could taste them in my throat."

The fury on his face faded to a wince. "Harsh but kind of deserved."

I nodded with a sad laugh. "Totally deserved, and then she told me she was done. My bear and I both knew she meant it… Like, really meant it. I tried to talk to her after that, and she pretended I didn't exist. It fucking broke me, man. I don't think I've ever felt that gutted, and I was literally almost gutted by my psycho of a mother." My breaths came out too fast and my words were too loud. This wasn't a conversation Emme needed to hear, so I attempted to pull myself together.

Kellan's hand landed on my shoulder, squeezing in what felt like understanding and support. "What are you going to do now, then? To fix it?"

That part I'd already decided on. "I'm going to get help. I've already arranged to see Dr. Whittier, that therapist in the city. My first, introductory appointment was a few days ago. She's apparently the leading expert in dealing with past trauma and repressed anger. Figured it was a good place to start."

Kellan's hold tightened, then he yanked me into his arms, hugging me so tightly that in normal circumstances I'd be tempted to punch him in the face. But today… today I needed this hug, no matter how uncomfortable it made me.

"You didn't punch me," he murmured with a chuckle. "Guess you really are changing."

"Don't push it," I growled back, slamming my hand against his shoulder, thankful when he finally released me. While I wasn't Slade's level of touch-averse, intense physical contact still bothered me.

We fell silent and resumed watching Emme, who was now

measuring flour and sugar. When she started to grate lemons, Kellan actually moaned. "Did you try her lemon tarts three days ago? Please tell me you tried them. They were actually one of the best things I've ever eaten, though as I mentioned already, second only to Emme's puss—"

This time I punched him, and it was all jealousy. He'd already mentioned how good our mate tasted, and I was a desperate shifter who was far from ever deserving to touch, let alone taste her.

"You ate all the lemon tarts," I reminded him dryly as he rubbed his arm. "Remember… you threatened to cut our dicks off in our sleep if any of us touched *the tarts…*"

Kellan rumbled out a deep laugh. "I think I remember that. I might have blacked out after eating the first one. But honestly, I will fight anyone who touches them this time as well."

This crazy bastard needed help.

Footsteps cracked against the floor as Slade appeared in the entry hall, dressed head to toe in black enforcer gear, his expression somber as blood streaked his cheeks and arms.

He'd been *interrogating* his evil twin again.

"He spill anything?" I asked when he halted in the doorway between Kellan and me, not touching either of us. This doorway had been built big enough to handle a damn truck backing into the kitchen.

The rasp that slipped from between Slade's pressed lips was so menacing my bear even poked his head up. "He's been well trained. I can't hurt him too much, in case it slides through the bond to Emme, but even so, nothing I've tried has gotten him to talk."

The dragon-dupe was currently stashed in our containment room —a noise-proof, magically reinforced cell behind the garage. Emme didn't know where he was, but she knew he was close—to keep their bond from flipping out. So far, she hadn't asked to see him, and none of us wanted her anywhere near the psychopath.

"He's said absolutely nothing?" Kellan pushed.

Slade sucked in a deep, heavy breath. "He spoke once to tell me that he'll only communicate with Emme from here on out. Since then, he's sat there staring at me, his dragon hovering just below the surface."

"She's in no state to deal with him," I murmured, my bear

rumbling as we watched Emme's heartbreaking routine once more. Back and forth. Measure and pour. Bake and repeat. Over and over.

Slade nodded roughly. "I'll figure out how to break him."

More footsteps echoed as Hunter joined us, his phone pressed to his ear. "I don't fucking care what it takes," he barked. "Find one of them. Fletcher Davenport, Blaine Rogers, Sorenson Thenguard. There's a fucking shifter out here who knows where one of them are, and I want them dead or delivered to my doorstep today."

He paused at the three of us perched in the kitchen doorway, and as if he knew exactly what we were doing, his frantic gaze darted through to Emme. His shoulders relaxed when he saw she was safe and relatively functional. "I'll expect an answer by tonight," he snarled as he hung up the phone.

We were using every contact and resource we had to track Fletcher and anyone associated with him. Normally, Slade would be our source for tracking, but he was entirely focused on Talon—it was a bit of an obsession for him. He'd all but lived down in the containment cell this week.

"They've gone to ground," Hunter bit out, running a hand through his disheveled hair. "All of them. Not a fucking sign of anyone, including Sorenson and Chelsea."

He'd made no secrets that he was going to end his best friend's pack the second he got his hands on them, which Sorenson no doubt knew. He wouldn't be coming back for a reunion any time soon.

"The bunker he had Emme in was state of the art," I reminded him. "You'd never even know it was there unless you had a tangible path to track. I barely knew it was there when I was standing over the top of it. If Fletcher is holed up in a similar place, we won't find him until he's ready for us to find him."

Hunter rubbed a hand over his face, processing my words, before he sucked in a ragged breath. "Has she said anything to anyone?" he asked, focusing on Emme, a hint of desperation bleeding into his tone. "I don't know how to help her. We've destroyed everyone involved, and half the council is terrified of us now, but it's made no difference. We haven't found the ones we really need."

The phone in his hand cracked as he squeezed it tightly, which would make his fourth replacement in a week.

"She's just... cooking," Kellan said, squeezing his eyes shut.

"Cooking, sleeping, and having nightmares. We're fucking failing her as mates."

I wanted to reassure him as he'd done for me earlier, but what could I say to make this better? We were her mates... her pack, and we'd let this happen to her.

And those responsible were still out there.

"We have another council meeting in an hour," Slade said flatly. "Are you going to tell them about our little prisoner?"

Hunter shook his head. "No. They've already proven their uselessness, though they've at least doubled patrols on the entrances and perimeter of the city. Along with adding enforcers to our family compound. Which gives us some breathing room to focus on tracking and keeping *that piece of shit dragon* from escaping."

When Emme added another tray of muffins to the piles of baked goods across the counters, Kellan couldn't take it any longer. With a low rumble, he headed into the kitchen and swept her into his arms. We were trying to respect her wishes, and if that meant giving her space, we did it... But for Kellan, there was only so much space he had in him.

Emme tensed briefly, *so briefly* that I doubted Kellan even noticed, but I saw it. When she tilted her head back and met his steady gaze, her whole body relaxed into his arms, as if she also really needed a hug.

"Hey, Golden," she said, her smile lifting her sad eyes. She did a doubletake when she noticed the rest of us in the doorway. "Oh, you're all here. Come and eat some of these sweets. I've made triple chocolate muffins and brownies, plus Nutella-stuffed cookies. Let me know how they are."

That was the longest sentence she's said in days, and as Hunter pushed forward, I was right behind him. Our entitled alpha didn't hesitate to sweep both Emme and Kellan up in his arms, dragging even our brother's feet from the floor.

Hunter tucked his head into Emme's neck and breathed deeply until the tension that had been shaking his muscles finally eased. Kellan didn't struggle in the embrace either, just accepting the hug without question.

Glancing over my shoulder, I clocked Slade hesitating in the doorway. The dragon was distancing himself from all of us, and though he hadn't said anything, I knew he blamed himself for the dragon—who wore his fucking face—forcibly bonding Emme. Along with the fact that he hadn't killed Fletcher when he had the opportunity.

"It's not your fault," I said bluntly as he backed away. "Don't hurt her by walking away now. Go in there and eat those fucking treats and get addicted like the rest of us. You can return to your torture sessions after we reassure our mate."

Even for one of his pack, it was a risk to talk to Slade in such a way.

But I was putting Emme first these days, even if it got my ass kicked.

To my surprise, Slade strolled into the kitchen, kicked out one of the kitchen stools to sit, and grabbed a muffin. I was a few steps behind, and by the time I sat and snagged my own muffin, Hunter had released them from his hug.

Emme looked dazed, her cheeks flushed in a ghostly semblance of her normal rosy glow. Her dazed stare moved about the room until she noticed the muffin in my hand, which resulted in a pleased smile tilting up her lips.

She pushed toward me, still avoiding my direct gaze as she'd done ever since our little blowout in Texas. "I know I've been a bit out of it the last few days," she murmured softly, as she reached out and started sliding cookies onto cooling racks. "I was working through *what happened*, and I'm sorry I shut you all out, but now that we're together I think it's time I told you everything."

I froze with the muffin halfway to my mouth, and I wasn't the only one waiting with bated breath.

"I've wanted to tell you all for ages what happened in the past, and what caused me to run from you in the first place. Weirdly, though, if I had told you this before I was taken, the story wouldn't be complete. I got more information from *Fletcher the fuckhead*."

Kellan and Hunter pressed in on either side of her, running their hands up and down her spine in a comforting manner.

"We did hear a little of this story from the Rogers pack," Hunter told her, and she blinked at him, showing clear surprise. Kellan had filled me in on what Donnie revealed, but I was more interested in hearing it from Emme. As was Hunter when he added, "But we'd rather hear it from you. Whatever you want to tell us."

Her throat bobbed as she swallowed roughly, and then she

nodded. "Yeah, that's probably for the best. That pack wouldn't give the truth, just the parts that worked for them." She released another deep breath and continued. "As you know, my mother wasn't exactly the nicest shifter in existence. I've told you that we moved around a lot until I turned about four, which was when we went to live with the Rogers pack."

Despite how delicious her baked goods were, the muffin ended up as crumbs in my hands. I already knew that hearing of her abuse and neglect would be a trigger for me, but I was determined not to make any of this about me. For once in my fucking life, I wouldn't let the trauma win.

CHAPTER 18

EMME

In the week since we'd returned home I'd fallen apart.

The moment I stepped into the entrance, and breathed in the comforting scent and vibe of *home*, my body and mind fell headfirst into bouts of suffering. The first couple of days were plagued with nightmares, none of which I remembered upon waking, but I was always left with a sense of loss as tears rained down my cheeks.

Kellan and Hunter were the best comfort through the night, and I'd have lost my mind without them. On the days I couldn't drag myself from bed, Kellan sat by my side and read to me, the same novel Finley had read to him when he was dying. My golden boy's voice wasn't as deep and rumbly as the bear's, but it was soothing and lyrical, weaving a tale of romance, betrayal, lust, and intrigue.

He even got a few laughs out of me, especially when he gave everyone their own "voice." It was all healing to my soul, until eventually I found the will to get my ass out of bed. After showering, washing my hair, and shaving half my body, I felt like a functioning shifter. Hunter ushered me downstairs in the hopes I would eat, and after I satisfied our entitled alpha's demands, I'd found myself helping Florence with her baking.

Then I'd started baking myself.

Using recipes from my time working in restaurants, I soon had cookies, muffins, and tarts lining the benches. The alphas started handing them out to family on our street, to their staff in Reeves Technologies, and the enforcers guarding the compound. Even Cora and Warrick left with two huge baskets when they visited, though I hadn't had the energy to do more than hug them and promise I'd catch up with them soon.

I just didn't know what to say to anyone.

I didn't know how to explain that while I was furious and broken over Talon's actions, I also didn't completely blame him. There was this annoying sliver of hope lingering in my essence.

I hated Fletcher Davenport with my entire soul, but my feelings toward Talon were more… complicated. He was here in the house somewhere, and I wanted to see him, but I was still too much of a mess to deal with the forced bond.

At least I'd finally found the mental fortitude to reveal the truth to my pack, even if they appeared to already know some of it. "It wasn't obvious at first," I continued, wishing I had more cookies to place on cooling racks to keep my hands busy. "The way they abused her. Or maybe I was too young to notice. But as I got older, there was no way to hide it."

None of them moved a muscle, as if they were afraid any interruption would stop me *again* from revealing my past. Little did they know that an asteroid could be heading for our house and I'd stand here until they knew the full truth.

"The bruises were always there, along with healing cuts and marks. Over the years her spirit was diminished, which ended up being a positive for me, as she lost her will to torture me in her spare time.

"One day, when I was maybe twelve, I caught Blaine biting my mom. That in and of itself wasn't odd, but I noticed that whenever he did this, she looked paler and weak afterwards. The bite marks stopped healing so quickly, and it was clear that she was suffering."

Slade's hard gaze caught mine, but his expression remained neutral as he took a bite of his second muffin. It stupidly pleased me to see them all eating my baking—pride at feeding our mates had my wolf preening.

"I didn't know at that time, but I figured it out soon after that Blaine was drawing on the energy of her wolf. Her shifter essence. He was taking it and making himself stronger and more powerful. Just before she died, Mom was all but contained to her room, speaking mostly in random mumbles."

Kellan, on my left side, drew in closer to me, as if sensing the worst was still to come. "In one of these rants, she cursed the goddess for the design flaw of allowing omegas to power an alpha. Without their consent, basically. An alpha, once bonded, could draw on our essence without asking for permission."

I sucked in another deep breath, my memories tainted with the spikes of fear I'd felt that day. I'd been unsure at the time if what she said was true, but either way, it changed everything for me.

"She said it was the worst when bonded into a pack of alphas," I managed to say, my voice roughened with unshed fear and pain. "It's an unusual bonding to start with, and it generally happens in times of crisis. She also told me that alphas will always crave more power and strength. That it's in your nature." I shrugged. "With the Rogers pack, that was absolutely the truth, and they ravaged her during her last years, drawing so much energy that she lost her wolf. On the day she died, she left a note saying her beast was gone, and so was she. Then she hanged herself. I had to cut her down, and in that moment I knew that my designation as an omega put me in a position to lose myself the way mom did."

All four alphas remained quiet, and even as I examined my hands, I felt their stares on me. My wolf lifted her head, enjoying the attention, but I was nervous to see their reactions… especially Finley.

"That's how you saved me," Kellan said suddenly, his voice filled with hushed horror, and I jerked my gaze up to meet his. "After we bonded, you used your essence to give me enough strength to fight the witch magic."

As impossible as it sounded, I'd all but forgotten that I'd shared my essence with him. As far as I could tell, there'd been no long-lasting or permanent damage from it. "I did, and I would do it again in a heartbeat," I said, letting my sincerity ring out.

Kellan shifted forward until our foreheads touched, the piercing blue of his eyes intense and desperate as they bored into mine. "No, you won't, pretty mate. Never ever again. I haven't felt any draw to take more of your essence since that incident, but we don't know if it truly could be corruptive over time. Especially once you end up bonding with all of us."

Against my will, my gaze darted to Finley, who had his head bowed, the remnants of his muffin nothing more than crumbs in his palms. Despite the small steps he'd made to lessen the chasm between us, we were still very far from being in any sort of *good place*.

I had no idea how he'd react to this revelation, when he'd been the one pushing for me to tell them all along. To explain so they'd understand my rejection.

As Kellan pressed his lips to my cheek, I let out a sigh. "I'm so sorry that I believed you'd all be the same as the Rogers pack. I was scared and uneducated, and my instincts were to run and protect myself at all costs. But I was wrong."

Hunter growled low and deep, and when I turned toward him I wasn't surprised to find myself caught in gold-tinted irises. "This is not your fault. The way you reacted was logical, and not telling us made sense—we could have reassured you every day forever that we were different, and even meant it, but if this power corrupts alphas over time, then there's still a chance it could happen."

When it looked like he was going to back away, I reached out and grasped his shirt. "Wait, there's more to the story. Fletcher revealed to me that he's the reason Mom died… She was one of his experiments. He told me he's been experimenting for years, and that Blaine and his pack were placed in my mom's life. They weren't corrupted by her essence; they came into the entire mating corrupted." As the anger washed through me, my voice grew louder. "And I'd bet my left tit that they weren't scent matches or even a proper pack. Everything was a ruse, and it cost Mom her life."

Kellan laughed in a harsh bark. "No betting of body parts, Shortcake. I'm quite fond of both boobs, but I do think you're on the right path with that line of thought."

There was more, and I hated having to say it out loud, but it was important. "Fletcher also said that Mom was just a placeholder while they waited for me to come of age to be bonded. He made it sound as if I was the one they wanted all along, but they couldn't do anything until I was old enough to claim my omega heritage. My mom's death was a catalyst that arrived just at the right moment. I ran right after, but it's weird that none of them ever tracked me down."

Heat rose in the kitchen, and it was impossible to tell who it came from, but a good portion was absolutely dragon in origin. "There's been a piece of this story I've been missing all along," Slade said, and I was so relieved to hear his voice I almost sighed. "And that piece was fucking Fletcher."

Of all the alphas, I'd barely seen Slade this week. Kellan told me he was with Talon mostly, which was in no way a relief, but I was worried about how he was handling everything that happened. I knew he'd take this hard, and I wanted to be there for him while he dealt with a new dragon, Fletcher's betrayal, and what happened to me.

Hopefully I was finally in a strong enough mental space to help my alphas now too.

"Was that the only piece you were missing?" I asked him, barely suppressing my happy sigh at being trapped in his glowing green gaze once more.

He considered his response before shaking his head. "No, there's more. One of them could be that mysterious shifter I was never able to identify. The one present at your birth. I showed you the footage of him crossing paths with the Rogers pack that same night. He has answers. I can feel it."

I remembered the shifter. He'd been a fairly nondescript looking male, and I'd never seen him before in my life. "You haven't found out anything more about him?"

Slade's voice edged into dark and brittle territory. "I've been failing monumentally at tracking lately. I know it's due to the sheer level of magic involved, and now that we're aware it's a Termaine witch, I'm not surprised. Their bloodline is one of the ancients, from the first of their kind, and they have proven on more than one occasion to enjoy darker magics."

Finley broke the silence as he finally abandoned the muffin, dusting off his hands on his sides as he said, "We're going to have to bring Jewels back into the ranks, aren't we?"

A part of me would forever be grateful to Jewels for what she did to save Kellan, but another part of me had really hoped I'd never see her again. Unfortunately, when no one argued, I knew that in this situation, she was our only chance to even out the playing field. There was no battling magic without her help.

"Magic protects Fletcher," Hunter rumbled, words as sharp as daggers. "But he won't stay hidden forever. Not only will he be desperate to keep his plan moving forward, we're also holding his weapon. Which he'll be wanting back."

Slade stood suddenly, that grim expression tugging down his features once more. "I need to break that bastard before we send him back in pieces."

My heart lurched at the notion of breaking Talon, and even worse,

Slade being the one to do it. Words burst from me in a rush. "Can I talk to him first?"

I didn't miss the look of horror directed my way from Finley, and I hurried to explain. "I have questions for him, and I need to know if there's a way to deal with this bond without one or both of us having to die. Fletcher has more knowledge than us, and hopefully that means Talon has more too."

Hunter shook his head. "If he's Fletcher's weapon, there's no way we can trust him in the same room as you."

That made sense, but it also wasn't the entire truth. "He's not involved in their evil plan as an equal. Fletcher treats him like… a pet. No, worse than a pet, he treats him like a weapon that he uses when needed. He called him dragon, it, or thing. *I* was the one who gave him the name Talon." My chest grew tight as I recalled that look on his face when he finally got a name. An identity and piece of dignity returned to him. "He's never been treated like a shifter, and while I'm furious about what he did to me, blaming Talon would be like blaming the knife for stabbing, instead of the one who wielded it. Talon might have been the blade that struck, but Fletcher was the wielder. All of which is to say… this is not black and white, and I need to talk to him."

There was complete silence in the kitchen, and then to my surprise, Slade was the first to break. He waved for me to follow him. "I can ensure he doesn't get free or hurt you." When Hunter made to follow us too, Slade shook his head. "The rest of you need to wait here. The dragon isn't going to talk with everyone there."

They all looked torn, but none of them argued with Slade.

In his current mood, it was far safer just to do as he instructed.

As I left the kitchen, I gave the mixer and ingredients one last look, relieved that I finally felt like I could move on to the next stage of grief. I'd been clinging to baking rather than dealing with what happened to me, but one could only hide for so long before reality forced them into the open. And it was now time to face my demons— starting with the one locked in this house somewhere.

"Can one of you take the tarts out of the oven when the timer beeps," I called back, not caring who responded.

Finley shouted, "No problem," at the same time Kellan hollered, "Mine! The tarts are mine and I'll fucking cut anyone who touches them."

With a final glance over my shoulder, I chuckled as I caught sight of Kellan with his chest heaving and arms out on either side of him, pointing his fingers at Hunter and Finley. "Don't even think about it."

Both alphas wore expressions like they couldn't believe this idiot was about to fight them over sweets, and I found myself actually happy for the first time in days. Being with my mates reminded me that I hadn't lost anything yet. We were all alive and together, and we would figure our issues out. One way or another.

CHAPTER 19

EMME

Hunter caught up to me in the entryway and drew me to a halt by wrapping his left hand around my waist. His right hand slid up to encase my throat, claiming me, as he tilted my head back to meet his gaze.

Hunger and heat pulsed from the alpha, and for the first time since I was taken, a flutter of arousal heated my core. My breaths quickened as my tongue darted out to slide across my dry lips, and Hunter followed every movement with predatory focus.

"If you need me, little omega," he murmured, his scent stronger as he leaned closer, "just call out. I will be there in a heartbeat."

His fingers flexed, and no one could have missed the low moan that slipped out from between my lips. A pleased expression flickered at the edges of Hunter's features. "I don't want to let you out of my sight. My wolf wants to claim you again."

Our bond pulsed as his need filtered through to me, and the tingles in his bite weakened my legs. "I'd like that too," I said, desperate to erase the last memories I had of being claimed. "I know I'm a mess at the moment, but I feel like I'm starting to work my way through it. There's a faint light in the darkness."

"You're doing just fucking fine," he told me, a rasp of truth in those words.

With a groaned huff, he leaned in and pressed his lips against mine, and I opened for him without hesitation, needing to taste him. It was a soft touch at first, but Hunter's dominance soon pushed him to take control. His tongue slid into my mouth, eliciting a whimper from me.

Neither of us were bothered that our pack watched. If anything, I was more relaxed with them there. By the time he pulled away, pressing a few lingering kisses to my lips, his hand flexing around my throat, I felt grounded and calm. The calmest I'd been in days.

"I needed that," I murmured, shaking my head to clear the drugging arousal holding me captive. "But we might want to wait a few minutes before we question Talon."

"Great work, Hunt," Kellan teased from the kitchen doorway, his grin lighting up my fucking world. "You've got our girl smelling like a candy shop again, and no time for us to indulge in our favorite sweet."

Finley, who'd been silently perched beside him, released a rumbly, scoffing sound, and I braced myself for his remark. "Speak for yourself, Golden. I've got all the time in the world right now."

My world ground to a halt, and I swear even the snow falling softly outside the windows of the kitchen slowed. *Did he just…?*

Kellan turned in the jerkiest of motions to gawk at his brother. "Did you just say…? You're just saying inside thoughts out loud now? That's fucking amazing! Don't forget what I told you about the two presents, okay? *Do not combine them!*"

I squint-glared at Kellan, wondering what the hell he was talking about.

Presents? Christmas presents?

It hadn't escaped my notice that there were decorations around the house, and I'd found myself enjoying moments by the huge, pine-scented tree, decorated and filling one corner of the living room. But no one had mentioned presents.

More importantly, what was going on with Finley Thornton and his new personality? "I only hit your balls when I took you down, right?" I asked, crossing my arms. "You didn't hit your head as well?"

Hunter let out an amused rumble, and even Slade cracked a smile. Finley met my gaze with a look I could only describe as determination mixed with a hint of desire.

"Look, I've said this before, and I'll say it again… when you were taken from us, Emme, my entire perspective changed. I stopped fighting the bond and started embracing it, because *I need you in my life*. More than that, I want you in my life." His eyes bored into me, and I was sucked into their velvety depths. "I want this bond, and everything it entails."

My insides swirled and tingled, and my chest ached like it was caving in. As much as I loved hearing that declaration, it didn't erase everything that had happened. The chasm remained between us, and it would take more than *pretty words* to fill it.

"While I appreciate that sentiment," I said, forcing my voice not to waver, even as my wolf screamed at me. "I can't just forget everything that has happened between us. My feelings and trust in this relationship were damaged. My feelings and trust in you *are* damaged. If I'm being completely honest, I'm not sure we can come back from this, Finley."

Even knowing I had to put the truth out there, and if his delicate feelings couldn't handle it then he was only proving my point, I still internally cringed and braced myself for his sharp reply.

But Finley surprised me for the second time in as many minutes. "You're absolutely right—I fucked up badly. Your rejection hurt me, but instead of being mature and giving you a chance to get to know us like my brothers did, I set out to push you away before you could leave me. It was an emotionally stunted response, and I regret the way I acted. I'm so sorry for the way I acted. You've told me before that it was my past trauma I was truly mad at, and you were right, *Ice*. You were right."

A fucking light breeze could have knocked me over. I stared at him, trying to understand how he could take his previously *nasty* nickname and make it sound so soft and loving.

"How will you fix this, then?" Hunter interjected, while I mentally floundered.

Again, there was no hesitation from Finley. "I'm going to ensure that I'm the shifter Emme deserves." His gaze never left mine, and I was so disconcerted by the weight of his sorrowful eyes that I almost crumbled. "I will prove my worth, and I will embrace our true family when I know I am worthy of it."

While I stared at this *body snatched* version of Finley, Kellan clapped his hands like a proud father and darted forward to hug his pack mate. "I knew you'd sort yourself out," he crowed, holding on tighter when Finley tried to shake him off.

The bear eventually gave up and accepted the hug, patting

Kellan's back a little harder than was necessary. "Early days yet," he murmured, but we all heard him.

For me, I was reserving judgment, but there was a stronger part now that hoped this was a true turning point for us. I could do nothing more than wait and see what the future held.

For Finley *and* Talon. For our whole quintet or sextet or *whatever* we ended up forming.

Slade, who'd remained quiet during Finley's revelations, finally spoke up: "We need to deal with the prisoner." His flat, frustrated tone had a new set of worries creeping in—Slade was retreating from us. From the bond.

Hunter must have had the same thought, as he dropped a final kiss on my cheek, nudging me in his brother's direction. "You two go and see if you can get any useful information out of the *asshole* while the rest of us continue threatening everyone we know until one of those fuckers tracks down Fletcher, the Termaine witches, the Sorenson pack, and anyone else involved."

I paused, having missed any updates in my week of baking. "There's been nothing on any of them since we returned? No sign at all?"

"Not a fucking hair sighted," Hunter rumbled, his eyes filled with storm clouds. "We can only assume they're all being protected by magic, which hinders our ability to track them."

Swallowing roughly, I fought down the anger pulsing in my core. Ever since Chelsea had stolen my will and delivered me to Fletcher, I'd been trying to understand her motives.

"There're so few of us left in the world," I bit out with a scowl. "Omegas were rare to start with, and Fletcher has helped inch us close to extinction. For another omega to betray us… Even if she was trying to keep her pack safe, there's no excuse. And where are they now? My bet is Fletcher was lying to her all along, and he took her anyway."

Which was the least she deserved, and I only felt a slight pang that her pack had gotten caught up in her deception. Hunter shrugged, as if he didn't give a shit either way. "If they're with Fletcher, they want to hope he keeps them hidden forever. Once I get my hands on the Sorenson pack, they're all going to die. There's no fucking explanation that could make what happened right."

Slade grunted his agreement, and I heard Kellan's, "Fuck yes," along with Finley's nod—all the alphas were on the same page about this.

"You don't think Soren and his pack deserve any grace?" I found myself asking, and I couldn't figure out why since I was pissed off with them too. "I mean, you'd run to protect me, right?"

Hunter snarled, the harsh, menacing sound ringing out through the room. "I would do whatever it took to protect you. Run, fight, end life as we know it on this planet. And if you were slated to die for your actions, I'd fight in front of you and die before you. But I already know I wouldn't have to deal with that, because you'd never make the same choices as Chelsea. You have integrity, and you would have fought at her side."

Heat filled the entryway as Slade and his dragon joined the conversation. "I agree," he said shortly. "Now, let's get down to the containment room and Talon. We're wasting time by letting that fucker recover."

Recover. That didn't sound good.

Slade, all decked out in enforcer gear, was a great distraction, but I hadn't missed the smears of blood on his arms and face. Had he been interrogating Talon for most of the week?

None of the alphas stopped us again as Slade led me down into the garage, and I wondered if we had to drive to these containment rooms. I'd been certain Talon was in the house, considering how relaxed our bond felt. Not that it mattered, since I trusted Slade implicitly, and if he led, I would follow.

"How are you handling all these new revelations?" I asked as we moved between the cars.

There was no response until he grunted. "And what revelation are you referring to, Emmeline?" When my full name spilled from the harsh lines of his lips, I swallowed hard. He was even angrier than I'd realized. "The revelation that when I left the cameras off during your prank, so I could experience it without any spoilers, it resulted in you being kidnapped and forcibly bonded. Or are you referring to the revelation that the shifter who forcibly bonded you wears my fucking face? A shifter who was clearly the call I felt to return to my place of birth all those years ago, and he was out there plotting against us the whole time." His breaths grew heavier, and I was sweating from the heat in the air. "Or maybe it's the revelation that if I hadn't stopped Hunter from tearing Fletcher into pieces years ago, you wouldn't be crumbling inside." There was another pause, and I searched desperately for what to say to reassure him that none of this was his fault. "I promised I would keep you safe," he continued, "and then you were taken under my watch and hurt worse than ever. There's not much I can say about how I'm handling all of these *revelations*."

It was one of the longest speeches I'd ever heard from him, and every single revelation broke my heart.

Slade picked up the pace, as if he could prevent me from responding by simply getting the heck away from me, but he was sadly mistaken. I started running to keep up. "We need to talk about this," I called toward his broad shoulders. "None of what happened is your fault, and I'm not sure it's fully Talon's either."

His grunting response didn't clue me in on what he thought of that, but he didn't sound happy. There was no time for me to force more conversation, as he paused before a slightly raised panel near the back of the garage. I'd never noticed it before, blending almost seamlessly into the wall, but it was clearly a door. There was no handle, just a keypad, and I covertly watched the code Slade entered for access. A whoosh followed, as if it were pressure sealed, then the panel slid into the wall.

Slade entered without a word, and I followed, breathing in new scents that weren't connected to the garage. I got hints of maple and metal. The hallway was white and shiny, giving the impression of a sterile environment, and lights flickered to life as we crossed under them, until we finally stepped into a large room with a barred area along one wall.

"This was designed to contain a dragon," Slade said, gesturing for me to step to his side.

I moved cautiously, searching for Talon in the barred-off section of the larger room. A shadow moved from the back of the cell, and when Talon stepped into the light, his expression was hard until he noticed me beside Slade. The moment I met his dark eyes, he slammed against the bars, his hands clutching them as he locked in on me like a predator.

It had been a week since I'd last seen him, and my wolf howled while the bite on my shoulder pulsed. Talon's maple scent amplified until I was drowning in it, and when Slade twitched beside me, I knew it was in response to my chocolate and honey tones swelling to match Talon's scent.

"Scent match," I breathed, unable to help myself.

I'd had the thought we might be when I first scented him strongly, but this moment here cemented it. Now that my wolf had returned and was back to full strength, her bond with Talon had strengthened too, and there was no denying it any longer. We were also a scent match.

How was it possible, though, and what did this mean for the quintet?

CHAPTER 20

EMME

"Mate," Talon breathed in his deep rumble.

Slade's returning rumble was stronger and more menacing. "Don't fucking call her that. You stole what should have been a sacred moment, and in doing so you condemned *my* omega to possibly being without a perfect quintet of power. *You* will pay for what you've done, but it will be so much worse if you keep calling her *mate*."

Talon didn't even glance at Slade, doing that thing where he visually consumed me until I was certain no one else existed in his world. A quick scan over the dragon revealed no injuries, or even tears in his black pants, fitted black shirt, and bare feet. He wore Slade's clothes, that much I knew for sure, and I didn't want to examine why that had my stomach flip-flopping.

No doubt being in an enclosed space with *two* dragon shifters was simply too much dominance and beauty for one omega.

I could barely keep my thoughts from clouding over with the imagery that identical twins were designed to provoke—

No. Holy shit. *NO!*

One of the twins had a touch aversion and the other was a psychopath who owed allegiance to an even bigger psychopath. The mental image of being caged between them as they took their pleasure, and gave me pleasure, was going firmly into the box where all my forbidden thoughts were stored. Never to be looked at again.

Talon pressed harder against the bars, one arm hanging through, his palm up as he gestured for me to step forward. "Mate," he growled it this time, and I was helpless not to step toward him, only halting when a firm arm wrapped around my waist.

Slade secured me in his hold and full-bodily lifted me to shift our positions so he stood between Talon and me. "Emmeline Anders," he snapped, dragging my attention up to his face. The menacing sounds of dragon rumble was a soundtrack in the background. "What is Talon doing to you? Tell me what's happening? I can't fix a situation without all the information and variables."

"He *is* my mate," I confirmed, the connection between us pulsing as Talon's bite tingled. "Our bond is not fully complete, but it's strong enough that I know we are goddess fated."

Now that my wolf was back and functioning, the incomplete nature of our tether drew her closer.

"You're only feeling this way due to the forced bonding," he said, and even I picked up on his uncertainty despite the statement.

Goddess, I hated hurting them. "It's a scent match, Slade," I repeated, forcing the words out. "Tell me you smell his sweet maple and—"

I was cut off by Slade's sigh. "Smokiness," he grumbled, honest as always. "Just like mine."

My throat tightened, and it spoke of how insane the tension was holding all of us, that it took me until this very second to realize *Slade was still touching me.*

More than touching, he had me plastered against his side, and he wasn't wavering in his hold—I was coming to realize that he handled touch better when he was the one to initiate it.

"It is smoky," I confirmed, my voice wavering as I tried not to squirm in his grasp. "It has hints of your scent, and he speaks with that same slight accent, which has to be *dragon related*, right?"

Slade looked like he was being tortured as he bit out, "Yeah, I wasn't raised around this accent. I've always held a slight lilt to my words. *Dragon related* is the most logical explanation."

My wolf howled, and I barely halted her need to rub against him, scent marking the shifter.

Slade's expression darkened and I wouldn't have been surprised if his dragon felt her need. "How can he be your mate when you already have four alphas? How does a fifth fit?"

Judging by the size of them, it was a miracle any of them *fit*, but since that wasn't his exact meaning, I forced my addled mind to focus. "I have some theories," I said, not sure if any of them were true. "But maybe it's best if we ask Talon. That's what I'm down here for after all."

Slade didn't release me for many long moments, which set Talon off again, as he growled.

"Fine," Slade finally snapped, "but don't get within touching distance. If he touches you, I will break both of his arms."

The murder-y nature of his tone had a natural fear response spiking in my chest, but I didn't try and pull away. Slade, who'd clearly felt the surge of my pulse, examined my face closely. "You have an instinct to fear my beast," he murmured, "but you also trust him. You trust us not to hurt you, don't you, Snow?"

"I trust you both completely," I replied without hesitation.

His expression tightened once more as if he didn't love that response, and then to my astonishment, he leaned down and whispered, "Don't move."

It was a command I couldn't disobey, and I wasn't even breathing as he shifted closer, descending from his lofty heights to press his lips to the corner of my mouth. Fire exploded through my body—not literally, though with a dragon you could never be sure—and it felt like I was burning alive as my stomach swirled and my core clenched desperately.

Slade's touch was over so quickly that I wondered if I'd imagined it, but as my tongue darted out to taste the spot, a lingering marshmallow sweetness remained, and it almost sent me to my knees. His eyes darkened. "Careful, omega. Don't push *me* or my dragon when we're in this state."

"Hard not to push a little," I choked out, the scent of my arousal filling the room, and when a hand slammed against the bars behind Slade, I was reminded that we weren't exactly alone down here.

Slade closed his eyes, and it appeared he was praying for the strength not to straight up murder his doppelganger. By the time he opened his eyes, he was visually back in control, and if I hadn't been standing close enough to see the faintest tremble in his hands, I'd have thought he was wholly unaffected.

Talon didn't help as he demanded his freedom. "Let me out. Now!"

Moving into his line of sight, I leveled a firm stare at him. "Until we can confirm that you're not a threat to our pack and the shifters of Golden Claw, you will stay contained." I glanced at Slade, who remained close to my side. "I'm assuming this room is protected from any sort of tracking spell?"

He gave a single, grim nod. "Yeah, this was originally designed for me. It's a contingency for the day I lose control completely. My brothers needed a place to contain my humanoid form until they figured out how to either kill me or repair the bond between me and my beast. It's the safest spot to keep him."

Slade leaned against the wall, and while he appeared to be relaxing, I tracked the tension in his broad shoulders. "I don't know how Blaine screwed up in imprisoning me, when he's had a dragon at his disposal to test on, but I won't make the same mistake."

"Blaine is overconfident," Talon said with a grunt, and I took it as a positive that he was offering up information without us even asking the question. "He believes himself untouchable. Alpha gives him too much rope, and he will hang himself."

I blinked and bestowed a small smile on him. "Nice work, Talon. That was a rather astute observation, highlighting the fact that your *Alpha* is not perfect."

He wore the flattest stare known to shifter to convey his thoughts on that.

"Anyways," I continued airily, sticking with our pretense of casual and friendly conversation, "let's ask the real questions, shall we."

Talon's arm remained stretched between the bars. "Take my hand and I'll answer any question you ask."

Slade was no longer the picture of false relaxation, his spine slamming straight as he reached my side in a single long stride. "Not a fucking chance. He could kill you in a heartbeat, Snow. Faster than even I could stop once his hands are on you."

Talon removed his intense stare from my face to glare at Slade; they stood close enough now that I had to gulp at their similarities. Clad in black, they were twin godlike statues of perfection.

"The omega is mine," Talon said, enunciating each word so clearly that he hit every damn letter. "Mine to keep. To protect. To claim. To use as needed. *Mine!* And a dragon does not hurt what is his."

Slade leapt forward, his fist slamming into Talon's face with enough force that the dragon's arm snapped between the bars as he was thrown back. I gasped, and before sanity caught up to me, I was against the bars, scrambling to reach the injured shifter.

"Slade!" I cried, shooting him an angry glare over my shoulder. "That was so fucking uncalled for. I've already told you he's been programmed by Fletcher, and he wasn't offering any violence toward me. There was no reason to react so brutally."

Talon didn't make a sound as he dragged himself up, his broken arm hanging awkwardly at his side. "I'll heal soon enough, don't stress, Emme." His voice remained even and calm, as if he didn't even register the pain.

Slade, meanwhile, filled the cell with extreme heat, and when I glanced up over my shoulder at him, a chill traced across my skin. Ironically.

He was out of control.

His eyes pinpoints of green.

Talon's arm wrapped around my center, dragging me fully against the bars. "You need to get away from him," he snarled. "He's not in control of his beast, and if he shifts here, he'll crush you."

Slade's gaze snapped to stare at the arm encircling my waist, and the fury in his expression grew as the air blistered. "Let me go," I whispered. "Let me go to him. It's the only chance we have."

Talon hesitated, his hold tightening, and I panicked just as he finally saw reason and released me. It took two strides to reach Slade, and my hands rose to hover between us.

I had no idea if my touch would send him over the edge, but there was a hope that my omega energy would soothe his beast. The dragon shifter's limbs trembled, and puffs of smoky air surrounded me, until the marshmallow of his scent was choked out by the ash.

"Slade, I'm going to touch you," I warned him. "You have two seconds to say no or shake your head or growl. Even an alpha grunt will stop me."

When no response was forthcoming, I moved slowly and lowered my hands toward his chest.

He released a harsh breath as my palms connected to his shirt, careful not to graze any bare skin. When I found no rebuff or increase in rage, I stepped closer and lowered my head to rest between my palms. I wasn't situated over his heart, but I could hear the rapid beats as we stood there in silence. It took a few minutes for those thuds to calm, and eventually Slade's hands swept up and wrapped around my back.

Thank the goddess.

"I would never hurt you," he breathed into my ear. "I would never have lost control and hurt you. But I would have killed him, which might have hurt you anyway. I believe you'd survive his death, as your bond isn't fully complete, but it's still a risk I shouldn't contemplate."

I wanted to reply but I was consumed by the feeling of being held against him in a hug, a mere fraction of his strength wrapped around me. My eyes burned until I had to bite my lip to force my emotions back under control.

If Talon hadn't cleared his throat, I'd have forgotten anyone else was even in the room.

As it was, neither of us moved, and I hoped Slade also wanted this perfect moment to go on just a little longer. Or forever.

CHAPTER 21

EMME

Talon slammed his hand against the bars of his cell and I jerked out of Slade's hold, taking two steps back. Slade didn't follow, and when our gazes met, I was relieved to see he was calm and contained once more.

"Why haven't you bonded with her?" Talon demanded, his unbroken arm wrapped around the bars. "Your beast is raging at your denial of the connection."

Slade's expression softened as he stared at me, only to harden when he turned to Talon: "My dragon isn't stable enough to bond." Even as honest as he was, it surprised me that he would reveal that *weakness* to his enemy. "There's a disconnect between us and I worry that if I tangibly tie myself to Emmeline, and one day lose myself to the dragon, I'll take her down with me."

I was aware of Slade's issues, and with the ghost of his touch still branded on my body, it hurt to know that we might never have more than this.

"My dragon's the same," Talon said casually, as if he didn't care. "But he's more stable with Emme. She's an omega, and their literal role is to calm and power alphas. In whatever means we need."

He wasn't technically wrong, but the way he said it instantly reminded me of Blaine and Fletcher.

"My role is not to power you, asshole," I snapped, wishing I was close enough to kick his broken arm. "My energy and essence is *mine* alone. If I chose to share it, that's one thing, but when you speak about *taking what's yours* then you're out of line, and I'll have no part in it."

Talon tilted his head, and it was so reminiscent of Slade that it *almost* derailed my angry tangent. "Why would you not want to share with your mates?"

I snorted. "Reverse psychology won't work on me, dickhead. I *would* share with my mates in a life-or-death situation, as I have already proven, but as you are all arguably more powerful than me to start with, there's no logical reason I should just share with you on the regular. Especially when I've lived through the damage it can do long term to a beast and essence. There's a risk that I'd lose my wolf completely and end up broken and wishing for death."

Slade's low, menacing growls indicated his dragon remained close to the surface.

When he pressed his hand to the middle of my back, his heat caressing my spine, I barely contained my groan. "Emme will never share her essence again," he said, his tone making it clear he'd kill anyone who tried to make me. "Not even to save one of our lives. We have no idea what we're messing with here, and until we know for sure the long-term consequences, we're not risking her." He pinned the other dragon with a hard stare. "If you cared about her or felt the true pull of a scent match, you wouldn't want that for her either. You'd want to do *anything* to keep her safe and healthy."

Talon's expression now held a hint of confusion, and I decided to take advantage of that by asking our most pressing questions. "How are you and Slade related? You look almost identical, which has me thinking you have the same parents? Or are from the same nest? I don't know how it works for dragons."

"Dragons have nests," Slade confirmed, his hand falling away from my back, and I tried not to mourn the loss. "I've never met any other dragons to know if we all look the same."

Talon snorted, and I debated breaking his other arm. For funsies. "We don't all look the same. Alpha has many old photos and books depicting our kind. We come in all shapes, sizes, colors, and facial features."

"Except you two are exactly alike," I reiterated.

His smile held an edge of menace. "Ah, yes. Well, I don't know everything, but I did overhear Alpha discuss us a few times. When he spoke about his *other* family."

I remained quiet, leaving him to continue. He just stared pointedly at me, his unbroken arm through the bars.

Fuck a duck. He'd stated his terms earlier, and I wasn't fulfilling them.

"You going to be okay, big guy?" I asked Slade, unmoving yet as I really didn't need another dragon brawl. "He's not asking for anything I'm unwilling to give."

Slade's exhalation held frustration, but he didn't stop me. "Fine, but if he tries anything *other than holding your damn hand* I will break his neck next. Which will require a much longer recovery."

If Talon's amused expression was any indication, he wasn't worried.

I stepped closer, and shadowed by his huge form against the bars, I felt small and oddly vulnerable. When our hands touched, my wolf perked up her head and growled *mate,* and it might have been a coincidence, but that was the exact moment the darkness in Talon's eyes brightened to highlight the bisects of green in them.

"You smell like chocolate and honey," he murmured, tilting his head to examine me. "Why is the scent stronger now than when you were in the bunker?"

Annoyed by the nerves sprinkling my stomach, my words came out rougher: "My wolf was broken and hiding while you held me captive." I breathed through my mouth to ease the thrall of the scent, but like with the rest of my pack, it had very little effect. "Being without my bonded mates forced my wolf to retreat and protect me, which was why I couldn't strongly scent you either."

Slade sounded reluctant as hell when he added, "Technically, this is the first time you've properly been together without outside forces impacting your beast and scents."

Yep, if we discounted those few seconds in the desert before Talon was knocked out.

Talon's hold on my hand tightened, and his usual hard expression eased. I was briefly met with what I could only liken to anime style *heart eyes.* "You are perfect," he whispered. "I've waited a long time for my mate."

"She's not fucking yours," Slade reminded him with a snap.

Talon ignored him, stroking his thumb over the fleshy heel of my palm. "We will rule by Alpha's side."

Annnd the moment was broken. "Nope. I will never side with Fletcher Davenport." I hoped he knew by how firm my tone was, that this was a hard line for me. "His views of the future, and *how* he's choosing to get there, doesn't align with my values. I'd die before I side with him. Talon, please understand how serious I am about that. I. Will. Die. First. And you will have no mate."

My statement was met with a dual set of snarls, so loud they echoed off the thick stone walls until it felt like the ground trembled.

"You hitched yourself to the wrong omega," I informed him sadly, ignoring their fury. "I'm not pliable and easily manipulated from my morals. What Fletcher did to my mom broke and reformed me, and I will no longer bend for an alpha with evil intentions."

The stroke of his thumb stopped, but Talon hung on every word, his stare unwavering.

"Think about what side of history you want to be on," I said, softening my tone. "But first, please tell me everything you know about Slade and you."

Talon's eyes darted briefly between me and the other dragon in the room, and I could *feel* his confusion. "All I know is that when the egg hatched, there were two of us. Dragon lore calls that—

"*Salatrina.*"

I swung my gaze to Slade, only to find him staring at Talon.

"You… you've heard of this before?" I asked, looking between them both. "You both came from the same egg?"

Slade nodded, looking like he'd seen a ghost. "Yes. It's a rare phenomenon that was mentioned maybe three times in the books and lore I've managed to procure about my kind. It depicts twin souls born to a single egg, who are connected in a way that defies the normal. That's all I really know, and to be honest, I assumed it was a myth."

Talon resumed his stroke on my hand, sending unwanted butterflies through my stomach. "Alpha said there are none left alive who truly know about our abilities, but that he believes we're joined in a connection that goes beyond normal quintets."

I thought over the implications of this and came to only one conclusion "This has to be the reason you're my scent match too. You and Slade were literally born in the same egg, as if you're two sides of a single coin. A yin and yang."

Slade, who had finally recovered from his shock, scoffed like he'd rather get run over by a truck than claim Talon as the other half of his soul. Talon, on the other hand, sent his *brother* a stare that was filled with longing, before it was just as quickly masked. "This pack life is not for me," he finally said, the life fading in his eyes. "I have a duty. I've been well trained to complete my duty. Alpha Fletcher will come for us soon, and then he'll return the packs to their former glory. He'll stand as the true alpha of the American shifters, and you all can either get in line or die under his rule."

That was the moment we lost him again, just when I felt like we were close to getting through to him. His unwavering loyalty to an alpha who most certainly didn't deserve it was frustrating as hell, but I forced myself to understand. Fletcher was all Talon had ever known.

Maybe with time we could show him what a true family looked like.

The battle ahead of us had exhaustion pressing on me, and I hoped tonight I'd actually sleep. "What was your normal day with Fletcher like?" I asked, shifting closer until our scents mingled. "If you weren't out fighting or killing for him, what did you do? Did he treat you well? Did you have family dinners? Family games nights? Watch television together?"

He blinked, his brows bunching. "I sat in my room until I was called for a mission. I had a gym to work out, and food was delivered once a day for me to consume in my beast form."

Slade's scent washed in from behind me, as he moved closer, and I wondered if he was feeling a draw to Talon too.

"That's not how you treat a shifter you care about. Or one who is family," I said, needing him to understand the truth. "In this pack, they spend quality time together. They joke and tease and have each others' back. They eat meals together, work together, race their cars, and show up to support their sports teams. They protect each other. You don't have to be alone all the time, sitting and waiting for your next *mission* to get attention." I lifted my free hand and placed it against Talon's chest, and his expression shuttered until I had no idea what he was thinking.

Despite everything he'd put me through, I wasn't immune to this shifter, but for either of us to ever move past the forced bonding, we both had to face up to the reality: Fletcher was an evil fuck, and we were true mates.

There was also the fact that I wasn't the only victim here, which Slade and the rest of our pack needed to accept, so we could claim our only possible future.

Forming a sextet.

CHAPTER 22

HUNTER

The entire time Emme was in our containment rooms with Slade and that *other fucker*, I paced the front entrance. Paced and yelled at whoever I could get on the phone.

Reeves Industries didn't exactly fall apart when I wasn't *in office*, but it always had more snags. If it weren't for the thousands of jobs that'd be lost across all of our facilities, I'd shut the whole fucking thing down. For now, my senior staff were handling the day-to-day, but when I returned, there'd be more than a few incompetent assholes on the chopping block.

I already knew I'd have to make an appearance tomorrow to ensure the launch of our new product wasn't a complete disaster. The magic-resistant, armored chest plates were about to ship out to the general population, and would change the face of the impending war.

These plates could be stitched into any shirt or worn over the top, with nothing more than a few easy-to-manipulate bands. It'd been in the works for a number of years, but I'd pushed up production. With all the magical attacks on our pack, I knew there was a battle on the horizon, and I wanted to create easily accessible and relatively cost-effective protection for shifters.

The *full* armored vests took longer to manufacture, and worked best when sized correctly to the purchaser. Custom-made didn't come cheap or easy, and while this new product wouldn't be quite as effective, it would still give us an edge during a magic war.

A war brought on by Fletcher. I should have killed that bastard years ago and dealt with whatever mental fallout resulted when you murdered your sperm donor. I'd have taken that fallout ten times over if it meant Emme never had to go through the last few weeks.

I had no fucking idea how I'd even missed all the signs that Fletcher was connected to our issues with the Rogers pack, but I should have known. It was a huge oversight, and it cost my pack too much.

By the time Emme and Slade slogged up the stairs, looking exhausted and emotionally shattered, I was ready to murder every fucking shifter who'd ever bothered either of them, including that rogue doppelganger in the containment room.

"Did you learn anything?" I asked, and neither of them showed any surprise to see me standing where they'd left me earlier.

When Emme stumbled into my arms, allowing me to support her as a mate should, a strong wave of satisfaction hit my wolf. Through our bond, she released a pulse of relief at being in my arms, and fuck, if I could bottle this feeling… I'd have many more billions.

Slade remained stiff, and I knew my brother well enough to see him trying to rearrange all his broken pieces. "We learned a little. He's much more receptive when Emme is close by. The main points are that Talon is a scent match for Emme, and that we were born in the same egg. Fletcher separated us at birth, but we're most definitely *salatrina*."

Fuck.

That word was immediately familiar, and swallowing roughly, I met my brother's wide-eyed gaze. Slade had gone through a ten-year period where he'd attempted to uncover every piece of information about his species of shifter, and I had helped out.

Salatrina meant… *twin souls.*

"Fletcher separated you at birth?" I huffed, unsurprised that the bastard had stolen that bond from them. "And kept you apart for decades…"

Emme snuggled closer, and I slid my palms down the back of her thighs to lift her up into me. When her long legs wrapped around my waist, securing her firmly against me, relief filtered through my essence.

"Your sperm donor is a real piece of shit," she mumbled against my neck, breathing deeply as she took in my scent, soothing her beast. "Not only did he make your lives hell growing up, he stole Slade's brother—his fucking twin soul—and kept him all but locked in a cage, trained to fight and obey. Talon has never been treated like a living being worthy of love or care. We have to help him."

My wolf howled in response, and I chose my next words carefully. "You really want to help him?"

Over her shoulder, I stared into Slade's eyes, which all but glowed green in the dim light. When Emme didn't immediately respond, he said, "We might not have any other choice. Talon is strong and well-trained. Our one hope might be to turn him to our side and show him that Fletcher is not the alpha he believes him to be."

I snarled, "Or even better, we kill Fletcher and forget he ever existed."

Slade shrugged. "Yeah, that's my plan too. I always worried that killing him would break the final shreds of your humanity, and if you broke, then I'd lose myself. But he signed up for death the moment he touched Emme. I'm quite looking forward to ending him."

"Get in fucking line," Emme mumbled, and I was relieved to hear the snark in her words. She'd been lost to us for days, but the pulse of her beast and essence was stronger, more like her old self.

"We can discuss our murder-list tomorrow," I said, running my hand up her spine and into her hair. "For now, our little omega needs to rest." I eyed Slade as I added, "Do you want to be alone, brother? Or do you need company?"

For three decades we'd held each other together and accountable. We checked in on the sanity of our beasts and fought our demons as a team.

Since our return from Texas, though, Slade had been pulling away from me, and from the pack. He was fraying around the edges, and I was done leaving him alone to deal with it.

"I need to fly," he said shortly, meeting my gaze with a steady one of his own. "I'll do some scouting, and then I'll hang out with my *twin* and see if he'll offer up any further information. I'm starting to think he might be the key to winning this battle."

I nodded, trusting in his instinct. "Well, you know where we'll be. If you need grounding or to share in pack energy, you know where to find us. Promise you won't keep fighting this alone."

Emme lifted her head, and I no longer had Slade's focus. It was all her.

"Promise us," she repeated softly. "Don't fight alone."

His chest heaved as he shared with her a look I'd never seen him share with anyone. Emme had no idea how precious she was to all of us. "I promise, Snow," he told her, and she sighed happily, as if she knew she could trust in his words.

Slade lifted his shirt to start stripping to shift and headed for the door. We watched him until he was gone from view, then I took the stairs up to my room. When I stepped inside, I thought Emme had fallen asleep, as she leaned heavily into me, but when I moved toward the bed she whispered, "Can we shower first?"

Through our bond I was hit with a surge of her need, and my own desperate desire roared to life. My dick kicked in my pants, and I willed the bastard to calm down. Emme was as fragile as I'd ever seen her, and she needed care and healing from me. As her entitled alpha, and a male who loved her more than my existence, I'd kill myself before I took more from her than she had the energy to give. Nothing would ever be forced or stolen from her again.

Keeping the lights dim, I set her down only long enough to strip our clothes off, before gathering her into my arms once more. Her scent exploded, and all I could feel was soft skin as she wrapped herself around me. The heavy throb in my balls joined in the pulse of my dick, but I was determined to only soothe her ragged soul.

Once the water reached her preferred temperature, I moved under the stream, and she buried her face against my shoulder. We stood under that fall of water for a long time, letting the rainfall showerhead do its job.

Tension slowly eased from her, and I tried to ignore how frail she felt in my arms.

She'd lost weight again. *Of course she had.* Those fucks had held her for a week, and we weren't there to ensure she was safe or fed. In the days since we'd returned, she'd started to eat regular meals again, but it wasn't enough to reverse the damage done. Not yet.

"I love being with you like this," Emme said, her lips brushing across my neck. My fingers flexed against her ass to shift her higher, stifling my groan as she ran her tongue over my shoulder, tasting me. *Goddess.* I wasn't strong enough for this.

The urge to slide my fingers lower, over her soft curves, until I could enter her heat and taste her desire, was almost too much to contain. When Emme moaned and wriggled against me, I gritted my teeth and prayed for control. "I know you usually soothe me in here, but, Hunter..."

She trailed off, and like the desperate asshole I was, I pushed for more. "Yes, what do you need, baby girl?"

She arched against me, and I swear to the moon I blacked out for a second. "I need to forget," she went on, shredding my control. "I need you to command me and destroy my body until I feel nothing but pleasure and pain. I want them both. I want it all."

My wolf surged forward, and my jaw shifted as I sank my teeth into her shoulder, over my bite. It was a reaffirmation of our bond. Now that we knew Talon was a scent match, I understood why his forced claim hadn't damaged our quintet energy.

Even if we didn't have all the information, it was clear that the twin soul magic made it all work. Somehow.

Emme gasped and arched into me, and as my jaw returned to normal, I lapped at the wound to seal it, enjoying the sweet metallic taste of her blood. When she thrust her hips, I slid my hands down her ass, spreading her cheeks as I moved, and let the tips of my fingers run back and forth between her ass and her pussy, unsurprised to find she was already dripping wet.

"I want to fuck you so badly here," I murmured, pressing my finger to the tight ring of muscles in her ass, swirling but not pushing too hard. If pleasure and pain were what she wanted tonight, I knew exactly what would destroy us both. "Have you ever been fucked here before?"

Her breaths came faster as she shook her head, tensing briefly before relaxing into my continued strokes. I slid two fingers through her folds, pumping them inside her tight, wet heat, before using her natural lube on her ass once more.

"You want this, baby?" I breathed, needing to hear her explicit consent. "You want me to bring you pleasure with an edge of pain?"

"Yes!" Her gasp was loud as I pushed harder, the resistance only lasting a second before I slid inside her ass.

Fucking hell. She was tight around my finger, and I wondered if I was about to come without even getting inside her.

"Oh fuck, yes," she choked out. "I want everything, Hunter. Please, please, fucking please just use my body and make me forget."

The throbbing in my balls grew. My dick was so hard that it was one pulsing ache between our bodies. Just the knowledge that I'd be inside her soon was almost enough to send me over the edge.

With my finger inside her virgin ass, I moved slowly, rocking her against me. "We're going to take our time," I whispered softly, and I loved the mewling cries she released as I slid deeper inside her. "If I do anything you don't like, you just need to say 'Red.' Do you understand, little omega? Red means I stop immediately."

I slid my finger to the first knuckle, and she rasped, "Oh yes, that feels so good."

"Do you understand, little omega?" I repeated, slowing my movement so she could focus.

Her nod was rapid against my chest. "Yes, yes. I understand. If I say 'red,' you'll stop what you're doing."

"There's my good girl," I murmured, and I wasn't surprised to feel her tighten on my finger. She loved praise almost as much as Kellan. "Now, let's get you cleaned up so I can spend the next several hours devouring you."

If the way she thrust against me was any indication, she liked the sound of that a lot, and it was with great reluctance I removed my finger.

I'd be inside her very soon, but first I would taste every fucking inch of her body, and edge her until she exploded all over my face. Then I would take her wherever she wanted to go.

A promise I intended to keep.

CHAPTER 23

EMME

After everything that had happened over the last two weeks, I was so ready to lose myself in Hunter. We hadn't really had a chance to be together since our *predator and prey* claiming, and I was ready to come from the sensation of his finger sliding in my ass. I'd never felt anything like it before, and goddess save me, I liked it.

When Hunter removed his hand from my body and lowered me to the ground, I barely stopped the pout from puffing out my lip. With a low laugh, he soaped up his hands with his body wash, the scent decidedly more masculine than my usual, and I loved that I'd soon smell as dark and spicy as Hunter.

His eyes were almost pitch black as he ran his hands over my shoulders, lingering on his bite, while ignoring the other two. When he washed down my breasts, he cupped their weight, his thumb brushing over my nipples in a maddening back and forth motion. His responding groan was low, but I heard and loved that he was as affected by all of this as me.

After driving me to the edge of my sanity, he continued down my stomach, over my thighs, and even dropped to his knees to soap up my legs, feet, and toes. This alpha on his knees was my *fucking undoing*.

By the time he finished cleaning me, my skin tingled, and my core throbbed in a steady beat that almost sent me to my knees as well.

Hunter shifted his weight to pull us under the water, and the deliberate way he removed the soap only increased my aching need.

"Please," I begged as I slid my hands into his luscious hair. "This isn't the pain I meant, Hurricane. I'm desperate here, and I demand you make me come."

The growl of his wolf was rumbly against my stomach, as his tongue darted out to swipe through the water cascading down my skin. He kissed and bit a path south, and I tried to drag his head to the *spot I needed*, but he was too strong to shift.

I'd handed over my control to this alpha, in my need to let go, which meant I got to suffer and enjoy every damn second of him edging me.

His palms wrapped around my thighs, and long fingers parted my center. He stared for many seconds, and it was only the hungry desire on his face that kept me from feeling self-conscious. "This is the prettiest cunt I've ever seen," he murmured, and all I could feel was awe and desire through our bond. Before I could reply, Hunter pressed forward, swiping his hot, wet tongue through my folds and inside me, cutting off all rational thought.

He flattened his tongue and ran it from my asshole all the way to my clit, and if his strong hold on my thighs hadn't been keeping me upright, my legs would have collapsed. The urge to scream increased as he continued this slow exploration of my body, until ragged breaths burst from me.

My vision darkened on the sides, possibly due to a lack of oxygen, as I struggled to *feel everything* and still breathe at the same time.

Hunter was relentless as he held me in place and devoured me. He deliberately kept the build of pleasure slow and steady, until my center throbbed in a heavy beat, and I was so close to tumbling from the top of a very intense peak.

My legs and thighs trembled and the pressure in my lower half caused the very real pain I'd been craving. A gush of pre-cum slid between my thighs, but Hunter didn't let any of it escape. His fingers captured what his mouth missed, and I could feel him sliding my release back inside me. Goddess, as punishing as the edging felt, it was also amazing, and he was definitely in the running to be called a good boy.

Only that wasn't his kink.

His was control, and I'd surrendered to him tonight.

Knowing it would be futile to beg, I bit my lip until I tasted blood and closed my eyes against the throbbing. He thrust his tongue inside as his thumb circled my clit, and this time he didn't back off. He pushed me over that damn edge and I came so hard that the back of my head hit the tiled wall of the shower.

When he made a move to check on me, I tightened my hands in his hair and locked my thighs around his face until he took the hint. He plunged his fingers inside me, pumping hard as his tongue circled my clit, and it was only seconds until I came again, my oversensitive nerve endings screaming at me.

By the time he stood and caught me in his arms, I was ready to pass out in sated relief and exhaustion. "Is your head okay, mate?" he asked, gently probing the small bump that would heal soon.

"It's perfect," I said, voice ragged. "I'm perfect. That was exactly what I needed." My head lolled against his chest as he supported my weight.

"Oh, we're not done, baby girl," he said, his right hand cupping my throat until he had my head angled back for a kiss. He worshipped my mouth, and I was drugged by the kisses, holding on to his thick biceps for stability. The kiss was transformative, and I wasn't sure I'd be the same shifter by the time he was done.

Hunter shut off the water as he lifted me out of the stall and onto the bathmat, drying us both in seconds. He kissed me again until I was a throbbing, needy mess, ready to explode at the slightest touch. When we entered the dark, cool bedroom, I headed for the bed, only to find wafts of caramel and cinnamon filling the space. Along with one of my favorite shifters.

"What are you doing here, annoying pup?" Hunter growled, as we both took in the near naked shifter, sprawled back in his black boxer briefs, watching us closely.

Kellan's lazy grin didn't match the violet flare of his eyes. "Training finished early, and my mate's siren song called me into the party." He propped himself up on his elbows, and my line of sight went straight to the pop of his abdominal muscles, thick and prominent in that position.

These alphas and their overachieving ways were really starting to grow on me.

"You wouldn't be thinking of keeping her all to yourself, right?"

Kellan added, looking between Hunter and me. "Sharing is caring after all."

Hunter's chest rose with a puff, but he didn't rebuke his brother. "Our mate wants to forget tonight," he murmured, brushing his hand down my shoulder, which sent a shiver through me. "She wants us to take control. Are you up for that task, pup?"

When his wolf's energy rose, Kellan's eyes darkened further. "Fuck yes. Whatever my Shortcake needs, I will be up for."

"There's my good boy," I whispered, because it wasn't a one-way street here. We all had our own needs and wants.

Kellan groaned, and palmed his cock through his boxers, the thick outline as obvious as his abs. "I think I just came. Lucky, I have a quick rebound time."

His refractory period was exceptional. Hunter's too.

I was one lucky omega.

Hunter nudged me forward and I crawled onto the bed, shimmying over to the center. Kellan immediately rolled into my left, his hands sliding along my tits, cupping them. His tongue caressed the left nipple before he sucked the hard tip into his mouth, sending a spark of pleasure all the way to my clit.

In response, I parted my legs, and he glided one of his hands down my stomach and into my core, finding very little resistance. He thrust into me, hard and fast, and my cry was lost in Hunter's mouth as he crawled in on my other side and kissed me.

"I will never get enough of you," he breathed, his tongue sliding across mine, leaving me with that drugged, desperate feeling again. "So sweet and spicy. And all fucking mine."

Kellan's thumb flicked across my clit, and between his touch and Hunter's words, I was spiraling into another orgasm, my cries filling the bedroom.

When he was finished dragging every last swirl of pleasure from me, Kellan released my nipple from his mouth and dragged his soaked fingers up my body, leaving my cum streaking over my stomach.

Hunter joined him in cleaning those trails, both of them lapping and groaning over my skin as they tasted my release. Kellan ended up reaching my mouth, and while his touch was softer than Hunter's, it was no less possessive.

Hunter continued down until he reached my pussy, his tongue

tracing through the remnants of my release. He slid his fingers toward my ass once more, using cum to lubricate me.

No one had ever been in my ass before, but I wasn't nervous or worried about it.

The snippet in the shower was enough to tell me that I was going to love anal, and I couldn't wait to be able to take both of my alphas at once. Eventually.

"It makes my wolf feral to know that your ass is going to be claimed by us for the first time," Hunter rumbled, pressing his big finger inside me, my ass muscles resisting for only a few seconds.

"I don't want to be an ass virgin any longer," I said around a gasp, the need turning my brain to mush.

The air was thick with the alphas' scents, and I grasped the back of Kellan's head when he returned to my nipples, sliding the sensitive tip into his mouth once more.

"Relax," Hunter ordered, as he slid his finger farther inside me, leaning down to lap at my clit.

My hips arched into his touch, and while there was a slight discomfort, the pleasure was greater… and different somehow. As my body loosened for him, Hunter added a second finger, and whatever resistance my ass had offered faded with each pleasurable thrust of his hand.

"She's going to come again," Kellan murmured, lifting his head to my mouth once more, as if he wanted to *taste my release* that way. The orgasm came barreling toward me, showing no mercy, and I screamed out incoherently as the two alphas held me between them.

When I was finally spent, Hunter slid his fingers from me, and there was a feral tilt to his gaze when he commanded, "Turn over and grab the head of the bed."

My limbs were jelly, but I was helpless not to obey as I shifted onto my belly, dragging my still shaky body up to clutch the dark timber slats of his headboard. The frame was thick and well-made, and I knew Hunter was about to test its durability.

When I presented my ass to them, twin groans echoed, and I looked over my shoulder to find them staring at me, hunger in their gazes. The alphas knelt side by side, staring like they were memorizing every line of my body, and I couldn't believe I got to call these beautiful males my mates.

The goddess had not let me down.

Kellan rubbed a hand over his face as he choked on another groan. "Damn, Hunt. It's lucky you're the entitled alpha, or I'd fight you for this honor."

"Don't fucking push me, pup," Hunter growled back, and Kellan was smart enough to shut up.

Hunter pressed in behind me, and I moaned at how good his hard body felt against mine. "You're such a good girl," he murmured, running his hands over my sensitive skin and through the mess my previous orgasms had left down my thighs. "Doing exactly as you're told. You want to come again, baby girl? You want me to fuck this sweet ass and bring you to another screaming release?"

"Yes," I sobbed, rocking against him, my body burning. Even better than the burn, my mind was hazy and dark, with no demons chasing me for once. "Fuck me until I pass out. Please."

He leaned down even closer, his weight near crushing. "Brace yourself, little mate."

The thick head of his cock pressed against my ass, and it was so much larger than his fingers that I instinctively arched away.

Hunter's hands landed on my hips, holding me in place. "Safe word," he reminded me. "Otherwise, I'm giving you what you asked for." *Red*. Yeah, I had absolutely zero intention of using any safe word.

He moved slowly, and the pain was biting until the pleasure won out, leaving me a breathless, needy, sobbing mess. As Hunter slid into my ass, my pussy clenched, too empty when I wanted to be filled.

"I've got you, pretty mate," Kellan murmured, pressing his mouth to mine, before he slid down my body until his tongue found my clit and his fingers filled my pussy.

"I want you inside me too," I cried, sure that was what I needed.

Kellan's chuckle tingled through my sensitive core. "It might be a bit much the first time, pretty mate, but don't worry. We'll work our way up to that very soon."

Hunter groaned, as if the very thought was too much for him, and with one final thrust he seated himself all the way in my ass. *Holy goddess of the moon.*

It was too much, and not enough at the same time, as I tried not to pass out. He gave me a few seconds to adjust, and then Hunter started to move, his firm grip keeping me in place. Not that I wanted to go anywhere else.

It felt good.

So fucking good.

I cried out as I ground down on Kellan's fingers and face, which only added to the pleasure. When I released the headboard to claw at the wall, Hunter's hand landed on my ass in a heavy slap that shot another burst of pleasure-pain through me, pre-cum seeping from me.

"Did I tell you to let go, omega?" he demanded, thrusting harder as he slapped my ass again, timing it with his movements.

"No," I groaned, gripping the frame again, which resulted in Hunter rubbing his palm over the sting of his slap, and praising me with all the perfect words.

As his thrusts got faster, so did Kellan's tongue, and he must have been near drowning down there, with Hunter's balls slapping him in the forehead—not that it appeared to bother him. These alphas might not be into each other sexually, but they were secure enough in themselves not to be bothered by sharing this way.

Hunter's groan stole my focus, and I looked up at him, finding his head back and the muscles on his neck and shoulders standing out harshly. "You feel so fucking good, baby. Your ass is squeezing my cock and I won't last much longer before I explode inside you. I want to fuck every part of you, every single night, for the rest of our lives. And eat your sweet cunt every single morning."

Kellan palmed his cock, the thick tip weeping as it rested against his stomach, visible above the band of his boxers. "Fuck," he groaned. "Can you finish, Hunt. If I'm not inside my mate in two seconds I'm going to fucking die."

That got a dark laugh from Hunter. "Wait your turn like a good boy. Good boys get the fucking rewards."

Kellan released a sound like he was dying and freed his cock fully to squeeze the thick base. The sight of his hand pumping sent me slamming headfirst into another orgasm, and Hunter followed a second later, groaning out my name as the heat of his cum filled my ass.

"This is how I want to die," Kellan announced when I collapsed on top of him, and I could feel his face and chest were covered in my release. "Drowning in your sweetness."

"You corny fuck," Hunter snorted, sounding breathless. "But... you've made an excellent point."

When Hunter slid from my ass, I groaned at the feeling of emptiness, which Kellan cured as soon as he shifted out from under me. He snatched me from Hunter's arms, dragged me into his lap, and thrust into my pussy so fast that I almost got whiplash.

His movements were rapid and desperate, our eyes locking as I was sucked into the turbulence of his beautiful gaze, until I came again so quickly it could have been considered magic.

Kellan's relief was obvious. "Thank fuck," he muttered, and I couldn't help but laugh and groan as he finished inside me seconds later.

By the time all three of us collapsed in a messy, sticky, amazing heap, I wasn't the only one ready to pass out. We probably needed to change the sheets and shower again, but that would have to wait until I could feel my legs. Maybe I'd just take a little nap first too.

"That was a perfect fucking night," Hunter murmured, and I couldn't have agreed more.

Fletcher might have stolen a lot from me, but he didn't take this.

CHAPTER 24

After being loved by my alphas into a near oblivion, followed by a nice long soak in the bath, which was thankfully large enough for the three of us, I managed to get a near full night of peaceful, uninterrupted sleep. No nightmares. No creeping sensation of dread. Just perfect slumber.

The next morning, Kellan and Finley had training, and Hunter needed to head into the office to deal with a new product release. He also had a council meeting afterwards, and I assured him I'd be totally fine. Today was the day I was going to ask Slade to train me.

Once I was alone and dressed, I searched for my phone, which I hadn't even looked at since I returned. I found it plugged in and charging beside my bed. Scrolling through my contacts, I dialed Slade. "Snow?" he said, answering on the first ring like he'd been sitting there waiting for my call. Knowing him, he had been.

"Oh hey, good morning," I said, swallowing hard at his deep, rumbly voice.

"Is everything okay?" he asked quickly. "I didn't expect you up early this morning."

Heat infused my cheeks at the realization that we'd been very loud last night, and no shifter would have missed what had been happening in Hunter's room.

Clearing my throat, I hoped my face wasn't as red as it felt. "Yep, everything is great. I just wanted to see if you'd consider starting my training today. Hunter said you were watching me anyways, since you all agreed not to leave me alone, so I figured what better time than now to start. I need to get stronger and fitter. I need to be able to fight in whatever war is coming."

Last night, when we'd left the containment room, I'd mentioned to Slade that I never wanted to be a victim again, and he'd agreed to start training me again. I wasn't sure he expected it to be this soon though.

"We can start today," he finally replied. "My enforcers will be at the training center, so we should be safe there. You've got thirty minutes to get ready."

"Amazing! Thank you!" I called. "I'll meet you downstairs."

Slade grunted and the line went dead.

Hurrying into my wardrobe, I tried to find an outfit suitable for training, knowing I'd need layers to counter the inclement weather. I paused at the new array of hoodies, surprised to find a lot more than just Kellan's hanging in the row.

It was easy to tell which item belonged to which alpha, from Hunter's huge sweaters, in black or grey colors, to Kellan's colorful hoodies with his favorite *Clawtine* branding on the back. For the first time though, there was an array of clothing from Slade *and* Finley.

Slade's were mostly leather jackets in brown, black, and charcoal, and when I sniffed them I groaned at the whiff of his scent, proving he'd worn them recently.

Finley had left me hockey jerseys and hoodies, and I was torn about how I felt seeing them.

It was nice to feel his effort, but I wasn't sure I was ready to wear them yet.

Deciding that today I needed to be strong on my own, I didn't choose any of the alphas' clothes, dressing in my own fur-lined gym pants, thermal shirt, and simple white sweater.

When I emerged from the wardrobe, I planned to head into the bathroom, only I got distracted by a new pile of car and bike magazines on the end of the bed. I had no idea how long they'd been there, as I could have easily missed them earlier when I raced in here looking for my phone.

The last time I'd received such a gift, there'd been no indication of who left them, and with everything that happened afterwards, I'd completely forgotten to even ask.

When I leaned down to sift through the pile, I caught no clear scent once again, but there was a new item: an origami animal sitting on top of the glossy cover.

It took me a second to recognize it was a cat made from orange paper, a white triangle under its tiny nose breaking up the color. It was intricately done, and I couldn't figure out how it managed to be so perfect and so tiny. Surely it was hard to fold a minute piece of paper into such precise lines.

Whichever of the alphas left this was excellent at their craft, and I found myself feeling a little enamored by this simple gift. I'd never been given much in my life, and to know one of them had taken the time to make this cat for me felt extra special.

Opening the drawer on my side table, I placed the cat carefully inside, keeping it safe until I got some shelves to display my treasures. The magazines I left to flick through later. Hurrying into the bathroom I threw my hair into a ponytail, before rubbing some tallow and honey on my skin to protect from the elements.

On my way out of the room, I closed the blinds, which had recently been replaced after Finley smashed through them, and turned the lights off to enjoy a brief glimpse of the red dragon eyes still on my walls. It was the only part of Slade's prank that remained, and I found them comforting. As if the dragon watched over me and kept me safe.

When my thirty minutes was almost up, I grabbed my phone and left the room, wandering toward the stairs. I absentmindedly swiped through my messages, finding a few from Cora which must have been sent when I was taken.

I'd been in no state of mind to read messages when I returned, but now that I'd crawled my way back into the land of the living, it was time to start checking in with my friends.

Bestie: Emme! What the fuck! War said that you've been taken again, and I'm losing my freaking mind. I don't even know why I'm messaging when I know you don't have your phone, but I needed a way to feel a connection. Even if it's only this. I'm holding out hope that you're fine and you'll be reading these messages soon.

> Bestie: Okay, your pack tore through Golden Claw, and now they're out in the human world tracking you. They lost it, Em. I mean… don't-even-fucking-look-at-them-or-they'll-kill-you sort of lost it. I've never seen any of them like this, and I'm eternally grateful that they're on the hunt. Whoever stole you is going to have big regrets. AND THAT'S JUST WHEN I GET MY HANDS ON THEM.

> Bestie: War has been keeping in touch with Hunter. They have a lead on your whereabouts in Texas. I'm fucking praying to the goddess you're alright. Please let me know the moment you can that you're alive and well. Whatever happened, we will fix it. I promise you. Whatever happened. You're still our Emme.

My throat grew tight at the evidence of her love and worry over me. It felt weird to have shifters who cared so deeply in my life. It was hard to break the habit of acting like I was alone in the world, but the truth was, I loved my new life, and never wanted to return to my old.

Never.

Hitting the button to reply, I spent a few minutes trying to fit everything I felt in a message, and when I reached the garage, I was still composing.

"You're getting better using the dyslexia font," Slade said, reading over my shoulder.

I jumped a mile in the air, almost hitting send. "Fuck, you need a bell. Don't be so creepy."

His lips twitched, but I didn't get a proper smile out of him.

"Do you see any errors?" I asked, holding out the phone.

He read it in like three seconds and I was both jealous and turned on by his skills. Sure, it didn't take much to turn me on around Slade, and reading wasn't an advanced or difficult skill, but for me he was the most capable shifter I knew—right behind Hunter.

"It looks perfect, Snow." He tilted his head and nodded. "And that reminds me that we should get started on reading lessons as well. I've been gathering resources to help."

Of course he had. "Yeah, I'm managing easier with the new font and background, but there's a lot of room for improvement. Though stamina and fight training are my highest priority, since I have no skills there at all."

Rudely, Slade didn't argue that point with me. Shaking my head, I hit send on my message to Cora.

> Emme: I'm so sorry, Cores. I've been a shitty friend. I'm sorry I worried you, but it means everything that you care. I hate that I've been slow to sort myself out since returning, but I promise I'm okay. Or I will be okay. I do have a lot to tell you, though. SO fucking much. Can we catch up soon? I love you, and I'm eternally grateful to have you in my life.

Slade waited until I slid my phone into my pocket to say, "The boys have a game today, but we all decided it would be safer for you to avoid major events. Until we have a greater handle on how widespread Fletcher's reach and control is."

As annoyed as I was that they'd *decided* for me, not to mention the disappointment at missing their game, I couldn't really disagree with their assessment. I didn't want to create a dangerous situation for me or my pack. "You four better not get used to making decisions for me, but in this case, I don't disagree. I just really fucking hate letting that asshole take away the things I love."

Slade was grim as he gestured for me to head for the G-class. "Yeah, here's hoping we can remove him from existence long before he ever gets near you again. I just need Talon to start cooperating."

"Did he tell you anything new?"

He opened my door for me, his expression shuttering. "Not much. He admitted that he's visited the volcano where our egg rested a few times, and agreed that was why I'd felt the pull to return. It wasn't the first or only time, but I ignored the rest after my initial search didn't pan out."

With a shake of my head, I pulled myself into the passenger seat. "I can't believe he was just out there all along, one half of your soul. Fletcher's scum, and a fucking liar. Blaine probably isn't even his son."

Slade grumbled. "It looks like that part might be the truth. Talon believes Blaine's mother was an omega... one that Fletcher kept until she *died*."

I nodded. "As I said, a fucking liar. I knew that bastard was part of the reason there are so few of us in the world."

My stomach twisted at the very thought of what he'd done to ensure he had a son. The thought of Fletcher imprisoning and raping an omega for breeding was enough to have me near vomiting in the car.

"Why is he doing this?" I choked out, feeling unstable as I tried to deal with this revelation. "Surely, he already has enough power and money. Hunter said he was rich and well-connected, but clearly it's never enough."

Slade's expression was shrouded in shadows. "He's not stable," he finally said. "He's spent too many years trying to break down our designations in the hopes of controlling us all. His power and money have corrupted his beast. They're no longer able to tell right from wrong."

He shut my door before I could respond, and I pondered this information while he crossed to get in the driver's side.

Once he was inside, I asked, "And you've still had no luck in tracking him or anyone else down?"

Slade shook his head. "I've spent days attempting to unravel the web he wove around himself and his actions, but when there's magic involved, it's almost impossible to figure this out digitally. Our best bet would be to release Talon and follow him back to his master, but I have one major issue with that."

I already knew exactly what that issue would be. "I'd have to go too, or my wolf might retreat again."

The engine roared to life, and Slade backed out in one skilled swing of the wheel. "Yes. Your bond is brand new, like with Hunter and Kellan. It takes weeks before the beast is okay with distance, so we can't let him go until yours settles."

There was also that unanswered question of what happened if we never completed the bond properly and cemented those frayed tethers between us.

Was there a chance Talon and I could never be apart?

CHAPTER 25

SLADE

Emme was quiet for the first part of the drive out to the training facility, as she fidgeted in her chair and kept messing with her ponytail. It would normally annoy me to have a shifter bouncing around beside me, but worry took over as my strongest emotion.

"You okay, Snow?"

Her head snapped toward me; her gaze moved over my face, and she let out a sigh. "I just have so many thoughts and questions. I hate the unknown more than I can express."

I felt the same way, which was what had led me to learn how to hack in the first place. If a shifter wouldn't give me answers, I'd track them down myself.

"You need a distraction," I said, returning my gaze, though not my focus, to the road.

That statement shocked her into stillness, and she sank deeper into her chair. "A distraction... What about a game of twenty questions?"

This omega constantly surprised me, and I could barely remember my mundane existence before she showed up. I'd take her form of chaos all day every single fucking day. "Twenty questions? Considering I know everything about you, I'm not sure I'm seeing the incentive here for me."

I was relieved when that elicited the response I'd hoped for and her airy laughter filled the car. My beast even rumbled in enjoyment over the sound. Our fascination with this omega increased every day, and my resolve to keep her safe, *even from myself*, grew harder to maintain.

"How about I get to ask the twenty questions, then?" she said. "Indulge me so I don't crawl out of my chair and throw myself from the window to get a reprieve from my thoughts."

The very idea of her being hurt had me crushing the steering wheel beneath my hands. "Okay, Snow," I bit out, trying to calm myself. "You can have ten questions. Make them count."

She thought about it for a second, tapping her finger against her chin. "When my wolf and I were broken and retreating," she finally said, the reminder bringing forth a surge of fire in my gut which heated the car, "I kept thinking about everything I didn't know about you all. And a few questions sprang to mind… Are you ready?"

All I could manage was a nod, which was enough for her. "Okay, first question: When did you learn to hack? And why?"

That one was easy, and I released my stranglehold on the wheel. "When I was around ten. I was always curious, and when I found myself with more questions than answers, I started searching for those answers myself. Computers, weirdly, have always been easy for me. Everything just makes sense. Code makes sense since it's all math and logic. Once I tapped into that world, I never looked back, able to manipulate and control from behind my screen."

She swallowed roughly, and I could feel her gaze burning into the side of my face. I liked when her eyes were on me like this. When she couldn't look away.

I wanted her obsession.

"You're terrifying at times," she choked out. "You know that right?"

I was also pleased by that assessment. "I know. Next question."

With a shake of her head, she recovered quickly. "What does it feel like to fly? Is it ever scary? Does your belly like swirl or dip when you dive fast?"

That question was more complex, and I searched for the words to describe the sensation. "It feels like power and freedom," I finally said. "And it's never scary. It's exhilarating, but at the same time, as instinctive as walking. My stomach never drops, as my body knows what's about to happen and adjusts. Soaring above the world is one of my favorite moments in existence."

Her lips quivered, and I tasted her desire and sadness before she got herself under control. "Sounds amazing. I'd love to try that one day."

I'd never taken anyone flying on my back, but if I ever did, Emme would be the one.

"Okay," she said, clearing her throat. "Dragon fire. What does it feel like to spew it from your mouth? Does it burn you?"

It made sense that she would be the most curious about my beast, and he was quite pleased to be holding her interest. *Bastard.* "Dragon fire burns in our center while in our beast form," I explained, "and when we breathe fire, that heat expands and rises until it spews from our mouth. I don't have to release it though, and it won't burn or hurt me. The heat is quite pleasant to our kind and allows me to fly at altitudes that would freeze any other creature."

She shook her head and muttered again, "Terrifying" before moving on to the next question. "Does your dragon have thoughts like yours?"

I nodded. "Yes, only with less empathy, and an ancient, cold feeling to them."

"*Less* empathy?" she breathed, and I couldn't help but chuckle.

"Believe it or not, it's the truth. Except for his pack, there's not a single living creature that the dragon gives a shit about. We razed villages to the ground in our search for you."

I looked away from the road to see her skin paling as she swallowed hard. "I don't want anyone to die for me. Especially not innocents."

To my dragon, everyone but our pack were ants, insignificant and disposable.

"Do you have any other questions?" I asked as the stadium appeared in the distance.

Emme was quiet, and when I looked over again, her cheeks were pink. Her scent wafted strongly through the cab, and now I was invested in whatever she wanted to know next. "Spill," I commanded, wishing for the hundredth time that my dominance worked on her.

Even though I'd absolutely go mad with power if I could control her.

"Uh," she started, and when I shot her a long stare, she hurriedly continued, "Your piercings... how does that work with your touch aversion? Is it the same as the tattoos? And... do they come across in dragon form?"

Of everything she could have asked, that wasn't what I expected, and I found myself *almost* taken by surprise. Though the pink cheeks made sense now. "I do enjoy pain with my pleasure," I admitted, relishing the deepening of her blush. "Self-pleasure that is, as I've never allowed another to touch me that way."

Emme choked on that statement, and she was basically fire-engine red now, leaving me with a desperate urge to see if that pretty blush extended down the rest of her body. After almost three decades on this planet, this was the first shifter I wanted to push through my touch aversion to be with. If only it wasn't dangerous for her, and maybe the entire world to do so.

"You're a virgin?" she asked, her breaths rapid though she didn't sound surprised. She sounded intrigued, and I could smell her arousal, which had my beast clawing at me.

"Yes, Snow. I've never found a shifter who I even wanted to try and overcome my touch aversion for." *Until you, little mate. Until you.*

She shook her head a few times, as if shaking off that comment, and then cleared her throat. "Back to the piercings…"

It was clear she wanted the change of subject, and I didn't fight her. "I held myself while Finley pierced me," I said, voice rougher as I fought a base instinct to devour Emme. In what way? Well, who the fuck knew. "Fin wasn't particularly happy about it, but I enjoy the sensation of the barbs in my dick. My favorite was while they were healing, but they still give pleasure-pain now as my body tries to reject them."

I was caught in the snare of her wide blue eyes, the pupils blown as her tongue darted out to moisten her lips. Pulling to a halt in the parking lot, I leaned in and murmured, "And my dragon's dick is barbed. It's designed to hook on to his mate, so we can stay inside until we've bred to our satisfaction. My piercings are in the *exact same position*, so it depends how technical you want to get in *coming across in my other form*."

"Goddess have mercy," she breathed, still unable to blink or move.

"No mercy for you, Snow," I replied, unsure what the fuck I was doing playing this game with my unstable beast, but I couldn't seem to stop.

Needing my own distraction now, I sucked in a breath heavily filled with her sweet scent, and looked around the parking lot. It was filled with cars, and I saw that my enforcers, along with Warrick's, were already here.

"Come on, Emmeline," I said, opening my door, desperate to cleanse her scent from my beast before he lost control. "Question time is over. Now we train."

On her side of the car, I cleared the snow under her door and she jumped out into the patch. "Thanks for answering my questions," she said, the flush of her embarrassment easing and her cheeks returning to a golden hue. "Ever since we got back from Texas, you've been distant. It was nice to feel close to you again."

My beast roared, but I shut him down fast. "I've always kept a certain distance between us," I said, reminding her of our relationship's limitations. Or maybe I was reminding myself. "With my dragon's instability, the most I can offer is protection and companionship. Not a full bond."

No matter how incredibly tempting she was.

Emme pressed her lips together, and when the shine of her eyes dulled, I wanted to kick my own ass. My intentions were never to hurt her, but it would be worse to lie when I wasn't sure I could ever complete this bond—complete it and keep her safe.

Reaching out, I caught her hand, barely registering the very mild negative response from the touch. Emme turned her torso toward me, though her line of sight dropped to our clasped palms. When she finally met my gaze, staring up from under her thick lashes, I couldn't logic away the need that roared to life in my body.

I wanted her. Every part of her.

Forcing out a long exhalation, I said, "It's not you, Emme. The goddess fated you to be mine, and she chose very well. There's no one else in the world I would want other than you, but despite our deepening bond, I haven't changed, and neither has my dragon. He's never to be fully trusted, and for that reason, I can't be trusted with you. You're too precious to risk. Do you understand?"

The blue of her eyes was piercing as she stared up at me, and though her expression remained neutral, her lower lip trembled. "What if it's a risk I'm willing to take?" she replied harshly, and I had to acknowledge the logic in that response.

"To some degree, it is your risk," I agreed, "but I'm the one who has to live with the consequences. You're my responsibility to protect. A responsibility I've failed at more than once."

She shook her head, her laughter bitter and broken. "I'm only here because of you. You've fulfilled your responsibility to me plus more. If you weren't beating yourself up so hard, you'd see that. You saved me when Blaine took us to Silver City, and then again in Texas when you were strong enough to knock Talon out and fly off with him before Fletcher returned. You're my fucking savior."

When she stepped into me, my dragon rumbled loud in my chest, and my dick kicked in my pants. The dragon's rage wasn't new, but the arousal was, and only ever around Emme. *Calm the fuck down, both of you.*

"Are you no longer afraid of what bonding to all of us would mean?"

Reminding her of why she'd avoided us for years was a low blow, but my resolve was crumbling under her scent, earnest expression, and those perfect freckles drawing my gaze. She was the drug I craved, and I'd probably have to kill myself to stay away from her for eternity.

Which I'd do if it kept her safe.

Emme gave my question great consideration. "I think I'm more afraid now of what it would mean to *not* be fully bonded in our pack. We're weaker this way, which is allowing Fletcher to take advantage of us. I won't stand for that any longer, even if it means I have to share my power between the five of you to defeat him."

The very thought was enough for the fires in my gut to flare, and I barely toned them down before Emme was scorched by the blowback of heat. I know she caught the flash of dragon in my eyes, her gaze drawn to my face as she gasped.

But she didn't back away.

My brave little omega took another step closer until she only had to breathe deeply for her chest to touch mine. I wasn't sure what would happen if she initiated the touch, and with that in mind, I released her hand and swung away, heading into the training facility.

Her exhalation of annoyance was audible from behind, but she followed without another word, as if she knew we were at an impasse. An impossible impasse. Unless something changed between me and my beast.

"Talon has the same instability," she piped up when we were almost to the training field, as if she'd been thinking it over on the walk.

I continued toward the middle which had already been cleared of snow. "Even more reason for me not to bond with you too," I bit out. "I'm the only one who can stop him from hurting you, so I need to keep a level head."

I paused at the scent of sorrow lacing her sweetness, but a glance back showed her neutral expression. Neutral bothered me as much as her tears.

Emme, for all her past traumas, was generally open with her emotions.

She never hid the way she felt, and I'd been craving that refreshing honesty from the first moment I'd seen her snowy white wolf prancing through the forest.

"Don't hide from me, Snow," I growled, pausing to stare at her.

She rolled her eyes. "You're a moody bastard. You know that, right?"

I couldn't even fucking argue that point. Lately my moods had swung on a pendulum large enough to hit the fucking moon. Which was what she did to me... turned my life into one of turmoil and beauty. My dragon wasn't equipped to handle it, and neither was the man.

"And how am I hiding?" she continued, hands on her slim hips. "I'm here, pushing you out of your comfort zone, where it's safe and perfect."

Leaning down, I let my lips linger near hers, reminded of that taste I'd had back in the containment room. "There's nothing safe and perfect around me, Snow. And I don't want you to hide your emotions from me. They're mine. Your desires are mine. Your tears are mine. I want them all."

She swallowed roughly and managed to say, "Even when you offer nothing in return?"

Ah, my poor Snow. "Yes. I'm a selfish bastard, but you already knew that. Now let's get you trained up."

She huffed, but I didn't give her a chance to respond. In the distance, Warrick and his enforcers were warming up, and my squad had just emerged from the obstacle course room dressed in their gear, with weapons strapped across their bodies.

As they approached us, they eyed Emme with curiosity but knew better than to get too close. "This is Emmeline," I said, meeting each of their stares. Most of them looked away, unable to handle the dominance of my beast. "We protect her with our lives. If anything happens to her, I will destroy the fucking world. Understand?"

Emme spluttered and opened her mouth to object, but she didn't get a chance over my squad slamming their fists to their chests in a loud thump. "Yes, Alpha Slade," they shouted. "We have our orders." And there would be no mercy for any who disobeyed.

When I turned to Emme, there was nothing neutral in her expression any longer, and I wanted to pin her to the icy ground and sink my dragon's fangs into her throat. Her fire was addictive, and I was a desperate, depraved shifter.

"Come on, sweetheart," I said, the endearment slipping out. "Let's get your training started."

Pink tinged her cheeks, and the fury in her gaze and obvious need to yell at me faded.

Not that I would have cared. Emmeline was the only shifter in the world who could speak to me in whatever tone she wanted and I'd just fucking take it. She had all the damn power here.

"Yes, sir," she muttered, and when she acted like a brat, I wanted to tie her to my bed and take control of every part of her body until she shattered under my touch.

A rumble filled my chest as she let the slightest smile linger around the corners of her lush lips. We were both aware of exactly what game she played. A dangerous one. "Run, Snow," I ordered gruffly, and with a wink she did precisely as ordered.

My enforcers fell in behind us, and I remained at her side, moving just above a quick walk. She was tall, but her fitness and running ability left a lot to be desired.

On the first trip around the stadium, we avoided Warrick's squad, but on the second they'd finished their warmups and were waiting off to the side. Warrick waved at Emme as she passed, and she managed to smile and return the gesture, even though she could barely breathe.

Improving her fitness wouldn't happen in a day, but I was pleased to see her pushing herself harder than she had last time. She was determined to strengthen herself, and the pride I felt didn't take me by surprise. It just added another layer to my already complex feelings for her.

By the time warmups and stretches were done, we were ready for drills and sparring. My squad teamed up with their usual partners, and I chose Horton for Emme, unsure I could trust myself to touch her.

"If you initiate more bodily contact than absolutely necessary for each drill," I warned the eagle shifter, "you will be permanently grounded." He nodded, his expression relaxed—he'd been expecting the threat.

Emme inserted herself between us like the little brat she was. "Don't listen to him. I will turn everything in his room to an odd angle if he hurts you even a little. And he knows it."

Horton's lips twitched but he saved his own life by managing not to smile. "That won't be necessary, Omega Emmeline. I understand a mate protecting his female."

Which was the exact reason he was one of my top enforcers. He understood the rules.

"Please call me Emme," she corrected. "I hate being addressed so formally."

Horton's eyes shot up to meet mine, and even though she deserved the honorific of the title, I wouldn't go against her wishes here. With my nod, he gave her a relieved smile. "Emme it is, then. You can call me—"

"Nothing," I growled. "She doesn't need to know your name. Now let's get to sparring drills. Emme has no skills to speak of, so we're starting at the beginning."

She glared at me while Horton chuckled. "We all started at the beginning, Emme. We'll get you trained up in no time."

With one last withering glare my way, Emme returned her focus to him, and I forced myself to walk away before I did something stupid like kill my top enforcer.

"What are you hoping to work up to?" I heard Horton ask as I strode off.

Her reply was exactly what I hoped and expected from her. "I want to be able to take them all by surprise," she said in a harder than usual tone. "I want to be a concealed weapon they never see coming. I want to be their worst nightmares."

Pride flared again as I acknowledged that Emme was, *and always would be,* my destruction. It was fitting that she might be Fletcher's too.

I couldn't wait to see it.

CHAPTER 26

EMME

After almost dying during training, I drowned myself in the shower for an hour, got dressed in sweats, and dragged my broken, ragged ass down the stairs and into the dining room. Hunter had already informed me that we were having a family dinner tonight, and anyone who missed it was going to be in *big fucking trouble*.

Now, while most of the time I chose to be in *his* kind of trouble, I also needed to eat and replenish all the energy I'd spent today trying not to perish, vomit, or cry.

It had been a close call on all three happening at the same time.

When I stepped into the dining room, four sets of eyes locked in on me, and *damn*, it was disconcerting to be at the center of all their attention. It hadn't happened many times before, as Finley usually avoided me and direct eye contact. Tonight, though, his gaze was locked on the hardest, the whiskey tones of his irises light and swirling.

"Hey," I said softly, a weird roll of nerves assaulting my stomach. "Sorry I'm late."

Hunter waved toward the seat on his right side. "Not late, little mate. You're right on time."

Trying to act completely normal, I managed not to stumble as I crossed to my chair, excited to sit and rest my aching thighs. My wolf healing wasn't fast enough to counter Slade's barbaric training.

Before I could grasp my chair, Finley jumped to his feet and moved the wingback from the table. He was dressed nicely tonight, in jeans, a white shirt, and a red and white flannel thrown over the top that brought out the auburn in his dark brown hair.

Our eyes met as my lips parted in surprise, and Finley responded with a gentle smile.

"I've never seen you smile," I whispered, blinking at him like a moron.

His grin grew and grew and *fuck me dead*, he had dimples. He'd been to the barber recently and I could just make out, under his thick, dark, and now well-groomed beard, gorgeous indents. In both cheeks.

When I'd been gawking for an uncomfortably long time, Kellan laughed and eased the tension. "You broke her, Fin. Nice job, bro."

Finley's smile never wavered, and it wasn't just the dimples. The amber and gold were bright in his eyes, and the bear looked... happy.

"I don't want to break her," he replied softly, answering Kellan but staring straight at me. "I want to protect and save her from whatever the world throws our way. I will not let anyone hurt my family again, no matter what it takes."

He leaned in even closer, and I barely breathed as he bopped me gently on the nose. "You're my family, Ice. Now and always. Whatever happens, *and whatever you choose*."

With that, he nudged me into my chair, and I remained shocked and speechless as he pushed me into the table. Hunter looked smug as he leaned back in his chair and swirled his whiskey around in his glass. "Everything in its own time. Just as I predicted."

As Finley returned to his seat, Kellan, who was on my right, leaned over and pressed his lips to my cheek. "You look absolutely gorgeous tonight, Shortcake. I love that color on you."

I glanced down to my plain black sweats, while remembering I'd left my hair stringy and wet from the shower. I shook my head at him. "You're crazy, Golden. I look like crap. Slade tried to one-up Fletcher and killed me during training today."

The joke fell flat as all four alphas scowled. "Too soon?" I said weakly, wishing they'd all get on board with me using *humor to deflect from very real trauma*.

"If we're discussing anyone touching, hurting, or stealing you away from us," Slade drawled, also twirling whiskey, though I hadn't seen him take a drink yet, "then yes, Snow, it's too fucking soon. There's never going to be a time that's *not too soon* in that situation."

Fair enough.

I'd never be able to joke about Kellan almost dying, so I understood how they felt.

Reaching for the wine Florence left for me, I took a long sip of the Moscato, enjoying the cool, sweet taste on my tongue. My body relaxed as Kellan started talking about their game today, and how they'd absolutely destroyed the Silver City Cobras.

"It's like they brought their backup players," he said with a snort as he took a swig of beer. "I had to do random drills out there just to keep myself from zoning out."

I hated that I'd missed the game. "I'm so sad I didn't get to watch," I admitted, pouting a little.

Finley smiled at me again, and *goddess be damned* he needed to stop doing that. It was like getting randomly electrocuted. "You really didn't miss much today. We destroyed them eight to one. And that one was accidentally knocked in by our goalie."

I glanced at Kellan to see if he was kidding, but apparently not. "Oh yeah, Coach almost reamed Carlson a new asshole. He was pissed, but in the end we got the W and that's all that matters."

"Fuck yeah it does," Finley called as he held his beer up for Kellan to *clink* from across the table.

I stared at the bear shifter and shook my head. "Has anyone done a DNA test to confirm he wasn't body snatched?" As soon as I said it, I immediately regretted it. "Fuck, sorry. Ignore me and my stupid questions. So, what's for dinner?"

From the corner of my eye, I saw Finley lean closer, and I braced myself for his response. "It's okay, Ice," he started softly. "I promise this is me, and this version of Finley isn't going anywhere."

While his promises didn't mean much yet, I was growing rather used to him speaking in kind tones to me. There was a softness I hadn't realized existed, deep inside the grouchy bear. "Okay," I replied, keeping my response simple. "That's good to hear."

Finley nodded, as if he understood everything I hadn't voiced out loud. "I'll back my words with actions, don't you worry."

We were interrupted as Florence hurried into the room, a massive silver tray perched on her shoulder. "Dinner's ready," she called, beaming. "It's pizza night."

She dropped the tray into the middle of the table, beside the plates waiting for us to use, and then added sides of garlic bread, breaded cheese sticks, and dipping sauces.

"Gerry and I spent all afternoon handcrafting these," she said with a hint of pride, and I took in the delicious-looking variety of toppings, steam rising up from the melted cheese. "I expect you all to eat everything. None of you have had a decent meal in days."

My stomach chose that moment to perk up and agree by rumbling loudly. I was excited that after weeks of missing meals and running on empty, I could focus on fueling up and growing stronger.

Before the alphas got on my case about eating, I scooped up three of the pizzas, selecting the meatiest ones with lots of cheese and swirls of BBQ sauce. There was no sign of a vegetable, and I couldn't be more pleased. I also grabbed two slices of garlic bread and a cheese stick to finish.

Food was literally spilling over the sides of my plate, and Hunter looked as satisfied as when he had his face buried in my—

Yeah, now was definitely not the time for those thoughts.

"Good girl," he murmured, taking another sip of his whiskey.

Ignoring him was the only mature response I could muster. I took a moment to inhale the cheese-meat aroma, already sure this was about to be a new favorite meal of mine.

It contained all the important food groups: meat, cheese, and bread.

The trifecta of nutrition.

When I took my first bite, I reminded myself that I could not moan, but *damn*, this pizza was about to give sex a run for its money. Okay, maybe not, but damn it was good.

"Delicious," I rasped, closing my eyes to savor the taste. "You all need to stop staring at me like I'm sprawled naked in the middle of the table and start eating these pizzas. The world won't end if you join me before I'm finished."

Hunter grunted, and I opened my eyes to find his were blazing gold. I stopped chewing as he reached out and brushed his thumb over my lip, swiping up a bit of sauce I missed. "Keep eating pizza like that, little omega," he rumbled, "and you will be naked in the middle of the table. We will eat our meal right from your delectable body."

My core clenched, and when I moaned it had nothing to do with food. Words failed me as I attempted to regulate my panting breaths, and somehow I managed to calm down enough to take another bite. When I finished my first pizza and started on my second, the alphas began to fill their plates, leaving plenty of the meat pizza on the tray of course.

For domineering assholes, they were so considerate that it broke me a little.

"I don't thank you all enough," I said, trying not to reveal how emotional this moment had made me. "I know everything is pretty fucked up, and there's a lot of danger out there still, but I'm so blessed to have you all as a pack. It's a fortune I never saw coming, but I want you all to know, I'm not running from it any longer. I don't care about the consequences; I am choosing you all. I am choosing and claiming this pac—"

Kellan grabbed the side of my chair and yanked me right into his side. He dropped his head into my shoulder and nuzzled along my skin. "Baby, we're the fucking fortunate ones. You're a gift and a blessing, and I don't care who we have to kill, we're going to make sure this world is safe for you."

Hunter's chest rumbled. "Couldn't have said it better myself. Now stop drooling all over Emme. She needs to finish her food." He leaned over and dragged my chair back into its spot, and while Kellan pouted, he let me go without an argument.

I spent the next ten minutes eating everything my hands touched, and by the time I was done, I was sure they'd have to roll me out of here.

"Florence has dessert still to come," Slade said, taking a sip of his drink. "Don't run away, Snow."

I shook my head. "Not only are my legs dead from training today, but my pants are also too tight for me to walk... let alone run."

Slade's gaze slid from my face and down to where the rest of my body was hidden by the table. "You're wearing sweats."

"Exactly," I said, and I couldn't help but laugh at his expression. "That's how much I ate. Enough to make *sweats* tight."

Hunter changed the subject before Slade could get more in depth about the current sweatpants' situation. "Okay, we need to discuss what our plans are moving forward with Fletcher, Blaine, and the witches of Termaine."

The lighthearted atmosphere vanished quickly, leaving behind a more somber and serious air. "What about our plan for Talon?" I asked.

Hunter's expression didn't fill me with confidence. "Talon is a complicated situation, so for now he remains where he is. Slade's monitoring him, and we'll figure it out eventually. I hope he can be used to our advantage."

"Only time will tell," Slade added, and that was all they'd say on the matter.

With more pressing issues to deal with, I decided to let it slide. For now.

"According to Talon, Fletcher is recruiting more witches to his cause," Slade continued, "and while we took out a chunk of his shifters during that attack in Silver City, he has many more where they came from too. He's been planning this attack for years, and he's a patient bastard."

"Did we confirm Blaine's mother was an omega?" I asked, unsure why it was important but I needed to know nonetheless.

Slade nodded. "Yeah, I think I tracked her down from a missing shifter report that was filed about a year before Blaine was born. It lines up."

My stomach lurched, and I hoped like hell I didn't vomit up all that delicious food. "He deliberately stole an omega from her family or pack, impregnated her, then killed her."

How the fuck was this real life?

No one spoke for many seconds, all of us locked in the horror of what had happened. The tension had my stomach whirling once more.

"I'm so fucking glad that when the council found you, Em," Finley finally said, his expression flat, "you were brought here to us. Imagine if *that fuck* got his hands on you. I can't…"

He trailed off with a slightly green tinge to his skin now too.

"I'd have ended up like my mom and Blaine's," I finished for him. "Used and abused, then thrown away once my power was spent. And there will be more like them. I'm sure of it."

Hunter slammed his glass on the table. "It will never fucking happen. We will kill them all before they touch you again. Whatever it takes."

"When's our meeting with the witches?" Finley asked as he leaned forward to meet Hunter's gaze. "We need magical help. We need spells to ensure that Emme remains safe, no matter what Fletcher or the Termaine witches throw at us."

Hunter nodded slowly, as if he couldn't help but agree. "Jewels is arranging for any loyal witches to join us and meet with the Alpha Council next week. In the end, unless they want to fall to the Termaine coven's rule, they need to take our side. In Fletcher's new future, witches will be under *his* witches' command. Goodbye freedom and unfettered power."

"Once we have magic on our side, we can ferret out these fucks," Kellan said, "since they're cowards and want to hide behind a witch's skirt. I say we take the battle to them. I'm sick of sitting back and waiting for them to come."

I agreed with him, and hoped the *loyal* witches did too, so they'd help us track Fletcher's safe house.

It was a better plan than releasing Talon and following him all the way home.

I might not trust witches and their motivations, but with a common enemy, there had to be a way we could all work together. Otherwise, we'd be crushed in this coming war.

CHAPTER 27

The next couple of days were both nice and odd. Life returned almost to normal, and Florence put up more Christmas decorations around the house, giving off the impression we were getting closer to my first Christmas in Golden Claw.

She'd even added a few strings of twinkling lights and a wreath on my door, which appeared after she noticed my admiration of the living room tree for the hundredth time. For the most part, I spent my days training, and texting with Cora as we tried to organize a time for us to catch up.

She was flat-out with work, wrapping up projects before the end of the year, and I was still scattered and tired, though overall my essence was healing. Piece by piece, day by day, I grew stronger and happier, helped along by a pack who never let me fall into my trauma.

Even as busy as they all were too.

Between hockey for Kellan and Finley, Reeves Industries drama for Hunter, and Slade training me, spending time with Talon, and keeping an eye on our security, we were running ourselves ragged. I ended most days tasting blood and vomit in my mouth as my body rebelled against the rigorous training regimen, but I refused to give up.

I had no idea when it was supposed to get easier, but so far there was no sign of relief.

A bright side I hadn't expected was how great Horton turned out to be. For an alpha, he was kind and patient, walking my unfit and unskilled ass through each different move and drill. Over and over. Until I eventually got it right.

"You landed a hit," he crowed, bouncing on his toes. "I'm so freaking proud of you."

This was my fourth session in three days, and when I'd dragged my butt from bed this morning, I'd almost cried at the thought of training again. But now I was so happy I'd pushed through.

"I can't believe it," I huffed, shaking my head. "That felt impossible when you showed me it earlier."

For over an hour now Horton had been teaching me a technique to use against a larger, stronger attacker, and I'd finally landed my first decent hit to his kidneys. This hit would loosen the attacker's hold, and then I could twist in a series of moves to break free and run. A lot of what they taught me was about escaping rather than fighting back. I'd always be smaller and weaker than an alpha.

Horton threw his arms out and leaned forward like he was about to hug me, until a low menacing rumble filtered through the grounds, halting everyone in their tracks.

And I mean everyone.

Slade's enforcers, Warrick's enforcers, and a third group training across on the other side of the facility, all whipped around to stare at the dragon shifter glaring our way from the middle of the field. Horton's brown skin turned quite pale as he flapped his arms and whirled, like he'd been attempting to fly in his humanoid form.

"That's enough training for the day, Snow," Slade called, his eyes locked on me.

He remained as emotionally distant as he'd been since Texas, but he was always physically nearby. Watching me. Keeping me safe. There was no doubt in my mind that when he wasn't standing at my side, I was front and center in all of his cameras.

To no one's surprise, our prank wars were on hiatus for the time being, and I tried not to miss the fun that had brought to my life.

"I'm not done though," I protested, still hyped up at successfully pulling off a semi-useful move. "I've got more energy."

Slade's flat expression indicated there was no point in arguing with him today. "You're done, omega. Shower and change in the locker room—I laid out an outfit for you."

I paused at that odd request. I generally showered and changed at home, but maybe we had to head to Reeves Industries today. Deciding I didn't care either way, I trudged off across the icy ground and headed for the locker rooms. I'd only used this facility once before to wash vomit off my shirt—*don't ask*—but they were impressive.

Huge, white, and clean, there were rows of showers along the back wall, and toilets near the entrance. The shelves were generally bare except for a stack of fluffy white towels, but today I saw the additional pile of folded clothes and black boots.

Excited to uncover what clothes Slade had chosen for me, I hurried into the showers and washed myself in record time. The toiletries were scentless and good quality, and when I emerged, there was nothing but my own natural scent in the air.

As I wrapped one towel around my body and the other around my hair, I wandered toward the shelves. On top was a sports bra and matching black panties, which I slipped on first, before I lifted a… *jumpsuit*.

When the heavy length unfolded, I saw that it was black like the boots, with pink flames up both arms, and gold stripes down the legs. On the back was my name, embroidered, and it finally clicked on what I held: a race suit.

Ahhhhhh! I started mentally screaming and cheering as I realized why we'd finished early.

Track day.

Finally, I would get to experience the Reeves pack racetrack, and lose myself in supercars and speed for a few hours. What a fucking excellent surprise.

Sliding the material up my body, I marveled at the perfect fit, zipping myself in and securing the button at my throat. The boots went on last, sliding over the pants, and when I checked myself in the mirror, I felt like a superhero.

Speeding Ticket Woman. There was no way to drive slow in an outfit like this—the gods would smite you right where you stood.

Using the hairdryer attached to the wall, I dried my hair and threw it into a quick braid to match the sporty, racer look I had going on. I finished tying the end as Slade strode into the room. "You ready to go, Snow?" he asked, and I glared at him in the reflection of the mirror.

"I could have been naked," I said, hands landing on my hips. "You almost saw my tits."

Maybe a glimpse of me naked would return the old Slade to me.

This new, cold version wasn't my favorite, and I hated the distance he maintained between us.

"I've seen you naked a hundred times," he said in the same flat tone. "Though, seeing it in the flesh does offer another element."

My mouth dropped open, even though I wasn't all that surprised he watched me through his security system. Part of me was now wondering if he watched me with Hunter and Kellan, but I was too chickenshit to ask him.

"Yeah, it's definitely different," I managed to say. "Your piercings are visually branded in my mind for that very reason."

He took a step closer. "Makes sense. Touch would bring a whole other element too."

Holy goddess. Was it hot in here? Did my fire-resistant suit just catch fire?

"There'd definitely be another element involved for you to touch me naked," I countered weakly.

The room grew even hotter until my reflection in the mirror turned foggy. "If I touched you naked, Emmeline..." Slade murmured, towering over me, and I focused desperately on his dark shadow in the fogged mirror. "...I would never let you go. You'd be naked all day every single day. I would claim your body until you begged me to stop. There's no middle ground for me or my beast. I'd consume you until there was nothing left, and even then, I wouldn't stop."

A throb strummed low in my core, and *what the hell was wrong with me* that I was instantly soaked by that promise. Or threat. Whatever it was, I wanted more.

"Trust me," he finished, as he backed up a few feet, "it's better for you that I keep this distance." He opened the door to the locker room. "Now, let's go. We've got an appointment."

On trembling thighs, with my hard nipples brushing against the stiff material of the suit, I managed to stumble toward him. "Maybe don't use all that bass in your voice when you're warning me off," I managed to get out as I passed him by. "My wolf likes the bass." *And I do too.*

Slade threw one long arm out across the doorway to stop me, and I couldn't help but meet his blazing gaze. "You look fucking magnificent," he murmured, setting my body on fire again with one stare. "I'm getting you a race suit in every damn color."

Have mercy on my horny soul.

My voice was a husky rasp as I replied, "You know what, I think I'd like to be consumed by you, big guy."

The green of his eyes flared as his pupils dilated, until there was no mistaking the beast behind the man. Before all hell broke loose, I ducked under the muscled arm blocking me in and strolled my ass out of there, Slade right on my heels.

I hoped from the back I looked calm and confident, because I was struggling to keep my expression neutral. Thankfully, I knew this place well enough now to navigate through the building without help, so I didn't have to turn back. When we reached the front desk, the multitude of shifters answering phones and typing on computers reminded me that this was a busy center during the day. They all called out respectful greetings for *Alpha* Slade, and he ignored them as he stalked behind me. Like a good bodyguard.

When we reached the car, he opened my door before I could, and I felt his stare burning into my face, which I ignored as I thanked him and slipped inside. Just because Slade was controlling the trajectory of our mating, didn't mean I had to play along. I wouldn't push him, but I didn't have to make it easier on him either. Eventually, he'd have to choose, and I wanted that choice to be me.

The drive from the training facility was quiet but not uncomfortable.

As the racetrack came into view, I found myself asking, "Is it Sunday? Why are we racing today?"

Slade's low rumble of laughter hit me like a punch to the gut. A punch that dripped lust straight into my veins. It was a real skill that this alpha could render me stupid and desperate with a single sound. "It's Thursday," he replied. "Do you know the date?"

I shook my head. "Nah, I haven't really paid much attention to days or dates since Texas."

My phone wasn't even here, as I'd forgotten it once again.

Slade remained relaxed, his hands loose on the wheel as he sped along the stretch of road that led to their track. "Today is special for two reasons," he finally said, but cut himself off before he could explain *what* those reasons were.

The stadium came into view, and I marveled at the sheer size of this facility. It was an oval design, spanning far into the distance, and when we drove through the open main gates, I pressed my face to the window to take it all in.

"You ready for this?" Slade asked as he pulled into a parking lot that could have easily held a hundred cars and switched off the engine.

I nodded, even though I had no idea what *this* was. As long as it was racing in some form, then I had no complaints. I'd used bikes and the open road to banish my demons before, and I needed that hit more than ever today. "I can't wait. I'm ready to lose myself in a race."

Having Slade's full focus left me breathless. Stupid charismatic asshole. "You're going to get as much race time and speed as you can handle," he assured me, "but that's not the only reason we're here today."

When he leaned in closer, I held my breath, wondering if he was about to kiss me. As his sweet breath washed over me, I froze in place, only to hear him say, "Happy Birthday, Snow."

My brain spasmed as I tried to comprehend what was happening. *Happy Birthday?*

Wait, whose birthday? "My birthday was weeks ago."

When I'd been held captive, if my math was correct. Not that it mattered since I hadn't celebrated a birthday in… well, ever. Most years I didn't even remember, let alone expect anyone else to.

Slade wrapped his fingers gently around my chin and turned my gaze so I was staring out the front windshield. A group of familiar shifters had appeared from *somewhere*, all dressed in custom race suits. Kellan waved a sign at me, and I took a second to read: *Merry Christmas and Happy Birthday, Pretty Mate. Let's fucking race.*

"We might have missed your birthday, Snow," Slade said, and I tried not to tremble against his touch. "But since today is Christmas Day, we decided to combine the two and take a day to celebrate how incredible you are. And how happy we are that you were born." I finally knew the two reasons, and they were too much for my fragile heart to handle.

Holy shit. *Don't cry. Don't cry.*

I mentally flipped out as I tried to contain my emotions. I was about to embarrass myself and bawl all over Slade. I wanted to get out of the car and run, or hide in the back, or scream. It was overwhelming, but somehow I kept it together long enough to say, "I don't have presents for you all."

Slade released me with a smirk, before he opened his door. "You're the damn present, Emmeline. Now get out so we can race."

I sucked in deep breaths, having no idea if I was mentally prepared for today, but wanting it all the same. A birthday-Christmas celebration was a first for me, and I couldn't let my past trauma ruin this surprise. For me or my pack.

CHAPTER 28

I wasn't completely under control by the time my door was wrenched open by Kellan. His smile as he reached over and unclicked my belt, before lifting me out the door, helped more than I expected though. Strong positive emotions were relatively new for me, and now they were everywhere... drowning me in their intensity.

"Baby," Kellan yelled. "Happy belated birthday. I've been waiting forever for you to get here."

He kissed me so thoroughly I forgot the time, place, and my existence. I loved when I was so close to my alphas that I didn't know where I began and they ended.

"It's nine fucking a.m.," Hunter growled from somewhere nearby. "You didn't even wake until eight."

Kellan chuckled against my lips. "Daddy Alpha is cranky this morning. He doesn't like waiting either."

Hunter's scent hit me when he wrapped his hands around my waist and lifted me away from Kellan.

"Mine," he grumbled, spinning me to face him. For once, he allowed my feet to stay solidly on the ground, so I popped up on my toes to bring our faces closer together.

"Best birthday-Christmas ever," I murmured, but they all heard me of course.

"A *birthday-Christmas* she forgot was even this month," Slade, the absolute freaking traitor, told them all.

That set off groans and cries, and I peered around Hunter when I heard Cora's soft laughter. She stood with Warrick and waved enthusiastically when our gazes met. Another burst of happiness almost took me down, and I found myself wiggling with excitement at what the rest of the day might bring. Racing, my pack, and my best friends, was all I wanted from life.

Hunter's wolf flared in his eyes as he took me in carefully. "Are you doing okay with all of this?" he asked softly, and as I stared into the dark depths of his beautiful, stormy eyes, it was hard to believe that not that long ago I'd feared this alpha.

"More than okay," I said, surprised to find that minus my initial freakout, I meant it. "Shocked, but super happy."

"Thank the goddess," he muttered, and then his lips pressed to mine, his tongue demanding immediate entrance. As always, he found absolutely no resistance from me.

It was a brief kiss, thankfully, or I'd be asking for a minute of privacy to deal with the throb in my core. When Hunter finished saying *happy birthday*, Cora and Warrick pushed forward, and my best girlfriend threw her arms around me.

"You look so freaking good in that outfit," she said as she hugged me tight. "Happy birthday and Merry Christmas, Ems. I'm so happy we're celebrating together."

My eyes burned, but I kept it together by burying my face in her shoulder.

When I pulled away, I examined her white race suit with green accents. "You look gorgeous, Cores, and I vote we get more of these suits." She enthusiastically nodded her agreement, and she wasn't the only one. I rolled my eyes at the alphas, who all looked like damn models in their suits, but I kind of liked the way they watched me. "And thanks for being here," I said as I turned back to Cora. "It wouldn't have been a celebration without you."

She waved me off like I was crazy. "You can't have a birthday party without your best friend. That's a fucking rule, and I let your alphas know as much."

Slade, the only one of us not in a suit, still decked out in enforcers gear, crossed his arms. "Warrick's life was in real danger when he delivered that message."

It was his turn to be waved off by Cora, who on occasion forgot he was a big, scary dragon. "Emme would have murdered you and she's the only one in the world you're afraid of, Alpha Slade. I felt fairly safe."

I waited for Slade to refute her claim, but he just smirked and shook his head, before heading down the tunnel that I assumed led through to the track.

Cora smiled brightly, and she looked so smug that I had to stifle my laughter. While it was at times terrifying to have Slade as a mate, I wouldn't change him for the world. Cora didn't mind dangerous males either, and I wondered what she'd say when she found out there were two of them. Talon remained a pack secret for now, but eventually the news would come out.

Golden Claw was going to lose their damn minds.

Kellan linked his arm through mine and started to lead me after Slade, but we were stopped when Finley stepped into our path. I looked over the bear shifter, his suit of gold and black making him look massive—his broad shoulders gave the illusion of nearly blocking the tunnel we stood in. Which wasn't as important as the somber expression on his face.

I waited for him to reveal his thoughts, but before he uttered a word, Kellan piped up. "I'll head on in and get everything ready. Fin will bring you through to the track, pretty mate."

Everyone else followed Kellan, and Hunter dropped a hand on Finley's shoulder as he passed. When we were alone, Finley inhaled deeply, and then released it just as slowly. His eyes were wide and a little glassy. I'd never seen him this obviously nervous before.

"Are you okay?" I asked, my heart hammering harder than usual. My palms felt clammy, but I resisted the urge to wipe them on my suit and give my own nerves away.

Finley lowered his gaze to meet mine, and his impossibly thick, dark lashes fluttered, hiding the whiskey depths briefly. "I wanted to wish you a happy birthday," he said, the gruffness of his tone deeper than usual. "But I don't want to make it awkward for you. Not now, or ever again. Especially not when we're celebrating your first birthday and Christmas with the pack. If you'd rather I wasn't here today, I can leave."

"No!" It was an instinctive reaction, but I didn't regret it. "It wouldn't be as special a day if our entire pack wasn't here."

Finley nodded, and I was relieved when the strain on his features eased. "Okay, well, I'm relieved to hear that. Happy birthday and

Merry Christmas, Em." The smile he shot me was soft and knowing. "How are you dealing with the surprise? If you're anything like me, you probably don't know what to do with a day dedicated to you."

He'd hit right on the confused emotions coursing through me. It was uncomfortable to have aspects of this day centered on me, but I appreciated it as well.

"I'm touched," I said, feeling an innate sense of gratitude, "that you all wanted to celebrate the day, even belatedly. It's awkward, but in a weird way. Like… I'm not used to these strong surges of excitement and happiness and nerves. It's like a fucking emotion-rave is in full swing inside, and I don't know if I'll cry, laugh, or throw up."

Finley's expression held understanding as he smiled. "Let them do this for you," he told me. "It's a day for them as much as it is for you. It will make all of them happy to shower you in love, attention, and presents."

I chose to ignore the presents part, focusing instead on the way Finley had phrased that last piece of advice. "*Them?* Do *you* not want to be here, Fin? Because I would understand."

Maybe. I had no idea really.

His expression shuttered, and I was taken by surprise when he pressed his lips to my cheek. It was a light touch, but it burned into my skin, and I barely managed to hold back my gasp.

"I don't deserve to celebrate this with you," he said, "but if my presence doesn't upset you, then I want to be here more than anything. Your first birthday with the pack is… a gift for me too."

The air was tinged in cherry-vanilla, and I had no idea what to say after that revelation. The relief I felt that he wasn't leaving was far too strong for the emotional distance between us, but it wasn't the day to deep dive into how fucked up I was. Nah, that could wait for tomorrow.

"Come on, Ice," he said, and I was finally rewarded with those dimples and a full-blown smile. "Let's not leave our asshole pack waiting any longer. They've been planning this surprise for a long time."

I fell into step beside him, and weirdly, there was a sense of comfort and calm between us. "You're sticking with Ice Queen," I said, not sure how I felt about it now that his tone had changed. "And here I thought you were trying to mend bridges."

Finley's smile never wavered, and dammit… I was addicted to

dimples. Just sign me up for life. "At first I told myself it was in reference to your icy heart, and how you could keep your true mates at a distance…"

Harsh but fair. "And now?"

"Honestly, I should have known all along that I'd chosen a name to represent one of my favorite places in the world. The ice is my peace, and all along, you were too. No matter how hard I denied it." *Peace.* Fuck, if I could have chosen to be his anything, that would have been top of the list. "Do you know how to skate?"

I shook my head, my reply rough: "Nah, my mom wasn't big on letting me out of the house. Or teaching me anything. Or allowing fun. I've never stepped foot on ice, except if I was in a city that snowed, and then it was just a pain in the ass as I tried not to slip on my way to work."

Finley nodded as if he wasn't surprised. "Yeah, I had a similar mother, but she let us out in our area. Mostly when she was fucked up on booze and additives. There was a lake out the back of our land, and during winter I lived out there. Fell in more times than I can count, after getting on there too early in the season." In my head I pictured a little wet bear, and it was too fucking adorable.

"My mother hated me being around," I told him. "Hence why she locked me in my room most of the time. If I hadn't had that sneaky escape into the garage below, I'd have lost my mind long ago." Mom had always been paranoid about me leaving the house, and I still had no idea why, or *who* she'd been hiding us from. The monsters were already inside.

"Our moms would have been friends, if they weren't complete narcissistic assholes," Finley said dryly. "But at least they're both dead. Silver lining."

A morbid but sadly true statement.

We were through the tunnel now, and I saw the others standing by an impressive lineup of cars, parked near the entrance to the track.

"Whoa," I choked out as I took in the full scene, "this is incredible. It looks like a professional speedway." I popped up on my toes for a better look. "You even have a drag strip and figure eight track. You've got it all."

Finley chuckled at my enthusiasm, and could we just say *Christmas miracle* at hearing Slade and Finley laughing today.

"Hunter designed and built this a few years ago," he said. "He got sick of us racing in the streets, and having to deal with pissed off enforcers and council alphas. It's been a weekend haunt ever since. Weather dependent."

The weather was mild again today, with perfect blue skies and chilly winds but no snow. "Conditions look good for racing," I commented, having no idea if that was true. I'd never done this in any sort of professional capacity. "I mean, once we get some heat into the tires."

The four Porsche GT3 R's in the lineup were from the garage, and I already knew they were running semi-slicks. Unless we wanted to die, we'd need to warm them up first.

Finley's wide-eyed and proud expression had me wanting to prance around with my damn fur puffed up. Apparently, all of his grouchy ways were forgotten with a few kind words and some dimples. I really needed to work out my fucking priorities here.

"Absolutely," he said, unaware I was mentally beating myself up. "This is one of my favorite weathers to race in. The NA engines love the cool air."

"Naturally aspirated love it as much as the turbos?"

That got me another slow, smirking grin, and my stomach intensely flip-flopped. "Turbos like it the most, but all engines perform better in cooler air."

"Very true," I said with a nod, sparks lighting up my veins. The car talk was turning me on, and more than that, it was Finley. The bear kept adding dirt to the chasm, and it didn't feel quite as vast as before.

Finley held my gaze for a few long seconds, but before he could say anything more, Kellan noticed our presence and started bouncing and waving as he shouted for us to *get our asses over there.*

As we headed for them, I found myself saying, "We need to do this more often. Just hanging out and chatting."

When he brushed his hand over the top of mine, a jolt ran through my body, and I choked back a gasp.

"I'd love that," he said softly, and it was clear he meant it. "I know I have a lot to atone and apologize for, Em, and to kick it off I was wondering if you might consider sitting in on a therapy session next week. I'll be delving into my past, and I'd like you there to learn a little more about me."

I blinked at him. "You've been in therapy?"

That was the first time I'd heard of it, and the knowledge brought forth another surge of hope. Therapy was the last thing I'd expected from the proud, stubborn shifter, but it was a tangible sign he was not just talking the talk. He was walking the walk. A sign that I could start to trust in the future he promised.

He nodded, and didn't try to downplay it at all. "Yeah, and it's been really helping. I think. Dealing with my past is not a linear journey, but I feel mentally stronger. I feel like I'm starting to accept and move through my traumas and learn healthy coping mechanisms. Rather than going straight for anger and violence. Rather than pushing those I care about away because I'm scared of being hurt. Honestly, I wish I'd started therapy years ago."

With my heart in my throat, I barely stopped myself from grasping his hand. Fuck, I was so proud of him. "If you want me to sit in on a session, just let me know the time and place. I'll be there. No doubt I need therapy too, and can I just say how proud I am of you."

I almost died as I caught sight of the splash of pink tinged high on his cheeks. He opened his mouth, but no words came out. I'd rendered him speechless, and it hurt to think that it might be because he'd never had anyone say those words to him before.

When we joined our pack, it cut off further deep and meaningful conversations, and I sucked in a shuddery breath as Kellan threw his arms around us both. "Race time!" he crowed, and I forced myself to focus on that.

Today we could pretend everything was perfect and that this was a normal birthday slash Christmas celebration.

Reality could wait for tomorrow.

CHAPTER 29

We lined up at the start of the track with Hunter, Kellan, Finley and me behind the wheel of the Porsches, our cars white and shiny against the darker tarmac. Slade was in his green SVJ and Warrick in a bright red McLaren Senna—I'd never seen one of those in real life before and I was giddy at getting to observe it on track. Cora rode shotgun with him, and she smiled and waved when she caught my eye from two cars away.

All of us were pumped. I could only liken the adrenaline coursing through me to how it felt when my alphas touched me. Like my soul was about to leave my damn body.

Kellan's laughter rang out as he revved his engine, and I barely resisted laughing with him. We'd already done two warmup laps to get heat into the tires, and now we all sat and watched the light. It was red, and I swear the anticipation of it turning green was next freaking level.

Hunter had shown me how to activate launch control, and while I'd never raced a car like this before, I'd been impressed at the way it handled in the warmup laps.

I turned to find Hunter, on my right, smirking and looking sexy as fuck in a car that rightfully shouldn't fit his huge frame. On my left was Kellan, and I chuckled as he bounced in his chair and shouted out that *Finley was going down*. The bear was on his other side, and I couldn't see his reaction, but I'd bet he was rolling his eyes.

When Kellan focused on me, he briefly calmed and smiled in his golden boy way. "Love you, Shortcake!"

I blew him a kiss, and then focused back on the track, feeling the change in the air as we got ready to race. My left foot was hard on the brake, and right pressed all the way down on the gas. The revs sat between six and seven thousand RPM, and I was desperate to feel the sensation of its launch. My breath caught as the light flashed on the red, and then dropped to the yellow, and then when it hit green I jerked my foot off the brake.

I'd expected to have to really handle the wheel to keep my launch straight, but it was so smooth that all I felt were the g-forces as we took off. Hunter, Kellan, Finley and I were side by side on the initial straight, with Slade's car pulling ahead so quickly I was trying to figure out if he had cheated. It was only when I remembered he had a V12, and we were in aspirated 4.0L six cylinders that it made sense why he had us on the straight. The McLaren was the same, pulling away in the straight with its V8 twin turbo. Though Warrick didn't have a chance of catching Slade, who was eating up the track.

The first corner didn't shift the order too much, though Kellan pulled ahead of the Porsches as he swung around it like a shifter with a death wish. Cora had told me he was a menace on the track, a daredevil with no regard for life, and I loved that about him. Even if it was slightly terrifying too.

Alphas were hard to kill, but a bad enough crash could definitely end their lives.

The first lap was over in a flash, and on the second I started to push harder, hitting corners with more speed, trusting in the impeccable handling of these purpose-built racecars. By the third lap, the more powerful cars had hit their top limits, while the Porsches were just getting started. Kellan and Hunter closed the gap, but Finley stayed with me, at the back of the pack.

I was determined that one day I'd be able to win one of these races, but for now I was satisfied by the experience of racing at all. By the time we hit the final lap in our six-lap race, Kellan was out in front, with Slade close to his ass, and Hunter bringing in third. Warrick finished out the top four, leaving me and Finley to battle it out for last.

At first, I thought he was going to ease off and let me win, which would have pissed me off, but when we closed in on the final turn, he met my gaze and I saw the glint of competitiveness in his. He might have stuck with me until now, but he wanted us to give our all for this final section.

Bring it on.

Pressing my foot harder, I clutched the wheel, hoping I didn't lose control and embarrass myself. Thankfully it was hard to do with a car this responsive, and as I lurched around the corner with my heart in my throat, I managed to come out of it alive, unscathed, and *out in fucking front.*

Almost as if I could hear thousands of cheers from the nonexistent crowd, I pushed my car all the way to the checkered flag, screaming in excitement as I lifted my foot from the gas pedal to allow it to naturally slow and drop down gears. When I closed in on the other cars, doors opening as everyone jumped out, I pressed the brakes to bring my car to a final stop.

When I jumped out of the car on shaky legs, I threw myself at the closest alpha, who, fittingly, was Finley. "That was incredible," I cried as his strong hands wrapped in under my arms and he lifted me up and spun me around like we were starring in a movie about princes and princesses and happily-ever-afters.

"You fucking killed it on that last turn, Ice," he bellowed, his bear rising to the surface. "You can really drive."

I was fully amped up on adrenaline as I focused on the bright hue of amber in his eyes and the dimples framing his exuberant smile. It was in that moment, for the first real time, I saw a chance for me and Finley. He must have caught a glimpse of the hope in my gaze, and his expression sobered as he lowered me to my feet but didn't let go.

It was only the shouts of our pack and friends that brought us out of the bubble. Finley bopped me gently on the nose. "Nice work, birthday girl. Now you better go and address your adoring fans."

I was reluctant to leave when we were mending chasms and filling canyons, but I couldn't forget that this was still early days. It would be foolish to let the ache in my heart, and the magic of a scent match, push *either of us* before we were ready.

"Thanks, Grouchy Bear," I whispered, and for once the name didn't trigger him into a snarky rage. Just like with *Ice Queen*, the tone made all the difference, and mine was filled with slivers of hope.

I turned away in time to get swept up by Kellan. "You did so good, baby," he crooned, planting kisses across my cheeks and over my nose. The last kiss landed on my lips, and *damn* was I starting to get the hype about birthdays.

"You won," I sang back, trying to catch my breath. "You're a fucking daredevil with a death wish, Golden. I think you took ten years off my life with some of those turns."

His face was lit up with adrenaline and lust, all of which he focused on me, resulting in one breathless omega. "I was never not in control, pretty mate. Never. I wouldn't risk what we have, not even for the thrill of a win."

He tilted his head over his shoulder and shouted. "Though win I fucking did. Come on over, losers. You can all get the next birthday hug."

Hunter was there in a heartbeat, his rumbles reminding us all that he was more deadly to Kellan's health than a racecar. "You'll be wearing your car around your fucking head in a minute," he warned as he reached for me.

Kellan reluctantly released me, and I wrapped my arms around Hunter's chest. "Nice driving, Hurricane," I murmured against his suit. "You're almost as scary behind the wheel as Kel."

He leaned down and buried his face in my neck, breathing me in. "That was nothing, little omega."

"You should see him on a dirt bike," Slade offered from somewhere to my right, which had my head jerking back to see Hunter's face.

"You ride dirt bikes?"

He shrugged, his expression neutral. "I used to compete when I was younger, but then I traded moto gear for suits. Now I stick with road bikes."

Slade on his Ducati was a core memory for me. Now I wanted to add Hunter to the imagery. "I'd like to see that," I said, thinking dirty thoughts.

Hunter's grin was lascivious. "Want to backpack for me one day, little omega?"

My insides tightened and there was a steady throb between my thighs. "Yes. Yes, I would very much enjoy that, Alpha."

Odds were between the bike and male between my legs, I wouldn't make it through an entire ride unscathed. Goddess willing.

Once Hunter released me, Cora wiggled her way through the alphas and threw her arms around me, careful not to touch Slade, who stood close to my left side. "I've never been so fucking turned on in my life watching you take on the boys like that," she breathed against my ear, and I heard Warrick groan in the background as he muttered.

"Fucking great. Not only did I lose to these bastards again, but now I have an erection while standing in the middle of the Reeves pack."

Cora threw her head back and laughed. "Don't worry, mate. I'll take care of that soon."

She barely got the sentence finished before she was snatched out of my arms and thrown over Warrick's shoulder. "Carry on without us," he said, as he stormed off. "I need to have a little chat with my mate."

Over his shoulder, Cora waggled her eyebrows at me, and I covered my mouth to hide my laughter. I couldn't believe I'd ever thought she was prim and proper. Sure, on the outside she held an air of refinement, but beneath that calm facade she was all fire.

"Have fun, kids," Kellan called, and then he grasped my hand, tugging on it gently. "Let's do presents while they're gone."

I planted my feet and shook my head. "This is more than enough present for me. I've never had a better day, and... anything more would be overkil—"

Finley caught my eye, and while his expression remained neutral, I couldn't help but recall what he'd said earlier. While parts of today would be too much for me, it made my pack happy.

And making them happy was one of my goals in life.

No one pushed me, and I found myself saying, "Thank you for one of the best days of my life. Let's do presents."

Hunter's hand wrapped around the back of my neck in a possessive squeeze. "Good girl," he rasped in a low voice near my ear. "You'll be rewarded for that later."

Okay, then. Presents were now the *second-best* way to end this day.

CHAPTER 30

EMME

Kellan led me into what he dubbed the "present room," which was actually a private parking lot on the other side of the main entrance. This one had metal gates to lock it off from the rest of the track, and at first I couldn't figure out why we were here, until we reached a large shipping container.

Crap. What had my insanely generous alphas gotten me for my birthday?

"Mine first," Kellan chanted as he dropped my hand to dash for the doors of the container.

He lifted the latch with his free hand and swung both sides open.

"Are you guys kidnapping me and shipping me off to another country?" I joked, trying to peer in through the opening. It was too dark to see much more than the first few feet in, and there were no visible presents there.

"If we could find a country where you'd be safe," Hunter grumbled, while Slade nodded and said, "Excellent idea."

Okay, then. No more giving them ideas.

Kellan disappeared into the depths of that massive unit, and I tried not to fidget as I waited for him to return. Slade stepped in closer until his heat caressed my spine, and I sucked down a groan when he pressed his hand to my lower back, as he'd done that day in Silver City. Grounding and comforting me.

Kellan was back in no time, wheeling a familiar but also unfamiliar motorcycle. Joy lit up in my chest as I ran my gaze over the newest

Ducati Panigale to come into my life. It was an almost exact replica of the one I'd lost in the blast, but I could tell that this was brand new, with a differently designed color scheme.

"Kellan, you beautiful alpha." I huffed in excitement. "Oh my goddess. You got me another bike? I don't even know what to say."

I was crying, which was partly why I hadn't wanted to do presents—it was just too much for me. These alphas seemed to crave my stronger emotions though, as they all watched my tears like they wanted to lick them from my face.

"Baby," Kellan laughed, and then shook his head as he caressed my face, wiping up the tears, "this is absolutely nothing, but I'm thrilled to see your pretty face this time when I hand over the dream bike." He turned to shoot the other alphas a gloating stare. "Dream fucking bike for our dream mate."

When he released me, I gave my bike all the attention she deserved. I brushed my hand across the silky paint, noting that this time it was mostly black with a few pink accents. Across the tank was a flaming pink wolf head, and the leather seat was wrapped in the same shade. "It's perfect," I rasped. "I love it, and I love you, Kellan Jackson."

His grin was so wide it almost split his damn face as he leaned over and kissed me. "That's not all, pretty mate." He left me to caress the seat as he grabbed a black and pink leather jacket with Shortcake stitched across the back and the same wolf and flames embroidered below, along with a black and pink helmet. Lastly, he had a set of hardcover books in a boxed set.

I stared at the books, and he shot me the cheekiest grin so far. "Now these are really a birthday present for me, because I plan on reading this spicy-as-fuck series to you every night, and then we're going to reenact the scenes."

The very thought had heat rising in my cheeks, which helped stem my emotional tears. "When is your birthday?" I asked him, realizing I wanted to make their days as special as they'd made mine.

"February twenty-first," he said with a smirk. "I'll take one naked omega as my present. In advance of course."

Which would be a present for me too. "I didn't realize I was older than you, Golden Boy," I teased.

His eyes lit up, but we were interrupted by Slade striding past us into the container. "My turn," he called.

Kellan leaned down to whisper, "To be continued, pretty mate."

I tried not to fidget as I waited for Slade to emerge, determined to give him my full attention too. In most packs there was a natural hierarchy based on dominance, but I didn't want that between the five of us. We were tied together for a multitude of reasons, and we all needed each other in different ways. Dominance didn't need to be part of that.

When the giant dragon stepped out from the container, he held two medium-sized black boxes.

He handed me the first one, and I ran my finger over the dark and shiny wood, which was interspersed with mother of pearl and gold accents. "There's so much I wanted to give you, Snow," he said, his face strangely vulnerable as he met my gaze. "But knowing how overwhelming this day was going to be for you, I kept it to two practical items." Of course my most logical alpha had gone for practical.

"The box alone feels like a piece of art," I said as I flicked open the gold clasp and slowly lifted the lid. Two pieces of jewelry came into view, displayed on the deep blue velvet lining the inside.

"Whoa, this is beautiful, Slade," I whispered, staring at a massive piece of carved emerald nestled at the base of a thickly woven gold chain. The emerald was in the shape of a dragon, with gold edging to create a pendant. It was large enough to near cover my palm as I lifted it. "But I'm going to need you to explain to me how it's practical."

Slade shrugged like I wasn't holding a very expensive jewel in my hands. "It's from a jeweler in Golden Claw who specializes in creating unique trackers. The smaller one is for you to wear day to day." He cleared his throat. "Not that any of us would care if you wanted to wear the larger pendant daily, but I know you'd be more comfortable with the other one for daily use." The smaller dragon was nestled in the velvet, and looked exactly the same, except it was the size of a quarter.

"Trackers," I said with a nod, switching to the smaller one, and handing it to Slade to put on me. Kellan took the box so I could lift my braid, and Slade's fingers brushed the back of my neck, sending shivers down my spine as he secured the clasp. "That makes sense."

Those fingertips, roughened from weapon's training so intense that not even alphas could heal the calluses, slid up to the edge of my jaw.

Then brushed the corner of my lips. "Do they have cameras hidden in them too?" I asked, breathless at his touch.

His grin was rueful as he released me. "Not yet, but give me time."

It didn't bother me in the slightest to be tracked by my pack, especially not under current circumstances. Popping up on my toes, I waited for Slade to lean down, and my heart hammered as he lowered his head. I moved slowly, giving him time to pull away if his beast reacted.

I felt the burn of the other alpha's gazes as they watched us closely, and while the dragon was tense, he relaxed as soon as my lips brushed his cheek.

I pulled back to find fire simmering deep in his eyes, but thankfully he distracted us both by reaching for the second box. With my pulse racing, I grasped it, noticing it wasn't as ornate as the first. This one was shiny, black, and required a thumbprint to open—just like Kellan's gun case.

I had no idea how Slade got my print, but the case clicked, and I opened the lid to find a pair of gorgeous blades nestled inside. There was more mother-of-pearl inlaid on their handles, along with embedded emeralds shaped like dragons in the hilt. There was a green-dragon theme going on here, and I liked that completely unsubtle touch from Slade.

"These are custom made for your grip," he told me, and I had to wonder if he'd taken an imprint of my hands when he'd stolen my fingerprint. One day he'd have to teach all of us the art of the stalker… he was pretty damn good at it.

"We can start practicing with them once I'm confident you won't cut your arm off. They're Damascus steel, magically infused, and sharper than anything you've ever worked with."

Kellan practically drooled as he leaned over and all but kissed the steel. "I've been trying for years to get *Froyde* to make me a set of these, but the bastard told me he was retired. How did you get him to cave?"

Slade shrugged. "I have my ways."

Kellan only nodded, like that didn't surprise him one bit. "Power of the dragon. Second only to power of the puss—" Hunter slapped him in the back of the head, and he just laughed like he barely felt it.

Slade closed the lid on my blades before anyone got stabbed, and I gently placed that box on top of the jeweled one. "I love both gifts so much. Thank you," I said, staring at Slade with all my feelings no doubt on display. The dragon nodded, but he looked pleased by my thanks.

"Your turn next, Fin," Hunter said, and I found myself staring at the bear as he flushed and hurried into the container.

Slade settled in at my side, his heat washing down my body. "When's your birthday?" I asked him as we waited.

There was a long enough pause that I wasn't sure he'd answer until he said, "The thirty-first of October."

I paused. "That's… Halloween." Which, when I thought about it, kind of made perfect sense. "Fitting for a dragon."

Slade shrugged like he really didn't care, and as it was a human-celebrated holiday, the significance no doubt meant very little to him. Which got me to wondering if any of them celebrated birthdays normally.

Today's effort would suggest they did, but these alphas often went above and beyond for me, without ever expecting anything in return. Which wasn't going to fly with me moving forward.

All of them would get a birthday this coming year, and I would make them all special. Somehow.

Finley's gift moved into sight then, and I straightened as a huge grill appeared at the end of the container, followed by the rest of a car being guided out by the bear.

He grinned as I gaped at the old Ford Bronco, which had once upon a time been a pretty sky blue, though now the paint was faded and patchy in places. "Holy shit," I said, blinking and gawking. "You got me an old car?"

Kellan stifled his laughter, while Finley's smile grew. "Well, I got a car that we can fix up together. If you… wanted to."

Be still my rapidly beating heart. Finley Thornton was a damn romantic.

Stepping closer, I fell in love with the car as soon as I ran my hand over her gorgeous, rounded lights. Finley watched closely, and I desperately tried to find the words to explain how much his gift meant to me. It was no more than the gifts from the others, but it was unique all the same. Especially when it came from the alpha who'd made no secret of how much he wished I wasn't in their lives.

"I love her," I said, blinking hard to ease the burn behind my eyes.

"I love old cars and fixing them up. And I love that you chose a gift which would give us time together. That's…"

Everything.

Finley's eyes were shiny as he swallowed roughly, his voice a low rasp. "I owe you so much more than a car, but I figured this was a great place to start. I can't apologize enough for how I treated you, Emme, and I will work every day to make it up to you."

Kellan coughed out a sob, and we all turned to find him wiping his eyes with his shirt. "Allergies," he croaked. "Fucking pollen is hectic during spring."

"It's winter," Finley noted dryly, though he smiled as he said it. Kellan flipped him off in response, apparently too *allergic* to speak. My sweet golden.

When Finley opened the door, I hurried to look inside, delighted by all the original parts and decent condition of the leather. "It doesn't start," he warned, his huge body crowding behind mine in the doorway. "She's going to be a challenge but I'm ready for it if you are"

"So ready," I burst out as I leaned in, noticing the joins up high. "Oh, and the roof comes off?"

Finley got even closer, and I was combusting in the small space. "Yep, she'll be the perfect summer car once we've restored her to her former beauty."

When I turned, he was so close we were almost chest to chest. "When's your birthday?" I asked softly, not wanting him to move away just yet.

His expression was the picture of serenity as he met my gaze, and I was struggling to remember what his scowling face even looked like. *How easily one forgets when one wants to.*

"The fifth of August."

I chuckled. "A summer baby. That must have annoyed your ice loving heart."

Kellan snorted, and Finley couldn't help but laugh along. "I enjoy the best of both worlds. Summer storms fit me just as well." Oh, how true that was. At least when we'd first met.

Finley's bulk kept me trapped between him and my new baby, until Hunter released a snapping exhale. "My fucking turn. You've all had your chance."

The bear looked like he was going to resist the order, so I reached out and brushed my hand across his chest, catching the way his eyes closed briefly before he stepped away.

When Hunter was my sole focus, I said, "You've already given me everything, Alpha." I pressed my hand to his shoulder and then ran it down until I felt his heart thundering under my touch. Our beasts nuzzling through the bond. "You convinced me to move into the pack house, coaxing my frightened, wary ass along until I was able to understand the gift of our pack. You saved me, Hunter Reeves, and I need you to know that *you've already given me everything.*"

His arms wrapped around me so fast my head spun, and when my feet left the ground, I sighed in relief. No doubt he'd felt my frazzled emotional state all day through our bond, and knew I needed a second of his strength holding me together.

"I haven't even started giving you gifts, little omega," he warned against my throat. "Prepare yourself."

Pressing my lips to his shoulder, I chuckled. "There's no way to prepare for you, Hunter Reeves. But I'm ready for whatever you throw at me."

He dropped me to my feet, and cupped my face for one last kiss, then headed into the container, emerging a beat later with a huge sack over his shoulder. "Okay, that once again is giving me kidnapping vibes, and I'm wondering if I should be concerned. That bag could easily fit a reasonably tall female."

"No kidnapping yet," Hunter replied with a smirk. "That comes later."

Heat flared in my body as he gestured for me to step back so he could place the sack between us. He reached in and pulled out a gift wrapped in shiny, black and gold paper. As he handed it to me, I noticed the tag with a large 1 on it, and I ran my thumb over the silky material.

"I wanted to give you the experience of opening gifts," Hunter said, watching me close enough to pick up even the slightest change in my expression. "I assumed you'd never gotten lots of presents before."

I shook my head as I unwrapped the paper, finding a shiny black phone case inside, custom made with my name printed on the back in pink.

"You didn't tell me your favorite color during our discussion after hockey," Hunter said, leaning in closer, "but I've noticed you favor pink and black."

Aw, he was such a good stalker. "I've never really claimed a favorite color," I said with a nod, "but I am drawn to pink and black. And this is so cute, even if it is a little late for my battered phone."

I loved that he'd gone for a practical and not over-the-top gift, which wasn't Hunter's usual style but fit me so well. "He'll have thought of the phone situation," Kellan said dryly from where he stood beside Finley, his hand on the bear's shoulder. I loved how close they were, a bond that had only strengthened since Kellan almost died.

"Thought of my phone situation?" I asked, turning back to Hunter to find him with another gift in his hand. Ah, okay. This was more Hunter Reeves.

Over the next twenty minutes, I opened dozens of gifts which included clothes, shoes, bags, and as predicted, a brand-new phone to match the case.

"How many gifts did you get me?" I said as he handed me number twenty-three.

"Twenty-six of course," Hunter said, bunching his brows like that was a ridiculous question. "You turned twenty-six, little mate."

I wondered if these alphas knew that today they'd repaired wounds they hadn't inflicted, and eased pain they didn't cause. They were the gifts, while the rest was just glitter on top.

Really lovely, and thoughtful glitter.

Hunter's next present was a pair of biker boots that had to be worth a fortune. I was instantly obsessed with the buckles and soft brown leather. Twenty-five was riding gloves, and twenty-six a matching leather jacket that fell to mid-thigh, and made all my biker girl dreams come true.

"I loved everything," I said, staring wide-eyed at the massive pile of gifts surrounding me. "I need to start working out gifts for you if I need thirty plus. When's your birthday, Alpha?"

His eyes darkened at my usage of the honorific I only pulled out on special occasions. "The tenth of October," he said, his voice a delicious rumble. "And you don't need to get us presents. We have everything we need with our pack."

"Fuck yes," Kellan called, "though if anyone wants to get me a set of gorgeous, one-of-a-kind *Froyde* blades, I won't be mad about it."

I locked that away to ask Slade about, since Kellan's birthday wasn't too far away.

It was going to be next to impossible to buy billionaires anything they didn't already have, but I had to at least try.

As I gathered up Hunter's gifts, I marveled over the fact that when I'd dragged myself out of bed this morning for training, I'd had no idea it was about to be one of the best days of my life.

The only way it could get any better, was if we got word that Fletcher and his witch had accidentally exploded in a workplace accident, and our world was no longer under threat.

CHAPTER 31

EMME

Finley volunteered to transport all my gifts to the house, leaving the rest of us to head back out to race.

Warrick even made it in time for the third race, with a slightly disheveled Cora along for the ride. They had a present for me too, which was a set of high-quality baking equipment, and as I hugged them both I found out their birthdays were in March and June. Which I added to the mental list I was making.

We raced all afternoon and I never won a race—or even came close—but I couldn't have cared less. It was a fucking perfect day, whatever way I looked at it.

When we arrived back home, Finley and Kellan took off for training, while Slade patrolled with his enforcers around the compound. Christmas didn't appear to stop Golden Claw shifters from living their normal lives, with the season bringing little more than a festive feel to the city.

"Just you and me, Emmeline," Hunter drawled after our pack had scattered to their various commitments. "Whatever should we do with our time?"

There was only one thing on my mind as I took in the breadth of his muscles in a tight black shirt and jeans—we'd ditched the race suits a while ago.

"Anyone else in the house?" I asked, attempting to sound casual, but it came out breathy. "Outside of our dragon hostage?"

Slade had been down to feed and water the beast, and I tried to shove away my guilt that Talon hadn't been part of the pack races today. No matter what my bond said, he wasn't one of us yet. And unless his opinion of Fletcher changed drastically, he never would be.

At least he was safe down there, and while it wasn't a five-star accommodation, he had a bed, a small bathroom, and got three-square meals a day. Slade kept him company as well, hoping to get more information from him, which was the best Talon could hope for.

"We have the house to ourselves," Hunter said, and the rumbling purr in his voice had me forgetting all about the dragon. "Florence and Gerry are at the Christmas Day football match."

My sports world solidly revolved around the shifter hockey league, but apparently there were other professional sporting leagues in the cities too. Florence was a diehard sports fan, and I wasn't surprised that a Christmas football match was one of her traditions.

I was keen to start my own Christmas tradition, in this huge, gorgeous *empty* house.

The light dimmed through the kitchen windows as the clouds grew heavier, suggesting our reprieve from snow was almost over. Hunter watched me with a predatory expression, and I stilled as a shiver traced down my spine.

When he stepped closer, I broke the tension by spinning on one foot and taking off, my socks slipping and sliding across the polished floors. Hunter let out a howl behind me, followed by a growl which caught and held my wolf. Through our connection, I felt his need to hunt me as he had the night we sealed our bond.

I wanted it just as badly, which was all that stopped me from turning back and throwing myself into his arms. As desperate as I was for release, there was no need to rush.

This slow, stalking build up was half the fun. It was ironic that once upon a time being stalked and taken by an alpha was my nightmare, while it now fueled my sexual fantasies.

My initial plan had been to race up the stairs, until I realized I'd have nowhere to go once I got up there. Changing tack, I took a left toward the back of the house, dashing past the games and cinema rooms. The tugging in my chest told me Hunter was close, and when I glanced over my shoulder, I found he wasn't even running.

Nope. The bastard stalked after me, and his smirk forced my panties to identify as a sponge and soak up arousal like it was their full-time job. *Keep up the great work.*

With no real plan in mind, I kept moving until I reached the glass sliding doors that led outside. I jiggled the lock, and when it finally opened, Hunter shouted after me, "Don't leave the compound, baby girl."

I had no intention of that, and I threw up a hand to indicate I'd heard him. As I raced into the back yard, icy air hitting me hard, I wasn't sure if it was fear or amusement that drove me faster.

Either way, I couldn't stop running until I was claimed. That was how this chase worked.

Near the back of the yard, I turned to see if I could find him, only to crash right into the damn alpha himself. His arms wrapped around me and my scream rang out as I tried to wiggle free. "Oh no you don't, little mate," Hunter laughingly growled, lifting me off the ground. "I caught my prey and now I get to claim you."

When his heat sank into my cold body, my fight died off, and I was ready for whatever he had planned. "You were letting me escape, weren't you?" I muttered, narrowing my eyes on his smug expression. "You didn't even run, which is rude, by the way."

Hunter threw his head back and laughed, drawing my gaze to the muscles in his throat and chest. "Oh, mate. I tried to drag it out as long as I could, but I'm a desperate, parched alpha. And you're my drink of choice."

A pulse in my core joined the pounding of my heart. I wrapped my legs around him so I could grind against his hard stomach. "Let's ease your pain, then," I said, licking across his lips and initiating the kiss.

He returned my gesture by capturing my mouth, his groans spilling between us as we kissed like there was no tomorrow. "I'm going to fucking devour you," he rumbled.

Yes. Please.

He started to run, and I could do nothing but hold on. We ended up inside, and Hunter all but kicked open a door near the glass sliders, bringing me into what looked like a storage room off the kitchen. "Sorry, little omega," he rasped. "I can't wait—"

I shut him up with another kiss, sliding my tongue against his, completely intoxicated by the taste of mocha. Hunter let me keep control for about two seconds, before he clenched his fists in the back of my hair and tilted my head to give him the access and control he craved.

I barely noticed when my ass hit a table, too caught up in his intoxicating kisses. He gripped my face, holding me in place, until he had every one of my nerve-endings humming.

I gasped for breath as he pulled away, and then frantically reached for his shirt, needing him more naked than he was. When his bronze muscles and tattoos were under my touch, I groaned at how good he not only looked but felt.

Fuck. I really didn't need any extra stimulation, already teetering on the edge of exploding from just staring at him. Hunter's expression turned serious as he looked me over, like he was memorizing every curve of my face. "I love you, Emmeline Anders," he said, giving me one of those rare glimpses of his more vulnerable side.

Pressing my hands against his chest, I straightened to kiss him softly, the touch almost chaste compared to how we'd ravaged each other before. "I love you too, mate."

Hunter's dark eyes darkened further until they were devoid of light. Slowly, oh so fucking slowly, he glided the zipper of my sweatshirt down, and I slid my arms free. He lifted my ass with one hand to remove my pants, leaving me breathless and clad in black underwear.

When I leaned back, resting my elbows on the table behind me, Hunter leaned forward and brushed his right hand down my throat, over my heaving chest, before coming to stop between my thighs.

"All fucking mine," he growled, his dominance in full force. "I share with our pack and no other. If anyone else ever touches you again, they will die."

"What about Talon?" I whimpered, unsure if bringing up the other dragon was a good idea in these circumstances.

Hunter didn't immediately snap, but he did mutter *"We'll see,"* before he shut down any further questions by pressing his lips to his bite, his teeth sinking in as he tore my bra off my body.

I arched into his touch as I cried out. "Please," I moaned, aware that begging was Hunter's kryptonite. "Please, Alpha."

His big chest rumbled as he gave my tits plenty of attention, sucking one nipple and then the other into his mouth. As he moved back and forth between them, his groans against my skin grew guttural, and my limbs trembled in response.

My panties were the next to be torn free, and then I was bare before him as he kissed down my body. His right hand remained around my throat, his claim visible, even as he sank to his knees before me. Right between my thighs.

Oh, fuck. My kryptonite, and I was fucking done.

My head dropped back as I cried out, and Hunter tightened his hold, keeping me in place as his tongue flattened against my pussy, sliding up to circle my clit.

As he lapped at my core, the desperate rumbles from his chest had me clenching my thighs on his face. Or at least trying to. His raised right arm and shoulders kept me from being able to do much more than slide one hand behind his head to hold him in place and arch against him.

Not that he was going anywhere as he did exactly as he'd promised and *devoured me*.

Hunter's tongue slid in and out of me until he flicked over my clit, and I came so hard that if he hadn't been holding my throat, I'd have fallen backwards off the table.

Worth it.

CHAPTER 32

TALON

The scent of my mate's arousal reached me in my prison. Along with the throbbing in my bite, it had my dick harder than I'd ever felt before.

Emme was the most desirable shifter I'd ever met, and she was mine, but my patience ran thin as I waited for her to understand there was no other possible future except the one where we were together.

They had me locked in a strong cell, but I could get out of here if I wanted. It'd cost me in energy, which was why so far I remained in place, but these alphas had no idea what I was capable of. The only one who could match me was my twin, and he'd let the rift between his power and beast widen to the point he was weakened by it.

Alpha wouldn't care that I was here. When he'd discussed plans with me, he surmised that my capture was a possibility, and that I'd use that time to learn their weaknesses.

So far, their weakness was *my* weakness: Emmeline Anders.

The connection I'd felt from the moment I sank my fangs into her was an instant bond and obsession, and now there was nothing else in the world more important than Emme.

I hadn't expected the intensity of it.

It fucked with my concept of pack and mate bonds, but I was coming to accept that I couldn't kill the rest of her pack if it meant I'd hurt Emme at the same time. Therefore they'd have to eventually join in with our plans, or they'd be the ones who'd spend their eternity in a cell.

When Alpha informed me of his intention to bond me to an omega, it was before Emme had joined this pack. We'd been under the impression that after her mom's death, she'd shunned shifter cities and alphas. Though I didn't blame her after feeling the intensity of our scent match… it was impossible to fight.

My beast stirred, his power ancient and filled with dragon fire. There'd always been a rift between us too, but as we'd had no other to connect with, I'd forced our closeness. I kept control, and so did the dragon. We were a team, albeit a fucked up one.

My brother let weakness into his soul, and in doing so, willingly brought a predator into their midst. Lucky for them, this predator needed them all alive, but luck only got you so far in our world.

Pressing against the bars, I struggled to keep my power contained. Dragons were different to other shifters with our essence as close as a beast could get to magic. We controlled energy and matter around us, and while I'd seen Slade use it to clean and purify his air, he hadn't bothered to use it as a weapon. Not even when he was *attempting* to extract information.

Missed opportunity for him there. Though, maybe like me, he enjoyed getting his hands dirty on occasion too. My biggest annoyance with my kin was that he'd gone too easy on me during his interrogation. For Emme, he should have torn me to pieces and stitched those pieces back together with a rusty piece of barbed wire.

I'd show no mercy to anyone who threatened my mate's existence.

Then again, maybe he'd feared that hurting me would hurt her too, and in that, I respected his choices. It was a losing battle anyway. Alpha had prepared me for all range of torture, and no amount of pain could compare to isolation. That was how I usually suffered.

Four white walls and nothing to break the monotony.

Slade had suffered under Alpha's control too, that much was made clear, but his wasn't about isolation. He'd always had his brother, Hunter, and for that I occasionally imagined killing them both.

Sometimes I even imagined killing Alpha, but he was the only family I knew, and everything he'd put me through was to strengthen me for the future. A future that would ensure the integrity of shifters remained pure. I owed him loyalty, and wouldn't let him down. No matter how torn my mind was.

Emme's scent grew stronger as our bond pulsed, and the throbbing in my balls and shaft reminded me that we hadn't claimed her fully yet. Before Emme, I'd had no sexual desires. I'd disciplined my body and shut down any base urges that didn't include killing.

With my mate, though, I'd have as much luck of rotating the Earth in the opposite direction as I would halting the flood of need scorching my veins.

Emmeline was mine to claim, and while I had no plans to ever take her by force again, I was confident she would eventually cave to the draw of our bond.

A door clanked in the distance, and like I'd summoned her with that thought, she appeared at the end of the room. Alone.

She hesitated in the doorway, and I pressed closer to the bars. "Mate," I rasped, reaching for her. "What's wrong?"

There was a reason she'd sought me out while her scent meshed with another alpha's and only a large shirt hid her nakedness. Seeing her in another male's clothing had me and my beast wanting to tear it to shreds and cover her in our scent, but I refrained.

For now.

The goal was to win her loyalty and convince her that Alpha's plan was the only way to ensure shifters survived. Not just survived but flourished as the strongest race in the world. Just as we were designed to be. She cleared her throat, rubbing a hand over her face, and I enjoyed the flush in her cheeks.

"There's nothing wrong," she finally said, though she grimaced, and the icy blue of her eyes was dull. She looked tired, and I was fighting the urge to drag her into my arms. "Nothing new is wrong," she clarified. "Your evil-ass boss is still out there planning to destroy the world. And the omega who betrayed me hides now as well, along with her pack. One of whom happens to be Hunter's best friend."

I knew all about the other omega. I'd been there for their initial negotiations, where she'd bartered to keep herself and her pack safe. Of course, that safety had only been from Alpha himself, and not from the Reeves pack. She should have taken that into consideration, but she hadn't thought further than not ending up in the *Omega Program*.

The problem was, now that they needed to stay safe from Hunter and his pack of lunatics, they were even more beholden to Alpha.

"Alpha will have them," I said, having no need or want to lie to Emme. "You won't find them until he's ready to release them."

Emme sighed and sank to the cold floor, resting her chin on her knees. My hackles rose at the sight of her in such an uncomfortable position, but if I made any move to help her, she'd panic and leave. Which was unacceptable.

"We will find him," she growled, peering up at me, and I thought she was fucking adorable. Even her little snarl was as cute as a kitten.

"You can try, and even if you do, he's prepared for any scenario. He knows your mates pretty well, and is well aware of what he's up against."

"And he has you," she shot back, tilting her head to stare me dead in the eyes. Not many had the dominance to do that, and I admired her spark and fire. More than admire, I craved it. "His guard dragon. Just out there blindly following orders."

With a shrug, I settled on keeping this affable. "Why fight when I agree with his vision for the future? Once his plan is in place, I'll take my rightful spot as a leader. With you by my side of course. I owe him for my existence, and the fact that it led me to you, Sweet Honey."

She blinked, as if she wasn't sure she'd heard me right. "Sweet Honey? Really? You're giving me a pet name like we're an old married couple?"

I had no idea why she made that sound ridiculous. As far as I was concerned, we were beyond married—she was mine—which Emme would learn sooner or later.

"We're bonded mates," I reminded her, my voice lowering. "And your scent is so sweet. You wouldn't know this, but I've been obsessed with honey since I was a hatchling. In the compound, before they taught me control, I'd escape and climb the trees to find the hives. It's fitting that my mate would be as sweet as that nectar."

Her lips trembled briefly, but then she pulled herself together, her next words barely a whisper. "I don't know how I'm going to forgive you for what you stole from me."

Guilt was about as familiar to me as sexual desire, but apparently I was getting a crash course in both. "For forcing the bond?"

I didn't play stupid. She'd already expressed to me how I'd hurt her, and why my actions were wrong. At the time I didn't understand, but I was a fast learner.

The fact that she was *mine* wasn't enough… I should not have forced such a sacred bond. A bond that would have been stronger if she'd chosen me as well.

Emme let out another sigh. "Yes. You took a special moment from both of us. If you'd have just given me a chance to get to know you better, I could have chosen to bond you."

I felt another crack in my chest, and fuck... I'd take physical pain over these emotional strikes any day. "I'm sorry."

I'd never said those two words before, but I truly meant them. "It was my only chance to bond with my scent match, and I fucked it up for both of us. It's just that what Alpha asks of me is usually for my own good."

She examined me for so long, and her stare was so probing, that *I* almost looked away. I'd never broken eye contact first—my dragon wouldn't let me. But we were both different with Emme. "Have you ever thought that maybe it's for *his* own good," she finally said, and it was another statement to settle far too deep in my psyche.

Needing a focus to keep my beast from destroying the house, I cleared my throat. "Grab a hairbrush," I said gruffly.

She blinked at me, and I enjoyed taking her by surprise. "Sorry?"

"A hairbrush," I repeated. "Grab one and I'll brush your hair again."

It was one of my favorite memories of our time together, the feel of her silky strands between my fingers, the honey and chocolate of her scent wafting toward me with each stroke. I'd thought about it far too often, wondering how all of that gorgeous hair would look curled around my fist, but that wasn't my reasoning for tonight. Tonight, we both needed grounding, and I knew this would work.

Emme glanced around the room, as if calculating what might happen if she got within touching distance. "Hunter's in his office on a call, and they have security cameras down here," she warned me, narrowing her eyes. "You wouldn't have much time to keep me captive."

I shook my head and couldn't help but smile. She really was fucking adorable. "I'm not keeping you captive. I'm trying to change the narrative between us. One step at a time, right?"

If her wary expression was any indication, Emme wasn't convinced, and my smile fell under my disappointment as she pushed to her feet and disappeared from the room.

Until she returned.

Not even ten minutes later she stood there with a black hairbrush in her hand.

When she shuffled closer, I remained so still that I wasn't even breathing. I'd break my own neck before I broke her trust this night, which she'd learn as soon as she was within touching distance. When she stood right before the bars, she reached to hand me the brush, and I moved slowly as I took it.

I savored the glide of our fingers, a reminder of how soft and delicate she felt. Her scent was everywhere, and my fangs ached with the desire to sink them into her again. And again. Mark every inch of her perfect skin and claim it as mine.

A desire I managed to contain as she offered me a tentative smile. "If you ever break my trust again," she warned me, her expression neutral, "then we're done. I'll figure out how to destroy our bond or lock you in the basement for the rest of existence. Most people don't get second chances in life, Talon. Don't waste yours."

My free hand drifted up, my fingers tracing across her cheek and over her lips. "You are my only chance in life," I whispered, leaning closer to breathe her in.

Her eyes widened, the blue encasing me near whole, but she didn't back away.

"Turn," I murmured, and she sucked in a ragged gulp, before obeying.

Ah, fuck. I liked that far too much.

She sank to the ground with her back against the bars, and I gently freed her hair from where it was trapped. With the first stroke of the brush, the tension lining her spine eased, and after ten minutes she was half slumped on the floor.

When her breaths evened out, I pulled off my shirt and draped it over her, annoyed at how awkward it was to cover her from within the cell. "One day, Sweet Honey," I breathed, tracing my fingers over her soft hair, "You will sleep in my arms. Until then, I'll keep watch over you."

There was no doubt in my mind any longer: I'd destroy the world before I let anyone hurt her.

The world and every fucking shifter in it.

CHAPTER 33

EMME

Finley might have needed therapy, but he wasn't the only one. How else could I explain the ease in which I'd fallen asleep beside the shifter who'd forcibly bonded me. My wolf was a relaxed fluffball, sprawled out and all but purring. The rhythmic stroking of the brush through our hair, and how careful he was not to touch me in any other way, soothed my exhausted body.

I hadn't seen Talon in days, and it had taken more of a toll than I'd realized. My trip down into the garage had been to see my new bike—Hunter had checked the security cameras and deemed it safe—but I'd found myself at the containment room door as soon as I stepped inside. Hit with an uncontrolled desperation to get inside.

Once I stood under the dark, watchful eyes of the dragon shifter, it was as if I could breathe again.

He should have been with us today, but this was a pretty nice ending to my perfect Christmas and birthday celebration.

I had no idea how long I slept, surrounded by his smoky maple scent, warm despite the hard floor beneath me. Eventually I roused to the sound of low rumbling tones.

"I'm taking her out of here," Hunter informed the dragon without inflection. "I gave her a moment to ease the strain on your bonds, but she can't sleep on a hard fucking floor."

"No," Talon snapped back, somehow keeping his voice low and modulated despite his annoyance bleeding through. They were both so busy trying not to wake me as they argued that they hadn't noticed

I *was* awake. "She'll leave when she's ready. You don't get to take her away."

When she's ready. That felt like a win from the shifter who struggled with the concept of consent.

Hunter gave that consideration. "If you want her to remain here with you, then you'll answer my questions." I barely suppressed my smile at how he lived up to his entitled alpha mantle. Not that I blamed him for using whatever advantage he had to keep our pack safe.

I expected Talon to snarl as he'd done when Slade questioned him, but he surprised me. "If I have the answers, I'll give them to you. Providing it doesn't place Emme in any danger."

The dragons didn't bother to lie. That was why Talon's apology before had gone a long way toward opening a connection between us. It didn't erase the past, but his more considerate attitude of late, was helping to heal wounds. Even if the scars would always remain.

"How did Fletcher manage to keep you a secret from us? Did mother… Donatella… know?"

Hunter didn't sound hurt over his family's betrayal, but he was good at keeping his feelings locked down. Even through the bond I got nothing more than a mild sense of annoyance.

Talon answered with ease. "We were kept in a large compound far from the cities. It has above and below ground facilities. I never left, unless it was to kill for him. There was no reason for you to know, and I never saw your mother there."

This was the second time he'd mentioned this "compound," and now we knew it was two levels. This was definitely where we'd find our enemies, and I wondered if Talon knew the precise location.

"Where's the compound?"

This question had Talon sighing. "I can't tell you that. If you went there, you'd be killed, and that would hurt Emme."

Hunter's growl was low, and he cut it off fast. "Did you know about us?"

"Yes."

I was desperate to look at Hunter and gauge his reaction, but I remained as I was, that rhythmic brushing of my hair keeping me calm.

"What happened with you and Slade at birth?"

The brush slowed in my hair. "That part I can't remember," Talon said, his voice unsure. "But from what I've pieced together over the years, we were born in the same egg. True twin souls. Alpha didn't know that would be the case, and he decided to experiment on us both. You know how he is with testing the limits of shifters and our world. He's drawn to figuring out the mystery behind everything. We were the last two dragon shifters, and we were his to control."

The sound of Hunter's wolf almost had me lurching up, but the brush started moving again, and my beast calmed.

"He's not a god," Hunter said gruffly, "no matter what he told you. He's an alpha who believes himself to be above all others, but I promise you, he bleeds red the same as everyone else. And I will not rest until that blood covers the floor under my feet."

I expected Talon to react negatively to a threat against the *alpha* he worshipped, but he just continued his story. "He tore Slade and I apart," he said. "This scar on my face occurred when we were in our dragon forms. My brother clung to me, but we weren't strong enough at the time to stay together. Slade's claws slashed through my cheek, leaving this scar."

Now I just felt sick, and wished I could kill Fletcher over and over again, until even his soul was destroyed.

"Why would you blindly follow that evil fuck?" Hunter asked, his voice softer as a weariness spilled through. It had me wanting to crawl over and wrap myself around him.

Hunter carried too much of our pack's worries on his broad shoulders, and while he made it look effortless, I saw the weight.

"He tore you from your brother. Your fucking twin soul. How was your life with Fletcher? Was it filled with love and respect? Did he show you care, Talon?" He scoffed. "How ironic that you only have a name because our omega's soft heart couldn't stand for you to be nothing more than a tool used by Fletcher. *She* gave you an identity. *She* gave you a pack. Not Fletcher."

The brush stilled once more, and the natural heat of a dragon shot up a few notches until I was toasty warm, bordering on sweltering.

"Alpha looks out for the entire shifter community. He has no time to coddle a fucking dragon shifter. I had all the training, food, and shelter I needed."

Hunter's laugh was a rasp of broken memories. "He treats the whole world the same way he treated you. As a possession or commodity to own, trade, or destroy. If he became a supreme alpha, taking us back to the past to live under his control, everyone would suffer the same way we all have as his offspring. Even Emme. He stole her from her pack and then forced her to bond to a stranger. Did Fletcher know you were a scent match at the time?"

Talon's chest was rumbling, so low I wasn't sure Hunter could hear, but I felt the fury of his beast through our bond. "He didn't know until after," he finally admitted. "They have the means to simulate a scent match, so he wasn't concerned about it."

Possibly Fletcher had guessed based on Slade being my match, but apparently he wouldn't have cared either way.

Hunter must have had the same thought. "He knew. He knew and he didn't fucking care. A scent match is a sacred, goddess-given gift, and he ensured you'd violate it through forced bonding. No doubt he wanted to see if it would impact your connection with Emme's wolf. Does your bond feel whole and complete?"

There was a disconnect between us, and I'd figured it was due to the way we'd bonded, and the fact that we hadn't consummated it.

"The bond isn't as strong as I expected," Talon admitted. "But we haven't sealed it completely yet."

Hunter's voice was louder as he moved closer. "And you won't be fucking sealing it without her express permission. If you ever force Emme into anything again, no matter how much you justify in your head that it's for her own good, I will bury you alive. Do you understand?"

To my surprise, Talon chuckled at the threat. "Fair enough. I might be new to this whole *pack* situation, but I'm a fast learner. Emme is our heart, and we don't hurt our heart. It makes sense."

"She's more than our heart," Hunter murmured, and his voice was so close that he had to be by my side. "She's our reason for existence. All of us were a fucking mess before she came into our lives. I thought an omega would bring stability to our pack, and don't get me wrong, she absolutely has. I just didn't expect the happiness too. Her light infiltrates our darkness, and while our pack always lived for each other, we now live for Emme."

We now live for Emme. I'd never heard five more perfect or devastating words.

His hands brushed over me, and I stirred, wanting him to gather me close. Which was exactly what he did. He slid his hands under my body and pulled me into his arms, nuzzling his face into my hair as he breathed deeply. "Love you," I mumbled, those words easy to say these days.

"I love you too, little omega," Hunter returned, his lips pressing to my cheek as he held me close. When I opened my eyes, I found Talon watching us closely, a yearning pulling at the corners of his expression.

"You can have a real family too," I said, shoving down the ache in my heart. "I've been where you are in the world, always alone and fighting for survival. I finally learned that it doesn't have to be this way. You can have more."

He pressed in closer, his yearning morphing into desperation. "Why can't we all rule at the top? We're the strongest alpha pack. We deserve to rule."

"Fletcher will never share power with you," Hunter said, his tone resigned. "You're a weapon, and he will dispose of you the moment your usefulness runs out."

Talon's eyes shimmered, and I couldn't tell if it was annoyance or anger. "He's the only family I've ever known. He's a hard alpha, agreed, but I'm not disposable. He's never thrown me away."

I looked up in time to see Hunter shake his head, and through our bond I sensed a new shred of sympathy for the dragon shifter. "I think I'm starting to understand the experiment with you and Slade," he said. "Slade, he tried to break through pain, with every touch designed to hurt him and create an unstable beast. He never could break our dragon completely though. No matter what he did, he couldn't get him to kill or fight for him.

"You, on the other hand… His treatment of you might have been an even worse form of control. He gave you nothing and no one, isolating you from the world so all you had was him. He forced your loyalty and used you as an experiment of how to turn shifters into monsters." Hunter's huff of laughter was laced in sadness. "I'm not sure which of you I feel sorrier for."

Talon's expression remained even, but the heat in the room surged. The pulsing of his dragon through our connection was stronger, and I sensed his struggle for control.

"Think about what we discussed here today," Hunter said, as he went to walk away, only pausing when Talon called, "Wait!"

I was once again turned to meet a darkly penetrating stare. "Will you come back to me, Emme?"

If tonight had proven anything, it was that I couldn't stay away from him. Not long term. "Are you willing to answer more questions?"

The desperate longing that tore through his expression almost broke me. "Yes. For you. Yes."

My heart clenched and I nodded. "Then I'll be back."

Talon clutched the bars, and I got the sense, even as Hunter walked away and left him there, that he would remain in that position for the rest of the night.

For the first time since we'd returned to Golden Claw, I was broken over the thought of leaving him locked down there in isolation. Slade might have a touch aversion, which I understood better now that I'd learned of his fucked up past, but Talon bore scars and triggers too. Including isolation. If we wanted to show that we were better than Fletcher, we couldn't hurt him in the same way. But when it was so risky to let him go free, I had no idea what the solution was.

CHAPTER 34

I hadn't been to a council meeting since that first day I was dragged to Golden Claw.

There was a sense of familiarity as I found myself surrounded by the strongest alphas in the city, only this time there were no onlookers—if you discounted the row of chairs that had been left for the witches on one side of the table, and the four chairs on the other for Slade, Kellan, Finley and me. Only entitled alphas got a seat at the main table, and Hunter was our representative.

With Sorenson missing in action, the only other alphas I knew were Warrick and Sissily, the second who had taken up scowling in my direction, as if my mere presence was ruining her life.

When the witches filed in, I wasn't surprised to see Jewels, along with four other unfamiliar females.

"Let's get this started," an alpha called as he stood at the head of the table.

He wore all white, which contrasted to his dark skin. While he wasn't as obviously powerful as Hunter or Warrick, there was a restless energy in his brown eyes that told me his wolf held a streak of wild. Those were the ones to watch out for.

"Thank you, Alpha Stenson," Hunter said, and I found my gaze lingering on my powerful mate in his dark gray suit. "We appreciate the full attention of the council."

The first time I'd met Hunter had been in this very room, when he'd all but leapt the table and crowded me into the wall. My life had flashed before my eyes that day, and while I remembered the dread, my feelings as I stared today couldn't be further from that.

My pack had only been in my life for a few short months, which was hard to believe considering how much had changed in that time. They'd shown me the truth: my mom hadn't been killed because her pack were alphas. She'd been killed because her pack were evil fucks controlled by an even eviler fuck. Her death was part of one big experiment, and the truth of that set me free. Cliché as it was.

There was still so much I didn't know though. Had Mom been aware of what she was getting herself into from the start? Why did she move us constantly in my earliest years? Who the heck was my father and how was he involved in all of this?

My train of thought was cut off as Hunter stood. "Now that formalities are out of the way, let's get to business. We're here, once again, to discuss the threat against my pack. An ongoing threat that the council has seen fit to ignore or dismiss for weeks, which resulted in our mate being stolen from us for the second time. We've been forced to take matters into our own hands, and if there is no action again, the next time we do, blood will spill."

Kellan snorted on my left side as he sprawled back, his hands laced over his flat stomach, and his big feet out in front of him swishing left and right. Like he was having the time of his life watching Hunter ream the council a new asshole.

"We're well aware you've taken matters into your own hands, Alpha Hunter," Alpha Stenson drawled. "And I don't know what you mean about blood *will* spill. We've had dozens of bodies dropped in our city since the omega arrived. You even took out council members who stood in your way. I don't honestly know why you're not the one on trial here today."

That had Slade sitting a little straighter, and if I was on the receiving end of his dark stare right now, I'd have run screaming from the room. Hunter handled it just fine on his own, as he leveled that alpha with his own stare, which lowered eyes around the room.

No one beat Hunter in a dominance battle. At least no one at that table, and Slade would always back him. "Her name is Omega Emmeline," he growled, his voice warning them all that he was at the end of his patience. Already. "Use her fucking title as her status in Reeves Pack warrants. And yes, I will drop the bodies of anyone who attacks my pack or stands in the way of their safety. No questions asked. If you're sitting here on this council, you should feel the same way about your pack. Otherwise, why are you wasting air pretending to be an entitled alpha?"

"You tell them, Hunt," Finley murmured from the other side of Kellan, and I leaned forward to see him. He'd slipped in late after practice, having had extra press commitments, and he'd only just made it in time. Despite the arctic temperatures outside, he was dressed in an old Celtics shirt, a pair of athletic shorts, and sneakers with white socks that barely contained his thick calves.

There was no mistaking him for anything other than an athlete, which was a worry when Kellan mentioned last night that Finley had been off in their last game. I took in the dark circles under his eyes, and hoped he wasn't sleeping even worse than usual.

As if he felt my gaze, his focus shifted toward me, and I was rewarded with a smile and faint dimples. I almost reached over Kellan to take his hand, but settled for returning the smile, until our attentions reverted to the meeting.

Alphas were yelling, annoyed by Hunter's reprimand, until Warrick brought their meeting back to order. "We cannot stand by idly any longer and allow one of our own to be targeted. The Reeves pack have been blown up and had their omega kidnapped twice in as many months. A traitor from our own damn council was involved in the last one, and I'm starting to believe we might have more amongst us. I don't like the way you're all turning a blind eye because this isn't directly your pack's issue."

Sissily sat straighter, her plump lips red and glossy as she smirked. "Usually, we go to the Reeves pack to destroy our enemies. It's just weird to have them need our help."

Hunter's rumble had gazes dropping once more. "We don't need your help, but you've all placed sanctions on our actions. You've reprimanded us for hunting our enemies on the council and killing off those who helped Fletcher and the Rogers pack. We've been warned that we'll be making enemies of the Alpha Council if we continue on our own, which gives me no choice but to involve you all." I scowled, having had no idea the council had issued such warnings. "Not that any of you have a fucking hope of taking us down, but for now we're choosing to keep the peace, which forces us to push this through diplomatically."

A lion shifter from the end of the table, with bushy golden hair and a full gold beard, stood. "Our pack is angry about everything you and your pack have been through Alpha Hunter," he started, voice respectful. "We're here to help, in whatever way we can. Hence why we facilitated a meeting with the witches."

Hunter looked unimpressed by the ass kissing. "You're here because you've heard the rumors that there's more going on than a localized danger to my pack. We're just part of a greater issue… one that's a threat to all shifter cities."

Sissily stood as well, looking around, while fluffing up her hair. "Come on, guys. It feels like a bit of a stretch that Alpha Fletcher, one of the greatest innovators and explorers of our time, is trying to usurp the current pack structure. Firstly, why would he want to, and secondly, where would he get the power to coordinate a task this mammoth across all cities at once. He doesn't have the power to govern tens to hundreds of thousands of shifters throughout our vast country."

Hunter moved out of his seat for the first time, and I wasn't the only one who hungrily watched him as he prowled down the table. Sissily and Jewels—who'd so far been quiet—were locked on to the alpha. At least Sissily had been until he reached her side, grasped the front of her suit, and dragged her closer. "Now, why does that sound like the sort of statement a traitor would make?"

She spluttered, her eyes growing wider as she looked around for help, but there was none forthcoming. "I'm not a traitor," she stammered, grasping on to his hands like she had a chance to break his hold. "Just speaking reason. Your father is legendary."

"A legendary bastard," Hunter shot back. "As anyone who'd ever interacted with him would know. I have no reason to lie, and the evidence of him taking my omega has been provided to the council. If you wish to hide your head in the sand until you're nothing more than a beta under his control, with witches up your ass, then feel free. But the rest of us quite enjoy the structure of our current packs."

Jewels popped to her feet, drawing the attention of the council. She wore all black today, and her light hair stood out nicely against the darker backdrop. "Maybe it's time to hear from the magical contingent in the room," she called, and a tingle of energy crossed my skin, along with the scent of sulfur, which wasn't as repulsive as usual.

Those tingles continued down into my fingertips, and it reminded me of Texas. More specifically, that final fight with Talon, when my shifter essence had surged until I was able to shove the dragon with more strength than usual. Odd considering my wolf had all but been in hiding. That surge felt a lot like this magic today.

Was it possible that there'd been magic in the bunker I'd unintentionally tapped into?

"You have the floor, Jewels," Hunter said as he dropped Sissily roughly into her chair.

He flattened a hand down his impeccable suit and returned to his own seat.

The other witches stood beside Jewels, each very different from the next. The first was a tiny redhead, with curves for days, wearing jeans and white shirt. Beside her stood a statuesque Black woman in a thousand-dollar power suit. Next an Asian female wore a loosely fitted, white linen pants suit. The final brunette had on a simple shift dress, though she bore a scowl that indicated she'd rather be anywhere but here.

Despite their differing appearances, they all had one thing in common: the power oozing off them.

"We're here today," Jewels started, "representing five of the ten most powerful covens in America."

"And the other five?" a councilmember asked from the middle of the table.

Jewels exchanged a brief glance with the Asian witch. "It appears they have aligned themselves with Fletcher. They want a change in shifter hierarchy. One where witches have more control over shifters as well, and can tap into your money and resources. They want to work side by side with one supreme alpha."

That set off chaos once more as the entitled alphas were forced to accept the truth of what Hunter had been telling them all along.

"Silence," Warrick shouted, on his feet, his handsome face creased in frustration. It took a few minutes, but eventually the room fell silent. "This information needs to go out to more than just our council. This is a serious matter for all shifters in our country."

"We're open to meeting whatever alpha councils you can bring to your side," Jewels added. "As you'll all need our help. Fletcher Davenport has powerful witches working beside him, as you already know, and they've clearly been planning this for years. Since the last war."

"Do you know where they are yet?" Hunter asked impatiently.

Jewels shook her head. "So far nothing we've done has been able to track them. They would have known this was coming and planned accordingly. Until they surface or use their magic again, they're all but undetectable."

Half the council spun in their chair and directed their gaze to Slade. "Also untraceable online," he confirmed. "Though I am narrowing the search grid."

"Bet the traitor dragon knows," Kellan murmured to me. "Be a lot easier if he talked."

Talon had already said he wouldn't share this information, but maybe we'd eventually wear him down.

"This will take a combined effort," Jewels warned everyone. "We can't participate without a binding magical agreement, which will require blood from all entitled alphas to ensure no one betrays the other party."

A few of the alphas jumped to their feet, the scent of their beasts wafting through the sulfur in the air. Slade edged himself closer to me, angling his body in front of mine. Kellan did the same on my other side, as Finley got to his feet to move behind us. Protecting our backs.

My pack surrounded me on the chance this chaos spilled our way, but I wasn't worried.

Until the redheaded witch looked right at Jewels, and when their eyes met she laughed and nodded. "You'll never win," she cried, turning back to the room. "Fletcher and our covens will rule you all."

Her hands plunged into her pockets to pull out two vials, and she launched them into the air so quickly that there was no chance for anyone to stop her. Jewels dove away from her, throwing up a field of energy, but it was too late.

The vials crashed into the ceiling and an explosion rocked the building. Bright lights blinded us as screams rang out when the foundation cracked. Before I could suck in a breath, the council chambers fractured completely and the ceiling came tumbling down on top of our heads.

CHAPTER 35

KELLAN

S lade moved a split second before the rest of us and covered Emme. I added my body as a shield over her other side, and Finley was quick enough to burst into his bear form.

His bellow rang out as he used his bulk and strength to keep the worst of the debris from hitting us.

The witch hadn't brought down the whole room, but she'd weakened the structure enough that if we didn't get out of here soon, we might not be so lucky. "I need to shift," Slade rumbled, surging to his feet, bits of drywall, tile, and wood flying off him.

"It's too unstable," I yelled, worried that his huge beast would bring the rest of the building down.

As I scanned the council, Emme started frantically shoving against my chest. "Where's Hunter?" she cried, trying to crawl out from under our alpha pile.

Jerking my shoulders, which ached from scattered rubble hitting me, I sent up a plume of dust. It was impossible to see more than a few feet in front of us, as chaos reigned through the room. Finley roared again, and I twisted to see his bear paws clutching Emme as he plucked her up from the chair. The blue of her wide eyes were stark against the white dust powdering her skin and hair.

"We've done this recently," she choked out to Finley, coughing through her words. "You can't just ferret me out of here while our pack is in danger."

The bear scoffed. Actually scoffed.

If we weren't in a semi-dire situation, I'd have been fucking thrilled to see my brother's snark and fire return. He was trying to change, and most of that was for the better, but it was a hard journey through the darkness and into the light.

"Shortcake, you're our number one priority," I reminded her, scanning the ceiling as another crack rang out. "Hunter will fucking murder us if we don't get you to safety first."

We all ducked at another fracturing crack, and this time a huge beam crashed against the table, setting off more growls and shouts. Which was around the time Slade lost his cool. "*I will fucking murder you both if you don't get her out of here. Leave Hunter to me.*"

Finley started to leave, and it was only Emme's cry that stopped him in his tracks. Slade and I were there in the next heartbeat, examining her for injury, but except for tear tracks through the dust on her cheeks, she appeared to be fine.

"I can't lose either of you," she rasped, her voice filled with her wolf. "Find Hunter but stay safe while doing it, Slade. You're my mates. I need you."

My soul temporarily left my body when Slade leaned in and pressed his lips to her cheek, tasting one of her tears. His nostrils flared as he breathed her in, dust and all. "A fucking building won't steal us from you," he assured her, and then he disappeared into the madness.

Finley took off again, and I was right with them as Emme wiggled against his hold. "I can walk," she said shortly.

Normally, a panicked Finley-bear wouldn't have released her for all the begging in the world, but in light of his recent determination to make amends, he immediately complied.

Emme popped up on her toes to pat his furry cheek. "There's a good boy."

Finley snorted and bumped me, resulting in my own burst of highly inappropriate laughter. "He doesn't understand the perfection of a rasped *good boy*," I told her. "But you can send all of his praise my way."

She didn't get a chance to respond as we reached the exit and I all but dragged her out with the multitude of other fleeing shifters. As we moved farther into the open, getting clear of the building completely, Emme paused as she noticed the enforcer squads pouring into the parking lot.

Or at least that was what I initially assumed she was gawking at, until she whispered, "Uh, guys. Are you seeing that?"

As I spun to stare over the top of the gathered crowds, I blinked at the shadowy beast on the horizon. "What the actual fuck?" I was genuinely bamboozled by the sight of a dragon hovering between two buildings, its black body blending into the shadows.

"Talon," Emme choked out, and I could feel her panic rising in our bond.

Finley wasted no time in snatching her up again, and now we were sprinting back toward the building, where there were two members of our pack with a chance of stopping Talon from kidnapping Emme once more.

Finley and I would fight, of course, but we weren't any match for a dragon, which left Emme in far too much danger.

"How?" she croaked. "How—what? How'd he get out here? Did they let him out?"

Oh, that was a good point. "Do you think this was all a coordinated attack to distract us so they could rescue Talon?" I asked, really hoping that wasn't the case. "Fletcher could have snuck into the city somehow too?"

"I really hope not," she murmured.

Me too, pretty mate. Me fucking too.

When we reached the doorway of the council building, I turned back to find the dragon exactly where we'd left him, hovering in the background but not moving closer.

"Emme!" The roar echoed from inside, as Hunter and Slade emerged from the debris.

Our entitled alpha was held up by our brother, his body littered in cuts and bruises.

Emme temporarily forgot about Talon as she raced for Hunter, pausing when she would have normally thrown herself into his arms. Her hands fluttered in front of her as if she wasn't sure where to touch. "You're okay," she sobbed, tears marking the dust on her cheeks again. "I thought we lost you."

Hunter didn't hesitate to wrap his arms around her, hauling her slight frame against his chest. Pain flashed on his face, but he hid it before she noticed. "Not a fucking chance, baby girl. This was a blatant attack though, and we have the witch held for questioning. The council will find out everything before she's disposed of."

"The other witches agreed to hand her over?" I asked, surprised. Those bitches usually stuck together against shifters.

"They had no choice," Hunter snapped. "Either she dies or they all do for bringing a traitor into our house. Jewels backed us, and since two council members were crushed to death in the attack, we have grounds to take our justice."

The attack. Right. "Uh, speaking of… Talon was just outside in the parking lot." I already knew I'd drawn the short straw in revealing this bad news. Emme had her head buried in Hunter's chest, and Finley was a bear. The lucky bastard.

As expected, I got the full slog of Slade and Hunter rage, and I managed not to piss myself. Like a fucking god. "He was hovering between the buildings, fluttering about in his dragon form, watching us."

"We don't fucking flutter," Slade snapped as he raced from the building, the rest of our pack right behind. When we reached the parking lot, the crowds were infinitely larger, but there was no sign of a giant shadowy beast.

"I'm going to need to hunt him," Slade decided, as his voice slipped dangerously low. "After I ensure you all get home safely first."

"Not a fucking chance," Hunter said. "I'm going with you."

Finley roared his agreement, and Slade sucked in a few deep breaths. His aura was giving *I want to knock you annoying fucks out and deal with this on my own*, but he managed to keep it to a rough grunt.

"I'll stay with Emme," I offered. "While the rest of you hunt down his ass."

"He can't leave without me," Emme reminded them, much more together now all of her pack were safe and accounted for. "Not unless he wants us both to suffer. We haven't been bonded long enough for it to settle, and the strain would be debilitating. He's close by."

Hunter tightened his hold on her. "Can you feel him through the bond?"

Emme closed her eyes and breathed deeply, while pressing her hand to Talon's bite. My annoyance flared at the sight of that mark, a permanent reminder of how the dragon had hurt her. *My perfect mate.*

I hadn't been down to see this Talon yet, too afraid I might try to kill him through the bars. Which was the last thing Emme needed. Dragon or not, I fought dirty and without mercy.

"The bond is pulling me toward our house," Emme said, her nose wrinkling. "We need to check home first."

Our car was parked in the lower-level lot, but Slade's bike was up here near the entrance. "I'll go on ahead," he said, eyes blazing. "I'm the best one to take him on anyway."

Emme shook off Hunter and stepped toward the dragon. "You don't have to fight everything alone. That's why you have a pack."

His expression softened just a touch. It was barely noticeable, but for Slade it was huge. "I'll be fine, Snow. You worry about these three idiots."

If this bastard wasn't a seven-foot-tall killing machine, I'd have totally flipped him off for that comment. "Come on, pretty mate," I said, wrapping her in my arms and thanking the goddess she was safe. "Let's find our pack's *psycho dragon the second*."

Her snort of laughter was soft. "Too soon, Golden. Far too soon."

I shrugged, sure there was never *too soon* when it came to bad humor.

Finley didn't shift back, his bear loping off down the road. The gathered crowds of shifters called out to us, asking questions, but the enforcers kept them away from the building. "Finley will run home," Hunter said shortly. "The rest of us need to figure out how to get into the parking lot."

It wasn't as hard as expected, as we found an intact set of stairs that led down to the undamaged lower lot. We all piled into the Mercedes and Hunter drove like a maniac to get us home in record time.

At the gate, our security team assured us there'd been no sign of a dragon in the skies, and to their credit, none of them showed any reaction to the question. Even though they knew nothing about Talon, and we didn't make a habit of checking in on Slade.

As soon as we parked, we burst out of the car and headed for the containment room. Emme was running as she all but slammed into Slade, who stood in the pathway staring at... Talon.

Who was *exactly where we'd left him*...?

Leaned against the bars, the dragon's darkly penetrating gaze locked on to Emme. "Are you okay, sweetness?"

Emme looked around like she was trying to figure out what had happened, only there was no sign of an escape. Everything looked normal. "Did—did you leave this cell and house?" she finally asked him.

Talon reached out a hand and remained silent. Slade had told us that the other dragon was much more receptive to questions when Emme touched him, and as our omega shuffled forward, Slade's arm shot out. He wrapped one giant as fuck hand around his twin's throat, and Talon never blinked an eye. If anything, he appeared almost *bored* by the punishing grip and lack of oxygen.

Scary psycho.

"Answer her question," Slade snarled. "How did you get out of the cells? And more importantly, why did you put yourself back into them? Was Fletcher behind the attack in the council chambers? Emme could have been killed, you dumb motherfucker."

Talon finally showed a sliver of anger, as he bared his teeth, nostrils flaring. The heat intensified until we all got a free sauna to go with our dragon fight. Add in a beer and popcorn and we'd have quite the show.

Emme huffed, and hurried closer, unconcerned that she stood beside two raging, mythical beasts.

"Stop it," she snapped, and fuck if my spine didn't slam straight at the command in her tone. Goddess have mercy on my sad, needy soul. And throbbing cock.

From here on out, Emme needed to use that tone in the bedroom. I would accept nothing less.

She shot a smirk over her shoulder at me, and I loved the sight of her palming my bite.

That's right, pretty mate. You're fucking mine.

"He's the enemy," Slade reminded her, and she returned her focus to the dragon war.

"This is getting us nowhere, Slade. We have to work together if we want a chance to win this damn fight." She took Talon's extended hand, which he hadn't dropped even under attack.

With an annoyed huff, Slade released his brother, and I studied the two of them while they stood close together. They did look scarily alike. Their faces were the same, but Talon's expression was darker and harder, along with the scar and shaved head.

Slade's eyes were more manic though, giving the impression his dragon was extra unstable.

When Talon tugged her closer, Emme went willingly. "Did you escape?" she asked, her voice calmer.

He didn't even try to lie. "Yes. I heard the explosion and felt your panic and fear. I had to make sure you were okay, and once I confirmed that, I returned here."

We all just stared at him, and I examined the bars allegedly holding him prisoner, but they all looked intact. "What the actual fuck?" Hunter snarled. "Why are you pretending to be locked up if you could leave at any time?"

Talon met his gaze without flinching. "I'm not pretending. It takes a lot of energy to manipulate the matter that encases this room. I won't be able to do it again for a few days. But it was worth it to ensure my mate's safety."

Emme threw her free hand in the air and shook her head. "As much as I appreciate that, I'd prefer if you remained in here. Safe." She huffed, her cute little nose wrinkling. "And with that, it's been a damn long day, and I'm going to bed." She pulled away, and I was surprised that Talon allowed it without a fight. It appeared that dragon-dude was on his best behavior too.

"It's lunchtime," Slade said, narrowing his gaze on her.

Lunchtime or not, there was plenty we could do in bed. "I'll tuck her in for a nap," I called, grabbing dibs. My nights lately had all been shared with Hunter, and I was ready for a little Emme alone time.

Slade and Hunter exchanged a look. "Okay, well, if this bastard is locked down, and I don't detect any lies from him," Slade said. "We need to get back to the council chambers and deal with the witch."

Thank you, goddess, for blessing me with this gift. No sharing today. She was all mine. "I'll keep her safe."

Emme's gaze heated as she felt the pulse of my desire through our bond, and I forced myself to breathe normally. Hunter shook his head, dispelling the notion I had kept anything from them. "Don't wear her out too much, annoying pup. She needs to rest. None of us are sleeping well these days."

"I'm perfectly fine," Emme growled back, her cute little wolf poking up.

When I held my hand out for her, she latched on and snuggled into my side. "Take me to bed, Golden," she whispered, her eyes darkening.

My favorite body part shot to attention, and I risked a glance at the caged dragon to find he looked mostly curious, without any obvious jealousy. *Interesting.*

Hunter and Slade did a sweep of the house before leaving, and I reminded them that Fin was out there raging around as a bear, and to keep an eye out for him. Then I took my mate up to my room, barely able to stop from throwing her over my shoulder and charging.

Emme didn't always love the way we carried her around like our own personal wolf plushie, and today she wanted to walk on her own. "Shower first?" she suggested, breathing in the scent of my room until she started to calm. My caramel and cinnamon tones were everywhere, and I loved that she needed a hit. Just like I needed every part of my Shortcake.

Emme's expression remained somber as we entered the bathroom, and she didn't even protest as I slowly stripped her clothes off, annoyed by the small piles of plaster, wood chips, and rubble that hit the floor too. She'd come close to being hurt again, and I was so fucking sick of my mate being in harm's way. I wanted to rage and crush the world around us.

In the shower, Emme leaned down and rested her head against my chest, and I did nothing but hold her. She was so tall that it had to be uncomfortable to bend her neck in that way, but she didn't show any sign of it.

"When did you start reading romances?" she asked randomly, her voice soft.

There was a hint of urgency in the question, as if she was worried if she didn't ask now, she'd never hear the answer. "Oh, and why all the plants? I'd really love to know about those too."

Smiling as I propped my chin on top of her head, I said, "Well, I honestly started reading when I first discovered girls. My brothers clued me in on the importance of romance, and while they didn't suggest the novels, I did my own research and concluded that female authors were all but giving me an insight into their minds... their wants... their needs."

Emme wiggled against me, and at first, I thought she was upset about the mention of "girls," not that any female existed in the world now except for her, but then she chuckled.

Needing more of that, I continued: "Funniest part was that it did teach me about romance, but it also opened my eyes to true escapism. I love the heart and soul that are woven into these stories, and the fact that I get spice as well… Sign me the fuck up. I've been hooked ever since."

"I love that," she mumbled against me, her soft lips brushing my skin, and I had to remind my dick that it was not play time. Not yet.

"And the plants." I thought back to when that had started for me. "I guess it would be from my mom. Dad taught me weapons, and Mom taught me to surround myself in greenery. She loves to garden. You should see their pack's house… I don't think they've bought groceries in ten years. She grows everything. They even have their own cattle. It's a full farm community in their area."

Emme was quiet as she absorbed that information, and then she let out a sigh. "You really did come from a good family, didn't you? I honestly thought they only existed in fairy tales. Even in romance novels the families are usually fucked up, hence why these main characters always have to save themselves."

I'd never thought of my family as anything other than fucking awesome, but the more I experienced the *real world*, the more I was coming to see that I'd been truly blessed. Growing up with them was a gift that I needed to be more mindful of. "I should ring my parents again soon," I murmured, holding her even closer. "They want to visit and meet you."

"I'd like that," she said, her voice low and relaxed. "I'd like to see a real family in action."

I pulled her up until she stood straight, and I could stare into her beautiful blue irises. "You do see one. Every day in our pack house. We're a real family, and you'll eventually accept our unconditional love, which is the sort of love you should have had growing up."

Her lips trembled, but she didn't cry.

She was so strong. It killed me that she'd been forced into that position, when her omega soul was soft and gentle.

"Let me take care of you, baby," I breathed, pressing my lips to her right cheek, and then her left, before slowly kissing across *my* perfect freckles and down to her mouth.

"Yes," she said, breathily. "Please, Golden."

I reached for my shampoo and lathered up her hair, slowly and gently, marveling at how beautiful she looked when her head fell back to give me better access. The long lines of her throat called to me, and I brushed my lips down the front as I finished off her hair.

By the time we were both clean, the aching sadness had left her body, and she smiled as she snuggled into our bed. We were both naked, and my dick was hard enough to punch a hole through the wall, though I didn't even bother palming the needy asshole. It was time to focus on Emme's needs.

"Will you read to me?" she asked, pointing toward our latest story. "I need to escape into a nicer fantasy world for a bit."

We were halfway through a series that I'd started reading during one of her nightmares. They were coming less frequently, thank fuck, but I was glad the reading persisted.

Reaching for the book, I smirked at the realization that we'd left off last night just before chapter twenty-seven. The perfect chapter for what I had planned.

CHAPTER 36

EMME

My head spun from the chain of events today.

So much had happened in such a short period of time, and I wasn't sure I understood the full reasoning behind it. Sure, the witch had made her agenda clear—she was on the side of Fletcher and the Termaine witches. But what had they hoped to achieve?

Was it destabilization?

Were they hoping to kill a bunch of entitled alphas and weaken Golden Claw's council?

Was it just a show of power?

Or had they been attempting to kidnap me again, and if so, why had there been no real effort?

I had all the questions, and no way to get any real answers.

"You ready to continue our story, Shortcake?" Kellan rumbled, settling back on his pile of fluffy pillows, dragging me against his side. It was the middle of the day, and after our shower I was exhausted, naked, and ready to curl up with my mate until our pack returned.

"I'm so ready," I murmured, rolling over to face him, draping my arm over his chest to enjoy all those gym and hockey muscles. As I traced the expanse of his bare, golden skin, a random thought hit me. "We should get tattoos." We were the only two—oh, and Talon—who didn't sport any ink.

Kellan let the book fall to his side as he turned his focus on me.

"What would you get? I've never been able to decide, even though Fin has drawn me up dozens of options."

It was still bizarre that Finley was the artist who created such incredible, lifelike tattoos on the others. Even though he only wore a few sentences—

"Wait, who did Fin's tattoos? Surely, it's not easy to write on yourself?"

Kellan laughed. "He's a talented punk, that bear. He did them himself, with Hunter helping through a few tough spots. Finley's a genius with a tattoo gun—all that angst and pain must be fodder for artists."

I couldn't help but join his laughter. "I can't draw a stick figure without help. Must have skipped my trauma."

Kellan dropped a kiss on the side of my head, his touch soothing as he ran his hand through my damp hair. "You have skills that are much more desirable than drawing on skin, Shortcake. Don't undersell yourself."

With a snort, I smacked him in the ribs, and he laughed so freely it sent tingles down my spine. "Now is not the time to discuss my head job skills, asshole," I said, still chuckling myself. "And when it comes to tattoos, I have no idea what I'd get. Maybe a symbol to represent our entire pack—I'd like it to mean something."

We remained in a comfortable silence for a minute or so, with Kellan's lips lingering against my temple as he held me close. "I'd like mine to mean something too," he finally said. "I'd love your wolf. My pretty mate."

This alpha knew exactly what to say to have me melting into a puddle at his damn feet—romance novels did him good. "I need one with all of us represented," I decided, already forming an image in my mind. "Our quintet."

Kellan's hold flexed against my skin. "But how is it a quintet with Talon?"

We'd all long stopped pretending he wasn't a part of the pack now, in whatever capacity it all played out. "The essence of a quintet remains complete, despite the extra member," I said, feeling more confidence than was probably warranted with the amount of information we had. "I can feel it, and while I don't know the future, the way forward is with the six of us. It's centered around them being twin souls, and whatever *their* specific bond entails."

Kellan didn't argue as he pressed kisses to my cheeks and over my nose, adoring me in his golden ways. "I trust you, pretty mate. I trust in our pack."

Kellan's faith was akin to a million-level boost to my own confidence, and I was glad we'd had this conversation. We both needed the reassurance.

Eventually he picked up the book, and I settled in to listen to him read. It was odd not having Hunter here with us, tracing his hand over my skin while Kellan read, as he did every single time I woke from nightmares. I had no idea what I did in my last life to deserve this pack, but it must have been huge. Like... I saved a burning orphanage or invented the vibrator.

Whatever I did, it benefited humanity greatly.

"Chapter twenty-seven," Kellan all but purred, resting the base of the book on his chest, holding it one handed while the other held me. "Hunter is going to be big mad that he missed this."

That piqued my curiosity. The story centered around a fae woman who was waging a war against the current king. She'd been living on the fringes of their society with the resistance and had gone undercover in a contest to find a bride for their leader. Her hope was to be chosen, and to destabilize the rule from the inside.

The last chapter we'd read was the dance, and she'd unknowingly found herself in the garden with the king himself. This wasn't their first time being alone, or the first time she'd noticed this annoying attraction between them, but it was the first time he'd shown a softer side. Which had confused her more than anything else that had happened so far. The king was the monster in her story, or at least in the stories she'd been fed from the resistance, and when he didn't live up to his reputation, it sent her confusion spiraling.

I related hard to the female main character as she traversed this forbidden love, wires-crossed, unexpected-soul-mate storyline. Torn between her heart and her duty.

The author was definitely leading us down the path of *if the king found a strong partner who'd help him fight for their people and the kingdom, then he would grow into a truly admirable leader.* Or maybe the author would throw a curveball and keep him as an asshole, and she will fall in love with him anyway. Maybe this was a villain love story.

Or maybe she was going to fuck her favorite guard, *Jere*.

The possibilities were endless.

This was one of Kellan's favorite series, and while he already knew the ending, he absolutely refused to spill one spoiler for me. Not even when I begged. On my knees.

Though he at least looked pained when I'd tried that.

"Shadows lined the king's face," he started, his low voice soothing, *"and all we had were the illumination of the fireflies around us to guide our way. In the dark, his beauty was even more unnatural. Those hard lines and perfect planes, full lips and defined cheekbones. The wash of silver hair littered with hints of shimmering strands, and I hated how he consumed my every thought."*

Kellan's voice, while deep, always took on this melodic tone when he read, like its own form of magic. I forgot everything that had happened today, and all the bad shit that would no doubt happen tomorrow. I got lost in this fantasy world again.

As they moved through the dance scene, stopping at the edge of the castle, Kellan's voice grew lower: *"'What spell do you have me under?' the king whispered against my lips, and my voice faded under the roar of desire unfurling deep in my stomach. Hot, unrelenting, desperate need.*

'It is you who have cast a spell, your majesty,' I replied, unsure if I was speaking truth or playing my part so well that not even I could tell what was real or not. 'And I don't know what—' My words were cut off as he kissed me. It wasn't my first kiss. Or even my second. But Lady Stars above, there was a very real sense that it could be my last. Pressing myself against his much taller frame, I tried to pretend this was all part of the plan. But there had been no way to plan for this. When his strong hands bit into my thighs, through the thick material of my gown, I ached to feel that firm touch on bare skin."

I leaned closer to Kellan and my breaths came out faster. I'd been so enthralled in the story that I jumped when he broke the moment with a laugh and kiss on my lips.

"The sexual tension," I groaned when he pulled away.

His eyebrows waggled, the deep blue of his eyes piercing into me. "You have no idea. No fucking idea. It gets so much better."

He continued reading, watching me between every sexually charged sentence as the king and the fae sent to dethrone him fought their desires. The next chapter was even more explicit, and as the king knelt before the female fae, running his hands up her bare thighs,

Kellan adjusted our positions so he could follow that same path on me.

On instinct, I parted my legs, breaths ragged as my limbs trembled.

Holy shit. Reading was the foreplay I didn't know I needed in my life.

"'So wet for me, Starlight,' the king murmured, his low groan sending shivers through my limbs until I was a languid, needy mess. 'There's only one path forward from here.' He remained on his knees, his tongue tracing the trail of his hands…"

Kellan's tongue glided over my skin, kissing as well, all the way until he brushed his lips over my aching core. My clit pulsed at the contact, and I arched against him, so wet that it slid between my thighs and down my ass cheeks.

"Next," Kellan whispered against me, "he ran his tongue along her pussy, lapping up all of her arousal."

I cried out as he flattened his tongue and slid it through my folds. I arched my hips, and he held me down, the book falling to the side as he used both hands to part me wide enough to wiggle between my legs again. "He circles her clit with his tongue," he rasped, apparently having the damn text memorized, and my hands tightened on the sheets in response.

One day these alphas would actually kill me via edging, and on that day I'd die a fucking happy, frustrated shifter.

Kellan's breath was hot as he huffed against my core, sending a clenching spasm of need through my stomach. My hips moved against him as I suffered through his slow, agonizing touches.

"He slid one finger and then another inside her," he continued, his thick fingers filling me and leaving an ache behind with each thrust. "Both of them knowing that this was forbidden but unable to help themselves."

At this stage, I was so damn wet that I could *hear* him finger-fucking me. I slid one hand around the back of his head and threaded my fingers in his blond strands, keeping him close.

"He didn't want to waste one drop of her release, so he slid his tongue down her sweet cunt, lapping at the spill of desire."

I gasped as Kellan's mouth joined his fingers, his tongue flicking across my clit. I was so close to release, but I wanted to hold out until we reached the climax of the story.

"Sadie knew this wasn't part of the plan, but as her body unraveled around his touch, she honestly didn't give a fuck any longer. The plan could wait for tomorrow. Tonight, she was taking her pleasure."

My body bucked against his thrusts, and as he moved his fingers harder and faster inside me, his dark-blue eyes met mine. Watching me, his tongue returned to my clit, and I was tumbling, crying out his name as my release coated his hand and face.

"Fucking delicious," Kellan rumbled against me. "I could live on your pussy and nothing else for the rest of my life, Shortcake."

Goddess be damned.

He drew out the orgasm, and when I collapsed on the bed, my limbs tingled in time to the spinning of my vision. Kellan crawled his way up along my body, the thick head of his cock bobbing tantalizingly before him.

He held his weight off me with his strong arms and stared down with a look that could only be described as awe. "You're so perfect, pretty mate, that I think you might have been written by an author and brought to life for me." He licked his glossy lips and groaned as he tasted me all over again. "Yep, my dream fucking shifter."

I threw my head back and laughed, my rush of happiness taking me completely by surprise. "My goddess. That's quite the line, Golden Boy. But I think I like it."

"I love you," he shot back. "I desperately crave you in a way that should scare you, mate. Are you scared?"

I responded by reaching out and wrapping my hand around his thick, heavy length, stroking from base to tip. "Not scared. *Happy*. You were a very good boy," I purred, stroking him gently as I watched his face to gauge what brought him the most pleasure in my touch. "And good boys get the rewards."

His cock jerked in my hands as Kellan panted, his pupils blown out. "Pretty mate," he groaned. "Please, baby. Please."

I wore a near permanent smirk as I continued to stroke him with one hand, while the other pressed against his chest to shove him onto his back. I moved to straddle his thighs, and he groaned, "Baby, have I ever told you that you can do whatever you want to me. Like… whatever. Just keep fucking touching me."

Sliding up his body, I released his length as I settled on his hips, leaning forward for a kiss. I sucked his tongue into my mouth, desperate to taste him, and angled myself until the thick head of his cock probed at my entrance. In slow, maddening increments, I sank down on him, my body still requiring time to adjust to his size, even after my orgasm.

Kellan gripped my hips, clinging on in a desperation that matched the tension lining his face and throat. But he never pushed me to hurry—if anything, he looked like he was enjoying the anticipation as I finally descended all the way.

Sitting for a second, to give myself a chance to adjust, my pussy tightened and clenched at the sensation of being this full. "I swear to fuck, you're so deep I can feel you rearranging my insides," I groaned as I wiggled my hips.

Kellan's hands slid up to cup my tits, his fingers brushing across both nipples until they were hard and aching. "Ride me, pretty mate. Take your pleasure from me."

My hips were already moving, swiveling and grinding against him as need stole clarity and conscious thought. "I want your pleasure," I managed to say. "This is your reward."

Okay, mine too, if I was completely honest. Still, I was determined not to come until Kellan did.

He thrust up into me, taking a little control as he continued to squeeze and caress my tits, sending me into a frenzy. My aim had been to watch Kellan fall apart beneath me, but I was the one losing it already.

Hunter never really allowed me control in the bedroom, and while I mostly enjoyed a more submissive role, it was nice on occasion to take the lead with Kellan.

Honestly, so far, whatever they chose to share with me sexually or emotionally was working, and I wondered about the dynamics when I was bonded to all five powerful shifters.

The thought of which all but took my breath away.

CHAPTER 37

EMME

"We're going to shift into our beasts for part two of warmups today," Slade yelled, and I leaned forward to suck ragged breaths into my lungs, pressing my hands to my knees in the hopes it would help keep me upright.

We'd only done three laps and I was wrecked. This shit had to start getting easier soon, right?

It'd been a few days since the attack on the council chambers, and while the witch had been taken in for questioning, she'd managed to kill herself in the holding chamber. Somehow.

She'd had no spells on her or means to stop her heart that they were aware of, but by the time they went to question her she was gone. Jewels had examined the body after, and was of the opinion that she might have been terminated by her coven. Again, *somehow*.

The other covens were being questioned, but so far, no evidence of another traitor had been found. Every time Jewels showed up at the house to update the alphas, the tingles in my limbs showed up with her, and I couldn't for the life of me figure out why my wolf was reacting so strongly to magic.

Not that I had much time to worry about it today, as I faced a row of half-naked shifters. At least until a broad chest encased in a black shirt blocked my view. "Time to shift, Snow," Slade commanded, leaning down to bathe me in his scent. He always finished warmups minutes before everyone else, but never showed sign of sweat, fatigue, or strain.

The literal only time I'd ever seen him fatigued was when we were kidnapped and he'd had to battle that magical house in Silver City for our freedom.

Despite the cooler weather, I'd come out today in a sports bra and long athletic tights. When my fingers skimmed the base of the bra, Slade's eyes darkened. "You're not going to turn around?" I teased.

His response was to lift his shirt, dragging the material up the full length of his ripped torso. Somehow, I managed to keep my tongue in my mouth. "Not a chance, Snow. I'm your security detail, remember? I can't take my eyes off you."

"Well," I choked out, "just call me your security detail then too."

And could I just say I was very happy with my new position.

His dragon tattoos now reminded me of Slade and Talon, as the dark and light faced off against each other in their beast forms. I had different theories about what this permanent mark on Slade's body meant now. I believed that a part of his essence had known all along that there was a missing piece of his soul out there. His twin soul.

When he dropped his hands to his pants, unbuttoning them, my gaze dropped with that movement. This was also the moment I had to lean down and shuck my tights off, which left me closer to eye level with beast number two. Which was still massive. Still pierced. Still terrifying.

Even if those piercings did form a ladder I needed to climb with my tongue…

"You're drooling, Snow," Slade drawled, and when I jerked my gaze up to meet his, I found amusement dancing across his features.

Words spilled from me in a rush: "There's a lot to take in. Too much really. That can't be survivable."

I stilled when I realized I'd said the quiet part out loud again, which happened far too often around my alphas. They had a way of flustering me until I was a disconcerted mess.

Slade's smile grew and I was graced with perfect, if not slightly predatory teeth. "You were made for me, Emmeline. There's no other shifter in this world who could survive what I can offer."

His words reminded me of our conversation in the car when he'd admitted he was a virgin. At first it took me by surprise, but with some time and reflection, it made sense, and I fucking loved that there'd been none before me. I was growing quite possessive of my pack—goddess help my soul.

"Surely, there'd be another out there who could handle you too, Slade," I found myself teasing. Maybe to lessen the tension. Or maybe I just was fishing for the answer. "An alpha female perhaps?"

The hint of his smile turned darker. "I'd kill any other female who touched me. Hence, not survivable. You are it for me, Snow. Now and always."

With that destructive statement, he stepped away and I felt his powerful energy wash over my skin as he called for his beast. I set my wolf free too and she arrived with ease, relieving tension I hadn't even known I was carrying.

I hadn't shifted for a while, and after years of suppressing my beast, it wasn't good to start doing that again. It weakened us, and weak could get me killed. Or worse, it could get my pack killed.

Slade's dragon straightened, impressive as always, and I noted that his scales were slightly greener today, shimmering brightly in the sunlight. His beast tilted its head back and roared to the sky, which must have been the signal for his squad to move. Some took off on wings, like Horton's eagle, while the land-bound creatures raced into the field. There were a couple of wolves, a bear, and a lion in his alpha squad. *Flight Squad*, as an ode to Slade's beast.

Slade didn't fly this time though, remaining by my side and moving gracefully on all fours across the field. My wolf loved being out here with him, letting out little yips, and the occasional howls. She all but purred when Slade's huge dragon head dipped, his snout tracing down my flank. Even knowing his beast could gulp me up in one bite, I felt nothing except this warm, fuzzy contentment.

We drew a lot of attention, from Flight Squad, and whichever other enforcers were out training today. Apparently none of them had seen the fearsome dragon's affectionate side.

I'd barely seen it, but I was officially addicted. With zero plans on attending a meeting, despite having an advanced case of the Slades.

My beast preened as she lapped up the attention of her mate. She'd be insufferable as she reminded me of all the times she'd tried to stop me running from our pack. *Yeah, yeah. You were right.*

The second part of warmup was over too soon, and I was pumped when I slipped back into my training gear.

"Let's break off into our pairs," Slade called, and as I moved toward Horton, I was stopped by a huge arm around my middle. "You're with me today, Snow."

Thrown off-balance, I reached out and clutched his arm, my gaze shooting up to gauge how he was handling the contact. There was no sign of his usual flinch or darkening green gaze, and it took him at least ten Mississippi's to move away from me.

Fuck, I really didn't need a warmup when Slade was around.

I was currently warm enough to melt into a puddle on the ground.

"Why am I training with you?" I asked, forcing myself to get it together.

"I want to teach you today."

Don't freak out. Don't you freak out.

"But… with the touching and…"

Slade crowded into my space, and it was so overwhelming I started breathing harder than when I'd been running. It turned out that standing in proximity to him was the equivalent of sprinting like my life depended on it.

"There'll be touching, yes, and I expect you to try and take me down. Fletcher is powerful. Blaine is a piece of shit, but he's well trained. You cannot let either of them get their hands on you."

Yes, sir. Thankfully I managed to keep that thought inside my head.

Slade backed away from me and fell into a familiar pose. It was the one I'd been practicing with Horton all week, and I quickly recalculated my stance for a much taller shifter.

When Slade grabbed me, there was no hesitation in his touch, and I was so nervous that I all but slipped over my own feet and landed in a tangle on the ground. The dragon shook his head, his expression serious. "Up, Emmeline. You can do better than that. I've seen you do better than that all week."

Grumbling and ignoring my embarrassment, I got back into position, and this time when he moved, I let my body fall into the series of steps I'd practiced. I nudged into him, hooked my foot behind his, tilted my shoulder for more leverage, and yanked him over the side so he'd lose balance. Slade being Slade, he barely moved, but I managed to knock him a few steps back.

Moving a wall of muscle would normally be reason to celebrate, but Slade didn't encourage celebrations in the middle of training. I'd heard him drill into his squad over and over that an early celebration when your opponent wasn't dead was a surefire way to get *you dead.*

With that in mind, I moved on to the next drill to knock out a grounded opponent. It did require a lot of contact, and my nervousness over that cost me as Slade moved faster than I could track, and encased both of my wrists in his massive grip. In less than a second, he reversed our positions so I was the one on the ground, under his mercy.

His huge body trapped me against the grass, and my instinct to struggle died off at the sensation of his muscles pressing against my curves. "You stopped fighting," he growled, as he lifted my hands above my head and secured them in one of his palms. His gaze was biting as his chest rumbled, and I made a weak, sad attempt to free myself.

Oh no, I'm trapped by a sexy dragon.

With a shake of his head, Slade slid one knee between my thighs, effectively pinning me to the ground, my hands still trapped by his above my head. He'd subdued me so fast that it was embarrassing, and his weight was too dense for me to even hope to buck him off.

I was his prisoner.

"What are you going to do now, Snow?" Slade asked as his gaze bore into me. "You're as vulnerable as you'll ever get. My weight is too much for you to lift. You're too weak to break my hold on your hands. And look at that," he lifted his free hand. "I can now do whatever I want with you."

My breath stuttered out from me, and as he pressed his knee into my core, demonstrating his statement, I barely kept a moan from escaping.

"Look, Scary Shifter," I huffed out in time to the steady throb between my thighs. "You're not giving me much incentive. I've dreamed about being held down by you like this too many times to escape now."

For the first time since I'd met the infamously terrifying dragon shifter, I witnessed him speechless. I'd have laughed at his astonished expression, but I was too busy trying not to erupt from just being this close to him.

"Slade," I whimpered.

His shock was replaced by a shadowed expression, and in a flash he was back on his feet. His chest heaved as he stared down at me, pupils slitted until all I could see was *dragon* in that green gaze. The part of the dragon that everyone feared.

The air sizzled, and with a growl he turned and shouted for Horton.

"Start her on the blades," Slade said shortly as the eagle hurried over, and then he was gone, leaving me with a strong sense that I'd pushed him too far.

Horton's gaze darted between me and his boss. "Everything okay?" he asked, reaching out for me. Just before our hands touched, a rumble rocked the ground, and while the dragon wasn't nearby, we both jumped away from each other.

"Let's give him a minute to cool off," Horton babbled, sounding nervous.

He ducked over to grab a case from the ground nearby and pulled out two practice sets of wooden blades. Somehow, I managed to focus long enough for him to explain how to hold them, even though most of my brain was still caught up on Slade.

That dragon was never far from my mind, and as I fought to push down my need and desire once more, I wondered how it would all play out.

Slade might be resisting, but the goddess wanted us to be together, and shifter help me, *so did I.*

CHAPTER 38

EMME

The rest of the week passed by in weird increments, going both fast and incredibly slow at times. We fell into a routine that had me training every morning, while the alphas went about their lives with work and hockey. Though one of them always kept an eye on me.

Every morning Slade dragged me out of bed to train with Horton, and every afternoon I came home to a new origami figure on my pillow, and a magazine on the end of the bed. A few of the intricate paper animals held the faintest hint of cherry, which led me to believe our resident bear shifter was the gift giver, and I found myself craving a deeper conversation with Finley again.

Like we'd had the day at the racetrack.

I wanted to know how he was able to craft animals from scraps of paper—my drawer now held a crane, swan, frog, fish, bear, unicorn, wolf, and a rabbit. I had a veritable range of creatures, all in various paper colors. So far, he hadn't doubled up on either animal or color of paper.

Finding these gifts were a highlight of my day as I stumbled in broken and beat-to-shit from training. Today it was a navy horse, and as I'd done with the previous ones, I quickly googled what an origami horse represented: freedom, strength, and courage.

Which made sense today.

Finley had asked me to sit in on one of his therapy sessions to delve into his past, and we could both no doubt use a little strength and courage to get through it.

I was nervous, even as I craved the knowledge of who Finley truly was. The good, bad, and terrifying.

His appointment was in two hours, which left me plenty of time to shower, change, and grab some food. I'd already said hello to Hunter in his office, and Slade was down in the containment room, where he spent most of his afternoons. I had no idea what he did with Talon now that the torture had stopped, and I was too exhausted from training to push and find out.

Hopefully they were using the time to chat and learn about each other, though most likely the broody brothers were staring, expressions hard and arms crossed, as they attempted to bond by murdering the other with their gaze.

As I undressed my aching limbs, I wondered if Slade was watching me via the cameras. There wasn't a single place in this house now out of his view.

So long, prank wars. You were fun while you lasted.

The glow-in-the-dark dragon eyes were my last reminder, and while one day I hoped to continue our game, until then I'd just have to be happy with the memory of all those googly eyes on *his* stalker wall. I wondered if he'd even noticed—he'd never mentioned it.

After my shower, I wandered into my wardrobe, unsurprised to find more hoodies from Kellan. He took great pleasure in swapping out whatever he'd just worn, leaving me with his scent. *Such a good boy.* In fact, my entire closet now smelled like all four alphas, in the best way possible.

A veritable sweets shop in my wardrobe. Except for maple, but we weren't going there yet.

Mate, my wolf grumbled.

She'd been trying to get me down to Talon all week, and all week I'd managed to resist. The fatigue from training was enough to keep me focused on eating, sleeping—with only the occasional nightmare—and destructing under the very talented hands of two alphas every night.

Kellan and Hunter had fallen into a very delicious pattern of dragging multiple orgasms from me before they both fucked me until I screamed their names. Passing out between them, sated, protected, and loved was the best part of my day. A shifter could grow very used to having mates like them.

Deciding to stay casual for the therapy session, I dressed in jeans, a plain white shirt, with Slade's leather jacket over the top. It hung to mid-thigh, but I loved how warm and heavy it felt.

Like the jacket had summoned him, when I left my room I almost slammed into the dragon himself, as he waited in the hall. "Oh, hey," I said, swallowing roughly.

Slade might drag me from my nice warm bed most mornings, and he might watch me in training like he was stripping away layers until he reached my soul, but he remained distant in every other way. Which made this visit a little unexpected. "What's up? Is everything okay?"

He took a long, slow perusal of my outfit, showing no immediate reaction to me wearing his jacket. "Where are you going?"

"Finley wants me to sit in on his therapy session this afternoon. Figured I'd upgrade the sweats so I didn't embarrass the pack."

Slade's expression flattened. "The therapist should be paying *you* to be in the fucking room. You're that far above her."

My brow furrowed as I processed his words. "If she's so terrible, why are we letting Finley go there? This is a huge and positive step forward for him. We can't risk him going to a subpar therapist." Not that anyone *let* Finley do anything, but my point remained.

"She's the top therapist in Golden Claw. Her specialty is dealing in past trauma."

Um, okay. So…

Slade noticed my confusion. "It wouldn't matter if she was the queen of all shifters. You are worth a hundred of her, and therefore she should be paying for your presence. Not the other way around."

I shook my head, even as it felt like I was slammed in the chest by a wrecking ball. "Maybe to you I'm worth a hundred of her, but out in the cities I'm no better than anyone else."

Slade shrugged. "I only care about you and this pack. Everyone else could fade from existence and I wouldn't lose a wink of sleep."

Okay, I was in love with my psycho stalker of a scent match.

My voice somehow remained even. "I think we've gotten off topic here. What did you come to my room for?"

"Reading," he said shortly. "I know you've found it easier with the adjusted font and background color, but I want to work with you to keep improving."

Slade's offer to help me with reading had been before everything went to shit. And while improving my reading was important to me, after spending years feeling stupid, it wasn't life or death.

"If you're busy, it can wait," I told him, only to find him shaking his head before I was even finished.

"I'm never too busy for you, Snow. It shouldn't have been put off this long."

He led me from the room, and we ended up downstairs in the library.

It was a room that I'd admired from the doorway but hadn't spent much time in. Everything was big and darkly masculine to fit the alphas who owned the house. Black wooden shelves lined the walls from floor to ceiling and were filled with thousands of books.

"Humans say if you own more than a thousand books you've got a library," I said, recalling that fact from my book-loving co-worker. "You guys have a few libraries in here."

"Twenty," Slade replied smoothly, and I tried not to freak out that there were twenty thousand books surrounding us. I focused instead on taking in the rest of the room.

There was no natural light, as it sat centrally in the house, which gave it a really cozy feeling, added to by the stone-lined fireplace roaring away in the corner, vented up through a stunning stone flue.

Warmth surrounded us as Slade led me to a long table, clearly used for research purposes. The *fun* reading would be done on the large, squishy couches dotted closer to the fire.

On the table sat a pile of books along with a laptop and tablet. "Sit," Slade commanded, pulling out the chair for me.

"Yes, sir," I said, snapping to attention in the way that usually had his eye doing a twitchy thing.

He shook his head. "You wouldn't call me *sir* if you knew how much my dragon liked it."

That had my wolf perking to attention, and I wasn't sure Slade and I were on the same wavelength when it came to our beasts. I absolutely wanted to use *all* the words his dragon liked. I wanted to claim both sides of this alpha. For once though, I was smart enough to keep that need to myself. We'd been so distant lately. I didn't want to ruin this time together.

I sank into the chair, and Slade pushed me toward the table. "Okay, let's do a bit of reading to figure out where we're at, and where to start."

He took a seat beside me and pulled the pile of items toward him, retrieving a dozen or so pieces of paper. The first one he handed me had a white background with printed sentences in black blocky text. When I stared at the words, everything started to move around, and I squinted in an attempt to focus. I finally figured out the first sentence and read it out loud: *The shifter broke the first rule of the treaty.*

"Okay," Slade said with a nod, making no comment on my obvious struggle, even as I felt heat in my cheeks. *Fuck, I hated this.* "Let's try a few different styles."

The rest of the papers were all different. Different colored backgrounds and different fonts. Surprisingly, I found some of them far easier to read, while others were even harder than the first white one.

"You do better with a green or dark-tinged background," Slade noted clinically, as if he was a scientist making a checklist. "Sans-serif fonts, at least point twelve or fourteen, and no italics."

A surge of excitement rocked deep in my gut at the idea that maybe I could keep moving forward with my reading once I figured out the foundations.

Next we worked on the tablet, and he continued to break down my difficulties, until eventually he had the perfect background and text for me. "Give me your phone?" he said, holding out a hand, and I tried to remember when I'd seen it last.

"Uh, I'm not sure…"

Slade shook his head. "Why am I not surprised? Have you even checked the group chat lately?"

That would have been a no. I'd been too busy training to think about anything else. "I'm always with one of you and you all keep me updated."

In truth, I loved our group chat threads, and I needed to make more effort to be in there. Especially if Finley and Slade were no longer ghosting as soon as they were added.

We spent another thirty minutes going through different programs, and I was shocked by how strong my reading was with the right background and font. I'd thought I'd test out as no better than a first or second grader, but I was actually much higher.

"You've been working harder than you realized over the years to compensate," Slade said, as he packed everything up. "Your reading level is good, Emme. You just needed to understand your brain better to help it shine. Now we can cater to that."

I barely stopped from squealing and bouncing in my chair over this unexpected boost to my day. "I'd really love to be able to read novels one day," I said, finally voicing a long-held dream out into the world. "The couple of audiobooks I could afford only whet my appetite, and while I love Kellan reading to me, I'd like to repay the favor."

Slade nodded. "You can use a reading tablet. I'll ensure it has the right font and background, which will come across in every book you download. I won't lie to you and say that reading is ever going to be super easy for you, but you've already proven your grit and determination. Just keep practicing and we'll have you reading novels in no time."

I waved my hand, feeling the burn behind my eyes as I fought back happy tears. "I need to work on spelling. Those pesky letters still want to switch themselves up, and I thank the goddess for autocorrect and spellcheck."

Slade, who was the closest shifter I'd ever met to a perfectionist, surprised me when he leaned down over me on the table, and rested his hands on either side of my body. *Caging me in.* "Don't worry about spelling, Snow. If you get your point across, I don't care if a letter is the wrong way around or you miss a comma. As long as you can express yourself, I want you to do that. Incorrect spelling and all."

As he moved back, he brushed a hand across my shoulders and left the room.

I needed a few seconds to pull myself together before I got to my feet and followed.

It had been a truly perfect hour spent with the enigmatic dragon shifter. I felt lighter as I stopped beating myself up about my differences.

Maybe it was time to embrace my true self and stop caring what others thought of me...

A freedom I'd never understood until this very moment.

CHAPTER 39

FINLEY

In my nervousness over therapy today, I started to focus on the fact that Emme hadn't worn anything of mine yet. Not that I'd expected her to, but I'd added my clothes to her wardrobe in case she wanted the comfort of my scent in the same way I craved the comfort of hers.

It was growing harder not to sneak into her room and roll around on her bed like I was channeling Kellan fucking Jackson. Instead, I snuck in to leave a few tokens of affection, using gloves while I made origami and handled the magazines. In the hopes she'd enjoy the gifts without feeling any obligation attached to them.

With our upbringing, gifts were often a double-edged sword causing us to overthink how to accept and thank someone for them. Especially with Emme and my tenuous relationship.

I'd loved origami since I was young, when Jiro, Kenzo's grandfather, had taken a lost, angry shifter and taught him productive ways to channel his emotions. When he passed a few years ago, we were both devasted, but his life lessons would remain for much longer than the shifter himself. Any healing I'd found since my family's death had come via that calm, strong male.

Kenzo retained a lot of his grandfather's traits, and I was honored to be treated like his family.

Jiro would have been disappointed in the way I acted when Emme came into my life, as I regressed into that same angry teenager. At least it did teach me that I still had a lot of healing to do, and trauma I needed to deal with.

Between origami, hockey, and therapy, I felt stronger and calmer. The only part of my life not in place was my relationship with Emme, but it also wasn't as bad as it could be either.

She was far too kind and forgiving, and as much as it worried me that fuckers would take advantage of her, I was also grateful she was open to me mending the bridges I'd burned between us. Having a chance was more than I deserved.

That day in Texas when she'd acted like I didn't exist remained front and center in my nightmares—hence why sleep had been even more elusive than usual lately.

I could never let that happen again, or I might as well cut my own throat and call it a day.

Emme was essential to my existence. Without her, there was no me.

It was only short of terrifying to know I'd be spilling dark secrets in front of her today, and I hoped Dr. Karen of the Whipsnar pack could keep it all on track. I'd only had a dozen sessions with her so far, but I found the eagle shifter easy to talk to. She had a calming and non-judgmental manner, and even when she asked hard questions and pushed me through my demons, it didn't send me spiraling.

I had no idea how she managed it, but if it helped me grow through my trauma, then I'd continue these near daily sessions for as long as it took.

"Hey," Emme said, breaking through my thoughts as she hurried down the stairs, jumping into the entrance hall. "I hope I'm not late! Slade was helping me learn more about my dyslexia and we figured out fonts that improve my reading."

Her face was flushed, her eyes lit up with a deep excitement. She looked so beautiful that it was hard to stare directly at her. Especially when all I wanted was to drag her against me and drown in her curves.

She pushed the wild strands of her pinkish blond hair off her face, and the piercing ice in her eyes held me captive. The first time I'd stared into her unusual eye color, I'd been hit with a sense of home that sent me into a downward spiral. Since that day, nothing had changed, except my stupid ass was no longer running from it.

"You're right on time," I assured her, already calmer with her presence.

My bear rumbled at me to step closer, but I knew I'd struggle to keep my hands off her, which was the last thing she needed.

She tightened Slade's coat around her, her slender form swamped by the massive jacket. If she ever wore anything of mine, I'd use that as a sign she had truly forgiven me. Until then, I'd be happy with the relationship we were slowly developing.

"Do you want to drive?" I asked her.

Her happiness shot up a few extra notches, and I felt that smile all the way to my soul.

"I'd love to," she said, moving closer, and my chest rumbled as her scent wrapped around me. "But let's choose one of the other reinforced cars today. The G-Class has had a good run lately."

I nodded, and she fell into step beside me as we headed for the garage. "What will you choose?" I asked. "The Rangey, Rolls, or Hummer?"

She took a long time to consider them all, her expression torn as she worried at her plush bottom lip with her teeth. I was so mesmerized by the movement that by the time she answered, I'd almost forgotten the question. "The Rolls. I've never driven one, obviously, and I feel like you deserve a little luxury before you delve into painful memories."

"Sounds like a plan," I agreed as we entered the garage, stepping into my happy place.

Or at least it had been before Emme.

Now, I wasn't so sure I could have a happy place she wasn't in.

As we headed for the Rolls, I was stopped by Emme reaching out and *grasping my hand.*

My bear roared and it felt like the world stilled around us. We didn't touch much in general, but today she pushed her pain and anger at me aside to offer comfort.

"Before we get to therapy, I just wanted to say that it's going to be okay," she said, her expression soft around the edges. My sweet fucking mate. Goddess, I would be protecting her until my last breath. "You're brave for taking this step and fighting your demons. I admire and respect that about you, and I want you to know that even though we haven't experienced the exact same upbringing, I do understand some of what you went through. The abuse, fear, and loneliness. I will never judge or repeat anything I hear in that room." Her lips twitched. "No matter how much you piss me off."

I couldn't breathe. The room started to spin around me, and if there hadn't been an omega grounding me to this Earth, I expected I'd just shatter into a million pieces and drift off into the universe. "Em," I grit out, voice guttural as I fought for composure. I hadn't cried in fucking years, and yet here I was, breaking apart like a damn cub.

Emme gave me a reprieve by simply squeezing my hand and stepping away. "I know, Grouchy. I know." My bear howled inside me, and I was so close to shifting that I felt the magic tingling across my skin.

I had no idea how I pulled myself together enough to stumble to the car, but it was lucky that Emme had chosen to drive. I was absolutely in no state of mind to deal with traffic. I barely managed to program the address into the GPS, while Emme patiently watched me fumble.

Once we were out of the family compound and heading downtown, she started up a normal conversation. Which I greatly appreciated. "How's hockey going?"

"Really good actually," I said, settling back into the chair. "We had a new transfer added to the offensive line, and he's working out well so far. Kellan has a mini-crush on the new bear, which should bother me, but I'm confident in my number one position."

A burst of laughter spilled from her as she stopped at a red light, a dozen or so shifters crossing the street in front of our car. "You two have a bromance that can never be broken," she said. "I wouldn't worry about losing him to another bear."

"We're pack and brothers," I said with a nod, having no doubts about our bond. "It's unbreakable."

Her responding smile was soft, and I found myself just staring at her while she looked out the front windshield. "I'm sorry I haven't made the last couple of games," she said suddenly, turning to meet my gaze. There was a tugging of guilt across her expressive features, and I fought the urge to trace a finger down her cheek.

Now that I was learning how to deal with the anger in my soul and direct it where it belonged, it was hard to remember when I'd resented her presence in my life.

"You have a lot going on, Em," I said, forcing my palms flat on my thighs to keep my hands occupied. "And your safety is the number one priority. Hockey isn't important when compared to everything else we're dealing with."

"Not true," she shot back immediately, and the lights changed green, but she didn't even notice. "It's important to you, and for that reason it's important to me."

Her statement was a gentle caress to my soul, but it also reminded me of bullshit I'd said in the past. Another sin to atone for. "I know you've listened to me bang on about how hockey is my life, and that I need it more than anything else in the world. To some degree, it did save me both in the past and now— "

The blast of a horn interrupted, and I barely restrained myself from ripping the door off this million-dollar car and beating the shit out of the impatient fuck behind us. Emme laughed as her hand shot out to press against my chest, and just like that I was calm.

She had magic in her soul this omega.

"Don't kill them, Grouchy," she said in amusement. "I was sitting at a green light. They're fine." Our car moved forward once more, and she added, "You were saying hockey saved you…"

"Yep, it did, and still does." I cleared my throat. "But I've also learned a lot about myself over the last few months. I learned that if Kellan had died when the witch magic hit him, hockey wouldn't have saved me. I learned that when the light in your eyes faded as I hurt you one too many times and you told me we were done, hockey wouldn't have saved me. I learned that hockey is now second to my pack. Every single shifter in my pack."

Her lip wobbled, but she kept it together as she shot me a look that seared into my soul. What I'd said was only partly the truth. Even within our pack, Emme was my number one, and nothing in the world could compare to her. I'd quit hockey in a heartbeat for this omega, which should have terrified me, but it didn't. I'd come to accept one undeniable truth: Emme was the heart of our bond, and I couldn't survive without her.

Before I could figure out how to express that without freaking her out—we were still early days into our healing journey—she turned into the parking lot of the therapy offices. We were a few blocks from Reeves Industries, right in the middle of the business district. The streets were teeming with shifters going about their day with work, shopping, or catching up with friends and family, and it wasn't the sort of place for heavier conversation.

"Are you sure you're really okay with me being here?" Emme asked once the car was off. "I don't want you to do anything you're not comfortable with. We have plenty of time to share our pasts, and if you're not ready, I'm happy to sit out here and wait. Therapy is usually done in private for a reason."

"Have you been to therapy before?" I asked, wondering if she spoke from personal experience.

She shook her head. "Nah. I wished many times for someone to talk to, but it would have been a waste using a human therapist. What do they know about our world and struggles? But I also couldn't use a shifter one, not while avoiding the cities."

At one point in time, I'd considered her weak and untrustworthy as she ran from the cities and her mates. But now that I could look at her situation without the cloak of my own trauma clouding my judgement, I recognized the strength it must have taken to keep herself safe.

To live amongst humans.

To suppress her wolf and her true self.

"I'm sorry you went through that," I said, hoping she'd hear the sincerity in my tone. "I think you're pretty fucking brave and amazing to have fought for your freedom the way you did. I wish I had half your strength."

Physically, I was a thousand times stronger than her, but mentally she had me beat. Hopefully one day I'd be the bear she needed and deserved—more than a broken shell of a shifter. And until I dealt with my trauma, I would fight not to taint her with my darkness.

Not ever again.

CHAPTER 40

EMME

Despite my every intention to remain impartial to Finley, I was already softening toward the bear. This new version of him was open and caring as he shared his pain and trauma, rather than using it to turn words into weapons.

Earlier when I'd reached out and grasped his hand in the garage, I'd been seconds from hugging him. It was only the worry that pushing too fast could set us back which stopped me—along with a small fear of his rejection. Though, for the first time, I didn't expect that to be the case.

When he got out of the car at therapy, I locked the vehicle and followed him. Driving such a magnificent piece of machinery should have been a highlight today, but everything dimmed beside Finley. The way he'd talked about his pack and *me*… there was no car on Earth that could compare.

"We're a few minutes early," he said as he held the glass door open for me.

We stepped inside to find the space decorated in a very neutral palette, with just a few ferns scattered around to add to the tranquil and calming environment. "Good morning, Alpha Finley," the shifter behind the front desk called. "Dr. Karen is almost finished up and will be with you shortly."

She beamed at Finley, exuding the sort of warmth that was rare to experience from a stranger. She looked older than us—if she was human, I'd estimate her to be in her late fifties. But as a shifter, she could be closer to a hundred. Her hair was a deep chestnut, with just a few strands of gold highlights, and her dark brown skin matched her eyes.

I'd never met anyone with such a genuine smile, and I wanted to walk closer and bask in all that maternal warmth. Or at least what I assumed was maternal, as I'd never had a real mother to compare it to. If I didn't get myself together, this poor receptionist was about to become the recipient of all my mommy issues.

Finley caught and squeezed my hand, drawing me toward the padded chairs along the wall. "She has a way about her, right?" he murmured near my ear, and I barely contained the shiver that traced down my spine.

"Her smile rolled me," I said as I breathed shallowly through my mouth to counter his scent.

If I thought the receptionist had rolled me, Finley flattened me dead.

His chuckle was low and warm. "Her name is Katya, and her family is one of the original founders of Golden Claw. She's ancient—not even I know her age, but she's beloved in this city. It's actually because of Katya that I chose this therapist."

Curiosity had me wondering if her age was the reason she exuded peace—I'd never met any older shifters before—or if it was her family line. Either way, it was curious to experience.

Finley and I sat in comfortable silence, our shoulders pressed together, as we floated in Katya's calming presence. A few minutes later, the therapist appeared in the reception area, leading out a blond wolf shifter.

"I'll see you next week, Caroline," she called, waving off her previous client before she turned to us. "Finley and Emme. I'm so happy to see you both. Come, let's get started."

It didn't surprise me that she knew my name, as I expected Finley had spoken of me, but she said it like we were already old friends. I'd also noticed her leave off the *alpha* on Finley's name, but he didn't show any sign of annoyance. This wasn't his first session, and I would guess they'd already established their wants and needs in greetings.

When we followed the therapist down the hall, I tried not to react to Finley's heat and energy sending tingles down my spine. I'd spent a long time denying my attraction for him, but I had always been drawn to the bear. It was a combination of lust, anger, need, want, and obsession. A true fucking obsession.

Even when I'd been doing everything in my power to ignore him, the obsession never went anywhere.

As hurt as I'd been with Finley, my heart and wolf had already forgiven him, especially with him showing up every damn day and putting in the work.

Filling the chasm.

"Welcome back, Finley," Dr. Karen said as she gestured for us to take a seat in a pair of plush chairs on the other side of the coffee table, "and welcome to you, Emme. I've heard a lot about you so far, and I am so pleased to see you here. I'm Dr. Karen of the Whipsnar pack, but please call me Karen. We're not formal here."

"Thank you, Karen," I said, sinking into the soft cushion. "It's lovely to meet you too."

She took a seat on the other side of us. I couldn't figure out how old she was, but I got the sense she had a few decades on us. Her light brown hair was pulled up into a loose bun at the back of her head, her olive skin was flawless, and her large blue eyes were framed behind dark-rimmed glasses. I eyed them for a beat, wondering if I'd ever seen a shifter with glasses before, and she laughed as she adjusted their frames on her face.

"I have a slight issue with focusing on smaller text after a few hours," she explained, somehow noticing my confusion. "It's rare in shifters but can affect eagles. It's related to our switch between beast and normal vision. I quite like them though."

I found myself smiling at her easy-going manner. "They do suit you."

"Well, thank you," she said as she settled back in her chair. "In regard to therapy today, I will catch you up quickly with what's been happening during our sessions. We've had quite a few sessions so far, delving into the earlier years of Finley's life. He wanted me to discuss with you our very first session." I swallowed roughly, and hoped they couldn't hear the way my pulse raced. I had no idea what she was about to say, and that made me nervous.

"I explained to him that the sort of deep trauma that Finley deals with isn't 'curable,'" she said with a nod, "in the sense we understand the word. It's a part of who he is now, but I also explained that I'm confident he will learn how to healthily channel his pain and move forward to a brighter future. That's what I'm here for, to provide him with the tools he needs to deal with triggers and regressions." She pulled her focus from me and met Finley's gaze. "As we discussed, you will most likely need years of therapy, maybe even a lifetime. But it won't always be this raw and hard for you."

Finley's expression gave me hope, as he made no pretense of shying away from that truth. "I'll be in therapy until I'm healed enough to never take my trauma out on Emme or anyone I care about again." He shrugged. "If that takes a lifetime, then so be it."

Dr. Karen looked pleased by his response. "Your determination is an excellent start," she said, "and the fact that you're here, willing and ready to open up to Emme, is the next step. You're not hiding from it any longer, and I'm already convinced that we can cut our therapy back to twice a week soon." When he nodded she continued.

"Today, Finley wants to take you through some of what he experienced growing up. We've spoken in detail about forgiveness, and what it can take to genuinely demonstrate remorse and show signs of change. Part of what he's revealing here today will hopefully help you understand him better, and explain the reasons he reacted so negatively to your *rejection* of the quintet."

"Even though my past is no excuse," Finley cut in, and Karen only smiled at his interruption. "I'm not excusing any of my actions, but I do hope that if you learn more about my past, it might bring us closer together."

"I'm ready to hear whatever you have to tell me," I said, wishing we were doing this in private, even though I sensed a professional in the room would be helpful.

Finley let out a deep breath. "Okay, great." He paused and wiped his hands down his jeans, and no one interrupted as he got his thoughts together. "My mother was an addict," he finally said, and I turned to give him my undivided attention. "At first it was alcohol with additives, but after the birth of my younger brother, she moved on to *shiftex*."

I flinched, having heard of the highly addictive powder, which was the only drug to alter a shifter's brain chemistry.

"When I was growing up, my father worked for a large factory, doing mostly forklift operations, and was gone for long hours. As fathers go, he was absent but not abusive."

In my opinion, remaining absent when your children suffered at home was a form of abuse. He had a duty of care to his children, and to his mate also, who clearly needed help.

"Mother, though, was always abusive," Finley continued, his voice flat. "It started small, just like her addiction. She hated being alone, so she'd wake me at all hours of the day and night, even when I was young and napping. She'd wake me in the harshest ways, by slapping my face or dropping a full cup of ice-cold water on me. I still don't sleep well, even though years have passed since I was roused from sleep like that."

He had been looking forward, his eyes glazed over as his mind drifted to the past, and I jumped when he turned to me suddenly. "The only night I've ever slept well was when we packed huddled around Kellan. I feel safe with my pack, and especially you."

My heart was in a stranglehold as I stared into his whiskey eyes, captured once again by the swirls of pain in their depths. "I'm here if you need me," I said, clearing my throat. "If you need me to watch over or sit next to you while you sleep, I can be that shifter for you."

The corner of his lips curled up, and the hammering of my heart eased. "I might take you up on that offer."

He returned to staring ahead. "One of the worst memories of my childhood was the feeling of being abandoned over and over again by the very shifters who were supposed to love, protect, and shelter me. From missing birthdays and school trips, to starvation when I was locked in my room for a week. There wasn't a day I didn't suffer under my mother, until eventually I gave up caring."

Finley spent the next thirty minutes detailing so much of his fucked-up past that I felt queasy by the time he was done. "The night my mom flipped out and killed Dad and Tommy, my brother," he rasped, his voice strained, "I ended up killing her before she could finish me off too. After that, I started to actively search for my pack. Well, once Kenzo dragged me out of my bear form. I was determined to find a family, and honestly, they're everything I could have hoped for.

"Hunter took in a broken teenager and supported my dreams of playing hockey. I'd never played much in a league, but I could skate better than I walked, and with Hunter's connections, I was soon trained up. Kellan joined me not long after, and for the first time in my life, I was content in my world."

My throat was dry as I considered that I was the first negative to come into his world since his mother, and I blew it all to pieces. No wonder he'd said that I reminded him of her.

"How did you find your pack?" I asked, desperately trying not to fall apart.

"There's a scent match registry," Finley explained, and while I vaguely knew about that, I wasn't aware it could be used by the general shifter population to find their packs. "After your first shift, your scent is loaded to the registry, and if you want them to, they will provide information on the candidates who could be a match. Or those who would make a strong quintet. Meetings are set up, and everything goes from there. I met with two packs before Hunter, and as soon as that asshole's arrogant face appeared, I knew he was my brother. My bear knows his pack."

Karen nodded. "Yes, our beasts are often in tune when we are in denial." She leaned forward in her chair. "Now, our time is almost up, but before we wrap for today, don't forget you wanted to explain what happened when she arrived in Golden Claw."

I thought I had a fairly strong understanding of why my arrival triggered Finley, so I was curious about what else he wanted to tell me. "My entire existence after my family died was wrapped up in finding the place I belonged," Finley reiterated. "In my pack I found the acceptance and support I'd been denied for most of my life. I'd really had no one before that —even my brother and I were kept apart by my mother's jealous and narcissistic rages. After their deaths, my pack was my family, and I was excited by the prospect of a final piece to our quintet. Only you… rejected us. It was like being thrown back to when my mother destroyed me. When I was alone and without an anchor in my fucked-up life. I was that damn broken cub, at the mercy of another who didn't want—"

He choked up, and I shifted toward him, grasping his hand. "I'm so sorry," I whispered, my voice rough from my unexpressed pain. "I'm so damn sorry. I was scared and uneducated when I was dragged here, and I wish I could take back those early actions that hurt you." As painful as it was, I didn't look away from him for a second. "It was never my intention to hurt any of you, I just wanted to survive. I'd been running on survival instincts for so long, I almost forgot that there were real alphas with real feelings on the other side of the pack I feared—who had done nothing wrong and shouldn't be punished for the actions of others."

Finley's eyes darkened, and I squeaked when he reached out with his free hand and gripped the base of my chair, dragging me around until we were face to face. I wanted to glance at Karen to gauge her reaction, but I couldn't tear my gaze from *him*.

"You did nothing wrong," he rumbled, sounding pissed but *not at me* for once. "Your reactions make perfect sense, and I should have focused more on figuring out why you were scared and running, rather than hating you for scars you didn't cause. Even a fucking idiot could see you were terrified, and not just a normal sort of terror, but a deep-seated fear that comes from true suffering." He moved closer until I could count every one of his thick, dark lashes. "I won't make that mistake again. I promise. I will be here with and for you, through every dark step. You won't ever be alone again, Emme. That much I promise—" I lost control and cut him off.

With my lips.

Against his.

Holy fuck.

CHAPTER 41

EMME

Before Finley even had a chance to process what I'd done, I tore myself away and sucked in a deep, ragged breath. Even as my instincts—*wolf*—pushed me to close the distance once more. *Stop it*, I growled at my beast, and she just shook her head as if to say, *That wasn't me.*

The shock on Finley's face was almost my undoing, and I frantically searched for a way to repair the damage I'd created with that stupid, *stupid*, move. "I am so damn sorry," I forced out through my tight throat. "That was… I just… there was so much happening and I temporarily lost my mind."

Holy fuck. I was acting like a fumbling teen who had never been kissed. I would be so fucking mad at myself if I'd just derailed the progress Finley was making.

He still hadn't moved, his eyes blazing as he stared at me. Shadows danced in the whiskey depths, darkening the color to a burnt gold, and I braced myself for his response.

"I'm sorry," I repeated, my voice breaking.

He lurched forward, both hands cupping my face as he held me in a stare so desperate and needy that it sent my heart into palpitations. "I've waited so damn long," he breathed, and then his mouth was on mine, and terrible idea or not, I kissed him back.

He tasted like sorrow and pain and *forever*.

I was consumed by his sweetness, and I wasn't surprised to find his kiss was almost as dominant as Hunter's. He took full control of the pace, as his tongue slid between my parted lips. "I've waited so fucking long to taste you," he repeated. "A fucking lifetime."

A million lifetimes.

I'd craved Finley—and the rest of my pack—for what felt like an eternity. I might have denied it when I'd run, but deep in my soul and essence, this was all I ever wanted.

The sound of a door closing registered in the back of my mind, and I'd completely forgotten that the therapist was in the room with us. A therapist who knew exactly when to leave the safe space she'd created. Finley and I were a scent match, and as a shifter, she understood the bond.

Finley slowly released my face, but his lips remained close to mine, as his hands traced down my spine. When he curved them over my butt, he flexed and hauled me into his lap. The sudden change in position had reality crashing into me, and I stiffened in his hold.

He stilled just as quickly, and angled his head to take in my expression, as our breaths mingled in harsh huffs.

Longing and need raged through me when he rumbled softly. "Too soon?"

Yes. No. *Maybe.*

"I don't know," I finally admitted.

With a sigh, he dropped his forehead against mine. "I won't stop working toward earning your trust and love, Emme. I promise. There's no rush."

For the first time, I believed him. "I have a whole bunch of hope for us simmering in my gut, Finley Thornton."

He crushed me into his chest, and the choked sound that burst from me was guttural.

He hugged like a bear, surrounding me completely, as he forced out everything I was keeping contained. My hands clawed against his chest, as if to push him away, but instead I found myself clutching his shirt like my life depended on it.

"I've got you, darlin'," he whispered against the side of my throat as he breathed me in. "I won't ever let go again. And I never break my fucking promises."

Sobs rattled in my chest, and my center cracked under the pressure of his overwhelming and consuming hug.

"Neither of us had enough hugs in our life," he continued in that low, soothing bear rumble. "But I will make up for that for the rest of your existence. I will hug you every damn second of every damn day until you know how precious you are."

My eyes burned, and squeezing them together did nothing to stem the hot fall of tears down my cheeks. His shirt absorbed the moisture, and I wasn't sure he knew how affected I was.

"I needed this," he whispered, a tone of reverence lingering in those words. "I need you."

A scream built in my chest, and I wanted to hide from this intense overreaction to a simple hug. But Finley wouldn't let me. "Let it out, darlin'," he murmured against my skin. "This room is soundproof. There's no one to know but me, and I will take it to my grave."

The pain swelling inside me built until it couldn't be contained. I pressed my face harder against him and howled into his chest. I'd always known that it was this shifter, out of all of them, who'd bring about my greatest emotional destruction.

Finley never let go, not until the constriction in my chest eased, and when I finally found a semblance of calm, I realized he was rocking me back and forth. The gentle, soothing motion helped to restore my equilibrium.

"I think we might have overstayed your appointment time," I rasped, my throat sore from the release. I felt utterly depleted, but also emotionally lighter than before we walked in here.

His deep chuckle reverberating through his chest added another soothing sensation to the rocking. "The doc has multiple offices. She'll be fine."

When I found the strength to lift my head, I stared into his eyes, and caught sight of a few tracks of moisture on his cheek.

"Thank you," he said, brushing back my hair as his expression softened. "I'm fairly sure that moment with you was worth at least a year of therapy all on its own."

I nodded as my lips trembled; our chasm now barely more than a deep hole. "Yeah, for me too."

His hands went around my hips as he stood with me in his arms, and I relished the last few seconds of being held by him, until he placed me gently on my feet. "Come on, Em," he said, sounding lighter too. "Let's get you home."

Katya wore her warm smile as we entered the reception area. "See you next time, Alpha Finley," she called. "It was lovely to meet you, Omega Emmeline."

"Lovely to meet you too," I called back. Finley gave her a respectful nod while holding the door open for me.

When we reached the car, I handed Finley the key, knowing I was far too unsettled to be controlling a powerful vehicle. He opened my door, and though we no longer touched, my awareness of him remained sky high. I *felt* him even without touch.

By the time the car thrummed to life, I was somewhat under control. "I'm proud of you," I said, as he pulled out into traffic. He shot me another one of those slightly broken smiles. "I know you haven't heard that much in your life, but you did fucking good, Grouchy Bear. You're loyal to those you care about. You play hockey like a dream, and bring old cars back to life, and throw down for your family. I know you weren't taught any of that from your parents, which means you did it all on your own."

He didn't have Hunter's ability to take his eyes from the road for an hour and not crash, but he did look back and forth a lot, as if attempting to unravel a hidden meaning behind my words.

"I was just surviving," he finally said, shrugging it off. "Until my pack came along. I owe them for a lot of what I have in my life."

"It was a team effort, but I understand what you're saying." It was my turn to shrug. "Not that I have much to brag about, but I did okay as a waitress with limited reading skills and a semi-decent driving ability—"

"Not to mention the best fucking pastry chef." Finley growled. "You've got a lot to brag about, Emmeline Anders. You're a survivor. You have strength that most would hope to possess. I wouldn't choose a different mate, not even if the goddess lined up every single female shifter in the world."

That statement was powerful, and it went a long way in reassuring me that he wasn't just making an effort because there was no other choice.

"I'm not ashamed of who I am," I told him. "I did what I needed to survive. Though…" I pulled a face. "…would it have been too much to ask that the rest of you weren't like the top fucking tier of alphas."

Finley flashed me dimples and a semi-smug grin. "If we're exceptional, then you have to admit you are as well. You'd never be a scent match otherwise."

I snorted. "Maybe the goddess knew that no one else could handle your arrogant asses and massive egos."

That kicked his smile up another notch. "You know that none of us care about success in the way of making money or having fancy titles. We care about loyalty and passion and showing up for each other. In that regard, you're more than our equal."

And now I was dead.

"We might have to switch your group chat name back to Care Bear," I murmured, only half kidding.

Finley closed his eyes briefly, before he shrugged. "You know what, if it comes from you, then I'll accept it. But if Kellan does it, I'll be forced to hurt him."

Kellan got threatened almost every time he was in the group chat, so I doubted Finley's words would deter him.

Our conversation switched to hockey for the rest of the journey, and we arrived home to find everyone waiting for us in the dining room. When I settled into my chair beside Hunter, I was filled with contentment from my bonds. Today with Finley had been a positive step forward in healing our quintet, and it had already seeped through to the others.

Kellan leaned over to press a kiss to my lips, his nose gently grazing my cheek as he breathed me in. "I can feel your happiness, pretty mate," he said. "Next time, I'll be the one taking you on a date."

Finley, who hadn't reached his chair yet, rolled his eyes at his brother. "It was therapy, you fucking moron. Our *pretty mate* will know when we go on a date, don't you worry."

My insides tightened as my stomach flip-flopped and my wolf howled.

Kellan gawked at Finley, his mouth open, while Hunter and Slade leaned back in their chairs, the former wearing a satisfied stare as he swirled his whiskey and murmured, "All in its own time."

For the first time, I believed that our entitled alpha had known how this would work out all along.

No wonder he was such a smug bastard.

CHAPTER 42

EMME

That night, after Hunter and Kellan wore me out by edging me closer to the art of double penetration—we weren't there yet, but we were so deliciously close—I fell into an exhausted sleep. Only to find myself startling awake not even two hours later.

The tendrils of a dream I couldn't remember coated my skin, and my body tingled as if energy or magic had caressed it. By the time I shook off the strange sensation, I knew I wouldn't be falling asleep for a while, and not wanting to wake the alphas, I slid out from between them.

Snatching one of their shirts from the floor, I headed for the kitchen in search of a snack—I might not have been baking much lately, but Florence's cookies were to die for, and a loaded chocolate chip sounded like the key to shedding the last of my dream.

The house was dark and quiet, and while I loved the sounds of my pack, the silence wasn't uncomfortable. Not when this place always felt like home.

My first real home.

As I passed through the front entryway, I caught a familiar clang from the garage. Without giving myself time to consider the consequences of my actions, I switched directions and hurried down the stairs. Low lights illuminate the vehicles, and I stopped to give my new bike a gentle caress. "Soon, sweet girl," I crooned, my gaze lingering on all her pink and black curves. "And this time I'll keep you safe."

Goddess, let that not be an empty promise.

"One day I hope you look at me the way you look at that bike." Finley's deep rumble washed over my back, and I spun to find him propped against a pillar.

He wore his overalls, and had a few grease stains dirtying up his gorgeous face. His hat was on backwards to hold his hair in place, a style which should be classified as a weapon against females everywhere. "It's a look of love," he finished.

Sweet fucking mercy. My voice turned playful even as my legs went weak. "Letting me help you fix up your car is a great way to build a look of love, don't you think?"

I'd offered once before, and it hadn't gone over so well. This time though, when Finley's gaze lingered on my bare legs, tracing up to the hem of the shirt that fell to mid-thigh, his expression was heavy with desire. "I thought you'd never ask, darlin'. Come on. Let's bring this old girl back to life."

This was the third time he'd called me *darlin'*, and in that low drawl of his rumbly bear it was as powerful as his backwards cap. Basically, I was screwed when it came to resisting Finley Thornton.

He held out a hand, and I barely hesitated before sliding my palm against his. When he tightened his grip, my body tightened with it. As positive as I was that standing here, *almost* naked and emotionally vulnerable was a bad idea, it was too late to turn back now.

Finley led me to the section of garage he used to rebuild his cars. His Ford still occupied the first bay, but in the second sat the car he'd gifted me for my birthday.

A broad smile ripped across my face. "She's here," I said. "And while I love her just as she is, with a few repairs she'll be spectacular."

"I haven't touched her," Finley assured me. "I've been waiting for you. Want to take a closer look?"

"Do dragons fly and cause mass hysteria?" I huffed, pressing my hand to my chest.

He rumbled out a laugh and led me around his Ford. He never let go of my hand, not even as he detailed the issues we faced with the Bronco, and what he had in mind to return her to her former glory.

"So, what do you think? Ready to get started on bringing her back to life?"

He stared at me, and I nodded. "Listening to you talk about cars reminds me of the few happy memories in my past." I wanted to share this piece of myself after he'd shared so much in therapy. "And I'm so fucking excited to do this with you. Where should we start? Tell me what you need me to do?"

I knew about cars, but I'd never been hands-on in repairing them.

Finley tugged me closer, and his unbridled enthusiasm caught on as I bounced briefly on my bare feet. When he noticed my lack of foot coverings, Finley detoured to a bag hanging on a peg on the wall, releasing me long enough to rifle through the contents. He emerged victorious with a pair of thick black socks.

"They're clean," he assured me, those dimples assaulting my senses as he knelt at my feet. "Now lift. I don't want you getting cold."

Even with climate control, the garage floors were cool, not that it was enough to bother me. Still, I didn't argue as he lifted my right foot, and then my left, dragging the thick socks almost to my knees. It was only as he adjusted the elastic on one that he seemed to notice his proximity to my vagina, barely hidden under Hunter's shirt.

Finley's hands tightened on my thighs as his gaze darkened and he breathed deeply. "Fuck," he groaned, closing his eyes as if that would help. "You're a temptation I would follow into hell and beyond."

I completely forgot the plan to move slowly as I was hit with an urge to thrust my hips until his mouth landed right on the ache in my core. All I could think about was the scrape of his beard on my thighs, and the flick of his tongue across my clit, as he buried his face between my—

With a startled growl, Finley launched to his feet. "Whatever you're imagining, darlin'," he winced, "please stop. Your scent is…" A choked desperate sound spilled from his lips and I shuffled back a few steps to create space.

I'd put the restrictions in place by telling him to earn my trust and repair the chasm between us, and yet here I was, flashing my needy vagina in his face like a selfish asshole.

"I'm sorry," I said, shame coating my cheeks in heat. "I'm not making this easy on you—I should go and put a few more clothes on."

As I turned, Finley lurched forward and caught my hand, twirling me back into him. "No. I don't want it to be easy." He pulled me closer. "I don't deserve easy, and more than that, I know that all of this buildup is only going to make it that much sweeter when I finally win you back. Keep making it hard, Em. Please."

I would challenge any damn shifter in the world to be able to say no to Finley when he was like this. "Okay, I can do that," I told him.

He kissed my cheek, and then moved to press another to the corner of my lips, before he released me and steered us back to the cars.

For the next two hours we worked in comfortable companionship, our conversations casual as we discussed our favorite vehicles and dream cars. "I've always been into the bigger trucks and off-roaders," Finley told me, leaning into the open hood. "While the track gave me a newfound appreciation for speed and competition, I'm the one you want with you if you're heading off the beaten track and need to push your car's suspension to its limits."

"I've always been into bikes," I said, handing over the tool he needed before he even asked. "Which had a lot to do with availability, speed, and price. The way I feel when I'm surrounded by these super and hyper cars indicates that maybe I just love anything with an engine that goes fast."

Finley tilted his head to the side to meet my gaze, and in the dim lighting his expression was wreathed in amusement. "We need to race again," he said. "This time just you and me."

The very thought had a jolt of excitement in my gut. "You want to get your ass kicked again?"

He threw his head back and laughed, his hands still buried in the engine. "Famous last words, Emmeline. I think I'll take that challenge. Name the place and time."

I found myself chuckling with him. "I'm ready whenever you are. Not this week, though, right? Kel told me you've got a road trip for hockey…?"

That sobered him as he returned his focus to the engine bay. "Yep, we've got three away games, which means we'll be gone Monday through Friday."

Before he could look my way again, I forced my features into calm, unbothered lines, which turned out to be a waste of energy. Finley noticed immediately. "We can stay if it upsets you," he said, and I got a hint that he kind of hoped I'd make them stay. "It's just hockey, and we're top of the division."

I narrowed my eyes on him. "Absolutely fucking not. I can survive a few days without you both, as long as my bond with Kellan handles the distance."

Finley released his hold on the car and took a step toward me. "You shouldn't have to survive. Come with us."

He paused in front of me, and I was about to agree before I remembered one glaring issue: "I can't leave without Talon. His is the newest bond. And on top of that, our connection remains slightly frayed and patchy."

Talon's bond did filter through bits and pieces of his emotions, but it wasn't as strong as with Hunter and Kellan.

The bear shot a frustrated glare in the direction of the hidden doorway. "Annoying motherfucker," he mumbled under his breath. "But you're probably right, which means we should just blow off these games and stay here."

I pressed my hand to his chest in the hopes of reiterating how serious I was. "Not a chance, Finley Thornton." His nostrils flared as he stared down at my touch. "You've already missed too many games because of me. It's not fair to you or your team for you guys to just blow it off. We can chat on the phone daily, and I'll watch your games on the sports network."

He didn't look convinced, and I was too tired to argue more tonight. "We can talk about it tomorrow," he finally said, before he glanced at the clock on the wall, which read two a.m. "Or today to be more accurate." He patted my hand on his chest. "Go to bed, Ice Queen. I'll clean up and get some rest too."

"Will you sleep?" I asked, noticing the fatigue on his features. "I can sit with you."

His stare was penetrating, and at first I thought he'd refuse until he said, "Yeah, okay. I'd like that."

In my relief that he wouldn't be alone, I was hit with another thought, one that might not go over so well. "Uh, I have a bit of an extreme idea that might help both of us and someone else."

Finley didn't even ask for any further clarification. "Works for me. Let me get cleaned up and I'll meet you… where?"

Forcing myself to remain calm I said, "In the containment room."

His eyes widened, and when his gaze flicked toward the door, I all but held my breath until he sighed. "Yeah, let's do it. Might as well get used to that bastard being around. See you in a minute, Ice."

While Finley disappeared to clean himself up, I raced up the stairs to pull blankets and pillows from the hallway storage. By the time I'd returned to the garage, arms filled, Finley was waiting in a pair of sleep shorts, and he hurried over to take the bedding from my arms.

I opened the door and strode through first, unsurprised to find Talon already at the bars, as if he'd been waiting for me all along. The fluttering in our bond flared as I drank in the sight of him after days of being apart. When his chest rumbled, I couldn't stop from rushing forward, Finley's protests lost as I hit the bars and reached for the dragon.

"Sweet Honey," Talon breathed, the growl of his dragon following again as he snarled, "don't take another step closer, bear. Give me this moment with her."

I breathed in his scent as he held me close, and even with the bars between us, I was comfortable in his touch. "You took too long to return to me," he rumbled, inhaling deeply against the top of my head. "I almost broke out again."

It had been too long, and it had affected me too, even if I'd been pretending otherwise. "I'll try and be here more," I said, knowing we both needed it. "But I wish you'd just give them the information they need to trust you. Then you could be free."

Talon shifted back to see my face. "I can't, mate. While I won't hurt you or any of your pack, I remain loyal to their enemy, and I see no reason to change that."

A spike of hurt at his statement had me pulling away to create distance between us. "You proclaim to be my mate," I said roughly, "and yet you would hand me over to an alpha who wants to hurt me. The alpha who killed my mother."

His expression remained hard and unyielding. "You are mine. No one will ever hurt you again. Alpha knows the deal, and he has assured me we will rule together."

Finley's laughter was broken and completely devoid of any humor. "You're one stupid motherfucker if you believe that."

The darkness in his voice reminded me of the Finley I first met, and I found I didn't mind his raging bear when it wasn't directed at me.

Not that I had the energy for a fight to break out tonight. "Let's leave the battle for later," I said with a yawn. "All of us need rest."

Even Talon looked exhausted, and it took a lot for the dragons to show weakness.

I directed Finley to set out the bedding beside the bars. "None of us should be alone tonight," I said as I slid down on the soft material, on the side closest to Talon.

The dragon's hands were in my hair not even a breath later, and I sighed at how good it felt when he played with the length. He grabbed the brush from last time, and started to run it through the strands until I was a relaxed puddle.

Finley watched us closely before releasing an aggravated sound. "Touch her in any way she doesn't like and I'll break your hand off."

He dropped down on my other side and stretched out his huge length. We didn't touch at first, until I reached out and pressed my hand against his chest. "Sleep, Grouchy," I whispered. "We'll watch over you."

Talon's dragon rumbled, but he didn't deny it, and to my surprise it took less than five minutes for Finley's breathing to even out as he went to sleep.

To stem the tidal wave of emotion crashing into me, I reached up and grasped Talon's hand, the brush stilling between us as I sought an anchor. In this moment, caught between the two alphas who'd hurt me the most, I was truly starting to believe that we might all be each others' salvations.

CHAPTER 43

TALON

My dragon demanded release.

He didn't fight my cage often, but when he did, it was often beyond my ability to keep him contained. *No, we would hurt her if we shifted. Have patience.*

He roared back, and the bass in that rumble suggested he was done with patience. It had been too long since she'd come to us, and now that she was here, we couldn't let her go.

When her hand went limp in sleep, I internally raged at the bone-deep exhaustion seeping through our bond. Wanting her to keep resting, I continued to slide the brush through her hair, unsurprised to find I was tired too. While I had more than enough time down here to get the few hours of sleep I required to function at full strength, without Emmeline it was an empty and restless slumber.

My gaze dragged over the male at her other side and I shelved my relatively minor urge to destroy him. As if he'd felt that flicker of a threat, his eyes slowly opened and met mine. He stared into the depths of my beast and didn't blink or look away. He held my stare as if he'd battled true evil before and had walked out the other side.

A sliver of respect had me inclining my head, and the bear appeared satisfied enough to close his eyes once more. I felt the calming of his beast, and as his hand drifted up to cover Emme's, which rested on his chest, he slipped into a true deep sleep.

I found myself stupidly invested in ensuring neither of them were awoken.

Alpha would beat the shit out of me if he sensed these softer emotions, and yet… this instinct to protect them was ingrained as deeply as my instinct to conquer shifters.

For hours I watched over them, my fingers tangled in the silky strands of Emme's hair, relishing in the moments I caressed a sliver of her soft skin or caught a waft of chocolate and honey. This omega held me in her clutches, and with that came the sort of power I wasn't sure she understood she possessed.

His energy reached me a few moments before he silently padded into the room. I never tore my gaze from the omega as he watched us both.

"We all look at her that way," Slade murmured, his voice so like my own. Dragon touched. "Like we would not only watch the world burn for her but be the fuckers who razed it to the ground."

That was where Emmeline's true power stemmed from. We would all turn villain the second anyone threatened her. I just had to ensure Alpha didn't make that mistake and force my hand against him. Surely, he knew better than to even try.

"What do you want, brother?"

Slade didn't physically react when I addressed our twin bond, but his scent flared. The connection bothered him, and for that reason alone I continued to remind him of it. "We might need to return to the volcano."

His statement was the first thing to capture my interest since Emme had entered the room. Reluctantly, I tore my gaze from her to meet his. "Why?"

He kicked his legs a few feet apart and leaned against the wall with his arms crossed. "We need to explore the twin soul connection, and my research indicates it might have to take place where our egg was found. With our ancestor's energy."

What he said made sense, but I wasn't interested. "I don't need to explore anything. I don't need you or the connection. My beast and I are copacetic, and I can protect my mate just fine."

Slade scoffed. "I detest a liar. You have a rift too, I can feel it. This might be our chance to claim our true strength and be the mates Emmeline deserves."

There he went, mentioning the one fucking thing that might get me to consider his idea. "What makes you think I won't run off to Alpha the moment you free me."

Slade's smirk was knowing, and I wished I was close enough to smack it off his face. "Because you obviously could have left any time you wanted. You're staying for her, and you won't hurt her like that. I may not trust anything else about you, but I trust that *you* believe you care about Emme."

Emme would have to travel with us, otherwise our new bond would cause her pain. Which meant there'd be no bars between us. "What happens with me after we figure out the twin soul connection?"

Slade looked like he'd rather kick me in the nuts than answer, but he had no choice. "What do you want?"

That was not as easy an answer as he might have expected. I couldn't return to Alpha without Emme, and yet taking her without her other alphas would cause her pain. I refused to allow her to return to the weak, broken shifter she'd been in the bunker. "I want you all to meet with Alpha. Hear him out. Hear his plan out. See if we can negotiate some sort of path forward that we all agree on." My fingers briefly tightened in her hair, but I kept my hold gentle enough not to wake her.

Slade's scent grew stronger as the room heated, and my beast lifted to the surface, searching for energy that I didn't understand. "I can't promise anything without speaking to Hunter, but you should know, if I'm in the same room as your *alpha*, I'm going to murder him. What he did to Emme... that must be punished."

A part of me couldn't argue. "That's between you and Alpha, but just know, I'm not the only shifter who would stand before him. You will have to go through all of us."

Slade glanced down at Emme. "Maybe you'll feel differently when we find our twin bond."

I couldn't quite figure out why he was so focused on this twin connection, and I had my doubts it'd make any difference to our power, but I was willing to give it a try. "Fine, I will agree to explore the connection with you, and in return, you will give Alpha your time and a chance to convince you of the new future for shifters."

We remained locked in a stare-off until eventually he grunted. "Fucking fine. I will choose the meeting place. Non-negotiable."

"I have to talk to Alpha, but as long as it's safe for both parties, there's no reason he'd refuse. He wants you and Hunter on board. You're his sons as well."

Slade's dragon soared to the surface, and my own thundered until I couldn't tell if he wanted to meet the other beast… or kill it.

"We're not his sons. We're nothing to him, and he's nothing to us. Sentimentality and a deal he made long ago has kept him alive all of these years. But that ran out the second he touched our omega. He should consider us his enemies at best."

The instinct to destroy anyone who was a risk to Alpha flared, but it was mild. Easily ignored. I was well trained to take out threats, but I found it harder to categorize this pack as a true danger. No doubt that would change the second they attacked him.

Then I wouldn't be able to stop myself.

"Don't be my enemy, brother," I warned him. "It won't end well."

The smile that tilted his lips was reminiscent of how I looked when a shifter was about to die. "It absolutely won't end well. *For you.*"

He left the room, but I knew he had eyes on us in here. I could hear the whirring of the cameras as they surveyed the containment cells. Slade and I were twin souls, but I didn't do technology. That wasn't for me, and I knew very little about it, even if I could easily tune in to its frequencies.

Having been deprived of the outdoors growing up, I preferred nature. Now, it was all I craved. Well, that and this omega sleeping so peacefully beside me.

Slade hadn't said when he planned for us to head to the origin of our birth, but just the thought of being outside, scenting the air and feeling the energy of the world around us, was enough to calm my beast. If we weren't removed from these rooms soon, I would have had to leave anyway.

For everyone's safety.

He was right, though, I would have returned.

I couldn't leave my sweet mate, not even for Alpha.

Despite being a prisoner here, my time wasn't the worst I'd experienced. Slade visited most days, and he was done with torture, so we spent our time in terse conversation. He told me about his life growing up with Alpha, and I told him about mine.

His had been far worse in regard to pain and torture, and mine had been far worse in regard to isolation and the expectation of complete obedience. Only one of us held loyalty to Alpha though, and I wondered if mine was due to my belief that the packs needed more structure.

That we were weakening in this current way of being governed.

Slade had suggested at one point that I should go out into the cities and see for myself, and as much as he pissed me off, it was a solid idea. I'd been trained to blindly obey, but in the end, I was stronger than almost all shifters in the world.

Alpha knew I chose to obey, and only because I believed in the agenda.

I'd placed my trust in his word that the cities were a mess and shifters weakening, but I was here now and could see for myself.

"What are you thinking about?"

My gaze jerked down to find Emme staring up at me, the piercing blue of her eyes softer as she blinked the sleepiness from her gaze.

"Could you show me around the cities?" I asked her.

Her brow furrowed. "What do you mean? You want to drive around and see Golden Claw?"

That was exactly what I wanted. "Alpha always taught me that we were stronger under a single, powerful alpha's rule, and I believe that he *believes* that. But I'm here, and I can assess for myself as well." My dragon rumbled in my chest, and for once it wasn't clear what his thoughts were.

Emme turned to fully face me, and as soon as her hand was removed from Finley, he started to stir. "I can take you into the city," she murmured, "but I'm not sure how it will prove Fletcher right or wrong. There are so many packs and shifters, and some are strong, while others hang on the fringe. But from what I know, the old ways were primitive, with many falling under cruel and barbaric rule. Now we have structures and new technology. We've advanced."

"That doesn't sound like advancement," I growled, just thinking about how confining buildings and technology felt. "We are beasts. Wild at heart. We need to live with the land for the sake of our animals."

"I agree," she said with a deep exhalation, "and we have both here. There are forests to run, and other packs to run with, but we also have a human side, right? Just catering to our beasts alone seems shortsighted."

Another truth, but for me the beast was the more dominant part of my personality. "Does Slade exist in this urban and technology driven world? I mean, does he thrive in it?"

Emme took a second to think that over. "Yeah, I guess he does. He wears suits to work at the office, which is this massive glass skyscraper, but then he's in his leathers when he trains and patrols with his enforcers. He also uses like a million cameras to keep us all under surveillance." Her expression softened, and I found myself happy to witness her deep respect for my brother. "He's a little of everything, which is how most shifters are these days. Your Alpha's plan would ensure that all these different sides of us were lost to the beast. Which feels a little… limited."

My beast was so strong that I never gave any consideration to the other side of being a shifter. For me, there were no other sides. There was my dragon, and then there was me waiting to release my dragon. "I'm not sure I have another side," I admitted, tilting my head back to stare into the darkened ceiling. I wanted to keep staring into her eyes, but I couldn't think clearly when I looked upon her.

I sensed her movement, and didn't physically react when she grasped my hand, holding on tightly. Fires lit in my center like we were about to level the world.

My gaze lowered back to her. "You are so much more than just your beast, Talon. Your life is just beginning, and there's an entire world to explore out there. I've been limited too. My life was about running and survival. I didn't pick up hobbies or interests. I don't collect plants or weapons like Kellan, I can't skate or create incredible origami like Finley. I wouldn't know where to start with inventing cool shifter tech like Hunter, and I sure as shit can't work a computer or fight like Slade. They're all far more well-rounded than me, but you know what you and I have in common…?"

"A mate bond?"

She chuckled. "Besides that, and just as a little aside, it's probably too soon to bring that up so casually."

Noted.

"What we have in common is time. We still have time to grow and learn about ourselves and our world. We have time to find hobbies and habits and become more productive shifters in this world. All of which could be lost under the control of your Alpha. There, we would be nothing more than his pack to control. We cannot let that stand."

"Even if it weakens the beast?" I questioned, unable to argue with a lot of her logic. "War could come for us, and most shifters have no idea how to survive it if that happens."

Finley was fully awake, listening intently, but Emme hadn't

noticed as she stared at me like I was the only shifter in the room. It was fucking intoxicating to hold her attention so thoroughly. "There's more to life than just surviving war. What if the Alpha's plan weakens our souls, Talon? What if it weakens our spirit? You can die in more than just a physical sense." Her voice wavered as she finished. "I was dying before I met my pack. I was slowly, day by day, turning into a shell. My spirit was broken, and I didn't even understand how badly I'd hurt myself and my wolf until I was finally set free."

When I met the bear's gaze over her shoulder, his eyes shone as he nodded his agreement.

For the first time, I started to consider that maybe… just maybe, I stood on the wrong side of this battle.

CHAPTER 44

EMME

The buzz of my phone reminded me that I hadn't checked it for days. There was never a need with one of my alphas in constant proximity, but Kellan and Finley had left this morning for hockey, and I was already feeling the strain in my chest from their absence.

My wolf whined, but she didn't retreat as she had the last time; my bond with Kellan was strained, but not debilitating.

Golden: We made it safe and sound. I hope you're all missing us. We're totally fine though. No sadness or tears, except from Finley when he got his bear paw caught in the door of our room. But I'M totally fine. *broken heart emoji* *Howling emoji*

My heart hurt even as I chuckled. My poor golden had been all misty-eyed when he'd left me this morning, even after kissing me stupid until I was breathless and throbbing. He'd been late for his ride to the airport, and it was all my fault, but there were no regrets from either of us.

Another ding sounded.

Yogi Bear: He cried for half the movie on the plane.

Yogi Bear: Kellan, I will not tell you again to change my fucking name. I'll even take Grouchy at this stage.

GOLDEN HAS CHANGED YOGI BEAR'S NAME

Golden: The movie was sad! Everyone cried.

Boo-Boo Bear: It was the Fast and the Furious. You were the only one who cried.

Boo-Boo Bear: Who the fuck is boo boo bear? These names are getting worse!!

The dings kept coming, and I was amazed to find that with the newly adjusted font, I kept up well. Definitely much better than before, even with the previously adjusted style.

Golden: Are you telling me that you know who Yogi Bear is but not Boo-Boo Bear? Blasphemy. You should be ashamed of yourself.

Boo-Boo Bear: I'm telling you that if you don't change my name, or show ME how to change my name, I will tell them all about the time you drank a bottle of tequila with additives and passed out in the locker-room.

GOLDEN HAS CHANGED BOO-BOO BEAR'S NAME

Finley Grouchy Thornton: I knew we'd see eye to eye on the situation.

Before I could reply in the text thread, though the boys appeared to be doing just fine on their own, Hunter popped into the conversation.

Daddy-o: Is Kellan sending out SOS signals with his eyes? Annoying pup doesn't want that story to get back to our omega, I bet.

And now I absolutely needed to know what happened.

Golden: Look, we all have stories to tell. Just remember that.

Slade: I don't.

Golden: Look, MOST of us have stories to tell, and I have a very long memory.

I quickly finished my message and sent it across.

Pretty Mate: Wait, I want to hear these stories. How long is your memory, Golden?

Finley Grouchy Thornton: It took him five minutes to remember our teammates' names this morning. They've played together for two years.

Golden: THAT'S DIFFERENT. Jones and Collins look the same! It's the blond hair.

Finley Grouchy Thornton: *eye roll emoji* They look completely different. And Collin's hair is brown. You're just too busy showing off to notice.

Golden: You say showing off, I say scoring goals. Same same.

I had no idea why I was laughing so hard, but some of the heartache that had been crushing me since they left eased with these texts.

Slade: You're making Emme happy. And that's the only reason I'm not flying to your hotel and smashing your phones under my damn boot.

Annndd there was my newest reminder that I was under constant, uninterrupted surveillance.

Which still didn't bother me.

Daddy-o: Can you morons focus for long enough to let us know what time your game is today. We want to catch it on the sports broadcast channel.

Finley Grouchy Thornton: Starts at six tonight. We'll be the ones in teal.

Hunter was no doubt also considering flying to the game and smacking them both up the side of the head.

Slade: I'll tap into the venue's cameras, and we can watch it in real time.

Golden: You guys better not pack huddle without us!! I almost died the last time you did that. Think of the children.

He was getting more ridiculous the longer this went on, and I was living for it.

Daddy-o: How do you really feel about death, Annoying Pup? I sense it's closing in on you again.

Finley Grouchy Thornton: *Image attached*

I clicked the attachment and found a photo of Kellan glancing timidly over his shoulder, as if ensuring Hunter hadn't somehow transported into the hotel room. He looked adorable, and my wolf and I were silently howling at how much it sucked to be apart from my alphas.

Finley Grouchy Thornton: It appears you've got him suitably worried. Nice work, Hunt. I might get a rest from his incessant whining about Emme tonight.

Golden: Wait! WAIT! Grouchy has been extra grouchy since we left, and I saw him looking at a photo of our mate on his phone. So. There. It's not just me.

The lurch in my stomach took me by surprise, but damn, that was kind of... hot. Knowing that Finley missed me too, even though he'd been such a different shifter lately, still took me by surprise.

> Pretty Mate: I miss you both! But, as an aside, I heard that Slade has a lot of photos of me on his stalker wall. If you don't mind googly eyes.

He hadn't mentioned the prank even once, and I was done waiting for him to bring it up.

My heart beat a little faster as I waited for his response.

> Slade: Oh, Snow. I will never share my stalker photos with anyone. They're safe and sound. Just like you are.

> Daddy-o: Yeah, that's not creepy at all, brother. Emme probably feels completely comforted.

> Slade: *shrugging emoji*

> Pretty Mate: I'm totally calm and fine. I'm not even remotely scared of Scary Shifter. What's the worst he could do.

I sent it and then immediately regretted challenging him like that. *Idiot.*

> Slade: You forget I can see you via the cameras, Emmeline Anders. You can't hide anything from me.

Leaning back on my bed, I flipped him off with both hands, and I wasn't surprised to hear a ding.

> Slade: I'm going to enjoy punishing the brat out of you, little mate. I'm going to enjoy it a lot.

And I was dead. Again.

Golden: You fuckers. You're going to naked pack snuggle without us, and I honestly don't love hockey enough to deal with this shit. *angry face emoji* This is goddess-be-damned unshifterly of you all, and I demand that you all stay in separate rooms until we return. *begging hands emoji*

Finley Grouchy Thornton: In completely related news, the game today is going to be very interesting as we think about you pack huddling without us. Hope I don't lose control of my bear and kill a few opponents.

Golden: Is it bad that I kind of want to see that? It's bad, isn't it? Hey, no one chimed in and said it's bad, so it's probably fine.

Daddy-o: Our plane is fueled and ready. One more fucking word from you Kellan.

Daddy-o: Good luck with your game today.

Pretty Mate: You are both amazing, and I'm so proud of you. Kick their asses today.

Kellan sent back a bunch of kissing emojis, and Finley sent one single pink heart. I might have stared at that heart for far too long before I threw the phone on the side table and headed into the bathroom to shower and get ready for the day.

When I was dressed in jeans, a shirt from Kellan that hung past my ass, and a hoodie from Finley, because he wasn't here to see me needing a hit of his scent, I ambled down the stairs and headed for the kitchen.

I heard voices before I entered the room, and wasn't surprised to find Hunter, Warrick, Cora, Slade, and Kassidy eating breakfast and chatting away. I eyeballed the pile of breakfast sandwiches before I greeted anyone, counting to make sure they had left me enough.

At Cora's snort of laughter, I glanced her way, and she wiggled her brows. "You owe me a hundred bucks," she said to her mate, and Warrick grinned even as he grumbled and slapped the note into her hand. "Should have known better than to bet on Emme not counting the sandwiches."

"I've made no secret of my priorities at breakfast," I said with a shrug.

Kassidy jumped to her feet, and I was struck by how gorgeous Hunter's sister looked in her skinny jeans and tight teal sweater. That family's genetics were exceptional, if you discounted the psychopathic tendencies of their father. "We've been waiting for you, Emme. It's girl's day. We don't want you wallowing without half your pack, so we thought we'd go out shopping."

I paused with a sandwich halfway toward my mouth, my gaze automatically finding Hunter, and then Slade, both of whom wore neutral expressions. "You two are letting me have a girls' day? What? With no security or anything?"

Hunter's lips twitched, and I had to remind myself that we had company, and it was not in my best interest to climb that damn alpha like a tree. "We arranged for one of the smaller stores to open just for you three. We'll wait outside, but you'll have a free run to shop and hang out with your friends."

Now it was my turn to smirk. "Like I'm a child and you're dropping me off at my friend's house to play?"

Slade placed his hands on the bench, and I swear he made the massive expanse of marble look small under his hold. "Exactly like that, Snow. Only this is an adult playdate and will include wine."

"That's how they got me here," Kassidy joked, reaching for another sandwich, undeterred by the stink eye I shot her way. She was a badass alpha and could hoover down as much food as the males. Lucky, I liked her.

"Sounds amazing," I said, excited by this prospect of a real girl's day. "I've never had an adult playdate with girlfriends. I can add it to the new experiences board."

"Yes!" Cora fist-pumped the air, and I noted that she was also in jeans and a pale blue, knitted sweater, the color lovely against her complexion. "I've been desperate for some good old-fashioned girl talk. I need to live vicariously through—"

Kassidy snorted, and Cora swallowed her laughter. "Okay, through one of you at least. The one with multiple mates. I know all about a single bond already."

Neither Hunter nor Slade appeared upset that I might share any of our lives with my friends. Which was good, since I had a lot to catch them up on—even if there were only three of us currently participating in the quintet bonding.

"Well, I'm ready to go," I said, snatching up two more sandwiches and wrapping them in a napkin. "Lead the way."

By the time Hunter dropped us off at the boutique chain of stores that we apparently had free run of, I'd finished my breakfast and was pumped as hell for this date. Despite the Christmas season coming to an end, there was still a tree and twinkling lights in the center of the store window, and I found myself grinning stupidly at their pretty decorations.

"You wear the most adorable expression whenever you see decorations," Hunter said, standing close enough that our bodies touched, and I was warmed from his energy.

I shrugged. "It's like winter. The snow covers everything until it's just a pretty expanse of white. It hides all the sins. Christmas feels like that too, like the lights and trees and presents are all so pretty and harmless that they shadow the bullshit out there. I wish it went for longer."

He leaned over and brushed his lips against the side of my head, until butterflies took off in my stomach. "We'll leave the decorations up at home for a little longer," he murmured, kissing me once more, before he led me where my friends waited near the entrance.

"Okay, I've set up an account instore," he said, addressing everyone. "Go crazy and buy whatever you want."

Kassidy fist-pumped. "I'm a strong independent shifter, you know that, but I will never turn down free clothes."

Hunter shook his head. "I've been trying to get you to accept my money for years, sister. Apparently, all it took was one girl's day and wine to seal the deal. I'll keep that in mind."

She patted his chest and batted her eyelashes. "See that you do. Now scurry away and leave us to our female shenanigans, big bro."

Hunter looked like he was barely restraining himself from an eyeroll. "I'll be in the car, and Slade is patrolling with his enforcer squad."

I touched my pocket, relieved I'd remembered my phone. "I'll text when we're finished."

Hunter's chest rumbled. He leaned down and this time his kiss landed on my lips, and I forgot my name for a few minutes. "See that you do, baby girl."

I almost wished he would come in with us, but I needed this time with my friends. Maybe I'd even get some advice about what was happening with my pack.

"Love you," I whispered, and the stare he gave me in return burned through my soul.

"I love you, little mate. Now go and have fun."

He slapped his big hand on my ass, the *mine* flashing as he pulled away, and I tried my best to ignore the tightening of my lower half.

That bastard knew what he was doing, and *fuck* if I didn't like it.

CHAPTER 45

EMME

"Okay," Cora said, as we made our way into a department store filled to the brim with not only clothing but bags, shoes, makeup, and accessories. "We need to know everything that's happening in your life. What's going on with you and the delectable Reeves pack?"

She pulled a dress off the rack, holding it up against herself.

"There's a lot going on," I admitted, "and I have no idea where to start to make it all make sense."

Kassidy leaned over a pile of jeans and waggled her brows at me. "So, you're happily bonded to Hunt and Kellan, but they mentioned a third bite this morning. Which one?"

Oh fuck. Were they aware of Talon's existence? I wasn't sure what information was out in the shifter cities.

"One second," I said, whipping out my phone and shooting off a text to Hunter.

Emme: Are the girls aware of the new dragon in our midst? Can I tell them?

It wasn't that I generally checked in with the pack before I talked to Cora, but this was bigger than simply sharing my life. Talon was *complicated*, and the revelation of his existence would shake up the shifter communities.

281

> Hunter: They don't know, but there's no issue telling them. They're in the trusted inner circle. Just advise them not to speak of it to anyone else.

I got the sense that he didn't want me to have to keep secrets from my friends, and I loved that about him.

> Emme: Thanks, Hurricane. *heart emoji*

> Hunter: Anytime, baby girl. Now, finish your shopping so I can take you home. We have plans.

I liked plans with Hunter. I liked them a lot.

Sliding my phone back into my pocket, I shuffled as they watched me closely. "Sorry," I said keeping my voice low as I eyed the staff behind the service desk. Who were thankfully far enough away not to be able to overhear. "There's been a new development in our pack, and I wasn't sure if I could share everything yet."

The girls must have picked up on how serious this was from my tone, as they huddled in closer. "When I was taken," I whispered, and my eyes darted to Kassidy, "your dad forced another shifter to bond me."

Cora gasped, her hand clutching mine as she stared wide-eyed at me. The shimmer in her gaze almost had me breaking down, but I held it together. Kassidy took a second longer to react, her expression turning brittle and angry. "We need to kill him," she bit out, which was comforting in the ways she reminded me of Hunter. "I've always hated that motherfucker, and if I could destroy him for you right now, Emme, I would do it without hesitation."

Fuck, these two were better friends than I could have ever hoped for.

"Yep, Fletcher needs to die," I agreed, my voice rasping as I fought down darker emotions, "but there's more to it than that. The one he forced to bond with me was meant to be in my quintet all along. He's a scent match, and another dragon. He's..." I gave a dramatic pause, because if there was ever a moment that needed one, it was this. "... Slade's twin soul."

Their eyes grew wider; I was genuinely worried that Cora's eyeballs might fall out of her head. "Wait, I'm sorry," she breathed, "I think I might have hit my head when we walked in here because I swear you just said that the scariest shifter in existence has a twin."

"Yep," I nodded, unable to suppress a smile. "We've got him locked in our containment room until we can figure out what to do with him."

Kassidy's previous anger slipped into confusion. "So, if there's a fifth alpha, how can a quintet work? Is Slade not part of it because the twin got in first? Or can you kill the twin off…? I mean, one dragon shifter is enough for all of us, right?"

The very thought of Talon no longer existing almost took my breath away. The devastation must have shown on my face, as Cora sucked in a deep breath. "Uh oh," she said, shaking her head. "You've fallen for him."

It was my turn to shake my head. "No, look, we're far from anything resembling a normal bond, and I'm not over him forcing the bite on me. But I also understand him a lot better now. He didn't choose this path, even though he agrees with Fletcher's plan. In some ways, he's as much a victim as Hunter, Slade, Kassidy, and… well, me. I have hope that eventually we'll work it all out."

Neither of them looked convinced, but they also weren't as visibly freaked out as they'd been a second ago.

"How's Slade taking it all?" Kassidy asked, her expression worried. "I know him fairly well. Or as well as he allows anyone to know him, and this is the kind of fucked-up that sends him spiraling."

"Yeah, he didn't take it well to start," I confirmed, "but he's getting better and dealing in his own way. At first, he was raging and focused on torturing his brother for information, but now… he's down there with Talon a lot more than any of us realize, and I think they're bonding. In their own way. Even though he remains distant."

Mostly with me.

Kassidy patted my arm, her expression filled with sympathy. "He's as much my brother as Hunter, and he's always taken on more burden and responsibility than he should. He'd be blaming himself, I'm sure, and trying to figure out how to fix the situation. He never wanted to bond to start with, and I bet this has only reiterated the risks he thinks he poses to a pack."

It was painful to hear, but I couldn't argue with her. Slade had made his position very clear. "He doesn't trust his dragon with me," I said sadly. "The appearance of his twin has made his own instability worse too, which means he's less inclined to get any closer to me."

Slade and I had been making progress before all of this happened, during our prank wars, but he'd been holding me at arm's length since Texas.

His distance hurt me and my beast more than I'd taken the time to really unwrap.

Ah, fucking hell, I was not about to start crying in a damn department store.

"In other news," I continued, forcing an upbeat tone, "Finley and I have made some real *positive* progress."

Cora jerked her head up, once again visibly shocked—we'd discussed Grouchy Bear before, and she knew how he'd reacted to my initial rejection of them.

"How did that happen?" she asked, but before I could answer, one of the sales staff strolled over, prowling along with a tray of wine glasses.

He was tall, thin, with dark hair and narrow dark eyes. He struck me as being part of the big cat shifters. "Ladies," he said, forced cheerfulness in his tone. "We're so thrilled to have you shopping with us this morning. We have a range of wine here for your tastes, and any additives you might need for *extra* buzz. If you require any assistance at all, please just wave us over. Otherwise, we've been told to stay out of your way and give you anything you need."

He didn't slow or breathe through the entire speech, and with a flourish placed the tray on a glass cabinet and hurried away. Hunter clearly had the staff shitting themselves, and they were keen not to spend too much time with us. *Good alpha.*

Kassidy and Cora didn't appear to notice or care, as they reached out and snagged a glass. I went for one with bubbles, hoping it would be sweet.

"So, Finley…" Cora continued. "I get the feeling this might be more shocking than the revelation that there's a whole other dragon shifter in our world."

That produced a rumbly shot of laughter from Kassidy as she took a sip of her red wine. "Agreed."

Rubbing my thumb over the condensation on the side of the glass, I shrugged. "It started when I was taken. Finley found me first, and he fought a damn dragon to get me out. He was stuck in his bear form for a bit, which happens during high stress situations—it's a trauma response from his past. Of course, the second he turned back into a lumbersnack, he started growling and huffing and puffing at me."

Cora's bark of laughter was very wolf like. "I don't know whether to love that you called him a lumbersnack or laugh at the fact that you're mixing up your fairy tales there."

Kassidy nodded along. "Lumbersnack is so fitting. I'm going to use that in the future. Consider it borrowed."

"Borrow away," I said. "I think I heard it in an audiobook once, and it stuck with me. So, yeah, he was raging away, and I honestly... I had enough. This part of me that had been trying to be nice, and hold on to hope... snapped. I proceeded to knee him in the balls hard enough that he probably tasted his future children..."

They both grimaced, and I wasn't sure if I'd gone too far with that analogy, until Kassidy leaned forward to laugh. "Balls in his mouth. Took me a fucking second."

Cora's lips twitched, but she managed to hold it together. "You're a brave shifter, Emme. That bear scares me almost as much as the dragon. He's got all this built-up rage."

It was the truth, but also... not.

"Yeah, well whatever he saw in my face that day, he knew I was washing my hands of him once and for all, and it scared the ever-living shit out of him. He immediately changed his actions, and he's continued to change them ever since. He didn't just say the words, he backed them up. He's even been going to therapy."

Cora looked impressed. "What does that mean for you and bonding with him?" she asked. "I assume, based on Hunter and Kellan, that you're no longer afraid of a completed quintet?"

That was the point I remembered she still didn't know the entire story. There'd been so much going on, and only my pack was aware of what had happened in my past. "Shit, I'm so sorry," I burst out. "I haven't shared all of my past with you yet. I've been wanting to tell you for ages, but I had to tell the alphas first. The reason I feared bonding with the pack was that omegas can share their energy with their bonded mates. Worse than that, they can have it forcibly taken. It happened to my mom and her pack, and in the end, they took so much that her wolf faded. I found her hanging in the street."

My words rushed out of me in a huge flood, and my legs felt weaker by the time I finished. It still kind of took my breath away to reveal my past so freely, when I'd spent so many years running and hiding from it.

The girls reached for me, their expressions filled with horror and sorrow.

As they embraced me with their warmth and caring, I forced myself to add, "There's trauma in her death, don't get me wrong, but I hated my mom. I don't feel her loss in the way you would normally with a parent. But I was determined never to follow in her path."

"What's changed?" Kassidy asked, her expression dead serious as she pulled back to meet my gaze.

"The Reeves pack is what changed," I said, feeling the truth in that. "I shared power with Kellan to save his life and it did nothing. He never craved more. He never tried to take from me again. Hunter and I have been bonded for weeks, and not even once has he shown any sign of wanting power from me. Not to mention I found out a bunch of shit about my mom and that pack, including the fact that they weren't her true scent matches. I've learned that my situation is never going to be hers, and I won't risk losing my pack on a maybe of losing my power. For them, I'd embrace a bigger fear than that."

For them, I'd give up everything.

CHAPTER 46

EMME

After our heavier conversation, we moved on to normal chats about our lives, and then we started shopping. An hour later, I found myself in the dressing room with a small pile of clothes to try on.

Cora and I finished at the same time and converged on the counter to pay for our items.

"I'm really happy to see you so settled in your pack," she said as she leaned against the bench. "You have this new glow about you."

Ah, the old glow of happiness. Or maybe it was copious amounts of sex. "It's weird, we've gone through the sort of drama and hardships a lot of packs wouldn't experience in a lifetime," I said, pushing my clothes toward the shifters behind the counter. "But we missed the normal dating and getting to know each other part. I only just recently learned their birthdays."

She shot me a lopsided smile. "In the first few months after finding your scent match, it tends to be more about our beasts and hormones than *dating* per se. You've actually taken it slower than most. From what I recall, War and I didn't even come up for air for weeks, and it was only later we started to converse about more than *what surface to screw on.*"

I blinked. "It still takes me by surprise when you speak so bluntly. There you stand all refined and proper, but on the inside you're just sass and sex."

She howled. "Oh goddess. That's so damn true. I like to keep everyone guessing."

"I'm starting to see that." And I absolutely loved it.

"You ladies are done already?" Kassidy called as she hurried over. "How did you try everything on so quickly?"

She dropped a pile of clothes so massive on the counter that I couldn't even see the sales staff behind it. "Uh, I don't think we had quite as much as you to try on."

She tossed her hair and fired off a satisfied smirk in my direction. "Look, big brother is paying, and while I normally wouldn't take a cent of his money, I've decided that today is about friendship. It'd be rude to refuse the gift of friendship."

"The height of rudeness," Cora confirmed with a smirk.

"I admire your independence," I told Kassidy. "When Kellan mentioned that you chose not to have a pack for no reason other than you didn't want one, I knew you were far stronger than me. You lose none of that by taking Hunter's gift."

Kassidy's smile faltered, and there was a hint of pink in her cheeks. "Well, there's a little more behind the reason than that. Some shit happened to me, and I decided I couldn't risk losing myself again. The last time it happened… well, yeah… it was fucked up."

"How long ago was this?" Cora asked, her concern shining through in her worried expression.

There was a pause as Kassidy's brow furrowed. "You know… fuck, it's been five years. Time flies when you're escaping from your mistakes."

She'd have been quite young five years ago, and I wanted to comfort her as I draped my arm around her shoulder. "You seem pretty damn strong to me. And once you learn how strong you are alone, you can have the same in a pack. If that's what you end up wanting."

Her smile held hints of pain and sadness. "I'm getting there."

Kassidy changed the subject as she moved on to plans for the new year, and what we hoped to achieve. Cora revealed that her and Warrick had started discussing the possibility of having a baby, and my heart clenched at the thought of a tiny shifter coming into this terrifying world. Shifters didn't have young easily, and it was a huge decision for any pack to make.

Which reminded me that with my fertile period approaching soon, and this time having copious amounts of unprotected sex, I would have to go to the healers for the potion to prevent pregnancy. I hated using magic, but there were no other choices except abstinence. Condoms weren't designed for our kind.

When all of our purchases were rung up and bagged, I shot a text to Hunter and not even a minute later he strolled into the store. He gathered up the dozens of bags like they weighed nothing, and piled them all into the back of the Mercedes.

"You certainly make life easier, mate," I said, popping up on my toes to kiss his cheek.

He turned at the last second so my lips landed on his, and the rumble of his wolf reverberated down my spine until my toes curled in my shoes. "You will never struggle through life again," he promised me.

My sigh was lost in our next kiss, and Kassidy groaned. "Come on, guys. I don't want to see my brother making out. Not to mention we're all lonely over here without soulmates."

Cora's face lit up as a Range Rover pulled in beside our car. "Speak for yourself, Kass. I've got mine right here."

Warrick exited the vehicle dressed in a suit and looking very suave. "We've got a council meeting," he explained, as Cora whistled and hurried toward him. "Members of all five cities are here."

I met Hunter's gaze, and he nodded. "Yeah, Slade is going to be at the house to take over security since I can't miss this one. Jewels, and our few allies in the witch world, will be there too. It's time to lay out a plan to draw Fletcher and the Termaine witches from their hiding spot."

"Won't Fletcher's council want to take his side?" I asked. "Or Blaine's?"

Hunter snarled, his expression lethal and furious. "Fletcher's council is Golden Claw—he's just never here enough to claim his spot. Not that anyone would have him at this point. He did himself no favors with the way he acted in the past."

"And Silver City with Blaine?"

Warrick spoke up. "We don't think so, but it's one of the questions we have for them today. So far it appears they're washing their hands of that pack. Especially since Blaine is the only one left."

I hated knowing they were going into that building again, even if it had been repaired since the magical attack. "Stay safe," I said. "After the last betrayal, I'm a bit nervous about these meetings."

"We'll be on guard, little omega," Hunter said as he pressed a kiss to my forehead, wrapping his arms around me. "And I'll be back in time to catch the game."

Kellan and Finley's game was tonight, and since we couldn't be there, I was determined to support them from here. "We'll be watching too!" Cora called, as she hurried over to give us one last hug. "Text me updates."

After promising I would, she grabbed her bags from the car and left with Warrick. Hunter drove Kassidy and me to the compound, dropping his sister and her many bags off first, before he followed me into the house. He changed into a suit and kissed me quickly as he raced out the door.

Once he was gone, I tried not to panic at what might happen during the meeting. Hunter was powerful and capable, and could take care of himself, but when you loved someone, worry for their safety appeared to be part of it.

Slade wandered into the entrance hall as a nice distraction. He smirked at the pile of bags around my feet. "Had a productive day I see."

I glanced down. "You know, it looked like a lot less in the store. Hunter did say go crazy and get what I wanted."

Slade surprised me when he brushed a hand across my cheek, leaving a burning wake in its path. He'd been so distant lately that I soaked up that one touch like it was a full-body hug. "This is nothing, Snow. One day soon, all you'll have to worry about is shopping, eating, and embracing your freedom. We can travel and see the world. Or stay right here in our home. Whatever you want."

I shrugged, my heart beating so damn hard that Hunter, who was well on his way to the council meeting, could probably hear it. "You've already given me everything I ever wanted. All I need now is Fletcher and his witches wiped off the fucking planet."

Slade's expression softened, and again it was such a rare occurrence that my parched emotions were desperate for another sip. "You're helping to heal all of us through your own innate magic, Emme. We can never repay that."

I wanted to tell him that it was the same for me, but I knew if I spoke, my voice would crack, and I didn't need this to get all weird and angsty.

Slade gathered up my bags, managing them easily in one hand, and I followed as he took the stairs three at a time to the second floor. In my room, he placed my new purchases in the wardrobe, and I decided I'd put them away later. Uninterrupted time with my most reticent alpha was too good to turn down.

"We have a couple of hours until the game," Slade said, as if he'd had the same thought. "What would you like to do?"

Usually, he was more of the *give an order and expect it to be obeyed* alpha, but apparently he continued to channel his softer side. "What if I said face masks and a pedicure?"

His jaw twitched and he sighed. "If that's what you want. I know you've been having a rough time lately. Or... we could practice reading?" He tagged on the last part with a semi-hopeful tone, and I managed not to laugh.

"I've been practicing my reading," I told him, "And I'm happy with my progress. Could we maybe try knife training instead?"

During my early morning sessions, I'd grown more confident with weapons, and Horton had suggested we move on to real—still blunted—blades soon.

Slade's relief was palpable, and I was *almost* tempted to go back to face masks just to stir him up. "Get dressed and I'll meet you in the gym," he said, leaving before I could respond.

After quickly using the bathroom, I threw my hair into a ponytail and dressed in black Lycra pants, a matching sports bra, and sneakers.

Slade was already in the gym, and I followed the sounds of thuds to find him in the back corner whaling on a boxing bag.

Oh. Fuck. Me.

He was shirtless, with just his gym shorts and sneakers on. He wasn't sweating, but I sure as hell was as I watched the play of muscles in his broad shoulders every time he slammed his fist into the bag. It swung hard into the wall, and when it returned, he smashed it again.

"These bags are made by a shifter company," Slade said, and even though I shouldn't have been, I was surprised that he'd already sensed me standing there. "They make it from a synthetic material which can withstand our strength." He was speaking words, that was for sure, but all I heard was static in my head as I drooled.

When he hit the bag one last time, catching it on the backswing, he caught me mid obsessive stare. "Uh, right? Very strong," I managed to say, as I sucked in a ragged breath.

Slade relaxed back into his stance, arms crossed over his chest to highlight both dragon heads. His gaze was heated as he ran it down my body, taking in my workout gear too.

"You ready to practice?" he asked, and I nodded roughly.

I already knew I was going to be utterly useless today, but we were here now, and I was still determined to learn how to fight… or at least hold my own for a few seconds.

"Can we use actual weapons?"

Slade's smile kicked up a notch. "You can, and I'll keep the wooden practice ones."

"What? Why?" I shot back, my annoyance cutting through the lust. "I'm never going to get better if you keep babying me. I'm a shifter. I'll heal!"

His smile disappeared faster than a drop of moisture in the desert. "I can't cut you, Snow. I won't fucking do it. If that blade slices your perfect skin, I'll probably plunge it into my own damn chest. So, just work with me here so I don't lose my shit and destroy the world. Please."

My fire died off, and since he so rarely said please, I knew I'd give him whatever he wanted. "Is that why you've been having Horton take point on my training? So you don't hurt me?"

Poor Horton though, taking all the risks. I needed to make sure he didn't accidentally stab me; otherwise he'd be a dead eagle.

Slade shook his head. "I don't trust myself to touch you more than necessary. My dragon is starting to crave the feel of your skin against mine."

The thudding of my heartbeat was loud in my ears. "Have you ever stopped to think that might be exactly what you're supposed to want. You said I was healing you all, in my own way, so why wouldn't I be part of healing the rift with your beast?"

I expected his immediate rebuttal, but he was slow to respond. "It's possible, but it's still a risk. I'm hoping everything will make more sense once we return to the volcano."

"You and Talon?" I asked.

"You will all have to come as well," he said shortly, "but only we will venture into the depths."

Before I could ask another of the million questions I had, he gestured for me to head back into the main part of the gym. "Let's get to training."

We moved past the machines and climbed into the training ring. It was an elevated square shape—ironically—roped off on all four sides. As I bounced onto the floor, I found it was hard with a very mildly spongy upper layer.

Slade picked up a case from a shelf on one wall, and I sighed as my beautiful blades came into view. "They're so darn pretty," I cooed, brushing my hand over the handle and hilt.

The embedded jewels were smooth as I wrapped my palm around one handle. "And fits so well in my palm."

"Like it was made for you," Slade said with a knowing smile, reminding me that he'd used his stalker ways to create these for me.

He retrieved a wooden practice blade, and we fell into a fight stance. It was getting easier for me to move my body the way I wanted, as my muscles, stamina, and wolf grew stronger with each lesson. I'd even managed to keep up with the back of the enforcer pack during our last lot of warmups.

My aim had been to get stronger, and as hard as each day was, I hadn't given up.

"Bring it on, big boy," I sassed Slade, and I was rewarded with his terrifying smile as he moved forward, the blade sliding toward me so fast I could barely track it.

When it touched my throat, I sucked in a rapid breath. "Good call on the wooden blades," I choked out, the blunt edge moving against my voice box.

Slade nodded, before removing the weapon and stepping back. "You move like magic," I whispered. *You are magic.* "Horton moves like an octogenarian compared to you."

His smirk appeared, and everything was right in my world. "Next time, don't leave yourself so open. Your throat is an easy place for anyone to inflict a quick death. Along with here." His hands slid down to hover above the joint of my hip and groin. He wasn't touching me, but I felt his heat in a *much more intimate place.*

"So, get your blades in position to defend yourself." He took a step back, and I shook myself from the daze. "Again."

Flames danced in his eyes, and I breathed deeply to try and maintain stability. As I brought my blades up, I nodded. "Yeah. Again."

And this time, I would be ready for his speed.

Probably.

CHAPTER 47

EMME

The Celtic Wolves lost in a very dramatic game that came down to overtime and one lucky shot that went in from their opponents. I watched from between Slade and Hunter, and if my mates hadn't been playing, I'd have been very distracted by Hunter's warm, hard thigh pressed down my right side, and the burn of Slade's energy on my left.

By the end, my wolf was whining in my essence, which had the alphas' gazes snapping toward me. The darkening of their eyes told me I wasn't the only one affected. Hunter barely restrained himself as he started to drag me onto his lap, until a pointed stare from Slade stilled his hand, leaving me to combust between them.

"The guys are going to be so disappointed," I said, as the highlights reel wrapped up the game. "They played so well though. The other team just got a lucky shot in."

"They'll be fine," Slade said, and if I didn't know him so well, I'd have assumed he didn't really care. But I knew better. His pack was his priority, and he was the first to suggest *murder* as an option for any players who roughed up Kellan or Finley. Even if he was also quick to move on from the losses and focus on the next win.

"You heading out to patrol?" Hunter asked, as the dragon got to his feet.

Slade's nod was abrupt. "Yeah, I'll do a fly around and check with the guards on Golden Claw's entrance. Fletcher won't lay low for much longer. I know his magical barrier only holds as long as he remains behind it, but then his plan to usurp the leadership of the cities goes nowhere. He has something big planned, and I won't get taken by surprise again."

"I can't believe none of them have popped up yet," I said, suppressing a shiver. I hated the waiting more than anything; I'd rather be facing them full-on. "Not Blaine or Sorenson or Chelsea… Where the hell are the rest of their pack?"

Hunter's wolf rose up with a deep rumble. "My *former* best friend won't hide forever. Even though I find it hard to believe he would betray me after all these years, the blame still lies with him. It was his pack… his omega, and it cost you dearly. For that, he will pay."

Slade leaned over and dropped a hand on Hunter's shoulder, the pair doing their silent communication. It didn't bother me, especially now that I knew how they'd suffered growing up and only had each other to lean on. "I will take care of it for you, brother. You shouldn't have to live with the memory of destroying a friend."

Our entitled alpha's expression hardened. "He was your friend too."

Slade shook his head. "I care about our pack. Everyone else is an acquaintance. If they live or die means nothing to me."

"What about Kassidy? Or Kellan's brothers?"

With a shrug, Slade straightened. "I don't wish them harm, but if it comes down to choosing their safety or my pack's, they'll all die." He brushed his hand across my cheek, in a move I was starting to associate with this shifter, and then walked out the door, taking his massive energy with him.

"If only he was kidding," Hunter murmured, shaking his head.

When his sole focus landed on me, the gold sparked to life in his eyes, and this time there was no one to stop him from dragging me into his lap. My core pulsed as I slid my legs down either side of his hips, my center pressed against his hard length.

"It looks like we have the house to ourselves," he all but purred near my ear. "Any ideas what we might do to occupy our time?"

I had so many ideas. All. The. Fucking. Ideas.

My body tingled, and my panties would have been damp if I wore any.

A fact that Hunter discovered not two seconds later when his hands slid down the back of my sweatpants to cup my bare ass. His groan was deep. I loved when he was vocal. That expression of desire from an alpha just *fucking did it for me.*

His kiss was forceful, as if he couldn't wait another second to taste me. I rocked forward in a desperate search for friction, while his firm grip explored lower and lower.

His fingers brushed over my dripping core and I gasped into his kiss. With another growl, he lifted my ass and stripped my sweats down as low as he could get them, along with his own. "I'm sorry, baby girl," he bit out, his beast heavy in his voice. "I can't fucking wait another second to be inside you."

He adjusted my body's angle and thrust into me in one movement. I cried out as pleasure and pain followed simultaneously, and I was huffing by the time he had me fully seated. "Goddess, you're too fucking big for that move," I groaned, even though I was already starting to shift my hips.

I'd been edged between two alphas for hours. This was exactly what I needed.

"You took me so well, baby girl," he rumbled against my throat. "So fucking well. My most perfect omega."

My hips arched, and he hit a spot inside that had stars dancing in my vision. Already.

Hunter jerked up my shirt to reveal the heavy fall of my tits, and if that look on his face was any indication, I should just ditch underwear permanently now. He latched on to my right nipple, rougher than usual, drawing the tight, hard tip between his teeth.

Bringing my legs tighter into his sides, I lifted higher and fell back on him, over and over, as he filled me completely. Needing an anchor, I threaded my fingers in his hair and held on as I rode my alpha, my core throbbing as release barreled toward me.

"Fuck, I needed this," I murmured, a small cry bursting from me when his teeth bit into my right boob. Marking me.

When his hands landed on my hips, his grip tightened, and as he said, "Let me, little omega," all I could do was hold on. He lifted me to thrust hard and fast, and my cries grew louder as I tried my best to exist in the incredible pleasure. I wasn't ready to fall. I wanted to feel this forever.

When Hunter slapped my ass, rubbing over the sting, I couldn't hold myself back any longer. My body tightened as I jerked against him, breaths forced from me in hurried gasps. "Oh, holy alpha. I'm going to come."

Hunter lifted his head, flares of gold surrounding his pupils. "Yes, you are. Come for me right now… I'm right there with you, baby."

My entire lower half tightened and I cried out, the release brutally perfect in every way. I loved long, drawn-out nights of foreplay but the moments where their need for me overrode their patience, were the times that really fucked me up.

As my body shook through the orgasm, Hunter groaned, finishing inside me as he growled my name. "Fuck, I love you, mate," he said, his tongue swiping over my swollen lips as he kissed me again.

I collapsed against his chest, my breaths ragged huffs. "That was unexpected but in-fucking-credible," I rasped against his shirt, laughing at our half-dressed state.

"You're incredible," Hunter shot back, and stood suddenly with me in his arms. He took a second to get our pants situated so he could walk while remaining buried deep inside me, my core still throbbing around his shaft.

In his room, he stripped us fully, and I groaned when he finally slid out of me. There were days I hated the sensation of emptiness after sex with my alphas.

Hunter distracted me with a shower. He cleaned me thoroughly, and then got me very dirty again. Until eventually we were ready for bed.

I slipped in under the soft sheets and found myself asking the very questions I'd had all those weeks ago. "What was your first invention?" Hunter jerked around to stare at me, blinking like I'd taken him by surprise. "Oh, and how did you manage to create a billion-dollar company when your father was such a fucking twat? Surely, he didn't enjoy you outearning him and no longer being under his control."

Hunter watched me shrewdly, but there was no nefarious reason for my questions. Just pure curiosity. Curiosity and the knowledge that I'd spent too long running from this pack when I should have been learning everything about them.

When he slid under the sheets with me, he wrapped his arm around my waist and pulled me against his chest. "Why the questions, baby girl?" he asked, and I had to chuckle.

"No reason, Hurricane; I'm just curious about you. I figured I should ask in this downtime of *not* fighting for our lives."

He considered that for a moment. "Yeah, makes sense. My first invention was actually the testing calculation they use now for scent cataloguing. I wanted to get out from under my father's control, as you mentioned, and I found a hole in our market. The original tests didn't give great match results, and as I wanted to find the rest of our pack, it was a double bonus. It made me my first billion in two years. Everything just went on from that."

I gaped at him. *First. Billion.* Yeah, I wasn't ready to deal with the concept of more than one billion.

"That's incredible. I'm so proud of you," I said, awed by my genius of an alpha.

He shrugged, like it wasn't a huge deal. "Honestly, I've always tinkered and used logic and maths to break everything down and find solutions to any problem. Slade was the one who figured out how to get it into the right hands without Fletcher throwing up his usual roadblocks. We had some close calls, but in the end, once it was all patented and ours, there was nothing he could do to stop me. I've been moving forward with Reeves Industries ever since."

Goddess, he was truly remarkable.

He turned on his side and faced me, his gaze dragging over my features. "I know you were forced to run for most of your teen and adult life so far, but if you'd had the chance to do anything, what would you have chosen?"

I stilled, trying to remember if I'd ever given a *career* much consideration. It just really hadn't been in the cards for me. I'd waitressed because it was a job I could consistently pick up anywhere, and they would often pay cash or only tips. And ask no questions. "I've never thought about it," I admitted, hating how pathetic that sounded. "Maybe something to do with cars or bikes. I enjoy being in a workshop, though I'm not trained in mechanical work. Or maybe baking. I do enjoy the art of creating food."

"And your sweets are damn delicious," Hunter added, the warm rumble in his voice like a spark of fire in my chest. "You are smart and capable, Emmeline Anders. You could do anything you wanted, but all I care is that you're happy. I support whatever decision you make, but just know, there are no limits. We have resources and money, and once I dispose of my father and destroy his fucked-up plan, you can take any path through life. Think about it." He tilted his head to the side. "There's definitely an opening for a bakery in the downtown now. Since Chelsea's Sweets *mysteriously* burned to the ground." He smirked over the word mysteriously, and I jerked up off his chest.

"It did? It fucking burned down? How did you guys manage that?"

That smug smile grew, but he didn't go into detail. With a shake of my head, I relaxed back against him again, and his phone rang as I rested my head on his chest. Reaching out, he grabbed it off the side table, and after a quick glance at the screen, he handed it over to me with a wry grin.

I wasn't surprised to find Kellan's name and photo popping up with a video call request.

"Hey, Golden," I said, pushing my damp hair back on the pillow. When his beautiful face came into view on the screen, a little of the ache in my chest eased. "We watched your game. Sorry about the last-minute loss, but you all played incredibly well."

Kellan bore no signs he was upset by the loss, his smile beaming. "It was an unlucky break, Shortcake. But seeing your pretty face takes my mind completely off it."

There was a low rumble from beside him, but I couldn't hear what Finley said as Kellan turned the phone to show the bear shifter perched on the other hotel bed. "Hey, Ice Queen," he said, gaze locked on the screen. Just like Kellan, he appeared unphased by the loss. "We're missing you. I'm not sure I want to stay away for the other games."

Kellan shouted from behind the phone he held. "Right there with you. Look at our mate, all snuggled up in bed. No fucking fair."

Finley's smile faltered briefly, and I felt a pang that we weren't quite at the place where he could express his need as easily as Kellan. But at least we had the possibility that we *would* get there eventually.

"I miss you both too," I said, letting my gaze linger on Finley's eyes which were less gold than usual as tension lined his features. "Are you worried you won't sleep?"

His struggles to sleep was a personal topic for Finley, and while his brothers knew, I wondered if he would brush it off in front of them. "I'm going to struggle," he admitted without any hesitation, and I stifled my sigh of relief that he was talking about it. Therapy was shifting all our perspectives on what was a weakness and what wasn't. *It's not weak to speak* was a slogan on Dr. Karen's wall, and I wholeheartedly agreed.

"I've grown used to having your calming energy near me," he continued, "and this distance bothers my bear. And me." He swallowed roughly. "A lot."

The urge to fly to them hit me hard, and when I turned to where Hunter was propped up on his pillow staring at me, I knew he'd take me if I asked. "Plane is always ready for you," he confirmed, picking up on my emotions through the bond.

"We can come to you," I said, pushing myself higher.

Finley shook his head. "No, Em. No way. It will cause you pain to leave Talon, and we can't take him out of containment. But..." his voice broke. "It means the fucking world that you would drop everything and fly to us."

I narrowed my eyes on him through the phone. "I know I don't have much experience with packs or loving families, but I promise, if any of you ever need me, I will drop anything and be there. Even if I have to crawl, walk, or steal a damn plane."

Finley's expression lightened as he made a deep, rumbly sound, and I could feel his bear in that response.

"What if I talk to you both until you fall asleep?" I suggested, not ready to let them go yet. "I could even practice my reading, if you guys don't mind me stumbling over words."

"Yes!" Kellan shouted again. "I just sent a new book to your reading app."

Finley's eyes shone, and he looked so happy that I was still considering getting on that plane and damning the consequences. "Yes, I'd fucking love that," he said, and his rumble was a nice distraction. "Give me a minute to get ready for bed."

He was still in his suit, and as he left the frame, Kellan turned the phone back on his face. When he came into view I blew him a kiss, and he closed his eyes and popped out his bottom lip. "Pretty mate, I'm going to need all the kisses when we get home. I demand one full day of your time. Finley will want the next day. Maybe we should set up a schedule."

"Not a fucking chance," Hunter said from beside me, his face popping into the video frame to glare at his brother. "Everyone will learn to share equally, or *I'll* make the schedule, and no one will like the way I divvy out Emme's time."

I wanted to laugh, but I also wanted to punch this dominant asshole in the side.

Kellan leaned into his camera, bringing his face much closer. "I'm a good sharer, Daddy Alpha. You already know that."

Hunter's lips twitched, and I knew our Golden had him there. "Just remember how quickly I can reach you, pup," he muttered, but there was no real heat in those words.

Kellan shot us both a wink, but further replies were cut off as Finley stepped into view, wearing only a pair of boxer briefs. He crawled into his queen size bed, making it look tiny.

"Open your app," Kellan said, drawing my attention back to him.

Luckily, my device was still in Hunter's room from when I'd been reading earlier this week, so I handed Hunter the phone while I grabbed it from the drawer. It powered up and the new book was already in the library.

It had a dark blue cover, with stars and a huge moon above the title, *A PackAge Deal: Shifter Pack Wars.*

"Shifters," I said, arching a brow. "Like us?"

Kellan's expression relaxed as he leaned back in his bed. "I'm not sure if they're exactly like us. I think this one is mostly about wolf shifters, and it's no doubt written by a human, but the part you might find interesting is that it's a 'why choose.'"

I wasn't familiar with that term, and as I squinted at him, he laughed. "It means that the female main character will end up with a pack of mates and she won't choose between them. Figured you might enjoy the concept."

Well, okay then. "I had no idea that was a genre," I said, excited to see what it entailed in this fantasy world. "Now I'm going to have to search them all out. For research purposes of course."

Hunter chuckled beside me. "You don't need to research, baby girl. You know exactly what you're doing." My lower half clenched at the reminder of what had happened downstairs.

Clearing my throat, I flicked the pages until I reached the first chapter. "Chapter one. *Being the outcast of a pack is never the role I expected to play. But here we were. Outcast. Rejected. And alone.*"

My reading was slow, and I stumbled over a few of the larger words, but overall I managed to keep the story flowing well. Years of trying to learn, and struggling along, had given me the skills to do this. If I had the right font, background color, and line spacing.

As I continued, Kellan's face was peaceful. When he shifted the phone toward Finley's bed, my throat tightened at the sight of the bear's serene expression, a hoodie in his hands.

Not just any hoodie—I recognized it as the one I'd worn yesterday, which he must have grabbed from my room before they left. As if he knew he'd need my scent to help him through.

Just the way I'd had to be in their clothes today too.

Fuck, away games sucked. Next time I was going with them, no matter what it cost.

CHAPTER 48

EMME

Over the next few days I forced myself to stay busy with training, visiting Talon, and baking—I wanted to surprise the boys with all the sweets when they returned. And every night was spent reading the spiciest "why choose" story on video chat.

The shifter tale was edging all three of us, but I at least had relief from Hunter.

Kellan and Finley got to suffer, though neither of them asked me to stop.

Their last game was today, and while usually they'd fly home tomorrow morning, they were taking the Reeves jet to get home tonight. These days without them felt like I was missing an essential part of myself, and the ache from my bond to Kellan was starting to drag deeper into my essence. It wasn't the same pain it had been the last time, but it still grew worse with each day.

The only silver lining was how close we felt after nights of reading and chatting.

I'd grown closer to Talon during this week too. The more time I spent around him, the more our beasts bonded. The connection between us hummed for that final completion, and as scary as it was, I could barely remember hating and fearing him.

When he looked at me like there was no one else in the world, and he only needed me to be happy, there was no hate in my heart for him.

Though I could never forget that we still had our greatest test to come: the day he had to choose between me and his Alpha.

My visit to the containment room this morning came with treats, as I brought a plate piled high with cookies, croissants, cinnamon buns, and a slice of cake I made specially for him.

"Emme," Talon murmured, gaze locked on me. "You came."

"Of course," I said, pausing at the dull edge to his voice. "I wanted to bring you some baked goodness."

He didn't glance at the plate. "I prefer honey," he murmured, forcing a smile, "but since you made them for me, I'll try the sweets."

I twisted the plate to bring the cake closer, the scent of caramel and honey wafting from the golden icing. "I made you honey cake," I said, my wolf perking her head up at Talon's mood too.

For the first time since I'd entered the room, a genuine smile lifted his lips, which should have been a relief… but it wasn't. There was a deep-seated unease in his beast, and I knew he'd been down here and trapped for too long.

"I'm going to talk to Hunter," I said, the urgency to race from here almost sending the plate crashing to the ground. "You need to stretch your wings."

Talon gripped the edge of the plate, keeping us both intact. "We have a trip to Europe planned once your other mates return. To explore the twin soul connection. I can wait for that."

I hated that Fletcher's way of punishing and conditioning him was to keep him isolated, and now we were doing the exact same thing. It had bothered me from the start, but now I'd grown to care for the big bastard, it was hurting us both. When we returned from the volcano, I would be insisting he stay in the house with us.

Either we learned to trust him, or he went back to the evil dictator —this couldn't continue indefinitely.

I slid down the bars to sit, and Talon joined me, staying close so our sides touched. We often sat like this, and our beasts would mingle, sending sparks through the bond.

"You want a taste?" I asked, holding out the fork.

His lips tilted up once more and I shivered at his dark gaze. "I absolutely want a taste." He turned and brushed his lips across my shoulder, another of the many touches he now initiated. "Then I'll try the cake."

I snorted. "Ah, such a cliché line." The tingles in my core indicated that cliché or not, I was a bit of a fan. Omegas must have been designed to require many, *many* orgasms. It didn't seem to matter how much sex I was getting; all of my mates elicited this response in me.

Apparently, the goddess gave you as much as you could handle, and for me, that was five alphas.

Talon took my proffered fork and slid it through the end of the cake, lifting the piece up to my lips first. Experience had taught me that arguing with an alpha trying to feed me was futile, so I ate his offering, relieved to find the cake was moist and flavorful. It was a new recipe, which always came with challenges.

Talon fed me bits of everything on the plate, and I groaned at the excess of sugar dancing across my tastebuds. When he was finally satisfied I'd had enough, he took his first bite of the honey cake, and I was pleased by his throaty sigh.

"This honey tastes almost as good as you do."

The only real *taste* he'd had of me was my blood during our forced mating. A memory I didn't relish. And while I'd never condone his actions, I had grown to understand the true core of Talon, and I had forgiven him.

Anger was a painful and draining emotion to hold on to forever. Once I started to release mine for Talon and Finley, I felt lighter, more at peace with myself and the future I was ready to claim.

Talon made short work of the rest of the sweets, and when the plate was empty, he didn't appear as drained as when I walked in. I stayed for another few hours, dragging a half decent conversation out of the generally reticent beast. Even if some of the answers to my questions were painful to hear.

It turned out that Talon didn't have a favorite color, had never celebrated a birthday, and he wasn't sure what he'd have done with his life if he wasn't enslaved to a looney alpha.

Each of those answers upset me, until eventually I stopped asking questions and just held his hand. "Your birthday is on the thirty-first of October," I said, my voice wavering. "Which is Halloween in the human world."

He considered that for a beat. "What's Halloween?"

While the day was a human tradition, most shifters still knew about it. "Oh, well, it's this night where humans dress up as anything they want. Could be monsters or celebrities or inanimate objects. They dress up, they celebrate everything spooky, and they go around to houses and ask for candy."

Talon's perfect face creased in confusion, the scar pulling against his lip. "Why would they do that?"

I shook my head. "Honestly, I'm not totally sure of the history behind it, but there's definitely a reason for the tradition. I don't even think it originated here in the States, but they adopted it and celebrate every year."

Talon still appeared confused, shrugging as he said, "As I've never had a birthday before. I don't imagine I'll even remember."

I made a vow that I would remember for him. The pack had made my day special in a way that I'd never forget, and I could do the same for each of them.

"Wait," Talon called, as I stretched out my legs, reluctant to leave but knowing dinner was soon. "When's your birthday?"

His expression was expectant, and I hurried to say, "It was on the twelfth of December. Almost a month ago."

Talon grew super quiet, and there was another drop in his energy. "I missed it," he said, a hint of question in his tone. "I'm so sorry, mate."

Technically, he had been with me for it, he just didn't know at the time.

Turning his way, I slid my hands through the bars. "No, it's totally okay. I never celebrated my birthdays either. My mom was *not nice*, and I usually forget the day too."

Talon didn't look convinced, his expression a mixture of anger and sadness that had my stomach lurching. "I met your mother once when Blaine brought her home. She wasn't fit to be blessed with a child, and that's all I'll say about that."

Where was the lie?

Even before the Rogers pack corrupted and drained her, she'd been an apathetic, uninterested, neglectful parent. "Did you meet anyone else connected to me?" I asked. "Did you ever meet my father?"

He eyed me for a few long seconds. "No, I have no idea who your father was, but I did hear Alpha refer to a Constantine and your mother more than once. I don't know if that's your father or just another shifter in your mother's life…"

Constantine. The name wasn't familiar, but it was a clue for Slade, who still worked on tracking the shifter from the security footage. Along with anyone else connected to that day.

"Thank you," I said, reaching through the bars to hug him.

Talon pressed himself into me, his strong arms banding around my back as the air filled with heat, and I felt a tingle of energy surrounding us. It washed over me like magic, but without any sulfur tainting the air. The prickling sensation in my essence seeped to my fingertip, and I was once again reminded of the time I'd shoved Talon in the bunker.

Today, though, it was all the dragon. "What are you doing?" I asked, pulling back from his broad chest. "Are you using magic—" I gawked as the bars came into view. Bars which were now *on the other fucking side* of me.

He'd pulled me right into the cage.

"What have you done?" I whispered, jerking my gaze back to his. "Hunter and Slade are going to straight up murder you."

Talon, looking pleased as fuck with himself, his arms around me again as he lifted my feet right off the ground in our first proper hug. "I needed you closer," he rasped, breathing in my scent like an addict getting his first hit of omega in months.

His smoky maple grew stronger with each breath, and I took the opportunity to fill my lungs even as I panicked. It wasn't that I was afraid of being with him like this, but it was still a risk.

But for real, I could get very used to being hugged by each of my mates. As our bond thrummed, I was once again a touch-starved shifter soaking up all the comfort.

The moment was shattered by the bang of a door as two enraged alphas stormed into the room. *Oh crap.* Here was hoping there'd still be a house by the time Kellan and Finley returned.

CHAPTER 49

EMME

Hunter and Slade reached the bars, fury drawing their expressions into hard lines.

I patted Talon's shoulder. "Put me down." I said, needing to defuse the situation, only to have him completely ignore that request and grunt.

Great, we were in alpha mode.

Hunter grunted back and Slade let out a growl that was menacing enough to bring every hair on my arms to attention. "Enough!" I snapped, and to my freaking surprise, all of them paused their dominance games to give me their full attention. An omega could go a little mad with that sort of power.

"Okay, we're going to solve this one with our brains today," I said, forcing my nerves to sink below my annoyance. "We already knew Talon could manipulate the prison, which means he's been very good so far. Let's not lose it because he suddenly decided I needed to be on this side of the bars."

"How are you managing this?" Slade bit out through his clenched teeth. Those pearly whites were lucky not to be cracking under the force. "I can manipulate smaller energies and atomic structure, but you're working with material that's not only filled with elements which weaken shifters but are also spelled."

Talon huffed, and I thought he was going to ignore Slade too, but he didn't. "As I've told you many times, you've allowed yourself to grow weaker by not repairing the rift between you and your dragon."

"And I've told you," Slade hit back, "that you have a rift also."

Talon shrugged, and I was lifted with the movement. "My rift isn't as deep as yours. My dragon and I fight on the same side, even when we're not as connected as we should be. You and your beast are as much enemies as you are allies, and that's why you're weakened. We should not be beholden to the same weaknesses as other shifters. Not to any elements, and not to magic. At our full strength, they would need something truly spectacular to take us on."

It was true that everyone in this city was afraid of Slade, but it hadn't seemed to extend to witches, who'd always thought themselves above *all* shifters.

"Can you put me down, please," I asked again, softer this time. "I promise I won't run away."

Moving so slowly it was almost comical, he let me slide down his frame, until eventually my feet hit the ground. His hand remained on my back, keeping us pressed intimately together, as our beasts enjoyed our sudden closeness.

"Thank you," I said, momentarily forgetting we had an audience as I examined his dark eyes. Just like with Hunter's stormy irises, there were hints of color in the darkness—Talon's hint was green.

He leaned into me, and our lips were only inches apart when Slade slammed his hand against the bars. "If you fucking touch her without her consent again, I will tear you into so many pieces all they'll find will be scales."

With a shake of my head, I pulled away, not sure if I would have refused his kiss.

"Don't forget where his loyalties lie," Hunter said, his gaze imploring me to come to him. No doubt he could feel my confused desire in the bond. "At the end of the day, he will heed to Fletcher's command, even if it hurts you. You've already lived through that."

He was right, and despite my softening feelings toward Talon, I couldn't grow complacent of a shifter as powerful as this dragon.

When I took another step away, Talon's wounded expression hit like a blunt object forced through skin, bone, and muscle until it embedded deep in my heart. "I'm loyal to you too," he rasped, and I was left with no doubt that he meant every word.

"I know," I assured him, "but the issue we have here is that my ideologies don't align with Fletcher's. I will never be like him. I will never sacrifice everyone in this world for power. It's inevitable that you'll have to choose between us, and right now I'm not convinced you'd choose me. Which means we cannot take this relationship any further. Not until I know for sure. Not until the trust is complete."

His expression hardened, and he was the one to back away now. "And you trust your pack like that?" he asked roughly. "Completely? Without reservation? Every single one of them?"

There wasn't a moment's hesitation in my response. "Absolutely. All of them, even Finley."

As I admitted that truth, the last of the chasm between Finley and me filled. It was a tangible sensation, just like that crack which started it all back in Texas.

Yes, he'd hurt me badly, but not even at our absolute worst did I ever believe he'd betray me. Berate me? Absolutely. Take immature little jabs and try to cut me down? Without hesitation.

But actually send me off to be hurt or killed? *Never.* Our trust had been building in the most unconventional ways, and now that we were on a path of healing and growth… the rest would fall into place.

"They're my pack and mates," I said, my voice rising as I defended them. "And I believe you are also, but until you cut final ties with Fletcher, your loyalty is torn. Which won't work for me. I've already grown up with a mom who couldn't put me first, no matter what I did, and I won't ever go back there again. Not even for you."

He stared in his way of seeing deeper than the surface, but there was nothing he could say to reassure me. We hadn't had our test of coming face to face with Fletcher yet, and until that moment, I'd always have doubts. After our trip to the volcano, we were tracking that piece of shit alpha down. Even if I had to fly on Talon's dragon to get there.

We couldn't live like this forever.

"You'll be free in a few days," I reminded him, stepping back toward the bars. "And I promise to visit again, but can you let me out now?"

"Move to the door," Slade ordered, before he pointed at Talon. "And you stay right the fuck where you are." Talon's gaze left me to clash with his brother's. The heat between them almost blasted off my skin.

"Watch how you fucking talk to me," Talon growled. "You're all alive because of Emme, but we've learned of magic that can sever mate bonds. I have the means to ensure that happens if you keep pushing me."

Magic could sever mate bonds?

My debilitating fear over that statement was enough to almost send me to my knees.

Slade, who never took well to threats, thrust his arm through the bars and gestured for Talon to *come a little closer.* Which he did, without hesitation.

I was about to double back and get between them when Hunter captured my arm through the bars. "No, Emmeline," he bit out, oozing dominance which didn't work on me. "They could kill you with one blow."

"Not a fucking chance," both dragons growled, and I almost couldn't tell them apart. The growlier they got, the more similar they sounded.

"She's the only one safe from us," Talon added.

Hunter still wouldn't let me get closer, but he also couldn't open the door without Slade. So we had to stand and watch Slade and Talon eyeballing each other.

Slade's arm jerked, his hand shooting toward his brother, who slapped it away before he made contact. He missed the other hand coming through the bars though, and Slade managed to smash his fist into his twin's face, sending him reeling back a few steps.

The hit was so loud I felt it in my bones. I was relieved to find Talon shaking it off like nothing.

"I'm letting her leave this time," he snarled, wiggling his jaw, but showing no other indication he was hurt. "But we'd better be heading for Europe in the next few days. I won't wait any longer."

"We'll leave Monday," Hunter informed him. "In three days."

Talon huffed, but he didn't argue. I felt the burn of his gaze on me once more, but unsure if I'd be able to leave if I met that stare, I shuffled to the door and waited for Slade to unlock it.

I didn't turn back to see the caged shifter until we were exiting. My heart broke when I saw Talon with his head hanging, fists clenched at his side. He screamed pain and dejection, and it stopped me in my tracks.

Slade backtracked to my side. "He'll be okay for a few days," he murmured, brushing his thumb over my cheek. "I'll keep him company. You can visit him too, but for now, give him time to deal with finally having you close and then losing you too fast. It's not easy for us to process that sort of loss. Dragons keep their most precious possessions in their claws."

Dismissing his reference of me being a possession, since I was used to it by now, I decided there was only one thing I could offer Talon.

Turning, I called out, "Tal!"

His head shot up, and the empty voids of his eyes sent shivers down my spine. He tilted his head in the animalistic way of dragons. "Tal?"

I forced a smile on my face. "Well, when you care about someone you give them a nickname. I'll be back later this evening, okay."

He didn't say anything, and I forced myself to swallow down tears as I followed Hunter and Slade from the room. Whether you called it karma or reaping what you sow, Talon was in the thick of his punishment.

I usually enjoyed when that happened to assholes, but in this circumstance, it broke my heart. Nothing was clear cut, and while we were growing closer, we still had a long way to go for true healing.

All I had was instinct guiding me as I navigated relationships with five powerful, damaged, and dangerous alphas. I just kept stumbling along and hoping we all made it out alive.

Alive was my driving need at the moment.

In the end, everyone I cared about had to be standing, otherwise I wouldn't survive.

CHAPTER 50

EMME

My phone buzzed through dinner, and expecting it would be the boys, I yanked it up and read the text.

> Beaten but still Golden: We're on our way home! Our plane will land at 10pm. I hope you'll wait up for us, pretty mate. We both need consolatory kisses and hugs.

> UnBEARable: You don't have to wait up for us, Em. We know you're tired and have a lot of shit going on. Kellan will crawl into bed with you anyway. And I… can wait. I'm a patient bear.

For some reason those last four words had me wanting to giggle and kick my damn feet under the table. These alphas screwed with my normal sensibilities until I had no idea who I was these days. Slade and Hunter both looked my way. "What did they say?" Hunter asked as he slid another crab cake on my plate. At this rate, I'd be too full to eat the main meal.

"Their plane lands at ten tonight. Kellan wants me to wait up, and Finley was telling me it was okay to sleep."

Hunter looked pleased. "I like when all of my pack is together." His chest rumbled, and through our bond his wolf relaxed. "Where they're safe and under my control."

"I've missed them so much," I admitted, rubbing my hand over my sternum. "It's weirdly empty here without everyone, and with our enemies still out there, I don't like us being separated. I'll feel much calmer when everyone's under the same roof."

Slade's expression remained neutral, and his eyes were empty. As they'd been ever since we left his brother in the containment room. He'd been back to deliver food and keep him company, but it was clear no one was happy with the current situation.

"I've been monitoring them from here," he said shortly, "and there was never any danger. But like Hunter, I'll sleep easier when our entire pack is back under my wing."

It didn't surprise me in the least that he felt that way.

Clicking to reply, I took a few seconds to consider what I would say, smiling sadly when my name popped up.

> Pretty Mate: I can't wait to see you both. Of course I'll wait up. Nothing could stop me from getting some pack hugs tonight. Safe travels and see you soon. *kissy face emoji*

> Beaten but still Golden: Awww, Shortcake. I am going to smother you in so many kisses. Don't dress up. You're only going to get naked.

A flare of heat joined the excitement, and I doubted anyone missed the surge of my scent or the wiggle I did to ease the throbbing down low.

Hunter chuckled. "Annoying pup is going to slobber all over you, isn't he?"

"I fucking hope so," I burst out, fanning myself with my fork.

That had Slade smiling. "Who knew there'd be a shifter who'd find his annoying ways endearing."

Pointing said fork at him, I let a slow smile form. "You forget that I saw you when we thought he was dying. You can pretend all you want, Scary Shifter, but deep down we all need Kellan's version of love." Slade shrugged, but he didn't deny it.

"Are you ever going to tell me what you thought of my last prank?" I asked again, expecting he'd ignore my question like the dozen times before.

He leaned in closer, the low lights from the dining room sconces giving his expression a slightly sinister look. "Oh, Snow. It's adorable that you think I'm going to spill that secret so easily. I like to stay on your mind, so I might keep this going for a little while longer."

Yeah, he really didn't need to withhold information to be on my mind.

The chime of my phone allowed me to wrench my eyes from Slade's penetrating gaze.

> UnBEARable: Carve out some time later for me too, Ice Queen. Please. I'd love to log in a few hours on your car.

> Beaten but still Golden: He'd like you to be naked too. FYI. Streaks of grease on your skin is an added bonus.

Goddess above. Kellan was going to be the death of us both.

> UnBEARable: Due to regularly scheduled bouts of being an annoying fuck, Kellan Jackson will not be arriving back to Golden Claw in one piece. Apologies for any interruptions to plans, but... he had it coming.

> UnBEARable: But also... he isn't wrong.

I pressed my hand to my cheek, unsurprised to find warmth under my touch. "Now, I need to know what brought that lovely pink to your cheeks," Hunter said, leaning forward to cup the other side of my face. "It's your color, baby girl. Especially when it coats your entire body."

A slow panting breath was all I could manage under the circumstances. "You're all going to be the death of me," I repeated for the group. "I feel like a fucking virgin thrown in to be sacrificed to the beasts. And we all know I'm no virgin."

Hunter snorted. "We don't know that at all, baby girl. As far as we're concerned, you were untouched before arriving on our doorstep."

Slade shrugged, and I didn't trust his calm expression. "Once they're all dead, it'll be like it never happened. That's how science works."

I blinked. "Uh, no. That's not how it works *at all*."

He just smirked, and I narrowed my eyes on him. "You leave those poor, defenseless humans alone. They're not even worth the few seconds it would take for you to track them down."

We remained in a stare-off, and all the time he wore that infuriating smirk. I made a mental note to talk to him about this again later, since I doubted he had time now to hunt humans. Not with everything else going on.

The door to the dining room swung open and Florence hurried in. "Dinner is ready!" she called, setting down a huge bowl of pasta, which was soon joined by bowls of cheese, chili flakes, and other toppings. "It's a chicken alla boscaiola, and it might be one of Gerry's best dishes."

Her eyes shone at the mention of the chef, and I swore I could see a twinkle of their budding relationship in her gaze.

"It smells amazing," I said, leaning forward to breathe in cream, garlic, bacon and mushroom. "Thank you both for all the incredible food. You take very good care of us."

She dropped a hand on my shoulder and squeezed briefly. "It's our pleasure. And soon we'll have our other boys home too, making sure they're eating right. I'll be back with the garlic bread."

Moving at her usual rapid speed, she was gone and back in seconds, placing the tray of crunchy bread beside the pasta. Garlic butter dripped down the sides of the toasted loaf, and my wolf let out an appreciative rumble. Hunter liked that response, and his beast joined in, as he pressed his palm to my collarbone.

As our entitled alpha, he held a strong connection with my beast, and she frolicked to the surface at his call. Hunter's black wolf was a powerful entity at the end of our tether, and I wondered how all of these connections would feel once our quintet was complete.

After a lifetime of loneliness and fighting every battle by myself, to feel them always there with me was an unexpected gift. I'd thought I'd hate it, but it had the opposite effect.

"Eat, mate," Hunter told me, releasing me from his hold.

They'd wait for me as always, so I hurried to fill my bowl and dig into the creamy dish. Both alphas got started after they watched me eat my body weight in food, and when we were finished, Slade headed out to patrol while I visited Talon again.

Hunter wanted to come too, but I left him in the foyer with a thorough kiss. "I'll be back up here soon and we can wait for our boys together," I said, and with a grumble he conceded that he had some work to get through.

"But I'll be keeping an eye on that fuck. If he pulls you into the cell again, I will remove all of his limbs. And break his neck."

With a chuckle, I patted his chest. "Okay, love. You can beat your manly chest if needed. I appreciate you going all entitled alpha for me."

Hunter shook his head. "I know you're patronizing me, little omega. And as a punishment, tonight might be the night that Kellan and I step up our plans for you."

My brain exploded and my panties disintegrated. *Poof.* Gone.

"Yes," I breathed, nodding like a damn bobble-head doll. "Yes. Please. I absolutely deserve to be punished." His very satisfied chuckle filled the room, and with one last toe-curling kiss, he left me to visit Talon while he got to work.

"Sweet Honey," the dragon rumbled, still propped against the bars as if he hadn't moved since I left. "You kept your word."

"Of course I did," I said, forcing myself to move casually, though my wolf was in one hell of a rush to get us closer. When she released a mournful howl, I almost lost control and shifted.

The ragged nature of this bond was wearing on both of us.

"You can shift," Talon said, straightening. "The room is too constrictive for my beast, but I'd love to meet your wolf."

As soon as he mentioned it, letting her go free was all I could think about. "I'd like that," I said with a nod. "Yeah, we'd like that a lot."

I briefly debated leaving the room to strip, before deciding not to make a big deal about it.

Naked for shifters was normal.

Talon's gaze darkened, and under that stare I quickly removed everything until I was clad in black underwear. "This feels a lot like foreplay," I found myself mumbling, and his gaze turned sensual.

"I'd say your instincts are spot on," he murmured. "I don't have any experience with sex, but I enjoy this feeling. I want to claim every inch of you, omega. Every damn inch."

Fuck me sideways.

Both dragons were virgins?

Annddd now I needed five cold showers and a lobotomy to stop thinking about touching them.

Together?

Wait. Nope. That went too far. Or… not far enough.

In a rush, I yanked off my underwear and called on my wolf, shifting into her form without any issue. When I straightened and stretched out all my limbs, Talon pushed against the bars, and my beast locked in on his scent until the pulse of his bite grew stronger.

"Oh, you are the prettiest wolf," he crooned, crouching down. "You're our perfect mate. Come here, sit with me."

My beast padded forward, proud by his response. She didn't have the slightest doubt that we would be a quintet of six—if the goddess designed it, then who were we to argue?

I was starting to agree, and had already decided that I would claim my entire pack.

No matter who I had to destroy to make it happen.

CHAPTER 51

HUNTER

Watching Emme via our security system was a poor substitute to real life, and while I could feel her through our bond no matter where she was, it was more potent up close.

The hum of our bond did put me at ease though, as it told me she was safe.

Even if she was with Talon.

I couldn't deny his connection to our pack. I felt the same *pull* toward him as the other members. His scent merged well with the group, and though none of us would bond him the same way as Emme—she was the center of our group for a reason—we would still have to bring him in through a quintet bonding ceremony. And list him on all official Reeves Pack paperwork.

There'd be an uproar from the community as they squabbled over how a quintet with six members could exist. It would no doubt throw everything out of whack for a while, and I hoped we had some form of explanation before it happened.

Not that I gave a fuck what other shifters said about us, but I was done with life being hard for Emme. She was confident that the six of us would form as strong a circle of power as a normal quintet, and the casual acceptance I felt toward Talon was a strong indicator she was right.

When my phone rang, I answered without tearing my gaze from Emme, who'd just shifted back from her wolf. She was chatting to

Talon, and the dragon stared at her like he wanted to eat her... In every damn way.

It was a look I was all too familiar with, and I couldn't blame him.

Our omega was delicious. *In every damn way.*

"Yeah," I said, already knowing it was Slade.

"He's stable," he said, giving me the update I expected. "She's fine to stay down there."

Over the time spent with his brother, he'd taken to sensing Talon's moods. They hadn't officially bonded, but we knew the twin soul connection was a mystical bond all on its own.

Which was about all the fuck we knew. It was a real pain in the ass how little of his heritage was out in the world, but at the same time, it might be what keeps him safe.

Knowledge was power, and we wanted no one to have the power to control the strongest beasts in our world. It was bad enough that Fletcher had figured out a way to garner loyalty from Talon.

"She looks happy down there with him," I said, having no doubt we were both staring at the same footage. He might be patrolling, but whenever he shifted out of his beast form, his focus was on Emme. The guilt he carried over Fletcher making it past our defenses was a weight I would take from him—if he'd let me.

"Her happiness comes second to her safety," Slade shot back, his dragon rumbling just below the surface. "Also, the car just picked up Kel, Fin, and Kenzo from the airport. They'll be there in ten."

My wolf let loose a howl, and I was pleased to have them back in Golden Claw. I detested my pack being scattered around the country. "That's excellent news. We'll see you before dawn, then. I want all of my pack to spend at least some time under this roof together."

He grunted, the line went dead, and I chuckled at his reminder that no one ordered him around. Still, he hadn't argued, which meant he'd make it home.

Shutting down my computer, I scanned through the security footage on my phone this time, relieved to find everything in order around our property. Ever since I'd found out my father was involved, I'd been fighting a deep-seated unease. Especially with that sneaky piece of shit missing in action, along with my mother and Sorenson. None of which sat well with me.

Once Fletcher regrouped and moved on to the next phase of his plan, he would slam the full force of his power and magic in our direction. I couldn't let my focus slip for even a second.

The guard house alerted me to Kellan and Finley's car arriving, and I waited in the foyer. Emme would be up as soon as she felt them, and then I'd get to steal her away for a night with Kellan. The annoying pup had been pining hard, begging me for photos of our mate, sending me crying emojis for days. He'd be all in for my plans.

Finley was welcome too, but from what I knew, they weren't quite there yet. Not to mention it was Kenzo's birthday, and he'd flown back last-minute with the boys so they could head out on the town for a few hours.

As the car pulled to a stop out the front, Emme burst into the entrance hall. "I'm so freaking excited," she said, jumping up and down. "I missed them so much."

The way her hair flew around her face had me desperate to thread my fingers through the soft strands. Hating any distance between us, I wrapped her in my arms, tucking her smaller frame against my side. "They missed you too, baby," I murmured, my wolf rising as I stared at her.

The icy blue of her eyes warmed, and the overhead lights illuminated the spattering of freckles across her cute button nose. Her smile, though, did me the fuck in.

When she'd first arrived in our world, her smiles had been forced, and I'd seen the way they were tinged with sadness. Now she showed real happiness, which was *every damn thing*.

She rested her head against my chest, and I pressed my lips to the top of her head, breathing her in. My wolf grumbled at the thought of her in danger ever again, and we were in agreement. My parents, Sorenson, Chelsea, Blaine, and any other fuck who'd ever hurt her was going to die. It didn't matter if I'd known them my entire life or they gave birth to me.

They'd touched my mate, and for that they were the enemy.

And enemies were eliminated.

Kellan exploded through the door first, and slammed into us with so much force, that if I hadn't been standing at Emme's back, she'd have gone flying. Not that he would have let her hit the floor—unless he wanted his ass beat. As it was, Emme's laughter as he hauled me and her off the ground was the only reason he didn't get knocked out anyway.

"Gentle with her, asshole," I warned, and he threw his head back to chuckle. His lack of fear was as annoying as it was refreshing.

"She likes it a little rough. As you're well aware, Daddy Alpha."

The goddess really owed me for taking this pup off her hands. "You're about to get it a little rough, and trust me, there's no pleasure for you."

Kellan didn't even answer, too busy burying his hands in Emme's hair, kissing her like she was the very air he needed to survive. Her scent burst to life around us, and I wasn't the only one groaning and adjusting my fucking dick.

Finley remained awkwardly hovering in the entrance, and I noted the look of longing on his face. "Soon, brother," I mouthed, and he nodded, rubbing a hand over his beard.

By the time Kellan and Emme broke apart, Finley had schooled his expression to one of amusement, keeping his pain locked inside. I was proud of my brother though, as he'd finally taken the steps needed to rise to his full potential.

When Kellan eased away a fraction, we could see how dazed and flushed Emme was. Her lips were swollen and pink, and when she sighed contentedly, I swear all of us wagged our fucking tails like good boys. Kellan was wearing off on us, but as long as it made Emme happy, I wasn't going to complain. *Much.*

When Emme approached Finley, he froze on the spot, as if any movement would spook her and she'd run away. He did manage to offer a tentative smile, which she took as encouragement. She popped up on her toes and wrapped her arms around his neck.

A gush of air escaped him, and his arms slammed around her back so tight that Emme let out a little squeak. Through the bond I could feel that it was mostly shock not pain. In fact, it was clear she loved his bear hugs as she clung to him. Her body relaxed.

"I'm so happy you're both back," she murmured against his shoulder. "We *all* missed you."

Finley lifted her off the ground, swishing her side to side in a gentle motion. "We played like crap because we'd rather be here with you. Hockey isn't worth the pain of these road trips."

I wasn't sure Emme truly understood the significance of that statement. Finley choosing her over hockey… It was all the evidence any of us needed that he was changing.

For the better.

Kellan sidled in beside me, throwing his arm over my shoulders. His eyes glowed as he watched them. If this were an animation, he'd have an exaggerated heart pounding from his chest.

"This could be one of the best days of my life, outside of when I first met Emme, and the first time we kissed, and the bonding, and the first time she touched me—"

He was cut off by my hand slamming against the back of his head, though I couldn't argue those points. Emme pulled away from Finley to shoot us a cheeky smile. "I'm so happy that I failed at my task to avoid packs and this life. I honestly couldn't live without you assholes. I really couldn't."

"Same!" Kellan shouted, and he was racing for her again, hauling her up into his arms. "And now we need to celebrate. You and me, naked for the next twelve to twelve hundred hours. What do you say, Shortcake?"

Emme wrapped her legs around him and clung on tight. "Sounds like a plan." Her gaze met mine. "You in, Hurricane?"

She had no idea how far in I was. It was the sort of *in* where not even death would part us. "All the fucking way, baby girl. All the way."

Kellan turned and headed for the stairs, and I paused to check on Finley. "You going to be okay, brother?" I asked him.

He nodded, watching them as they raced up the stairs. "Yeah, I'll just shower and change before heading to Kenz's place. Emme and I aren't there yet, and that's okay. I'm learning patience, and I'm thrilled that she's let me in as much as she already has."

I slapped a hand on his shoulder. "We're all proud of you. Just know that."

Finley reached up and wrapped his hand over the top of mine, his head lowering, but I caught the shine in his eyes. "Thanks, Hunt." He shook his head and then cleared his throat. "Now go and love on our omega. I want her to be happy… above all else."

With that, he shuffled off to his room, and I knew he'd be okay. Eventually.

My pack was strengthening in ways that had my alpha energy settled and satisfied.

Now all we needed was to eliminate our enemies.

CHAPTER 52

EMME

Kellan raced up the stairs with me clinging to him like a damn monkey, and I already knew it'd be a waste of breath to insist on walking. Through our bond, his love and need bled into my desperation, leaving me panting and on the edge of losing my damn sanity.

After his greeting downstairs, not only were my panties absolutely ruined, but my sweatpants might be as well.

"I'm not sure I can wait," Kellan groaned, all but sprinting along the landing and busting into his bedroom. Florence had already been in today and freshened everything up, leaving it cool and scentless. I hated the evidence that he'd been gone for days, but he was here now and I would enjoy every second of our reunion.

We didn't make it to the bed. He brought me down on the soft, thick rug, his mouth landing on mine, and I groaned into the kiss. Kellan wrenched back, panting against me. "Goddess of the shifters, pretty mate. My dick is literally trying to bust through my suit pants."

"Well, you better get naked, then," I suggested between laughs. "We don't want you to have to perform with an injury."

Kellan groaned again and kissed me in long, drugging kisses that rendered me mindless and frantic with desire. It took me many seconds to realize he was trying to wiggle out of his clothes without separating our bodies.

"I don't care what Coach says, I'm not leaving you again," he vowed, his pants almost to his ankles as he tried to kick off dress shoes. When they didn't come off easily, he focused on tearing his shirt open, the buttons flying around the room. "When you were reading and got to the spicy scenes, Finley and I had to take turns jerking off—" He narrowed his eyes on me as a slow smirk tilted his lips. "Separately, Shortcake. Get your mind out of the gutter."

That sent me into fits of laughter, my body heating at the mental image he'd painted. My alphas loved each other like brothers, which was okay with me. I wasn't mad about being the sole focus of their sexual needs.

"Well, tonight you won't have to take care of anything yourself," I whispered, leaning up to kiss him as Hunter entered the room.

Our entitled alpha paused, taking in what was no doubt an interesting scene. Kellan, pants around his ankles and shoes on, crowding me into the rug while he kissed every part of my skin he could reach. I whined when Kellan was lifted full bodily from me, an unexpected growl tearing from his throat as he turned on Hunter.

The entitled alpha let loose an even more impressive growl, laced with dominance, which halted Kellan in his tracks. "You're half fucking rabid," Hunter snapped at him. "Pull yourself together. I know you won't hurt Emme, but you're also not getting anywhere fast in this current state."

Kellan sucked in a ragged breath and lifted his head to rumble out a howl. "I was actually getting there *very fast*," he muttered

Hunter shook his head. "Don't worry, annoying pup. We have all night to love on our omega. And I think it's time to *love her together*."

Not even ten seconds later Kellan was completely naked, I was completely naked, and we were both on the bed staring at Hunter. When our Golden wanted something, he moved fast.

Hunter took a step closer, and the wild energy of his beast rose around us. What I felt from them through the bond turned me mindless. "Please, *please, please*." Yeah, I was already begging, and I didn't even care. If these two didn't destroy my body *right the fuck* now, I would detonate into a million pieces and scatter about the universe.

Yes, I was dramatic when I was horny, but the need was… *Gah.*

The gold in Hunter's eyes deepened and he continued his slow prowl, shedding clothes, until every delicious inch of his skin was on display. The tattoos flashed down his arms, and I was drawn to the *mine.* As always. "Is this what you want tonight, little mate? You want both of us?"

When he asked questions in that deep growl, I had to squeeze my thighs together.

"Yes, we want," Kellan said, waving his arms as if to hurry him up. He stretched out next to me, his hands cupping my tits. "Get your ass on the bed, Hurricane. You're testing my limited patience."

Hunter silenced him with a single look, but Kellan put his focus into exploring my skin in tracing, teasing touches. His hold firmed up down my stomach as he cupped my core. His fingers slid through the arousal, spreading lubrication down to my ass. I groaned when he returned to my pussy and thrust two fingers inside, stretching me to his touch. He thrust hard and fast, the wet sound of my arousal loud in the room.

That snapped Hunter into action. He was on the bed in a flash, crawling over the top of me, his huge body covering mine as we kissed. He pulled away too fast, but my protests died off as he slid down my body and batted Kellan's hand out of the way.

"Mine first," he grumbled, flattening his tongue to run it in one stroke along my slit, his fingers tracing my ass. When he plunged his tongue inside my pussy, his finger pressed to the ring of muscles at my ass, entering me and sending me straight to the edge of release. He'd been big into ass play lately, and I was growing addicted to the feeling.

Kellan returned to my tits, cupping and dragging them closer to lick from one hard nipple to the next. Back and forth. When he panted and groaned, my walls clenched at the sound of alphas expressing their desire. I fucking loved it.

Hunter's finger in my ass was soon joined by a second, the stretch and burn familiar, and I was so horny there was no need for any other form of lubrication.

Hunter knew exactly how to play my body until I simmered on the edge of release.

Hovering. Dying, desperate, and breaking into pieces.

"Your scent," Kellan rasped, his teeth marking me between kisses. "It's everywhere. I want to bathe in it."

I couldn't speak, reduced to pants and moans.

Hunter's tongue flicked across my clit in a maddening rhythm, and every time I was about to topple over into a blazing release, he changed the pace. If his huge shoulders weren't keeping my thighs apart, I'd have locked his head between my legs to keep him in place.

His laughter vibrated over my core. "You will come so many times tonight you'll lose count, little omega. And you know I always keep my promises."

"St-Starting now?" I choked out.

Another chuckle, and he moved his fingers deeper in my ass as his tongue slid against my clit. If I'd thought the buildup was intense before, it had nothing on now. When the swirls of pleasure finally exploded, I screamed and briefly lost touch with reality.

After Hunter drew out my orgasm, he lifted his head, and I wasn't surprised to find his face and chest soaked in my release. Kellan pouted as he stared at his brother. "I need a taste, Hunt," he whimpered, lurching forward as if he was going to lick Hunter for a hit.

Hunter took pity on him and backed away, and Kellan slid into the spot between my thighs, his equally talented tongue caressing my sensitive flesh until I clutched his hair and screamed into another release. Kellan ate me like a shifter who'd been starving for years.

As I sucked in ragged breaths, Hunter moved up the bed, and when he kissed me, I tasted the sweet muskiness of my cum.

"Come again, little omega," he ordered as Kellan slid two fingers inside me, curling them to stroke my g-spot, and I came instantly. "Good girl," Hunter murmured, always pleased when I obeyed. My body jerked against them, hips moving to the rhythm they set.

"I think you're ready," he murmured, and despite having just come three times, my entire core clenched. I knew exactly what he was talking about.

"Oh, she likes the idea of that, Hunt," Kellan groaned, burying his face again, his fingers sliding deeper. "She likes that a lot."

My fourth orgasm ripped through me, and it was a miracle that I could still count. Hunter slid his hands under my thighs and flipped me over to straddle him. "I've had your delicious ass already, baby girl," he rumbled, "so I think we should give our Golden a try. What do you say?"

I nodded, unable to form coherent words.

Hunter released my weight, and I gasped at how hard his cock felt as he pushed slowly inside me. I had no idea how this was going to work with alphas of their size, but I was a shifter, and I'd heal fast. As

I slid down his thick, pulsing length, my breaths caught in my chest. That feeling when they entered me would never get old… the fullness took my breath away.

When I was fully seated, Hunter moved slowly, and as desire built within me again, I started to ride him in time to his strokes. When I was panting and breathless, my scent so potent it was drowning us, Kellan moved in behind me. He ran his hand down my ass, gently stroking me.

My body was sensitive from multiple orgasms, nerves alight, and when Kellan's finger pressed against my ass, he found very little resistance. He pumped in and out of my ass in time to Hunter's thrusts, and my next orgasm coated them both. Kellan used that release to lube up his dick. When he removed his fingers, I was desperate for him to replace them.

Hunter slowed so Kellan could press against me, and I cried out at that first push of cock into my ass. He moved so fucking slowly it could be classified as a form of torture, and as the sensation of fullness grew, I worried that I'd overestimated my ability to handle this.

"That's it, baby. Relax into the feeling," Hunter murmured, drawing my attention to him as I huffed and moaned. He cupped my face, tilting me forward, his tongue dancing with mine as we kissed. "You're doing so well, mate. You were made to take us, and look how perfect you are. Fucking perfection. This pussy, and that flawless ass. Goddess be damned, mate. You are *fucking perfection*."

His praise washed through me, and by the time I was *full* of alpha, tingles of pleasure had burst to life *everywhere*. The need to move had me arching against them as a "please" slipped out.

"Please what, little omega?" Hunter growled, tilting his head to stare into my eyes. "What do you want from your alphas?"

"Everything," I gasped. "I want and need everything. Please."

Kellan moaned. "Your ass feels so fucking good, pretty mate. The way you hug my dick, like you were made for me. Every fucking time Hunter moves I can feel it too, and buried in your ass like this, I don't even care."

"You're fucking me so good, Golden," I praised him, wanting his needs met as thoroughly as mine were. "Such a good boy, taking my ass and making it yours."

Both alphas groaned, and Kellan's normally smooth thrusts grew more frantic.

"Oh, baby girl. The goddess knew what she was doing with you," Hunter growled.

With each claiming word, he thrust into me, and Kellan timed the snap of his hips for whenever Hunter pulled out, so there was no break in the rolling cascade of pleasure. The tingle of my impending release ran from the tips of my toes to the top of my head, and as my body adjusted to the size of *two* alphas, they figured out how to move at the same time, the dual sensations too much to contain.

I came screaming so hard that I almost blacked out, my vision graying out around the edges. Hunter growled my name and jerked inside me, Kellan right behind him, which set me off again. And again.

Eventually I did lose track of my orgasms, as promised, and with exhaustion dragging down my limbs, I collapsed in a sated, sticky mess between the two of them.

Okay, *group pack sex* was my new favorite version of sex.

CHAPTER 53

A dream woke me. It had been a while since I'd been drawn out of sleep so abruptly that I couldn't relax enough to fall back asleep. It hadn't been like the days after I was forcibly bonded, when I'd come awake screaming. This just felt like a more run-of-the-mill dream, where the anxiety of our hidden enemies kept my mind from fully shutting down.

Neither of my mates moved as I crawled out from between them, desperate to pee, drink some water—I was dehydrated for a very good reason—and maybe grab a snack. Only a few aches remained in my body, the reminder of my night of absolutely mind-blowing sex.

My healing abilities were improving, which was what I'd hoped would happen after bonding my alphas. My pack was strong, and I got a boost of that strength through our bonds. I would argue that the alphas had adapted some of my calmer temperament too.

It wasn't that they were less dominant, but their beasts felt calmer.

Even Slade's. Despite the way he continued to hold himself back.

When I finished in the bathroom, I slipped on one of the shirts off the floor, realizing it was Hunter's when the scent of coffee surrounded me. Padding silently through the hall and down the stairs, I let the moonlight guide me to the kitchen. Florence or Gerry had left a pantry light on, making it very easy for me to find the snacks.

I headed straight for the container of baked goods, only to pause at a loud crack and rustling from outside the windows over the sink. Creeping in that direction, I peered out into the darkness, unable to track any movement. The rustling came again a second later, but it wasn't as loud, as if the culprit had moved further away. When a grunt and burst of laughter followed, I relaxed, recognizing that deep rumble. Finley was home.

Abandoning my snack, I headed for the front door, pushing down my annoyance at him being out until almost dawn. My stupid brain flashed right to the last time he'd stumbled in the door drunk and smelling like a damn florist. He'd assured me nothing had happened during those nights out, and I believed him. He hadn't cared about hurting me in the early days, that was for sure, so he wouldn't have lied to spare my feelings.

It meant everything to me that he'd remained loyal from the moment I arrived in Golden Claw, and in the hopes of our reconciliation, I doubted he'd fuck it up now. Still, it was hard to completely dismiss my worries.

When I reached the front door, there was a heavy thump against it, and I could hear his voice clearly. "—get to bed, and I need her, brother."

My stomach flipped and I pressed in closer.

"I know, Fin," Kenzo mumbled, sounding almost as drunk as Finley. "You need your mate, which is completely understandable, but... brother, you can't drag that gift up to her. I swear to the goddess, Hunter will kill you." He started to laugh, and I was filled with curiosity about what was so funny.

"She's sooo beautiful," Finley said, his words muffled, like his face was pressed to the door. "She deserves the world, and I owe her all the gifts."

Another thump, this one louder, and my curiosity won out. I flipped the deadbolt and disabled the alarm. When I pulled the door open, two massive shifters straightened on the small front stoop, comically trying to fit together. And they weren't the only thing needing to fit.

Finley, covered near head to toe in what looked like mud, had a tree clasped in his hands.

It had to be ten or fifteen feet tall, and the bright green foliage was dotted with blooming white flowers, which should not have been so vibrant in winter.

"Ice!" Finley called, sounding happy. "My queen. There you are, darlin'."

Swirls of desire and excitement kicked to life in my stomach. When he drawled *darlin'* to me... on top of the full effect of those gorgeous eyes and dimples.

Lethal. Fucking. Combination.

"What's happening, guys?" I asked, trying to sound casual, though I felt anything but.

Kenzo swayed forward and almost toppled down the stairs before he caught himself. "Fin brought you flowers," he declared, puffed up like a proud parent.

Pressing my lips together as hard as I could, I tried not to let my laughter spill free. "I see that. Your *flowers* are lovely, thank you, Grouchy." Finley beamed, and I let loose a small chuckle before I got myself back under control.

"We need to find a thingy to put the thingy in—" The bear shifter said, swaying as he examined the thick base of the tree.

Don't laugh. Don't laugh. "Do you mean a vase?"

He fucking beamed again. "Oh, you are so smart, baby. Yes, a vase." He glanced down and squinted at the base once more. "Or maybe a bucket? I'm not sure there's a vase big enough for this one."

"I think you're right. It's very impressive." More laughter bubbled up inside, and I would pop soon if I kept holding it in.

Finley's smile faded into the saddest expression I'd ever seen and I no longer wanted to laugh. "A simple bouquet of flowers was not enough," he whispered, his gaze intense. I wasn't sure he'd blinked since I opened the door. "You deserve the biggest flowers in the world. I'm so sorry I hurt you, baby. I'm so damn sorry. I have something else for you upstairs in my room with the magazines."

My chest tightened at him calling me *baby* again. The first time I'd thought it had just slipped out, but he'd used it again, so casually. Not only that, but he'd also just confirmed he was the one to leave the magazines and origami. I'd suspected, of course, but it was nice to know for sure.

Kenzo snorted out such a loud laugh, that these idiots would wake up the street if they weren't careful. "That's a secret," he boomed. "She'll know you made her the origami too."

These two were hilarious, and I was happy that I'd been out of bed to see them like this. Swaying together, holding a damn tree that would topple most shifters.

"Happy birthday, Kenzo," I said, remembering why they'd gone out in the first place. "Do you want to come inside?"

He shook his head. "Nah, I've got two beauties waiting in bed for me. Which is exactly how one should end their birthday. But I'll see you both at the family BBQ."

He pointed slowly at Finley, and then slowly at me, before shaking his head like he forgot what he was saying. With a final slap on Finley's shoulder, that sent the bear stumbling forward until his tree got caught on the doorframe and rained white petals on us, Kenzo left.

My focus returned to Finley, who was patting me down with one hand, while the other clutched the stuck tree. "Oh, shit, sorry darlin'. I got you all dirty."

Fuck me. His deep rumbly bear voice had my body waking up in a way that should be nearly impossible after the night I'd just had.

"You're totally fine, Fin," I said, helping him untangle from the doorway, so he could fit himself and his "flowers" in the house.

Together, we got the tree into the kitchen, and he waved off my help as he dropped it into the large sink, resting the branches against the windows. It was right around the time he started filling the sink to use as a vase that I lost it, leaning forward to laugh until tears ran down my cheeks.

Finley glanced over his shoulder, and his smile was soft as he watched me. "I love it when you laugh," he whispered, his emotions blaring across his face. I read regret and despair and hope and *love* all wrapped up in one longing stare. "Your eyes were so sad when you first arrived. Every time I looked at you, I drowned in your pain."

That knocked the laughter from me. "Your eyes were the same," I replied, my voice hushed. "I felt this instant connection, even as my heart ached."

With the tree now chilling in the sink, water covering its roots, Finley headed toward me. He was so dirty that mud covered him from the ends of his boots to the tips of his forehead. He didn't appear to care as he wrapped his arms around me and hauled me up into him. "I missed you," he breathed, burying his face into my throat. "Fuck, I missed you so much. Please don't ever leave me. I swear to the goddess, I will follow you. I don't even care if you go where it's eternally summer and they've never even heard of an ice rink. I'll take up surfing, and we can live in the sand. Just please... please, darlin'. Please never leave me."

Deep in my heart, I'd suspected that Finley would be the one to wreck me in a way I'd never recover from. He'd hated me so intensely, or at least he'd tried to, and it appeared he loved just as fiercely. When he was like this, with no pride or hurt feelings between us, I could admit that I loved him too.

I'd probably loved this asshole from the first second I stared into his eyes. Now that he was showing up in the ways I needed, I didn't have to deny it any longer.

"I won't leave you," I promised, voice thick as tears hovered on the edge of my control. "Fin, I need you in my life. Now and always. I had no idea how truly broken and empty I was before I found this pack. You're all—" I choked out a sob. "You're the greatest fortune I've ever received."

He wrapped himself tighter around me, as if we were imprinting into each other's skin. I had grown more used to hugs, but there were times, like tonight, when it tore me apart once more.

My wolf howled and she was happy. So goddess be damned happy.

With the sound of her joy in my head, I sobbed silently, and Finley lifted his head from where he'd been huffing in my scent like he'd die without it. When I saw a tear slip down his cheek, cutting through the mud, my sobs were no longer silent.

"I haven't really cried in years," he admitted, sounding almost confused.

I coughed to try to catch my breath through the tears soaking my face. When another tear slid down his cheek, I reached up and captured it. Pressing the muddy, salty drop to my tongue.

Finley's eyes darkened, and I groaned as his lips landed on mine, our tongues coated in our sorrow. We kissed for so long in that dark hall, leaving mud on the shiny floors, and fractures in our hearts.

"I love you, mate," Finley breathed against my mouth. "I have loved you from the first second I stared into your beautiful, icy blue eyes. *My* ice. *My* mate."

I'd barely gotten myself under control when the tears started again, and Finley kissed them away. I was so caught up in this pivotal moment between us that I didn't even notice him carrying me up the stairs until we were in his room. I'd never stepped foot in his space before, and there was no time to notice anything, as he whisked me into his bathroom.

"I'm going to clean you up," he warned, still kissing my cheeks, his beard marking my skin in ways I'd dreamed of. "Then we're going to sleep in the same bed. I can't sleep without you, darlin'. I hope you don't mind that I'll need you forever."

"I don't mind," I promised, feeling the sort of peace that was terrifying when we were still in so much danger. Everything was going so well in my world… too well.

That anxiety dream had happened for a reason, as I sensed the impending doom that would steal all of this happiness from me. No matter how hard I fought to hold on to it.

CHAPTER 54

EMME

I woke surrounded by warmth and the scent of cherry, vanilla, and chocolate as our beasts slept symbolically beside us. Finley held me tight, my back plastered down his front, his leg tangled between mine. One big hand pressed against my stomach while the other sat just under my boobs. I wouldn't have expected this position to be so comfortable, but I was relaxed enough to fall asleep again.

Then I heard a familiar voice whisper from nearby: "This is what they mean when they say they witnessed a miracle, and were eternally changed from the experience."

"You're a moron," Slade said flatly to Kellan.

There was a grunt, and Hunter added, "Tell us something we don't already know, but our annoying pup has a point. This has been a long time coming."

I heard feet shuffling closer. "Though I will say, there's not enough of our pretty mate to go around," Kellan said, more loudly. "We need to sleep in shifts. I'm taking the first one right now." Our bond hummed as he moved closer, and I didn't even have to open my eyes to know he was about to climb in on my other side.

"I will kill you," Finley rumbled, pissed off and half-asleep. "Leave now and you might get to keep your fucking intestines inside your body."

As usual, a threat just set Kellan off in laughter. "Ah, Grouchy Bear. There you are. I was almost going to change your group chat name to Care Bear again. Specifically, whatever one of those little plushies is the soft-hearted one."

Amusement flickered through my tired brain, as I'd suggested the same thing recently.

I tried to force my eyes open, but I hadn't had enough sleep lately and my eyelids refused to cooperate. Finley buried his face in the back of my neck, my hair no doubt everywhere since I hadn't braided it back before bed.

"Ignore them," he whispered, his breath tracing over my skin and sending shivers down my spine. I wore one of his shirts and a pair of way-too-big-for-me athletic shorts, and the bear shifter was pressed *very* closely to me.

He let out a low, deep groan as my scent intensified.

In fact, all the alphas did, and it was only when Kellan yelped that I pried my eyes open in time to see Hunter haul him off the bed and out of the room. "Give them a damn minute," he yelled as he went, and Kellan shot back that this was *deprivation of his sexual liberty.*

Slade smiled, and I was not awake enough to deal with his devastatingly handsome face on top of everything else. "Family barbeque starts at five," he said. "Since you've slept half the day away, you'll only have a few hours to get ready. Attendance is mandatory. It'll be our last before we head to Europe."

I managed to get my arm out from the blankets to salute him. "Appreciate you not waking me for training today, sir. We'll see you outside soon."

His big chest lifted as his dragon rumbled. "Don't call me sir unless you want to experience the consequences."

Before I could respond—and ask for details—he followed Kellan and Hunter from the room.

"Fucking brothers," Finley grumbled again, draping himself farther over me. As I folded to his hard length, I couldn't quite remember why we weren't mated yet.

I'd honestly never felt readier, even knowing I was trusting in faith and gut instinct. There hadn't really been enough time for Finley to prove this new attitude was here to stay, but I was okay with that. Gut instinct rarely let me down.

Accepting we'd bond soon had contentment flowing through me, and I wasn't sure if Finley felt it, but he relaxed too. "I slept so soundly," he said, rocking me slightly in a comforting way. "With you in my arms, and the therapy techniques I've been working through with the doc, I can feel the change in my essence and my beast. Our moods are less erratic, and I'm dealing better with disappointment and pain." The rocking slowed, and I turned in his arms, wanting to face him.

He didn't let me create any distance between us as he shifted his face closer to mine, and I was momentarily distracted by how ridiculously good these alphas looked first thing in the morning. Between those whiskey eyes, outlandish lashes, messy hair, and his beard, Finley was devastating.

"You're the biggest key to my healing," he said, expression serious, and all my focus returned to his confession. "Without you, it would have taken months of therapy to even come close to where I am now."

I was hit by a moment of panic that he'd already planned on stopping, and I found myself blurting, "Don't forget what Dr. Karen said: there's no *cure* for our trauma from the past, but there is moving past it with time and hard work." I regretted my statement the second it was out, knowing I'd overstepped.

I was relieved when Finley nodded and shuffled even closer. "I will never consider myself cured, because I don't have a disease. Or at least, not one with a cure. My brain is forever altered by my life experiences, which is what makes me the bear I am today. But the weight of the trauma is lifting. I can see the light through the mists of my past, and I'm ready to walk in the sunlight. If that makes sense..."

"It makes perfect sense," I replied, my unease already calmed by his reassurance. "When life got hard for me, it felt like I was drowning in shades of gray. An entire world of gray and endless rain and sorrow. But now there's so much warmth and color... it's quite overwhelming."

He nodded, and anything more I was going to say died as his hands slid down my back, stopping at the curve of my butt. "Did I get you flowers on my way home from the bar?" he asked suddenly, tilting his head as if the night was just coming back to him. "It was on my list of presents to make up for being such a dick to you."

Amusement had my lips twitching. "Yeah, in a manner of speaking..."

He squinted, as if he wasn't sure what I meant. "In a manner of speaking?"

His hands tightened possessively, and my wolf howled as need roiled inside me. Finley leaned in closer. "What are you thinking about, darlin'?" he murmured, and I groaned.

"I love when you call me that," I told him, my brain too frazzled to be anything other than honest.

His responding grin was wicked, showcasing those perfect indents of dimples, and I was *totally fucked*. "That's good to know. And…" His lips almost brushed mine. "…I remember everything from last night. I really just wanted to see your reaction to my *gift* again. I like making you laugh."

His lips crashed against mine right when a shout rang out from downstairs. "There's a fucking tree in my sink."

A laugh bubbled from me, and Finley held my stare for about five seconds before he snorted into rumbles of laughter too, shaking the bed, me, and my freaking nerves.

More shouts echoed from below, and all I could see was the image of him stuck in the doorway last night, covered in mud, while petals rained on us.

"They better not throw my flowers away," I choked out between heaving breaths as I tried desperately not to pee myself.

Finley couldn't even speak he was laughing so hard, and when he eventually calmed, he rubbed a hand over his face. "They wouldn't dare, but if they did, I'd kill them and then head my ass back over to Old Jim's nursery and dig another one out."

Oh crap. Somehow, I knew *Old Jim* was not going to be happy with Finley when he found out what he'd stolen from him.

"Well, thank you for my flowers," I said, sobering. "I've never been given flowers before, and that was certainly a spectacular start. And thank you for fighting your demons to be in my life."

His chest rumbled as a heavy hand landed on his door. "Hey, Fin, you better get downstairs before Florence and Gerry send your tree through a chipper," Kellan called, sounding amused. "I can get our omega ready. No worries."

Finley's sigh gusted his sweet scent over my face. "Golden missed you so much when we were gone. I suppose I can share with him since I got to sleep with you for like seven glorious hours."

They really were glorious, and genuinely restful. For a shifter I'd initially thought was all rage and attitude, Finley had a surprisingly calm and tranquil aura.

"Let's do it again soon," I told him, finding myself taking the initiative to lean in for one more lingering kiss. Kellan, having exhausted his limited reserves of patience, burst into the room and bounded across to us.

He launched himself over the bed, most of his weight landing on Finley. "Brother," the bear said, slapping his hand on Kellan's shoulder. "Perfect timing."

Kellan pulled away and squinted suspiciously at Finley. "Okay, I'm with Shortcake here. I think we should do a DNA test on you. I'm worried that the witches dropped a doppelganger in our midst."

Finley scoffed as he shoved Kellan half off the bed, crawling out after him and standing all lumbersnacky in a pair of shorts. "This is just me with a full night's sleep. You can thank Emme for my amazing mood. The fact that I'd usually be kicking your ass and I'm not, speaks of my growth as a shifter." He sent a wink my way. "See you soon, darlin'."

Kellan remained gobsmacked as he watched Finley wander into the bathroom, and when he turned back to me, his eyes were wide and very blue. "I never thought I'd see the day. You're a miracle worker."

Shaking my head, I held my arms out for him to crawl into the spot Finley had just vacated. "Nope, this is a credit to Fin's hard work and the magic of a true mate bond. Not even a grouchy bear can fight against that forever."

Kellan's hands slid up under my shirt to tangle in the back of my hair as he pulled me closer. I lifted my leg to wrap over the top of his hip. "How are you feeling about this progress with Fin?" he asked me. "Are you having any worries or issues with the pace that it's moving at? If you're not ready to bond, you don't need to rush. Our bear is *not* going anywhere. You're literally all he talked about while we were gone."

And there they went, reminding me how lucky I was to have this pack.

"I've forgiven him," I said, knowing I truly meant it. "My connection to him has always been there. Even when I was denying my feelings, I couldn't shove him completely from my mind. I love him, Kel, and I think we can make this work. When the goddess finds the right time for us to bond, I'm ready to take that step."

His whole face softened as he dropped his forehead to mine. "Aw, pretty mate. I'm so happy to hear that. Fair warning, though, Finley is going to love you until you're consumed. It can be overwhelming to be part of his life, but if it ever gets to be too much, just let him know. His comprehension of boundaries is skewed from his fucked upbringing, but he responds well to honesty."

His words reminded me of how Finley had held me last night, as if he wanted to imprint on my very soul. Which really wasn't a problem for me.

After my own *fucked* upbringing, I craved that sort of thorough and unconditional love. A love I never had to question.

In that way, Finley Thornton and I had a lot in common.

CHAPTER 55

EMME

Despite his promise to help me get ready, Kellan was summoned by Hunter to haul the grill and coolers of meat and drinks into the street to start prepping for the barbeque. Everyone was expected to show up today after weeks of the event being postponed or cancelled.

I didn't have any experience with this barbeque yet, but I was excited to see it all in action.

While Finley was in the shower, I pulled myself out of his comfortable bed, and I took a second to look around his room. From the moment I stepped foot in this house, there'd been two rooms off limits to me: Slade's and Finley's. I hadn't been sure I'd ever get to see this one, and I took my time taking it all in.

The walls were white, and like all the bedrooms, there was a bank of windows along one side. Heavy curtains in the same shade of blue as my eyes blocked the outside world, and when I pulled their thick length aside, weak sunlight filtered in. It looked super chilly out there today, and if I had to guess, there was more snow on the horizon.

Leaving the curtains open, I perused the many shelves that covered the walls, ending up in a corner set up like a tattoo studio. Artwork was pinned to corkboards, and the stainless-steel tables held sealed boxes of equipment. I still had no idea what was required to tattoo shifters, and it was a relief to know I could ask Finley questions without getting my head bitten off.

Maybe I'd even ask him if he'd work on the tattoo I had brewing in the back of my mind.

Examining the sketches, his artistic talent was abundantly clear, from landscapes, dark symbols, and insanely detailed animals. There were even a few portraits, and I paused at a bear standing next to a familiar side profile, freckles dotted across her nose. *My* nose.

Whoa. I blinked at this new piece of evidence that I was important to Finley. He'd drawn us staring out into the distance, expressions pensive.

We didn't have many photos together, other than the few on my phone from the night we'd celebrated at Luxuria, and I couldn't stop staring at his drawing. It was so much more than a photo; it was his heart on paper, and I was about to break down if I didn't get out of here.

Tearing myself from the art corner, I focused on his shelves again. I'd have expected Finley to be minimalistic like Slade, but he was far from that. The first shelf was filled with hockey trophies—hundreds more than Kellan, as if Finley had never lost or misplaced even one. They were all shiny, not a lick of dust across them, and each had its own space to shine.

He was proud of his achievements, and I was determined not to let him give up hockey for me. No matter how hard it was for us to be apart.

The next shelf was filled with books, and I scanned the spines noting they were mostly non-fiction: Biographies, self-help, history. He appeared to enjoy reading about human wars, and I noted five or six on the *art of origami*. I loved that while the origami was recent, the magazines first appeared before he made the choice to fight for us. As if even back then, he couldn't quite manage to hate me fully.

The next set of shelves had glass doors protecting the treasures inside. Everything looked old, and I guessed this held significant pieces from Finley's childhood. There were multiple pairs of old skates, shards of pottery that had been broken and repaired with what looked like gold, and some sports memorabilia.

Along with shelf after shelf of origami, surrounding the largest paper flower I'd ever seen in my life. It must have been created using multiple differently colored papers, until it formed one massive bloom. It looked older as well, the colors fading around the edges.

"Jiro, Kenzo's grandfather taught me."

I almost threw myself through the glass in surprise. I turned to find Finley leaning against the doorway of his bathroom, a towel slung around his waist, and I wondered how long he'd been standing there watching me snoop through his room.

"Kenzo's grandfather taught you origami?" I repeated.

He nodded. "Yeah, he was born and raised in Japan and emigrated out here with his pack when Kenzo's father was young. He didn't have a complete quintet until they arrived here, which was no doubt why he'd felt the urge to leave his home."

I returned my gaze to the pieces of his past he held most precious. "I'm glad you had them in your life," I murmured, pressing my fingertips to the edge of the glass. "I get the sense you might not have fared so well without them."

He cleared his throat, and I glanced his way in time to see his expression tighten. "I wouldn't have survived without them. Or at least I wouldn't be the functioning shifter I am today. Despite how poorly I showed that side of myself when we first met."

I waved him off, and not because it wasn't a big deal, but we were moving on from it. The only way forward was to let go of the past.

"You're doing just fine, Finley Thornton. You show me your strength every day. We both have traumas we're working through. And while I know this is an individual journey for both of us, it's comforting to know that someone else understands."

He took a step closer, and I was much more aware of how naked he was, just a towel covering him as droplets of water fell from the ends of his damp hair to his broad shoulders.

"Healing means taking an honest look at the role you play in your own suffering," Finley said, but in my distraction, I almost didn't hear a word of that very sage advice.

As I followed a drop of water, I found myself asking, "What do your tattoos say?"

Finley glanced down at his chest as if he'd forgotten he even had tattoos. He pressed his hand to his ribs, right over the cursive writing. "This is advice Jiro gave us all the time: *Fall down seven times and get up eight*. He wanted me to know that it didn't matter how many times I fell, as long as I kept getting up. As long as I kept fighting."

That statement hit me hard. My knees were weak by how real it felt. "And the other one?" I managed to rasp.

His eyes never left mine. "Well, I have two more now, but I'll leave the third for another time. The second is a hockey quote: *Leave it all on the ice*. It has multiple meanings for me, but mostly it's the way hockey was my therapy and salvation."

I loved that one too but was slightly distracted by a search for the third tattoo. Wherever it was, it was either very small, on his back, or hidden beneath the towel.

Finley chuckled as he shook his head and turned to enter his wardrobe, reemerging a minute later dressed in jeans and an old hockey jersey. "Would you like to do something with me today, before the barbeque?" he asked.

My nod was enthusiastic as I really wasn't ready to give up our bonding time. "Yes, I'd love to. If you don't think the guys will need our help."

"Nah, Hunt already messaged and said that we should keep hanging out for a few hours."

With a muffled snort, I said, "We might need to change his chat name to *Cupid* at this rate."

It was fairly adorable the ways our big, growly entitled alpha kept his pack safe. We couldn't have asked for a better leader of our quintet.

Finley grimaced. "You might need to make that suggestion. You're the only one Hunter won't kill over a cute nickname."

Now, didn't that just make a girl feel a tiny bit special.

"So, what do you want to do today?"

Finley's slow smile had sparks firing through me. "Dress warm and I'll take care of the rest."

Well, that worked wonders in distracting me, and I was excited by this plan, whatever it was. As long as we kept hanging out, I'd be happy.

"Okay! I'll meet you downstairs."

Ten minutes later we were in Finley's big truck, heading out of the compound. A few family members waved as they hauled chairs and tables around, and I was doubly excited for the event after our outing.

Finley controlled the big truck with ease, and I was extra

comfortable in the nicely heated seats. When he casually reached out to take my hand, I flinched, taken by surprise. Despite my reaction, he didn't pull away. Instead he threaded our fingers together, his huge, callused palm sliding against my own. Every part of my body clenched, right down to my toes in warm socks and furred boots.

I'd dressed similarly to Finley, in jeans, with layers of shirt, sweater, and one of his hoodies over the top. As I'd guessed earlier, it was icy today.

When he turned onto the road that led to his hockey stadium, I settled back, enjoying the silent but relaxed ride. There was no music or distractions, just the two of us, with Finley's thumb tracing a path over my palm.

"You have a calm soul," he said, with a contented rumble. "I've searched for calm my entire existence."

"Me too," I admitted, before we fell silent again to enjoy said calm.

When the rink came into view, Finley pulled into a spot near the players' entrance, and before I could open my door, he was there helping me out. When the breeze cut through my hoodie, I tried not to shiver. Finley grabbed a sports bag from the back and looped his arm over my shoulders, his heat chasing away the chill.

"Come on, darlin', let's play some hockey."

We ended up in the locker room, and I wasn't surprised to find them fancy and clean, the same teal, gold, and white of their jerseys filling the walls in stripes and logos.

The Wolves were the top team in the league, which meant plenty of money to keep everything in peak condition for the players and spectators.

"You know I can't skate, right?" I said, feeling the need to put that out there. "I don't even mind just watching you. You're kind of magic on the ice."

"I'm going to teach you to skate," he said as he pulled a gorgeous pair of white skates from the bag. "This is the gift I had in my room for you. I think I mentioned that this morning when I stumbled in from the bar." A slight pink tinged his cheeks while I gawked at the shiny, pretty skates.

Finley nudged me down onto the bench and knelt before me to remove my boots. His hands were gentle as he slid the skates on my feet, focusing as he laced them up. "This should be the right size," he murmured, checking everything closely.

"They feel perfect," I assured him, having no idea if that was true or not as this was my first time wearing a pair of skates.

It was cute how nervous he seemed, that blush remaining as he slipped guards over the blades and got his own skates on. When we were both ready, he helped me hobble to the ice.

At the entrance to the rink, I glanced across the smooth expanse, and tried not to let my nerves get the better of me. Shifters had near perfect coordination, but this was still a frozen bed of water. It felt unnatural to try to traverse it on skinny metal blades.

I'd already accepted that I'd be on my ass more often than not today, but this was important to Finley, which made it important to me. I'd fall a hundred times, as long as he was there to help me up again.

"Are you nervous, Em?" he asked when I hesitated. "You're the ice queen, you have nothing to worry about."

"I'm not sure I'll be any good, but I'm willing to try," I told him.

He helped me remove my guards, and he stepped out first, gliding so effortlessly that it was exactly like magic, as I'd said before. I eyed the ice, my adversary for the day, and took one last fortifying breath.

The first step wasn't too bad, but as I brought my other foot down and pushed forward, I misjudged the slipperiness and started to wobble. My arms went out for balance, but there was nothing to grab on to. A little shriek escaped as I started to go down, but Finley caught me long before I hit the deck.

He hauled me closer, low chuckles rumbling his chest. "I'd never let you fall, darlin'," he said patting my back. "Not ever."

My heart hammered from the close call, or maybe it was being in his arms like this, but either way... Ice skating might be for me after all.

CHAPTER 56

Finley was a bear of his word, keeping me from landing on the ice as he patiently taught me the basics of skating. My wolf didn't want any part of it to start with, but once she realized we'd have our mate's hands on us constantly as he kept us from killing ourselves, she was a much bigger fan.

But like… same.

By the end of the session, I made it all the way around the rink without needing to be caught. When he guided me off the ice, I was all pumped up on adrenaline. "We need to do this again soon."

Finley's grip firmed across my hips. "We can come here whenever you want. This is all of my fucking fantasies come to life… minus one."

The heat in his voice, and the way his gaze locked onto me, had me feeling a little hot under the collar myself. "What fantasy is that?" I had to ask. Which got only a smug grin from him, and I fought down a needy sigh. "Okay, well, if you won't tell me that, then what's your third tattoo say?"

Finley's laughter was a nice reminder that it was okay if I was annoying and pushy. He wasn't going to turn on me. "I think I'll keep both of those a secret for a little while longer. I quite like being on your mind."

I grumbled under my breath. "You're never far from mind." Which only had him smiling harder.

He kept his hand on me as we headed for the lockers, and I said, "I still don't know how you managed to tattoo yourself. Especially words. That must be so hard."

"It took a long time, and a lot of practicing in a mirror to get all the details right," he admitted. "The guys helped as well. Hunter is actually pretty good with the gun, as he is with most things he tries. Annoying fucker." His indulgent smile lessened the harshness of that statement—we all knew he loved his brothers.

"Would you tattoo me?" I asked, and for the first time since we'd put skates on our feet he stumbled.

"You want a tattoo?" he asked.

As if there was any question when faced with how stunning his work was. "Yeah, I'd love one. I've been playing with this idea, but without an ounce of artistic ability, I can't do more than sketch a few stick figures and hope for the best."

Finley got us moving toward the lockers again. "I can draw up anything you want, and I'd love to get my ink on your virgin skin. But... it's fairly painful. The ink is infused with magic, which cuts through your natural healing abilities. The pain can last for a few weeks to months, depending on the size and location, until eventually it's an oddly numb spot."

Without even having to ask, he'd given me the answer to a question I'd had for a while. It annoyed me to know magic was involved—witches were officially on my shit list—but I couldn't say I was surprised. "I think I can handle it," I said, hoping that wasn't a lie. "I mean, not now when we have all this shit going on and have to head to Europe, but soon."

Finley looked pleased. "I can't wait to get my hands on you, Emmeline Anders. I have so many ideas." The way his gaze caressed down my body had my pulse speeding, and my scent filling the damn locker room as we entered. No way he was only referring to tattoos in that statement.

Whatever had shifted between us early this morning, with his lovely *flowers*, was still in full effect, and neither of us were backtracking. We were diving headfirst into it.

Finley helped me out of my skates, and goddess be damned, it felt so good to take them off. I could finally wiggle my toes, and when he used his talented fingers to rub out a few spots on my feet that he somehow knew were aching, I barely suppressed my groan. "Skates take some getting used to," he said with a chuckle. "I think I've permanently changed the shape of my foot by now."

I laughed with him. "I have no doubt with the amount of time you're on the ice."

My boots felt so good when I slipped them back on, and I was one happy shifter as I followed him from the stadium and hopped into the truck. After closing my door, Finley crossed to the driver's side, and I swore the desire between us was its own beating heart, thudding in the air.

I was struggling to remember that bonding was special, and we shouldn't rush it.

"You're making this damn hard," Finley groaned as he started the car, startling me from my depraved thoughts.

"Hard?" I repeated, and then I smirked because I was about to be such a cliché. "What's hard?"

He closed his eyes; another groan reverberated through the cab. "Every fucking part of me is hard." His laughter was strangled, and then with zero fucks given he grabbed my hand and placed it on the front of his jeans.

Well, now I'm deceased.

Under my touch he felt thick, hard, and huge like all the alphas.

Choking on air, I almost used his dick as a handle to drag myself across the center console to straddle him. My underwear was soaked, and my scent turned just short of obscene as our eyes remained locked together. Finley's chest rocked with need.

"We don't have time," I breathed, my annoyance seeping out in those four words.

He fisted the front of *his* hoodie and jerked me closer, kissing me like I was his last chance for salvation. My hand remained in his lap and I stroked his length, lost in his sweet taste on my lips.

Finley slid his hands down to pop the top button on my jeans. "I need to touch you," he murmured, voice growly. "Please, Em. You're sitting here in my hoodie, drenched in arousal, and I can't leave without touching you."

At this point, I'd all but forgotten we sat in the parking lot of a hockey stadium where anyone could stumble upon us. "Yes, Fin," I gasped. "Please. I need *you* to make me come."

With my consent given, he snapped into action, opening my jeans fully and sliding his hand down the front of my panties and over my bare pussy. His touch was firm and sure, and when he stroked through my wet heat, his cock kicked hard under my hand.

"I always knew you'd be the death of me," he whispered, without any heat in that statement. "And when it's my time to go, this is exactly what I want to be doing."

As I opened my mouth to growl at him for even mentioning his death—*unacceptable*—he slid one thick finger inside me, cutting off my ability to talk. Rocking my hips up, I rode his hand, softly moaning as his thumb stroked my clit in time to the thrusts.

In my mindless state, I continued to rub him through his jeans, and he finger-fucked me until I was gasping and seeing stars on the edges of my vision. Overwhelming pleasure stole my ability to breathe.

"Seeing you fall apart like this…" Finley's rumble had my eyes snapping open to meet his dark gaze. "…is the best sight of my existence. You're so beautiful, Em. So damn beautiful. You're the best part of this fucked-up world. I will never stop fighting to be by your side. To be worthy of being by your side."

My core clenched on him, as his brand of love completely rolled me.

He didn't dirty talk or praise like Hunter, and he wasn't a *good boy* wanting to please like Kellan.

Finley just straight up showered me with unfiltered and pure adoration.

When I shattered and clenched around his finger, he moaned and called my name, and his dick jerked under my touch.

Well, that was one for the books. I'd just made Finley Thornton come in his pants, which had me raring for round two… or ten.

His fingers slowed even as his thumb stroked my clit a few more times, dragging out the full spectra of pleasure. When I fell limply against the chair, he slowly slid his hand free, and I watched greedily as he lapped my release from his fingers, eyes closing as if he savored the taste.

"Goddess, so fucking sweet," he rumbled, which had another one of those needy whimpers falling from my mouth. He caught the next one on his lips, and I loved the scrape of his beard against my skin.

"Thank you," he said when we finally parted. "For trusting me with your pleasure and body. I'll never make you regret that decision."

My wolf and I were sure now that we never had to worry about pain from this particular alpha again, at least not one he deliberately inflicted. He'd proven himself to us both.

When I glanced down at his lap, I glimpsed the wet patch darkening the denim, which he was wholly unconcerned about. He just laughed. "Yeah, that's not the first time you've made me come in my pants like a fucking teenager learning how to use his dick. It's just the first time you know about it."

A smile lit up my face as I relished that little ego boost. Even when he'd "hated me" he still wanted me, which pleased me more than I expected.

"I have a change of jeans in my bag," Finley said, as he reached for the button. "Think you could reach over and grab them while I clean myself up?"

"No problem," I said, propping myself up on shaky knees, my body still shuddering through the aftermath of my orgasm. I found the spare jeans in a few seconds, and turned to find Finley sliding out of his jeans and boxers, thick, muscular thighs and long legs sprawled out in front of him.

No part of me wanted to look away, so I didn't. His dick jutted proudly in front of him, still hard and thick, perfectly fitting the overall *big boy* size of the bear. These alphas were too much for this omega, and yet, I would die trying to *fit* them.

"You'll make a bear blush if you keep staring like that," Finley drawled, and I jerked my gaze up to find dimples and a smirk. He reached out and caught my chin. "I didn't say look away."

"Couldn't even if I wanted to," I replied cockily, though the breathiness of my voice kind of gave away how overwhelmed I was.

He sucked in a quick inhale, before shaking his head and releasing me to slide on the clean jeans. I had to give myself a quick pep-talk about not jumping him, while Finley started the car and tossed his stained clothes in the back.

"Come on, Em," he said, pulling out of the lot. "Let's get you to your first family barbeque. Our pack wants to show you off to the whole family group."

A hint of nerves broke through my dick-drunk brain. "What if they don't like me? They all know I tried to run and rejected you guys. I'm assuming they don't know the reasons why, so... in those circumstances I'd hate me too."

At some point I started babbling, and only calmed when Finley reached out and took my hand. "If they don't love you, then they're fucking idiots. You are entirely loveable, Emmeline Anders. Every single part of you. Not to mention I'll be front and center to remind them to mind their own business if needed."

Just like that, my fears eased. It didn't matter what anyone else thought of me, as long as the members of my pack knew the truth.

About halfway home, in the middle of explaining to Finley about all the cars that came through the garage growing up, I jolted in my seat. Hit with a jab in my bond to Kellan and Hunter.

"Something's wrong?" I gasped when Finley swung toward me. I pressed my hand to Hunter's bite, trying to figure out what it was.

The car picked up speed as Finley snarled. "I felt it too. You've got a stronger connection... Can you tell more specifically what's happening?"

My mouth went dry as nausea swirled my stomach. "I don't... They're not in pain, but it feels like they're in trouble. Hurry, Fin. Hurry."

He flew through the streets, and when we reached the tangled mess of the security gates, I felt the blood drain from my face. This was just like my first almost kidnapping.

Please let them be okay. Please.

"What the fuck is going on?" Finley's gaze scouted the landscape, and there was no sign of the guards.

"They're down near our house," I bit out, grabbing his arm to urge him on. "There's magic all over the area. Can you feel it?"

His focus snapped to the street, as he peered through the windshield. "I don't want to take you down there," he said, his voice filled with bear rumbles. "It's too dangerous."

"Our pack is down there," I yelled, too panicked to do anything else. "I have to be there, and we need to move now. *Please.*"

His expression torn, he finally slammed his foot on the accelerator, the powerful engine shooting us forward toward our pack. And whatever was waiting for us at the end of this street.

CHAPTER 51

EMME

The roar of the engine was loud, but it didn't drown out the sound of my own thundering heartbeat. There was no sign of Slade's dragon in the air, which hopefully meant this wasn't a worst-case-scenario situation. The discomfort through the bond was mild, but I couldn't stop rubbing my hand over my bites as I silently urged Finley to hurry. Even though he was already foot to the floor.

Further along the street, shifters came into view, gathered in a huge group. Finley hit the button to open his window, and his scowl deepened as he sniffed the air. "You're right, it's magic," he bit out. "Fuck."

My wolf lurched forward, but I managed to block her before she forced a shift. In her form, I was better at fighting and had some resistance to magic, but I didn't want to change yet.

Not until we assessed the situation. Though I did wish I had a weapon.

"I need my blades," I said, hands flexing in my lap. "I know I'm still learning, but they're infused with metals and stones that help deflect magic."

"There's no time," Finley said shortly. "If Slade's dragon isn't loose, then they're holding them with a spell. We have to get to our pack."

He slammed on the brakes when we were a dozen feet from the motionless group of shifters, most of whom had their backs to us. We were out of the car in seconds, and while there were at least thirty shifters in my line of sight, I couldn't see my pack.

But I felt them out there.

With a growl, Finley shifted into his bear, the force of the change shredding through the clean jeans he'd just put on. I waited for him to approach, and when he was at my side, his bear paw wrapped around my shoulders.

"I won't run off," I promised, easily understanding his beast. "Let's find our guys."

We set off toward the main group, who remained stationary, and I didn't need that roiling stink of sulfur in the air to tell me magic was involved. I could feel it in the churning of my gut. My body and wolf were sensitive to magic, and it only grew stronger with each day I spent in the cities. And each alpha I bonded.

Maybe it was a normal part of being in a quintet, and if we all lived through this, I'd ask one of my alphas. *No.* Not if. *When* we lived through this, because any other option was unacceptable.

Sliding through the gaps in the crowd, I noticed a few familiar faces including Kellan's brothers, and Kassidy. My panic spiraled when I spotted children too. If any of those precious little ones got hurt… *No.* They weren't after the kids. Everyone here would be okay; I'd make sure of it.

Finley's growl stole my attention, and I focused on what had drawn his wrath. "Is that fucking Sorenson?" I snapped, familiar orange hair coming into view.

Along with the rest of our pack.

The tiger shifter was an entitled alpha, but he had nothing on even the weakest alpha of the Reeves pack. Yet here he stood, holding all of them in stasis.

Including Slade, who was the only one bound by a shimmering silver rope, wrapped from his throat down to his ankles. As he struggled, burn marks shone on his skin under the bindings. Whatever was in those ropes was both painful and debilitating.

As my gaze ran across my pack, I finally understood why I'd gotten a sense of discomfort but not injury through my bonds. They were being held, and fighting the spell, but except for Slade, none of them looked injured.

Sorenson, who'd been pacing back and forth and ranting at Hunter, took a few seconds to notice we were here. At his growl,

Finley took off at a speed no normal bear could achieve, and the tiger shifter turned quick enough to flick a small glass vial at the bear's feet. When it cracked, a spell rose and coated Finley's fur.

In his bear form, he held some resistance to the magic, which slowed him, but he managed to make it a few more feet to slam against Sorenson, knocking them both down.

Sorenson cursed, and his expression turned thunderous. From where I stood, he didn't look well, with haggard features and dark rings under his eyes. He was weakened too, trying to shove the bear off, but not moving him at all.

His fury blasted in a surge of heat as he shouted, "You're going to die, Finley."

Finley remained limp, and the irony was that it was Sorenson's spell holding him as a dead weight on top of the tiger shifter.

Sorenson continued to shout. "The witch will be back in seconds, once she's obtained her leverage. I just need you to give *them* to me, or they'll kill my whole pack!"

He roared and wiggled, but the giant bear was too heavy.

Meanwhile, I was fighting the sort of rage I'd never experienced before. How. Fucking. Dare this piece of shit put my entire pack in danger again to protect his weak bitch of a mate. Stepping into the open, I strode right over and booted him in the side of the head.

"You have two seconds to tell me what you want," I snarled, "or I'm shifting and ripping your throat out."

His expression didn't calm, but he stopped struggling as he stared up at me. "You," he finally choked out. "You're the one I need. You and the dragon. Alpha Fletcher has Chelsea and the rest of our pack in his compound, and he's… experimenting on them. I struck a deal that if I return with you both, he'd let us go. He knows I can get in and out of this city without detection, and decided it was worth it to get you back. I'm sorry, but I had no choice!"

"Who is the witch?" I asked, trying not to let my panic show that one of those evil bitches was somewhere in this city, getting *leverage*. "How did she get in undetected?"

His eyes bored into me as his lips curved into a mocking smile. "Yeah, you'll find out soon enough. I'm not going to be the one to spoil the surprise and get myself killed via magic. I'm just trying to survive. Trying to ensure my pack survives."

Crouching down near his side, I let my voice lower until the true fury in my soul spilled out. "There's no surviving for you or your pack," I whispered, the even-tempered part of my omega essence long gone. Fuck with my pack and I would channel the goddess herself to take you down. "Chelsea signed her death warrant the second she used me to keep herself safe. It's not my fault she expected the devil she bargained with to honor their deal. There's no help for her… or for you."

A scuffing behind us had me turning to see Hunter fighting the magic, his face bright red as his eyes glowed gold. He opened his mouth, and I swore I heard, "Kill him."

Sorenson confirmed it when he let out a mournful, purring sound. "You can't mean that, Hunt. We've been friends since we were young."

Hunter's face only grew darker, and redder, as he fought the hold. I found myself rising and hurrying toward him. When I touched his chest, a sticky residue clung to my hand as the magic coated him like slime. To contain this many powerful alphas took strong magic, and I wondered if we were about to meet one of these *ancient* Termaine witches?

"Kill him," Hunter managed to rasp again, louder this time.

Slade's roar filled the air and he burst free from the ropes binding him. A piece of the magical debris hit me, and I flinched at the burn. Slade had been enduring that pain… Now I really was going to follow Hunter's command and kill Sorenson.

As the dragon tilted his head back and roared to the sky again, the burns were already healing. With a flash in his glowing green eyes, he strode forward and rolled Finley off Sorenson. He wrapped his hand around the traitor's throat and lifted him from the ground.

"How dare you threaten us," Slade thundered, his voice guttural and brimming with his dragon's rage. "Say your goodbyes, tiger."

Sorenson couldn't say anything as his eyes bulged, and with another squeeze of his hand, Slade crushed the shifter's throat. He didn't stop there either, lifting his other hand to palm the tiger's face. With a sickening crack, he ripped Sorenson's head right off, not letting go until the jerking of the tiger's limbs ceased.

Feeling satisfied but slightly ill by the graphic death, I faced Hunter, unsure how he'd take the death of his friend once it was too late to go back. He'd told us all that they would die for what they did, but it might have only been his anger talking.

I hoped he didn't regret the decision now. Not that anything would have stopped Slade in that rage-filled moment.

Hunter's expression remained cold and indifferent, and when he finally burst through the spell, he scooped me into his arms and held on protectively. "Baby," he growled, "are you okay?"

Tilting my head to examine him, I was relieved to find none of that sticky magic on his skin any longer. "Of course I am. I didn't even get touched. Are you okay?"

He buried his face against my neck. "Yeah, I am now."

Slade dropped the tiger's body and head, which rolled a few feet away to sit there like a macabre trophy. "Will that kill the rest of his pack?" I asked, unsure how it all worked for semi-complete quintets.

Hunter's shoulders lifted in a brief shrug. "It's different for every pack. It depends on who the heart is, who holds the strongest bonds, and how weak their beasts are. I personally hope they're all gone now. It'll save us tracking their disloyal asses down later."

Slade strode over to us, wiping his hands down his black pants, which only removed a fraction of the blood coating the dragon. He examined me as closely as Hunter had, and appeared satisfied that I was okay. "What happened?" I asked them. "How did Sorenson even get in here?"

"He called for a meeting," Slade said shortly, "then ambushed us with magic. There was no sign of the witch when he entered, and no unauthorized magic came into this city. I still can't feel them."

Hunter growled, and his hold briefly tightened on me. "So, how the fuck did they do this?"

Slade's lips thinned, and it was clear that he not only didn't know, but he was pissed about it.

As I peered around Hunter to check on Kellan and Finley, who were starting to stir also, there was a surge of magic in the street once more.

Slade's eyebrows drew together as he glanced above the heads. "Jewels," he murmured. "She must have felt the spell—"

He broke off, and I wondered if we were all struck by the same thought. Jewels was in the city, but hadn't come until the attack was over.

"What if the witch helping *is* Jewels," I bit out. "That might be how they made it into the city without any detection. You all consider her an ally, and she's in and out of this fucking place like she owns it."

Hunter opened his mouth as if to deny the possibility, but he couldn't voice the words. If there was any witch in the world he trusted, it was Jewels. Well, as much as one could trust a witch.

"I always wondered why she put up with our shit for years," Slade rumbled. "But I could never find anything damning on her. If she's a traitor, she played her game well."

Too fucking well.

Jewels strode into the crowd, using magic to drag a shifter along beside her, while keeping one hand wrapped around her captive's throat. A captive I knew very well: Cora.

My lungs seized as I frantically examined my friend, only breathing again when I noticed the small rise and fall of her chest.

Hunter stepped forward, angling himself to hide me from witch view. Slade did the same, and I felt the rise of their beasts. "What are you doing, Jewels?" our entitled alpha called, his voice carefully modulated.

From the sliver of view left to me, she didn't look very happy. "Fletcher made me an offer I couldn't refuse. I'm sorry, but if I had to choose between a future where magic rules or one where shifters use and abuse our power, then I know where my loyalty lies." She met my gaze from where I peeped between the alphas. "Just hand the dragon and the omega over. She never deserved you anyway."

"Not a chance," Slade said, casually. As if he wasn't concerned at all. "You'll have to kill all of us first, and we won't go down easy."

No! I would throw myself at Jewels in a heartbeat before I let any of them get hurt. We all just needed to live to fight another day.

Jewels' faked sadness morphed slowly into annoyance. "Don't threaten me with a good time, dragon. I have the power to kill you. I mean, how do you think I managed to keep you all in stasis like this? Hmmmm." She tapped her chin. "It might be thanks to that energy I took from you four."

Slade slammed his hand against his chest. "It returned to us. I felt it."

Her snort was a tad deranged. "You felt the touch of energy as I pretended to slip it back, but you were too distracted to realize I never truly returned anything. You're too freaking powerful to notice the small loss, but for me it was immensely useful. It also allowed me to cater my spells specifically for you all. It was clever of me to enhance that spell on Kellan until he was too weak for any other option than you all to consider sharing your strength. It worked out even better than I planned, except I hoped he would die. Little shit." She did a fake bow, as if we'd given her a round of applause, and my heart lodged in my throat as my gaze shot to Kellan, who was glaring and moving his arms, though the rest of him remained locked in place.

"The cost of doing business, I'm afraid," Jewels continued.

Hunter's fury sent heat pouring from him, scorching my face, and he kept shuffling back to get us further away. He probably thought I was about to sacrifice myself to save Cora and my alphas.

Most likely he was right.

She was my best friend, and they were my heart—no one was fucking dying for me today.

If Fletcher wanted me this badly, then he'd get me.

I had too much to lose.

CHAPTER 58

SLADE

The roar of my dragon was deafening inside my head. We were too close to our family to shift without risking injury, and I couldn't step away from Emme as she was the most vulnerable and the one this bitch wanted. A bitch who was going to die.

The fact that she'd stolen my energy. *MINE.*

I'd been too distracted by my mate and Kellan at the time to properly inventory my power, and that had me ready to blast the entire street to cinders. It took every ounce of my strength, every scrap of control I'd built over the years, to keep a hold of my destructive fury.

My body shuddered when Emme pressed her hand against my spine, and I wished now wasn't the time she chose to initiate touch.

Today… we were out of control. Today… was the root of all my fears.

My dragon could destroy everyone who stood here in seconds.

It had happened once before when I was fifteen, when Fletcher had taken his torture a little far. He'd cut me until there wasn't any part of me which didn't bleed, all in a bid to force my dragon out. He'd wanted me to kill for him, but I was no one's fucking puppet.

I'd endured the torture, which went on for so long that I believe this was the first time I started to associate any touch with pain. Ironically, I now quite enjoyed pain when it was done right.

That day had a lasting effect on me, severing my bond to my

dragon, who blamed me for holding him back. Not that I cared about killing Fletcher, but there were others being contained near me. Hunter for one, along with other prisoners chained against the walls of his torture cells.

By the time Fletcher was done, the rage of my beast had me confusing friend with foe, and even as we healed over and over, the canvas of my skin repairing for his butchery, I never broke.

Not until he brought an omega female to me.

She'd looked about twenty and was naked and blank faced. Fletcher sent her in there to clean the blood from my skin, and then he'd told her to hug me. That full-bodied touch, soft and gentle, had been the last crack in my control. Somehow, he knew all along that an omega was the key to my destruction.

I'd shifted, and Fletcher got exactly what he wanted: the omega torn to pieces and the building torn down around my beast. I'd almost lost Hunter that day. I definitely lost myself. I should have fucking killed Fletcher too, but when I'd finally shifted back, he'd offered me a deal. If I forgave all his sins, there'd be no more pain and Hunter would go free.

I forgave nothing, but for Hunter, I kept the sick bastard alive.

As long as we were free from him, I didn't care. I should have expected that he'd find other ways to fuck us over.

The rumble in my chest echoed around the street, drawing Hunter's attention. Whatever he saw in my expression had his features tightening. He nudged Emme's touch away as he leaned down to murmur to her, too low for me to hear over the roar of my beast.

"You have signed your death warrant, witch," I informed her, the fires building in my chest.

She smiled broadly, and her tone was heavy with amusement as she said, "You always were my favorite, Slade. I fought Fletcher when he hurt you, and ensured he turned his attention to the other lizard. You should thank me."

The knowledge that she'd been in my life manipulating behind the scenes had claws appearing at the end of my fingertips. Not to mention her casual reference to Talon and his suffering under Fletcher's *care.*

"I will thank you by taking your life," I promised.

She chuckled. "You're never going to win if you can't even figure out the most basics of information about who I am, and how I've been manipulating behind the scenes…"

I hadn't kept up with Jewels' life for many years, not since she initially passed all my surveillance tests. When she started assisting us, and didn't ask for more than her usual favor or cash, I accepted her role in our lives. *Another fucking mistake.* Clearly, I'd missed a vital piece of information, and I wondered if she was somehow connected to the Termaine witches who were supposedly behind this…

As more of our friends and family started to break free from the spell, Kellan hurried over to stand with us. We'd had to fight harder to break the spell due to her use of *our* energy, hence why she'd been so fucking happy to steal from us.

Jewels needed to die, and I needed to figure out how to make it happen without Cora as a casualty. Not that I cared about her personally, but she meant a lot to Emme. I couldn't be cavalier with her life when it would break my mate to lose her.

The crowds of shifters pressed in closer to us, and if I let my beast free, they'd be crushed or worse. I needed a distraction so I could back away.

Jewels watched me carefully, and her hand tightened on Cora's throat as I moved. "Don't do it, dragon. Just give me what I want."

"Talon is in our containment room," I informed her. "I'm happy to go and get him."

And return in my beast form, which you fear, don't you, witch.

She shook her head. "Call him, omega!" she shouted. "Call your mate, or everyone here will die. Starting with your best friend."

Emme's low sob was audible, but then cut off immediately. Our mate was strong. She would be figuring out how to get over there without Hunter stopping her.

Jewels stepped forward, and Cora moaned, her eyes closed though her heart beat strongly. "It's simple," the witch said. "Give Fletcher what he wants, and he'll reward you."

"You're not leaving here," I promised, and she threw her head back to cackle, giving me a few seconds to step away.

Hunter sensed what I needed, and kept shuffling Emme back. Kellan and Finley were now keeping her caged in too. I locked eyes with Kassidy, who stood near a group of family members, and I jerked my head to tell her to get them back.

She did exactly as I asked, having grown up with me as well.

Everything was falling into place, and as I finally found myself in clear grounds, my dragon roared as shadows danced on the edge of my consciousness. The shift was fast, and in my beast form I headed right for the witch, who shook Cora in front of her, but my dragon didn't care.

"No," Emme screamed from behind us, but she was still caged in by Hunter, Finley, and Kellan, and couldn't move. If anything happened to Cora today, Emme would never forgive our actions here, but as long as my mate lived, I'd accept her rage with pleasure.

Cora was a friend and ally, but I'd kill everyone here to save Emme.

My own pack included.

Flames burst from my parted jaws, and Jewels threw up a strong shield to prevent them from touching her. She'd thought Cora would work as a hostage, and if it was only Emme she faced, she'd have won immediately. But my dragon's priority was to kill the witch, no matter who stood in the way.

Jewels dropped her shield and threw a vial of magic at me. I swung my tail out at the same time, sending the witch and her hostage flying. The vial hit my chest, burning against my scales, but the pain barely registered.

Cora flew off into the sidewalk, hitting it hard, and Jewels landed much closer to me.

Unlucky break, witch.

I slammed my front claws and weight on her, and she managed to get another shield up in time to prevent me crushing her. It was a battle of strength then, and Jewel's expression turned ashen as magic poured from her raised hands in a bid to counter my weight.

My essence was in that magic, and I was going to take great pleasure in flattening this fucking thief.

A roar echoed in the distance, and deep in my chest, where I'd recognized Talon from the first moment we battled in the sky, I felt my twin's approach. Emme must have called him after all.

Now we might have another enemy in our midst.

I had no idea which side he'd take today, and if I had to battle him and the witch, the odds dipped out of my favor. When Talon landed with a thump beside us, my dragon roared at his brother, and that hollow of fire in my gut expanded.

What's Alpha's witch doing here? Talon growled.

Now, if I'd been in my humanoid form, I'd have jumped a damn foot in the air at a random voice in my head, but my dragon reacted as if he'd been expecting it.

There was this immediate connection between our beasts, as if their ancient souls recognized one another, and knew they'd been separated far too long. The only other time we'd met in our beast forms was during our first battle, and we'd bonded a lot since then.

Talon had never shied away from probing at my dragon, at my essence, connecting with the parts of me I both feared and admired. He'd created tethers, and they were all coming to fruition today.

Brother, my dragon replied. *Do you know this heinous creature? The one who must be squished. She threatened our mate.*

Talon roared, and I felt hope that I'd found the key to ensuring his loyalty. *Well, let's ensure that doesn't happen again*, he said.

This time, when his dragon's power probed at my center, I opened myself to the bonding, and the surge of energy between us swelled out of control. There was no way to stop the wave of darkness, and with the witch slipping out from under my grip, I fell into the abyss of what Talon had just awoken between us.

Until I was no more.

CHAPTER 59

Hunter held me back as I screamed and clawed at him. Kellan and Finley remained near us, the former's expression torn, while the bear growled.

But neither interfered.

I sliced my nails through Hunter's arm, my wolf fired up at hurting our mate, but it was a fucking scratch. A scratch was nothing to Cora dying at the hands of that magic wielding lunatic.

When Slade's tail hit the witch, Cora flew off to crumple hard on the ground, and I froze to stare at her, begging for her to open her eyes. She remained sprawled against the curb, unmoving. *My fault.* My fucking fault.

Another shifter I loved had been hurt.

Fletcher wouldn't stop until he got his hands on me and my power.

"Emmeline," Hunter growled. "I don't want to hurt you. Please. Stop fighting me."

"Let me go to her," I shouted, and he flinched at my rage—I was pissed and he knew it.

"Let Slade take Jewels out first," he countered, his voice unnaturally calm. As if he hoped that the calmer he was, the more it would filter to me through our bond. *Not fucking likely.* "If you race over there, you'll be close enough for the witch to grab you."

I snarled, and the force of it tore at my throat. "I don't fucking care!

I swore after Kellan that no one would ever get hurt because of me again."

Hunter's grip remained unyielding as he shook his head. "That wasn't your fault, and neither is this. You're not hurting them, Fletcher is. When we get our hands on him, he'll die for his role in all of this."

I scoffed, because I got mean when I was terrified and devastated. "You haven't found him in weeks. He's had a witch inside playing you *for fucking years*. He's ten steps ahead, and eventually he'll get what he wants, since evidently we aren't evil enough to play this game. Especially without knowing all the rules. Our lack of knowledge is what he's using to take us down."

Hunter's face could have been carved from stone, but I saw a flicker deep in his stormy eyes to suggest I'd hit a nerve. But he did not relent and let me go.

Talon! I mentally screamed for him again, not sure it had gotten through the first time. There were flickers along the incomplete bond, and I decided then and there that if we survived this, I would *fully* seal the bond with all my mates. The disconnect in our quintet kept us weak.

We could sort out the logistics later, but to survive we needed to be a whole circumference of power. No more excuses. No more fear.

When my strength was spent, I went limp in Hunter's hold, conserving my energy for when I might have a chance to break free. We watched as Jewels battled Slade, her shield preventing his claws and body from crushing her. Which was the least she deserved.

Even before finding out she'd been trying to kill Kellan rather than help him, I'd never liked the witch. For two reasons: one, magic was the worst, and two, her cold, calculating stare made me uneasy.

Fletcher probably had sleeper agents everywhere, and I wouldn't be trusting any witches or other shifters ever again.

A spark shot through Talon's bite when his beast burst from the wall of the garage, momentarily tangling up in the metal before he got free. My initial reaction was relief, which was insane when Jewels was here to drag him and me back to Fletcher. I'd called him anyway, to keep Cora safe, but I wasn't sure what choices he'd make here today.

When he landed next to Slade, Talon's darker beast nudged his head into his brother, and it was as if time froze for seconds as the two stared into each other's eyes. There was a soft humming of energy in my bond, and then the street was flooded with a light so bright it rendered me blind.

Energy exploded a moment later, knocking us all to the ground. Hunter cushioned my fall, and I pushed at him, needing to see what happened. As the light faded, I found Slade and Talon's beasts on the ground, while Jewels had used magic to shoot herself into the air, hovering above them.

"What just happened?" I asked, voice shaking as Hunter dragged us back to our feet.

"I have no damn idea," he said, moving us a step closer to his brother, "but their energy is shattering the air and smashing into our pack bond."

I could feel it too, like dominance pressed our beasts into the ground.

Most of our friends and family were still down. Even Finley and Kellan struggled to get to their feet. My eyes watered as I examined the dragons, while Hunter kept his focus on Jewels hovering above the street. She moved in our direction, but didn't descend close enough to touch any of us.

I stifled a cry when pain shot through Talon's bite. It almost felt like I was being marked again, the tendrils of our bond knitting together. *What was happening?*

When the last of the light faded completely, and our eyes recovered from the flare, I could finally see what had happened to the dragon twins. The sight drew a harsh gasp from me.

"What in the ever-loving fuck," I breathed. I opened and closed my mouth, having no idea how to explain what I saw, and Hunter followed my gaze to find Slade and Talon in their *new form.*

"This is impossible," Hunter murmured, his grip weakening on me. "*This* is what twin souls means? They're definitely two sides of the same soul."

Slade and Talon's beasts had merged together. Into *one giant beast.*

Standing twice the height of their individual dragons, the beast was a kaleidoscope of black and green scales, forming patterns that were so complex it was hard to describe them. A massive pair of black wings spread out on either side of it, like a damn plane had landed in our city, but that wasn't the craziest part of all. There were *two* freaking necks and heads. Two. Giant. Dragon. Heads. Like it was the dragon version of a two-headed Cerberus.

"Slalon," I whispered. "This has to be the reason we remain a quintet. Two shifters, one essence."

Hunter grunted, having recovered from this *insanity* much faster than me. "You might just be right, little omega. There's only a single energy inside them in that form, which means we can form the perfect power of five."

I felt lightheaded as I nodded. "Yeah, they feel the same to me, too. I can sense Slade's calculating personality mixed through my bond with Talon."

As the dragon straightened to its full height, both heads shot in different directions, which sent Jewels off in a flurry of magic, until she disappeared completely from the street—not ready to take on the super-dragon. "Slalon scared her away," I said with a snort.

Hunter grimaced at me. "We need to work on that name, but it'll do for now."

With a shrug I said, "It's better than Talade."

"Debatable," he replied.

"We'll circle back to the name," I said, keeping my focus on the sky. "Do you think Jewels is properly gone? Can I help Cora now?" My best friend was still in a crumpled heap, and while she was clearly alive, she was also hurt.

As soon as the dragon's dominance died off, everyone in the street got back to their feet, and Kellan and Finley scrambled to me. The pair wrapped me up in a messy group hug, which included a lot of bear fur.

"We couldn't move," Kellan growled. "What in the actual magical bullshit is happening here? Did the witch make the dragons morph into one super dragon? Or was that them?"

I snorted, and they turned to me. "I called them super dragon in my head too. And I think that was all to do with them. I could feel my connection to Talon solidifying as they merged, like parts of his essence were being repaired too."

All along, I'd thought the tattered nature of our bond was a result of the way we'd bonded, and that we hadn't connected on a sexual level. But now… I was sure it was due to the disconnect between him and his dragon. The same disconnect Slade felt.

Which might have just been repaired as they connected as twin souls.

Finley hugged me to his side, and I ran my hand gently over his fur until he shifted back into a giant, naked male. "We have to kill her," he growled, finally able to speak. "That fucking traitorous witch. I don't care what it takes."

"We will," Hunter assured him, and he leaned closer to me. "Let's check on Cora."

Thank the goddess. As I headed for her, there was a thud from behind us, and I jumped as Slalon tried to take a step and crashed down to the ground.

"Shit," Kellan burst out. "We're going to need to help our brothers figure out their new giant body."

The dragon tried to walk again, falling once more, and the ground moved under my feet as I headed for Cora. The three alphas remained right on my ass, discussing the best way to get Slalon back into their separate forms.

When I reached my friend, I dropped to my knees and brushed my hands over her arm, which was thankfully warm to the touch. As I turned her toward me, I caught the scent of magic coating her skin, and it felt like the same spell that had knocked Kellan unconscious.

Which meant we'd need Jewels to reverse it...

"It's not the same," Hunter said, reaching down to touch her lightly. "I believe this is just a knockout spell, but... I feel her pain."

"What pain?" I asked, frantically scanning her. "Where is she hurt?"

The steady thump of her heart was strong, and I could see no injuries.

"It's her wolf," Hunter rasped, his eyes flickering with gold. "Her wolf screams in agony."

I gasped as my eyes locked on his. "Warrick?" I whispered. "Do you think War is...?"

I couldn't even finish that sentence, overwhelmed by the very thought, as tears burned my eyes. Kellan and Finley knelt with me, wrapping their arms around my shaking shoulders.

That was why Cora lay here alone... Warrick would have come for her if he was able. Jewels must have hurt the alpha to get to Cora, and now her wolf screamed.

For her mate.

CHAPTER 60

EMME

Warrick's face filled my mind until all I could see was his handsome smile. He was one of the best entitled alphas I'd ever known, up there with Hunter. Then there was Richard, Sierra, and Marcus. The rest of the pack could have been hurt too, after they'd welcomed me into their home when I'd had no one…

"Don't cry, Shortcake," Kellan said softly, rubbing his hand up and down my spine. "As soon as we know it's safe to leave, we'll get to the Annandale pack house.

"I've already sent a message to the council," Hunter called, focusing on Slalon again. "They're sending enforcers and healers there… and here."

When I batted at my tears, Finley caught my wrist, his touch gentler as he wiped my cheeks. "You did not do this to them," he whispered, the rasp of his bear in his voice. "Fletcher was coming for all the pack cities, okay. You just happen to be the omega in his sight today. But eventually we were all going to suffer." His lips brushed my cheeks. "I'm choosing to believe the Annandale pack were just knocked out."

The soft cadence of his tone was strangely soothing, and I decided to hope for the best, despite expecting the worst. "Okay, I'm manifesting that they're all okay too."

My energy remained flat as I glanced around the street, noting that while a lot of shifters were watching the spectacle of the dragon, many of them had also taken off back to their homes. Thankfully, I couldn't see any of the children any longer.

"Why aren't the enforcers here already?" I asked, angry that we'd been alone in dealing with this attack. Again. "Surely this strong of a magical disturbance should have registered, especially since they're usually patrolling near our street."

Hunter's boots hit the ground hard as he paced. "They've been working around the clock, so we gave them the afternoon off. I figured with this many alphas in the street, we should be safe. We didn't anticipate it would be Jewels' magic, which is registered and accepted in Golden Claw, to take us down."

"She stole our fucking essence!" Kellan rumbled, sounding very un-Kellan like. "Stole it and used it to bypass any security measure we would have against her."

"She didn't see the super dragon coming though," Finley added, his lips twitching. "I mean, who could have seen that coming?"

Kellan's fury eased into a stare of contemplation. "I swear I've read a book where two magical beings joined together in that way. They ended up being crazy powerful and saved the world."

We all turned to take in the giant beast, in time to see him fall down again.

"He's a work in progress," I said quickly, and despite the situation, even Hunter smiled at that.

"They haven't changed back yet," Kellan noted, still staring. "Do you think they're having an issue with that?"

Finley laughed. He'd kept his hand against my face, thumb sweeping gently over my cheek. "It's an issue I have a lot of experience with, and for me, Emme is the key to transitioning back. It'll probably be the same for those two."

I stared at the dragon, and then down at my friend. "Cora will be fine until healers arrive, right?"

Hunter nodded. "There's nothing we can do for her. She's trapped by her wolf, but isn't in any immediate danger."

I'd bet she was going through exactly what I had after I'd been stolen and forcibly bonded: her beast retreating to keep her sane.

"Then I need to help the dragons," I said, and Hunter got straight in my face.

"Don't even think about it," he snapped. "You can't keep risking your life for others. I don't care who they are, or how important they are to us. You are all that matters, and you need to remember that without your influence, the rest of us will make sure there're no shifters or cities left for anyone to save."

"Correct," Finley said, backing him up.

Kellan just stared at me with an expression so broken it was as if I'd already been cut down.

"Talon and Slade are my mates," I reminded them. As much as I loved their all-encompassing way of loving me, on days like today it was a fucking pain in the ass. "I won't take any risks, but I know they won't hurt me. Think about the role I play here in our pack, the way I fit with the rest of you. I might not fight with my fists, but I'm just as essential to our survival—"

A bellow rang out down the street, and Cora stirred. My heart soared when a beaten and bleeding Warrick stumbled toward us, pushing through the shifters still standing around.

"CORA!" he shouted again, and the anguish in that one word had my eyes burning.

Cora's arm twitched, and I knelt beside her again. "He's bringing her back," I said in a rush, just so happy to see them both alive.

When he fell to her other side, his glowing eyes were locked on her face as he leaned down to press his cheek against hers. Her lashes fluttered as she rasped, "War…? Wh-what happened?"

I squeezed my eyes shut, so relieved to hear her voice, and got back to my feet to give them some space. Finley and Kellan stepped in on either side of me, Hunter at my back, and I was grateful for their strength surrounding me.

Especially when Warrick said, "They attacked us at home, baby." He lifted her upper body into his arms. "A magical bomb detonated when we stepped out the front door. It knocked me out, and when I woke, you were gone." His voice broke. "Marcus was the closest to the blast and… he didn't make it. I left his body with Richard and Sierra and got over here to you."

"Marcus is gone?" Cora sobbed, and I pressed my hand against my chest, wanting to shatter apart with her.

I'd feared it was Warrick her wolf mourned, but Marcus was almost as bad. He was one of their quintet. A brother. Their family. My best friends were suffering, and I couldn't help them.

Tears streaked Warrick's face too as he held her—mates locked together in grief.

Eventually, they got to their feet, and I had no idea what to say as they stared at me.

"Where did the witch go?" Cora asked, her voice growing harder.

I shook my head. "We don't know. She transported herself out of here as soon as super dragon appeared."

They both blinked at that, and I pointed toward the other side of the street, where Slalon had finally figured out how to use his giant body. The huge wings were spread wide for balance, and he had started to move more easily.

Warrick narrowed his eyes on the beast. "What in the goddess' design is that?"

"They're twin souls," Hunter said, with a shrug. "Slade and his twin, Talon, merged during battle. We don't know what it means or what this form is capable of, but I would guess it's a much stronger beast than their individual ones."

"When the fuck did you find a second dragon?" Warrick growled, and I got the sense he was pissed we hadn't shared that information with him.

I met Cora's gaze, wondering why *she* hadn't shared it, but she only shrugged. "You trusted me to keep that part secret and I did."

Goddess, I loved her for her loyalty and true friendship.

Warrick's expression softened as he glanced down at his mate. "You're too good for our fucked-up world," he told her, and I could see his utter relief that she was alive and relatively unhurt. Unlike Marcus. When he returned his attention to us, it landed on me: "How does this other dragon fit with you?"

"Talon is one of my mates too," I said, not caring who else heard. We were pretty far past keeping secrets, as the dragon-size hole in our garage wall could attest. "We believe we can still form a completed quintet. It's not about numbers, but energy and essence. Together, Slade and Talon are considered one essence."

No one looked at me like I was crazy, and in fact, both Hunter and Warrick nodded.

"The quintet is only *five* because the essence of our beasts and bond works best with that number," Warrick said slowly, as if he was thinking it over as he spoke. "If their essence is one, then you'll be a quintet. A very powerful one."

His voice broke, and we fell silent at the reminder that his pack would never again be a complete quintet. I felt helpless against the sorrow that they'd forever carry. "Jewels will pay for what she did," I said forcibly, anger tainting my sorrow. "I don't care what it takes, or how many holes we have to dig to find her. This is the last death we'll ever suffer at her hands."

Warrick's wolf rose until it was clear in his gaze. "On that, we are in complete agreement." He wrapped his arm around Cora, drawing her tighter to his side. "Now, we need to get back to our pack and update the council. Call if you hear anything about the witch... we will be ready to take her down."

I took a step towards Cora, who stood there looking broken. Her expression was filled with anguish, and I had to suck in a deep breath to be able to say, "I'm so sorry about Marcus. I wish I could offer you both relief from this pain, but just know that I'm here for you. Whenever you need. *Whatever* you need."

Cora reached out and I clasped her hand, relieved that she didn't appear to hate me for the role I played in this. At least not yet. Maybe once her shock eased up, she'd feel differently.

"I have no idea how we navigate forward without *him*," she rasped. "But I do know we need to be together. I'll call you soon, Emme. Please stay vigilant. The witch could be back at any time."

Warrick's chest rumbled. "Call me later," he said to Hunter, and then they headed down the street toward their car.

When their car vanished from sight, there was a shout, and enforcers poured into the street, racing for us. The shout hadn't been to alert us to their presence, but to the magic filling the air, turning the skies darker.

"Get to cover," Hunter shouted to any friends and family still here, and most of them took off, though I noticed Kenzo was nearby, along with Kassidy.

Alarms were sounding around Golden Claw as their warning system for witches came into effect. But it wasn't a single witch this time.

The sky filled with them, and Jewels hovered dead center, her hands wrapped around Fletcher's shoulders. The evening sky was dark enough at this point to showcase the huge, red-tinged moon. An eerie backdrop to their arrival.

Jewels smirked our way and carried Fletcher across the street, the alpha staring greedily at our super dragon. Without thought, I raced for Slalon, fearing that their lack of control in this new form would make them an easy target. Even with their size and magical resistance, there were enough witches to truly make this the fight of their lives.

CHAPTER 61

EMME

A magical blanket pressed down over the street, almost sending me to my knees, and I had to fight the oppressive energy as I sprinted. Kellan kept pace on my right, Hunter on my left, and I didn't even have to look back to know Finley guarded the rear.

Up ahead, Slalon swiveled both heads, blasting fire in two different directions, which took out any witches floating too close. A few stronger ones erected barriers, leaving the rest to turn into blackened corpses falling to the ground with sickening thuds.

The enforcers around us started to shift into their more magically resistant forms. Those with wings took to the air to fight the witches above, and I spotted more than a few of Slade's squad. They were highly trained fighters who worked well together, and the witches were unprepared for such a direct attack, which gave us time to get to the dragon.

Leaping over shifting wolves, cats, and bears, I reached the tip of the dragon's tail, which was nearly as round as my whole body. Slalon's heads were still working as weapons in the sky, and I shouted out to let them know I was there. "I'm climbing on your back now."

They didn't flinch as I ran up their spiked tail, surprised by how easily I traversed its length up to the broad back. Their wings lifted higher and wrapped closer to me, as if to offer protection and support. At the junction of their body where the two necks split, I slowed and leaned down. "Okay, alphas," I said, keeping one hand on each neck, the scales near scalding under my touch. "I think we need to get you separated. I know you're strong in this form, but you're also stuck here on the ground while the witches are up there."

They continued to spew fire in hot arcs, the heat scorching my cheeks. Jewels and Fletcher were the only ones still in our vicinity, her shielding strong enough to keep them safe. She didn't flinch as members of her coven were destroyed around her, her focus only on us.

"Dragon," Fletcher called, the sound of his voice sending shivers down my spine as I was thrown back to the night I met him in the old house. "You're being called to return to your Alpha. You, your brother, and your mate."

"You never even gave him a fucking name," I snarled, finding my voice. "I won't let you take Talon. I don't care if it costs my life. He's mine now, and I will fight until my last breath for him!"

Mine. They were all mine, and I was done with this motherfucker trying to split us apart.

Hunter, on the ground, moved in on the left side of Slalon. Finley and Kellan were on the right.

I stood in the center of them all, the heart of our quintet.

Technically, an omega was the weakest of any pack, but I was strong in ways that not even Fletcher understood. Even after all the years of experimenting on us, he'd missed the fundamental truth: we stood outside of his dominance and were not his to control.

"You need to separate your essence," I said again to Slalon, "so we can take him on as a team."

This time it was clear they heard, as a shimmer of energy traced over my skin. Needing to jump ship, I leaned forward and called, "Head's up, Hunter," and without waiting for his response, threw myself off the dragon.

Hunter's reflexes were quick enough to catch me before I hit the ground, tucking me in close to his chest. "For fuck's sake, little mate," he groaned, his nose tracing along my neck. "Could you stop trying to give me a heart attack..."

I patted his chest. "No one is dying on my watch, Hurricane. Not today."

Behind us, the dragon's essence grew stronger, but they hadn't shifted back yet, so I wiggled out of Hunter's hold. "We need to help them," I said, and Hunter joined me as we pressed our hands to the massive chest, their mate and entitled alpha working together.

Through our bond, Talon's dragon nuzzled against my wolf, and Slade's beast was there too, his touch colder as he ran it gently along my flank. My wolf dug deeper into their combined essence, right to the place where they were joined, a connection that should have been honed from birth. These two had been cruelly torn apart, left to live without half their essence, always at odds with their beasts. But that was over forever.

I called to my wolf for help, and she knew the exact spot to nudge between them, which was all they needed. With another burst of that blinding light, the dragon heads both roared, and I was tugged away as they split. Instead of the two dragons I expected, I was left staring at two naked males. Two huge, ripped, gorgeous, and furious naked males.

Oh holy goddess.

Kellan, who must have been the one to yank me out of the way, whispered in my ear, "Well, fuck. Even I'm impressed by that. Do you want the one with the hardware or without?"

Both. There was no other appropriate answer to that question.

Tattoos. No tattoos. Piercings. No piercings.

They were twin souls, and I wanted them both.

The tingle in Talon's bite grew stronger as he stared at me. "You need to make a choice now, mate," I said, meeting his gaze. "Where do your loyalties lie? With that bastard hovering above us, hiding behind a witch's skirts? Or with us, your pack who claim and love you…?"

His unwavering stare left me for Slade, and as he looked upon his twin, his expression filled with longing and love. We might not know yet what exactly happened between them when they merged, but it was clear that they were closer, bonded in ways they hadn't been before.

Slade took a step toward him. "You can't have it both ways. You're either on the right side of shifter history, or…" His expression grew harder. "Or you're dead to us."

My wolf howled, and I almost stumbled back at what had felt like a blow.

Talon's expression turned lethal. He stepped away from our pack and headed for Fletcher.

I clenched my hands so hard my nails bit into my palms, as I watched the psycho alpha steal my mate. "I'm the one who's been there for him since birth," Fletcher said with a gloating smirk. "I trained, and fed, and cared for him. I'm the one who offers him a future where he rules, as dragons should. He knows where his loyalty lies."

When Talon drew closer, Jewels dropped the alpha, and the dragon automatically reached out and caught him, setting him gently on his feet.

"Pathetic," Hunter muttered. "Too weak to fall a dozen feet without help."

Fletcher's gaze cut into Hunter. "Ah, here's my most disappointing son. You could have had it all, and you gave it up to be an entitled alpha of *four*. Tell me, son, has your precious Alpha Council been helpful in this battle against me? With all of their rules and protocols? All of those hoops to jump through?"

Hunter didn't rise to the bait. "I'll take being your most disappointing son as a compliment. Why are you even fucking here, Fletcher? You must be one stupid alpha to come here outnumbered and without your army. Your witches have failed. Now we get to kill you."

Fletcher's laughter was high-pitched and creepy, as if the final strands of his unhinged mind were unraveling. "Jewels would never let that happen. She's the strongest witch in the world, and we've been planning this for a long time. Ever since she helped me mastermind the last war with her mother."

Most of my pack and the enforcers around us watched Fletcher, but I was staring at Jewels, who had just been outed as a fucking *Termaine witch*.

Her face hardened, and as she narrowed her eyes on Fletcher, there was only hatred in her gaze. "Actually, I think I might let you clean up this mess alone," she called, her eyes going dark as she turned briefly to stare into that eerie moon. "I don't think I need you anymore. Or any shifters." With that, her magic pulsed against us, and she vanished the same way she did before, taking that oppressive blanket of energy with her.

Fletcher flinched, and immediately looked around, his face a shade of pale that didn't look healthy. The sky was clear and empty as witches either bailed, or were already burned and twitching on the ground. He started to back away, until his gaze settled on Talon, and a spark of life returned to his features.

"Shift and get me out of here," he demanded, grabbing for the dragon. "We'll get your mate later."

Talon stared at me, his expression unwavering and hard, but I still had faith in him.

"She'll be in pain," he murmured, voice flat.

Fletcher struck him across the face with a closed fist, which had my wolf raging to the forefront. She burst from my skin, and I launched myself at the alpha, needing to tear him to pieces. Fletcher used his dominance first, seemingly used to fighting alphas, but I wasn't slowed as I slammed against his chest. Clamping my jaws around his throat.

I jerked back in one motion, following the instinct of my beast to tear and shake.

Fletcher recovered fast, and smashed his fist into my chest, forcing air from my lungs as he pummeled my chest. When I landed on my side, still in wolf form, winded and injured from the blow, the street filled with a menacing rumble. By the time Finley reached my side and started checking for injuries, heat scorched the air around us.

"You're okay, darlin'," Finley said, helping me up.

My wolf whimpered as we shook off the pain, and I nodded to assure him that I'd live. Fletcher, who'd remained in the same position, was already healing, his throat closed up.

He was strong, that much was for sure, but he'd made a mistake when he hit me.

Slade and Talon now held his arms, keeping him trapped between them as Hunter stalked forward.

"I'm your alpha," Fletcher spluttered to Talon. "You were supposed to learn their secrets, not join their fucking team."

Both dragons rumbled louder, until it felt like the vibration rattled my aching bones.

"You. Hit. Her," Talon seethed, his teeth clenched hard so that his words were barely audible. "You hit my mate. You hurt her."

I whimpered again, wishing I could comfort my alphas, who now faced off against the asshole who'd raised them.

"She attacked me," Fletcher argued, his eyes widening. "I was simply defending myself."

Talon met my gaze for a long minute, and I silently promised that I would have his back forever. *Mate. Pack. Forever.*

With a nod, he turned back to his brother, and with one strong inhalation, their muscles tensed and they yanked. Just as Hunter reached out with his claws and swiped.

The three of them tearing Fletcher Davenport into two very dead pieces.

CHAPTER 62

TALON

Alpha hit her. My fucking mate. *MINE!*

He had promised me from the time I agreed to his plan, that when he presented me with a mate and we bonded, she would be safe from the repercussions of any battle.

He promised she would be safe and protected.

Mine. Always mine.

Emme was more than just a mate—she was my scent match.

My every *fucking* thing, and Alpha had hit her.

My vision blazed red, and my dragon raged as we watched her pretty wolf struggle to her feet. The alpha tried to argue that she'd attacked first, but it was all white noise in my head as rumbles spilled from my chest and the fires in my gut burned hot enough to scorch the earth under my boots. *We must end it now.*

The voice wasn't my dragon. It was my brother.

Tearing my gaze from Emme was hard, but this was a decision I wanted to make with Slade. The joining of our essences, and hearing his voice in my mind, was the second-best moment of my existence. Meeting Emme was the first.

When our souls bonded, whatever ragged, empty spots had been between me and my dragon vanished. The broken tendrils in my soul mended, along with the tendrils in my mate bond.

I felt whole and entirely un-alone for the first time ever. How it should have always been.

I don't need the alpha any longer.

As that revelation struck me, I knew there was only one way to keep Emme safe from him. Only one solution left to me. *He has to die.*

Slade nodded, just the smallest incline of his head. *Are you ready, brother?*

Yes, I hissed back.

We knew how to dispose of an enemy—we'd been born to destroy as a team. If we still had dragon hordes, we'd have been their warriors.

I tensed my muscles, and didn't even bother with a goodbye for the alpha who'd raised me. He'd never truly given a fuck about me. The second he touched my mate, he'd destroyed my final loyalty to him. I didn't care if she attacked first; he should have let her tear his head off.

On the count of three, I said to Slade. *One, two...* I inhaled. *...three.*

Fletcher opened his mouth, but it was too late. I yanked, and Slade did the same. With a little help from Hunter, it was almost too easy to tear the shifter in two.

Blood spattered the air around us, but none of us flinched. Warriors wore the blood of their enemies as a warning to others, and we would warn them all. Five alphas protected our pack. Our mate.

Emme, who was back in human form, hurried toward us. Kellan had given her his shirt, but she was tall for a female, which left a long expanse of legs on display.

My mate.

Slade smirked at my side, and in sync again we dropped Fletcher's remains on the ground and stepped forward so Emme wasn't walking through that scum to reach us.

"Holy fuck," she cried, her eyes wide and glassy. "He's dead."

Kellan caught her and lifted her into his arms. "There's pieces of Fletcher all over the ground," he said casually, and I was reminded of why I fit with this pack so well.

None of us were afraid of getting our hands dirty, and we'd fuck this world up to keep Emme safe.

"Okay, that's gross, but good point," Emme said, her little nose wrinkling up. She turned back to us. "Are you all okay?"

"Fine," Slade said, wiping a hand over his face, smearing the blood. "His death was a long time coming."

Hunter grunted as he nodded. "Yeah, the world would have been a better place had we killed him years ago. I figured it was either loyalty to me, or some threat against my life that kept you from attacking him, and honestly, I don't even care anymore." He opened his arms. "Now please give me my fucking mate before me and my wolf lose our shit."

Kellan didn't argue, and when he shifted Emme forward, we all caught her wince.

Hunter got to her first, his hand brushing over her chest. "Are you okay, baby girl?" he said. "I don't think he broke anything."

She pressed her hand to her chest. "Nah, it's just a bruise, and it's already healing. Not that it matters. I'd take way more than a broken bone to ensure that asshole was out of our lives for good. I honestly can't believe it's over." She sank into Hunter. "I feel like I could sleep for a week."

Unable to help myself, I took a step forward, desperate for a hit of her calming energy. "I just need a minute to hold her," I rasped, hoping the entitled alpha understood and didn't fight me.

If they put me back in my cage without this touch, I'd be likely to destroy the rest of their house.

Hunter huffed, and *thank the goddess*, handed her over without fuss. She settled against me, and when her hand pressed to my cheek, everything that had felt off-center righted itself. "I'm so sorry, Tal," she whispered, pushing herself up to kiss my cheek, uncaring of the blood I wore. "You had to make a terrible choice, and I'm so grateful you chose us. I will always choose you. I promise."

My dragon's roar was filled with pride and contentment. We had claimed our mate, and proven our worth, and she chose us. *Always*.

"Mine," I breathed against her skin, taking in her sweet scent. "You're mine, sweetness."

She dropped her face against my chest. "I can't believe you and Slade turned into a super dragon. You need to tell us all about being Slalon."

I heard my twin laugh at that, and I was equally as amused. "We have so much to tell you," I confirmed, and she settled at that statement.

After a few minutes, Kellan said, "Why don't I take Emme inside and help her get cleaned up. We can all regroup soon."

Hunter looked torn, until eventually he nodded. "Yeah, I need to speak to the council and enforcers."

Emme mumbled as her eyes fluttered closed. "I keep thinking

about Cora and Warrick, and everything they went through. Can one of you find out what's happening with them too."

Hunter prowled closer, and her eyes flew open to meet his dark gaze. "Yes, we'll find out. All you can do is offer them support and give them the space to grieve as a pack."

A choked sob escaped her, and I wished I could kill Alp—Fletcher all over again.

"You're right," she swallowed roughly, and Kellan stepped forward.

It took every ounce of my control to release her, and I wouldn't have for anyone who wasn't part of this pack. I'd have murdered them for even suggesting it, but they were hers too.

When Emme settled against the blond alpha, she let out a sad laugh. "I can walk, mates. I don't care if there are bits of Fletcher on the ground. He deserves to be under my fucking foot."

Kellan kissed her cheek, and like the rest of us, was too weak to resist her. He dropped her gently to her feet, and the pair of them strolled into the house. Emme only looked back once, but it was enough to settle my beast.

"I can handle the council," Hunter said, stepping right into his role of entitled alpha. "You all get everything out here cleaned up, send our family messages that it's safe, and then let's meet up in the living area. We have a lot to discuss."

Despite my stronger dominance, I felt no desire to fight him for his role, and accepted his orders without worry.

Unsure if they wanted me back in my cage or not, I hesitated until Slade indicated I should stay with him. It took over an hour to deal with the carnage of the street, and I met more than a few shaken family members, including Hunter's sister, who'd stayed to fight.

She showed not one sliver of concern over her father's death. "Wish I'd been the one to kill him," was all she said, before heading back to her house.

When we were done, Slade told me to follow him. "You can bunk with me," he said as he led me up the stairs.

I blinked, our bond flaring strongly inside. "What? No more containment room?"

He shot me a flat stare over his shoulder, a smile playing at the corners of his lips. "No more containment room."

That confirmation settled my beast even more. "I thought you hated others in your space?"

We'd had a lot of time to talk when I'd been his prisoner, and I'd quickly learned how he kept his world in order. How he kept his dragon under control.

"I've spent too many years missing a fundamental part of myself," Slade explained with a shrug, even though I could see how tense his muscles were. "I won't do that again. We need this bond, and we need to figure out how to exist in our combined form. Which means we'll be sticking together for a while."

My chest warmed at the thought. "I'd like that, brother. And my dragon likes it."

Slade turned to meet my gaze. "Mine too. For the first time in my life, I'm not at war with him, broken and fearing what we might become in the future. We are as one."

It was the same for me.

When he faced me, I took in the tattoos on his chest, and noticed a change. "Was it always like that?" I asked, gesturing to the twin dragons. Their scales were closer in color, and there was a shining white wolf between them now.

Slade stared down for many seconds, and then squeezed his eyes shut. "This is how it should have always been. Not a battle. A joining of two souls, with our mate right between us."

I pressed my hand against his chest, and he didn't flinch. "We're forever joined. You will never be broken or alone again, Slade."

It was a promise to my brothers and my mate.

My pack.

They had no idea how far I'd go to keep them all safe. Whatever it took.

CHAPTER 63

EMME

Leaning against Kellan in the shower, I struggled to fully comprehend everything that had happened out in the street. *Fletcher is dead.*

It took at least fifteen minutes for my body to stop shuddering, as I finally accepted that I was safe, and so were my pack. My alphas had gone through a traumatic experience, with at least three of them having to deal with the death of a parent. Or the closest thing they had to one.

For me, all I felt was relief.

Fletcher had been out there causing death and mayhem for years, all to be the supreme ruler. The money and power weren't enough for him, and he didn't care who he hurt on his climb to supremacy.

I still didn't really understand why he spent so many years experimenting on shifters, and maybe it didn't matter anymore since he was gone. His death was a huge win for the shifter world.

Most of us would sleep easier at night, even those who'd had no idea there was a devil waiting in the darkness.

"You okay, Shortcake," Kellan asked, his voice low as he stroked his hands up and down my spine. "You don't have to act strong in front of any of us. That was a fucking lot. I'm here if you need to fall apart."

Aw, my sweet alpha. "I'm weirdly okay," I said, snuggling into his chest. "I mean, I'm not okay about what happened to Cora's pack, and that our guys had to destroy the only father they'd known, but other than that, we got out of it easy."

Kellan tucked his head on top of my shoulder, a comfortable position with our five-inch height difference. "Almost too easy," he murmured.

"Well, Blaine and Jewels are still out there," I offered, knowing it wouldn't completely be over until those two were destroyed.

Kellan pressed his lips to my shoulder, and I closed my eyes to enjoy his touch. "Yeah, they are. Jewels, the fucking snake in the grass, will be an issue, but Blaine's not powerful enough to do anything now that his pack and father are dead."

"We need to find the compound," I decided, unease growing at the thought of what we might discover there. "Talon can show us, and then we can ensure no shifters are being held prisoner."

Kellan's touch stilled. "Maybe we'll figure out what Fletcher was trying to achieve with his experiments and secret plans."

I wondered if we were better off not knowing. "At least we're aware now that Jewels is our enemy," I said, my wolf rumbling with need to kill the witch. "If she shows up again, we'll be alerted. Plus, we have a super dragon in our pack."

When he pressed his lips to my shoulder again, I shuddered under his touch, and this time his tongue swiped through the water beading on my skin. "Let's worry about that tomorrow," he murmured. "Today we're alive and whole. We have everything, and with Slade and Talon, the pack feels stronger. Can you feel it through the bonds?"

I nodded, comforted by how strong it felt. "I wonder what will happen when I complete the bond with the entire pack. Will I be able to freely share power? Will you all grow more powerful? Could I lose my wolf?"

Kellan growled and his chest rumbled. "Not a fucking chance, Emmeline Anders. Your wolf is sacred to all of us, and we'd die to protect you both. There's no amount of power in the world that would be worth hurting you for. You never have to fear us."

"I don't," I assured him, having no doubts. "I promise. But if I needed to share my essence to keep one of you alive, I'd do it without question. If you refused, I'd force you. Never think this is your choice alone. I get to die for you all too."

His hold tightened until it was almost painful, and I was fucked up enough to enjoy the sensation of his strength against me. "Stop it. Just fucking stop it. That's never going to happen, and I refuse to let you put those words into the universe. Don't make me gag you, Shortcake. I'll fucking do it."

My laughter was muffled against his body, as he clung to me with desperation. "And what exactly are you gagging me with? I might enjoy that."

His groan was a low, dragged-out echo of suffering. "Oh, baby. You're the most perfect form of torture known to shifters." His hand slid down to cup my ass. "But we don't have time for fun. The guys are already in the house, waiting for us."

He shut off the water and dried me thoroughly, before patting my ass. "Go and get into comfy clothes."

We were in my room, so it was easy enough to duck into my wardrobe and grab soft black pajama pants and a matching tank. When I emerged, Kellan waited for me wearing sports shorts and a navy hoodie. He held a similar hoodie in his hands, and I laughed as he draped it over my head. "You need to live in my clothes now," he declared as he stepped back to take me in. "I love seeing you in them."

Rubbing my hands down the soft fall of the material, I enjoyed the wafts of his scent that came with each stroke. "You might have to take turns with the other alphas," I warned him. "If the amount of their clothes in my wardrobe is any indication, you're not the only one who wants to cover me in their scent."

Kellan's smile broadened. "But I was the first one to get you in my clothes, and no fucker can take that from me."

Golden had been the first to throw himself all-in and not care about the consequences.

Which almost got him killed. More than once.

"I love you, mate," I said, as he took my hand. "I don't say this enough, but thank you for taking such good care of me from the first time I saw you in the forest. You changed my life, Golden."

His grip tightened and he yanked me into his arms, his lips surprisingly gentle against mine. As we kissed, his hands cradled my face, holding on like I was precious.

"I love you too," he said, pressing more kisses to my lips, and then up over my nose to my freckles. "You changed my whole damn existence, baby."

Our kisses ended when we had to head downstairs to find the rest of our pack. Kellan held my hand all the way, only releasing it when we reached the living room. The alphas were all clean, and smelled like themselves and not battle.

When Talon approached me, I noticed he was dressed in Slade's clothing—all black of course—looking younger and less violent than usual, as if a weight had been lifted from his shoulders.

"No more containment room," I said, staring into dark eyes with a lot more green intersecting them now. I sighed when he cupped the back of my head, pressing his lips to my cheek. "No more prison at all. You're finally free, Talon."

"When you were with me, sweetness, it never felt like prison. It felt like having a family for the first time in my life."

My chest ached at that sad, fucked-up statement. "Always," I repeated for him. "You will always have a family." The other alphas didn't argue, and there was a real sense of pack in the room today.

When Talon released me, he took a seat beside Slade, and Hunter led me to the large sectional. He sat and pulled me down until my head was in his lap and I was horizontal. "You need to rest," he said as way of explanation.

Kellan dove in under my feet, dragging them onto his thick thighs, and Finley shrugged and dropped right in front of me on the floor, leaning back and stretching out his long legs.

Even though Christmas was long passed by now, the tree and lights remained up, as Hunter had promised. With the fire roaring beside it, everything just felt peaceful.

Hunter played with my hair, tracing it through his fingers, while I watched the lights twinkle against the shadowy wall. Red, green, silver. Festive in a way I'd never understood until I'd been part of a real Christmas.

"We don't usually decorate for Christmas," Hunter said, digging his fingers a little harder into my scalp, which dragged a soft groan from me. "But we never want you to miss out on anything, baby girl. Whatever you want or need, we're here."

I laughed softly. "I haven't missed out on one thing since you all dragged me into this world, and aptly demonstrated how stupid I'd been to run in the first place. It's like Christmas every damn day."

As if proving my point, Kellan started to rub my feet, and Finley leaned back so I could run my hands through his thick hair. With

Slade and Talon watching over us like giant dragon sentinels, it was kind of perfect.

"Tell us what happened when you bonded," Hunter said, staring at them.

My eyelids were drooping with exhaustion, but I really wanted to hear this story, so I forced them open.

Slade stared into the crackling fire, his expression pensive. "As I've said before, I've always felt like there was a part of me missing. There was a rift between me and my beast, and while I blamed my upbringing, I now know it was much more than that."

My chest rumbled. "Fletcher still didn't suffer enough," I bit out.

Slade leaned forward, resting his elbows on his knees. "He didn't, but in the end, his death was justified, and the world is better off without him."

"Abso-fucking-lutely," Kellan hollered.

Ignoring him, Slade continued: "When I first saw Talon, there was a new surge of energy from my beast. It was strong, and made it harder for me to retain my usual control. Everything was off kilter, which resulted in me screwing up more than usual. Which was unacceptable when I needed to protect our pack. I kept missing information, getting taken by surprise, losing my edge."

"You aren't the sole one responsible for this pack," Hunter reminded him, but there was no bite in his tone. He wasn't pulling entitled alpha rank, just pointing out that we were a pack, and we protected each other.

Slade met Hunter's gaze. "Yeah, I know that, Hunt. I know, but my instincts to protect are deeply ingrained."

Talon rumbled his agreement, shifting forward on the chair. When they sat side by side like this, they were so similar. Beautiful shifters, carved by the gods themselves.

"With Talon, there's a sense of peace," Slade said. "Of completion."

"Yes," Talon agreed, dropping his hand on his twin's shoulder—Slade didn't even flinch, which almost had me shooting up straight. "I felt the same. It was like… coming home. Between Slade and Emme, I found the pack I'd been searching for. I put my energy into Fletcher for years, and gave him my loyalty and respect, but he wasn't my family. He was my captor."

It was a hard-fought realization from Talon, but one that essentially saved all of us.

"And the rest of us?" Finley asked. "How do you feel about the rest of the pack you've found yourself in?" There was no anger in the bear's tone, and I was proud of Finley for asking so calmly, with rejection a huge trigger for him.

"You're pack and family too," Talon said, as blunt and honest as his twin.

Finley relaxed under my hands. "Thanks, brother. We feel the same about you."

Kellan, who was still rubbing his thumb into the arch of my foot—the boy knew how to massage—groaned. "As much as I love all this pack bonding, and I can't wait until our quintet is complete, is anyone else really fucking hungry? I could kill Jewels just for screwing up our barbeque."

Finley laughed, dropping his head all the way back. "Might be time to give up the family days, Hunter," he said. "We haven't been able to complete one since Emme came into our lives."

My chuckle was cut off by a huge yawn, and I shook my head to clear the daze. "If you're all hungry, I can cook for you."

Florence and Gerry had a day off today, and I was thankful they'd missed all the danger and drama.

"Em, you don't have to cook for us," Finley said, turning to face me. "We're more than capable of feeding you and ourselves."

Forcing myself up into a seated position, I dropped my legs down on either side of his shoulders. "What if we do it together," I offered. "A proper, family pack meal, where we all contribute. What do you guys know how to cook?"

When Talon's laughter filled the room, I wondered if I'd ever heard him sound so free. "I've never cooked a meal in my life," he told us all. "I was mostly only allowed to eat in my dragon form, while hunting the grounds. I'm not sure I'll be any help." He shuffled his ass forward on the couch and turned a pleading stare on me. "But can you please make the cookies and honey cake? Or any of your sweets. They're the best thing I've ever eaten."

That set Kellan off groaning about starving to death again as he got to his feet. "You have the best surprise coming your way, brother. Shortcake's cookies are second to her actual cook—"

I smacked him in the gut and he let out an oomph, which didn't halt his amusement.

As Slade and Talon turned their penetrating gazes on me, I

couldn't ignore the shiver that raced down my spine at the thought of twin dragons.

I'd been unsure if I could handle one of them in a true bond, and now it was two...

Goddess give me strength.

CHAPTER 64

EMME

After we spent a few hours cooking and eating together as a pack, feeling lighter than we had in weeks, I crashed out between Hunter and Kellan, only to wake far too early.

I headed out of Hunter's room and found myself in the doorway of Slade's bedroom, staring at the twins sleeping side by side. *In the same freaking bed.* My ovaries burst into flames, and I died a thousand deaths as I watched them like I was the stalker.

Fitting, considering how obsessed I was with my alphas.

They slept the same way, their huge bodies sprawled back, one arm flung up above their heads, and the soft sound of breathing filling the room. They slumbered so soundly, I knew they had finally found peace. If it wasn't for the fact that my best friends were dealing with the loss of one of their pack, I'd say that I'd finally reached the pinnacle of happiness.

I couldn't help Cora or Warrick tonight, but tomorrow I'd be there to do whatever it took to get them through this.

Turning away from the twins was hard; it took every ounce of control not to crawl in between them. For the first time, I was almost certain it wouldn't bother Slade if I did, but they deserved their time to bond. Just the two of them.

Knowing exactly why I'd been drawn out of bed so early, I headed straight for the garage, noting that there was no obvious draft from the section Talon had smashed through. The alphas had patched it up somehow, and cleaned the debris. Leaving our garage as pristine as it could be under the circumstances.

As I passed my bike, I picked up on the telltale signs of a shifter working on an engine. Finley's presence called to me, and I was ready to finish what we'd started at the hockey rink.

I needed him tonight.

Finley must have heard me coming, and was already waiting, hip nudged against his Ford. I surprised us both when I leapt at him, and he straightened in time to catch me as my legs wrapped around his waist.

"Ice Queen," he breathed. "What are you doing down here, darlin'? You were exhausted, and that wasn't enough sleep."

The concern on his face was almost my undoing. "I just… needed you."

He stiffened, and I pulled away from his chest to catch his expression. It was one I'd never seen before, a stare wreathed in devastation as he stared unblinkingly at me.

"Fin," I whispered, pressing my hand to his cheek.

In a rush, he spun and set me down on the hood of a car. It wasn't his huge Ford, and I was too focused on him to notice anything other than the cool metal seeping through my underwear.

He slid his hands up to cup my face. "I've waited so long for you to come to me like this. I swear… I've never needed anyone the way I need you." His whiskey eyes consumed me as he held my gaze. "It's an obsession. I'm fucking obsessed with you, mate. I can't sleep without you, and when I do, I dream about you. There's nothing else on the planet as important as you are to me, and I *will never* fuck this up again. I swear. I swear on my life. On the love I have for my brothers." He dropped to his knees, his breaths shallow as I pushed myself up to see him. "I need you to forgive me," he begged. "In all ways before we can take this step."

It was my turn to reassure him, as I reached out and pulled him back up to stand. "Baby, I have forgiven you in all ways. We're going to bond tonight, mate." I made sure he could see and feel my sincerity. "We're going to bond our souls and our beasts, and we'll be joined forever. I want that more than anything."

Finley's chest rumbled as he pushed me back, cradling my head as I went down. He leaned over to press his mouth to mine in a hard, claiming kiss. "I want that more than my next breath," he rumbled. "I want to consume and own you, darlin'. I hope you know what you're signing up for here, because I only see this obsession growing with time."

A shudder traced across my skin, leaving goosebumps in its wake as I registered his poetically perfect words. And, I mean, would he even be one of my pack if he wasn't semi-stalking me? Obsession and stalking were part of how we loved.

"I hope you know what you're signing up for," I teased back, sighing and arching as he kissed my throat, tasting my skin. "I mean, it's not stalking as much as *lovingly observing you without your knowledge*. I'll be taking no notes on that."

Finley continued to kiss and taste me, the loose neckline of my pajama shirt allowing him to reach the swell of my breasts. When he lifted his head, his pupils were blown out. "My bear wants to keep you in our cave for eternity. Just ours to love and protect and *fuck*."

My core pulsed, and if he wasn't inside me soon, I'd probably lose my mind. "Fuck," he groaned, and I was coming to learn that nothing got me off faster than seeing strong, powerful, dominant alphas fall apart.

Finley traced his fingertips gently over the bridge of my nose. "Kellan raves about your freckles, and while I'm most certainly a fan, it's your eyes that I crave. My perfect Ice."

"Whiskey and ice are our eyes," I said with a chuckle. "Sounds like Hunter's favorite drink."

Finley's smile grew. "It's one of mine too." With that, our conversation was done, his lips returning to my throat as he tasted me in slow, delicious swirls of his tongue. My body grew heavy and languid under his touch, legs moving restlessly against the energy building beneath my skin. His weight held me down as he *very thoroughly* explored my body, one of his hands dragging off my shirt, leaving me half naked. My panties were gone just as quickly.

The metal of the hood heated under my skin, as Finley's hands slid over me, learning through touch. His gaze traced down my face and body, taking in every inch of me, and the feral want in his expression had me throbbing and wet. "Touch me," I pleaded, my core clenching around nothing, which was sadly depressing.

Finley's grin was sharp, and I loved to see that hint of his darker side once more. He'd been on his best behavior for so long now that I almost forgot the fire and wicked humor that filled his core. "Are you begging me, darlin'?" he murmured, looking pleased by this turn of events. "An alpha could grow used to that."

I arched up against him, my scent sprinkling the air ferociously, while desire coated my thighs. Finley's mouth caressed my chest, and my hands went into his hair as he sucked one nipple between his teeth. I clawed at his shirt, needing his naked skin against mine.

He helped me tear it from him, and I sighed as broad shoulders came into view. I ran my hands over the thick muscles, loving how big he was all over. Finley was just the most delicious big boy and I fucking lived for it.

He stroked my tits, and as he moved lower his hands remained cupped around them, brushing my nipples. The scrape of his beard over my stomach had me gasping, and I was so sensitive already that I knew it wouldn't take much to make me come.

Finley was controlled as he explored, and when his breath brushed over my core, he licked up the pre-cum already sliding down my thighs. Pressing my hands into the hood, I worried I was about to just slip right off this thing.

Finley continued lower, reaching the arch of my foot, which he kissed and touched. With a groan, I wiggled my toes in his face. "Grouchy, please." I was about to beg. On my damn knees if needed.

His laughter rumbled over my skin. "Patience, Emmeline Anders. I've waited a long time to get my hands on you, and I need to learn every inch of your skin. I want to know where you're ticklish, which touch gives you goosebumps, and where I can find your strongest scent. I need to know it all."

I was panting hard, and when he finally rose, his hands wrapped around my hips. In one swift movement he flipped me over and slowly lowered me against the hood.

From this new angle, Finley continued to explore, touching every inch of my scar. That mark represented some of the worst days of my life, but apparently not to him. "This shows your strength and resilience," he murmured, kissing down the ropy length. "This is a battle scar, Emme. You wear it well."

My eyes burned, but I was thankfully distracted when he continued exploring. When he reached my ass cheeks, his touch firmed until I was arching and all but shoving my dripping core in his face.

His groan was loud. "Fucking hell," he rumbled. "I can't…"

He buried his face in my pussy, devouring me. "Fuck, you taste so damn good," he growled.

Small gasping cries spilled from my lips, and I pushed back as he plunged his tongue inside to fuck me, while his fingers caressed my clit. The slow buildup had me so on edge, all it took was a few strokes until I tumbled over.

"Finley," I cried, the force of the release launching me flat against the hood. On the shiny surface, I couldn't get traction, but the bear's strong hold kept me in place as he lapped at my release, face buried between my thighs until I was completely spent.

All I could hear were delicious rumbles, as if he was the happiest bear shifter in the world. Which was fitting, as I was the happiest wolf shifter.

CHAPTER 65

FINLEY

I'd been through a lot of fucked-up shit in my life, and I'd done a lot of fucked-up shit too.

But I must have done something right to be gifted this mate.

Her taste was sweet, and so uniquely Emme, living up to every one of my expectations after I'd spent days listening to Kellan rave like it was a nectar of the gods.

My brother was right, though he may have underplayed it.

If she'd let me, I'd just fucking move in down here and live with my mouth on her pussy. Emme might not mind, but my brothers would have something to say about it. I'd just have to learn to enjoy my time with her, along with sharing her with them.

"Fin," she moaned, her raspy voice sending another pulse of desire through me. When I flipped her over to her back again, she threaded one of her hands into my hair, while the other pressed hard against the car.

Being here with her in the garage felt right. This was *our spot*, and to claim my mate for the first time, surrounded by engines, made perfect sense to me.

Changing pace, I buried my face and inhaled, my tongue and mouth moving faster as I attempted to keep up with the sweet nectar dripping from her. It was too good to waste, and I'd rather not have to lick the damn hood of the car. I loved cars, but not that much.

When her thighs tightened around my head, she jerked her hips, riding my mouth. I dug my hands into her luscious ass and pulled her even closer. Everything about her was so soft and lush, and I was going to die one very happy shifter. *Eventually.*

I certainly wasn't ready to leave this world now that I knew this perfection waited for me every day.

"Holygoddessfuckinghell," she cried out, arching and grinding against me as she came hard on my tongue.

I hadn't even had a chance to slide my fingers into her slick heat, too caught up in tasting her for the first time. Not to mention my hands weren't the cleanest after tinkering with cars for a few hours, and quick healing or not, my omega deserved better.

As she cried out again, I barely suppressed my own groan—my balls were heavy and throbbing, my dick so hard I could have hammered in a fucking nail in one swing.

Desperation to slide inside my mate clawed at me, rising with my instinct to hunt and claim—to steal her away to our cave for the rest of eternity. "Em," I murmured, lifting my head to find her sprawled back in a heap, her cheeks nicely flushed as her lungs heaved.

"That was amazing," she huffed, "holy goddess. You know how to eat your mate."

A rumble rocked my chest. She had no fucking idea how well I could eat.

Pushing myself higher on the hood, I hovered over the top of her. "Are you ready for me to claim you, darlin'," I drawled, loving the way her eyes darkened and pupils flared every time I used that pet name.

She nodded almost frantically, and I leaned down and pressed my lips to hers. She didn't hesitate to open and taste herself, and fuck if that didn't have my dick kicking even harder in my pants. Odds were, I wouldn't last very long the first time, but this was only the beginning.

I planned on being inside her for most of tonight.

"I'm ready, Grouchy," she said breathily, wearing a satisfied smile. Sliding my thigh between her legs, I nudged them farther apart, and hoped we wouldn't slide off this fucking hood before I managed to claim her.

Her hands fumbled with the button on my jeans, and I helped her get them undone and down so I could kick them off. I wore no underwear tonight, and when her eyes locked on my dick, throbbing and leaking for her, she looked as desperate as I felt.

"I swear," she mumbled, "my vagina is not equipped for these alpha cocks."

As I planted my hands on either side of her head, I lowered until I could brush the head of my dick through her wet folds. *Fuck me.* "You take us so well, baby," I murmured, and managed to hide my grin as her pupils flared again. Our girl liked a little praise, and I liked that look on her face. "You and your pussy are perfection, and we couldn't have asked for a better mate. You're built for us, just as we're built for you. Goddess blessed."

With each crooned word, she arched into me, until I was positioned right at her entrance, her warm heat wrapping around the tip. "I'm close to my fertile time again," she warned suddenly, and I paused.

"Do you want me to stop?"

As impossible as it felt, with her already hugging my dick, I'd stop mid-fucking stroke if she asked.

She shook her head roughly. "Oh, goddess no. I just wanted to let you know. I shouldn't be able to get pregnant this early, but I didn't want to force you into anything you're not ready for…"

Her babbling was endearing, and if that was her only concern, well… I thrust my hips into fucking heaven and had to count to twenty not to come from that first stroke. "I want to fill you with my cubs," I rumbled, pulling almost all the way out and slamming into her again, holding her close so she didn't slide up the hood. "I want a million babies with you and our pack, and I would start tonight if you were ready."

She didn't say anything as she clutched me, wide eyes locked on mine, and I got her moans and cries, which were fucking wrecking me.

"Please," she finally whimpered. "Fuck me harder, mate. Please."

The begging from her pouty lips, and the half-lidded stare she wore, shredded the final vestiges of my control. My balls slapped against her ass as I fucked her hard, and she embedded her nails into my biceps until she drew blood. The prick of pain mixing with all the pleasure had my balls tightening, tingles flaring in the head of my cock.

Buried inside my mate, my bear raged as he fought to claim her, and I wished we could get closer than this. I wanted to climb inside and claim every part of her. I wanted to own and pleasure this omega for the rest of my existence.

Emme's eyes widened, her pants and cries growing louder. "Holy shit," she choked out. "I'm going to come, mate. I'm going to come."

I released my bear and he rose to partially shift our jaw. I bit Emme's shoulder, right beside Kellan's mark, and the blood that filled my mouth was sweet and metallic. My beast roared, which drew her wolf to the surface, swirls of energy connecting us. While I remained locked onto her, Emme bit me as well, sealing our bond.

We remained locked together, our beasts joined in my mind while I kept thrusting into her body, adjusting my angle to bring her the most pleasure. I felt her in my essence settling within me, and for the first time in my existence I understood what a true home was. Our beasts nuzzled briefly before fading, and my jaw returned to normal as I pulled away.

But the connection didn't release us.

Emme cried out and clenched around me, milking my cock as she came, which sent me right over the edge. I roared her name and released so much fucking cum she dripped with our combined release. I liked seeing her like that, filled with my seed… my essence.

It was all hers.

Trying not to collapse on her, I braced my feet on the ground to keep us in place, with my hands on the hood. "Shit, baby," I groaned, heart hammering as my muscles quivered from aftershocks. "I've never been this happy in my life."

I hoped she had no objections to me staying buried inside her for the rest of the night. "We're bonded," she whispered, and her voice broke.

Panic smashed through my mental bliss, and I was hit with so many emotions from our new bond, that I couldn't tell what caused the sob in her words. "Are you okay? Did I hurt you?"

I leveraged myself higher to check her over, and she stopped me with a gentle brush of her palm across my cheek. "I'm absolutely amazing, and you could never hurt me." Her pupils were still dilated as she sucked in air. "That was intense and incredible. It's just… a lot. There was a point I never thought we'd make it here, but we beat the odds, Grouchy. We made the hard decisions, and you put in the work, and this is our reward."

She was my reward, and I would never take her for granted.

Determined to remain buried inside her, I slipped my hands under her, and pulled us up to stand together. She got on board with the plan quickly, wrapping her legs around my hips, and settling close.

We both moaned as she slid all the way to the base. I'd never felt this sensitive after sex before—I was hard and ready to go again. When it came to Emme, I doubted I'd ever get enough.

She rested her head against my shoulder, her arms wrapped tightly around me as I strode from the garage. She barely stirred, and I felt her exhaustion deep in her essence. Neither of us had slept well lately.

When I reached my room, I sat on the edge of the bed, and when she attempted to slide off, I held her tighter. "I know you're tired, darlin'," I murmured, "but I need to be inside you for a little longer. While we sleep." When she woke in the morning, she'd already be primed and ready for me.

Emme blinked, her lips parting as her tongue darted out to moisten them. Her cheeks pinkened, and she looked fucking adorable. "How'd I know you'd be the kinky one?" I smirked at that; she had no fucking idea. There wasn't any part of this shifter I didn't want to claim. "But yes, Finley Thornton, I would like to sleep with your massive cock buried inside me. However that works."

Well, okay then. My bear bellowed, and I really hoped I could keep from fucking her long enough for us to get some sleep.

When I sprawled onto my back, she parted her legs wider, letting them fall on either side of me, and her hips arched for me to slide deeper. She rested her head against my chest, and I pulsed with a need to fuck her, but her exhaustion won out. There'd be plenty of time to love her when we woke.

Palming the back of her head, I pressed kisses to her forehead and traced my fingers over her soft skin. Her eyes were closed, her beast settling beside my bear, all of us snuggled like a true pack.

I didn't expect to sleep as I savored this moment I'd dreamed about for a long time. But with Emme's scent surrounding me, and the comfort of being inside her, I drifted off into what would end up being the best sleep of my life.

If I hadn't believed in the goddess blessed scent matches—which I absolutely did—this moment alone would have proven me wrong.

Emme was my endgame, now and always.

CHAPTER 66

EMME

I woke aching and needy, and it wasn't until I felt the warm chest under my cheek that I remembered what had happened last night. Finley was sound asleep, his breaths even, and he looked relaxed in a way that was rarely visible on his face.

As if it was only in sleep his demons left him alone.

There was one body part that was far from relaxed though, and it was buried deep inside me, throbbing as if he'd been rock hard and teasing my inner walls all night.

A surge of pre-cum seeped from me, and I wasn't surprised to find that I was really fucking turned on by sleeping with him inside me. When he mentioned it last night, I'd almost come again just from the thought alone.

Finley and I bonded.

A month ago I'd never have believed it, but our beasts were curled up together, and I could feel his essence pulsing through the newest bite on my shoulder.

A sense of completeness followed, and with each member of my pack I bonded, my essence and energy strengthened.

Sex with Finley had been so fucking good, and I could still feel the way he touched and tasted every inch of my skin.

Unable to resist, I leaned forward and pressed my lips against his, the beard scratching nicely across my cheek. He didn't open his eyes, but his lips curved into a smile. His hand crept up to the back of my head, and he deepened the kiss as he rumbled, "Good morning, darlin'."

My core clenched around him, which drew a groan from the bear. "A very good morning."

Finley's eyes opened; the whiskey depths darker to match the need in his expression. He thrust deeper inside me, right when a loud knock echoed through the room.

"Fuck off," Finley growled, his gaze locking me in place.

He flexed his hips again, moving slower this time, and I really had been edged all night, because I could have come instantly. If the dilation of Finley's pupils were any indication, he wasn't far behind. He moved faster, his hands tightening on my ass to lift me higher for a better angle to slam up into me.

There was another knock, a much heavier one. "You need to get downstairs," Slade growled, sounding pissed off.

"Dragon or not," Finley snarled back, veins prominent on both sides of his neck as he drove into my body, "I'll beat the fuck out of you."

"Holy goddess of orgasms," I choked out, trying not to scream. It was impossible to stay quiet when this felt so damn good.

At this angle, Finley hit a spot that sent fireworks through my body.

"It's an emergency," Slade finally said with a sigh. "Two minutes or I'm coming in there to haul you both down myself. I don't care if you're naked and mid-fuck."

Finley didn't slow, choosing instead to reach between us and rub his thumb over my clit until I was hurled into an intense orgasm, finding the release I'd been chasing all night.

"Mate," Finley rumbled, drawing out the pleasure with long, slow thrusts. He closed his eyes as he came too, and when I collapsed against him I could hear our hearts pounding, loudly and in sync.

As I caught my breath, I had to ask: "Have you ever done that before? Slept inside a female?"

Why I asked when the very thought had me wanting to descend into a rage blackout, I'd never know. But ask I did. "Never, baby," he assured me, probably feeling my sudden rage through our new bond. "I've never even slept beside a female before, and in all honesty, I'm fairly sure we were both virgins before last night. As far as I'm concerned, there's been no one for either of us."

My anger faded under my amusement. "Well, Hunter and Kellan might argue the virgin thing, but I agree. There has never been anyone I cared to remember before you guys, and you're definitely the first to be inside me all night." I swallowed roughly. "Which I liked… a lot."

He closed his eyes briefly, and our bond was filled with his desire. "I fucking loved it," he growled. "We might need to keep testing the theory though. Just for like… every night for the rest of eternity."

This time I laughed. "Well, Kellan likes to sleep with his hand on my ass, and Hunter claims my thigh or throat, so maybe sleeping inside me will be your thing."

The satisfaction on his face was undeniable—he liked that idea.

It wasn't that we'd forgotten about Slade, but it did take a crack of magic against the house to haul me out of bed. I frantically searched through my bonds to ensure everyone was okay.

"Fuck, I guess that was what Slade was carrying on about?" Finley rumbled as he grabbed shorts and slipped them on. He handed me his shirt and I quickly buttoned up the flannel lengths.

"We need to move fast," I said, racing for the door with Finley right on my heels.

Before I hit the stairs, he wrapped his hands around my biceps and hauled me off my feet. "Me first," he growled, his bear rising.

There was no time to argue, so I stayed on his heels all the way down to where our pack stood in the entrance hall, blocking the door. I didn't notice the stranger in our midst until Hunter stepped aside and I found myself staring at a familiar face.

Well, if seeing a photo counted as familiar. It was the male from the grainy security footage Slade had showed me weeks ago. The shifter who stood outside my place of birth.

"You," I said, wrinkling my brow as I tried to figure out what was happening.

"Hello, daughter," he replied, his eyes meeting mine. His *icy* blue eyes.

Even as I froze, there was a part of me that accepted this information, as if I'd known all along.

"Excuse me," Slade growled, edging in front of me protectively. "Are you saying Emme is your biological daughter?"

The shifter nodded, crossing his arms over the plain linen shirt. His feet were bare, and his hair was long and unkept, as if he'd been living rough for a while, but there was a dominant wolf in his stare. He was an alpha.

A powerful one.

"Yes. She's my daughter," he continued, his voice harder as his impatience spilled out. "I have spent decades trying to keep her safe, but unfortunately the time for hiding or concealing powers has expired."

My head spun, and I couldn't quite figure out what he meant. "I don't understand," I finally murmured, peering around Slade to meet his disconcerting stare. "Why are you here? Why did you bring magic to our door?" I had no doubt that the surge I'd felt before was from him.

"My name is Constantine," he said, and I blinked at the name Talon had revealed to me. "I'm half shifter and half witch, and I'm going to need your help to save the world."

Slade snarled. "Shifters and witches can't breed. You lie."

Constantine shook his head. "Ah, if only that were true. We can breed, and we can wield magic. Just like your mate will be able to."

Your mate. He was talking about me. "Why would you need my help?" I asked, my anger rising toward this *male* who'd left me alone with my mother. "And why the hell would I help you after twenty-six years of absence?"

He never looked away, and I hated how much of myself I saw in his features. Even his hair was light blond with a hint of strawberry. "The witch you know as Jewels has enacted a curse. She's been planning this for years and was just waiting for the right time. A time where she could steal the energy of the alpha her family bonded decades ago, on the night of a blood moon." He paused, and I was reminded of the eerie glint to the sky last night. "Fletcher anticipated this of course, and he had her bound not to harm him. But that didn't stop others from striking the killing blow. Now we're all in danger."

All my worries and fears from yesterday raged to the forefront, and I knew this was the other side of the coin. We'd felt like we got off too easily, and clearly that had been for a reason.

"Danger from what?" Hunter asked, his wolf rising as his patience ran out. "What does this curse do?"

Constantine released a slow breath, still staring at me like he'd seen a ghost. "If we can't stop her by the strike of the next full moon, she will lock our beasts inside us and they'll be hers to control. We will never shift freely again. Even worse, all witches will be able to control the packs. For all intents and purposes, they will be the supreme alphas."

The silence was heavy as we processed this, and I knew that most shifters would die before submitting to a witch in such a way. We couldn't let this happen.

"You're a witch," I said, wishing my voice wasn't trembling. Hopefully he sensed it was ninety percent from anger. "Why should we trust you?"

He didn't hide from me in any way, his expression open. "You're also a witch, Emme. Which side of yourself do you feel most loyalty to?"

I didn't even have to think about it—the fact that there was any magic in my veins had me wanting to slice them open and bleed out. "My wolf. Always."

Constantine's smile held hints of fatigue. "Same, daughter. I have always felt the same, and I have a lot more to explain to you. Not that we have much time to waste."

With my pack closing in around me, I knew this was a pivotal turning point for the shifter cities. The point where we were once again at war, and this time we stood to lose autonomy over ourselves and our beasts.

As I stared into eyes that were mirrors of mine, I did the only thing I could and stepped back.

"Well, *Father*, it appears we have a common enemy. We accept your advice and help, and we will figure out how to take them down together."

Alpha energy raged around me, but no one countered my statement.

If what Constantine said was true, we had one chance to save ourselves and our packs. But it would require me to trust another parent. One who'd already let me down for most of my life.

Goddess help us all.

You can read the conclusion to the Shifter City Fated Mates in *A Bond of Trust* link. For more information on this and all future releases, follow me on Instagram, join my Facebook group The Nerd Herd, or subscribe to my newsletter.

WHAT TO READ NEXT...

I've had a lot of readers contacting me asking for what to read next. Try my complete (MF) romantasy series, the Shadow Beast Shifters. Rejected- Book 1

My father made a terrible mistake. One I'm left paying for.
  As a wolf shifter growing up in a strong pack, I should be living

my best life. But after my father tried to kill our leader, I'm labelled an outcast, traitor, less than dirt.

When I can't take pack life any longer, I run, but apparently they don't like losing their punching bag. Torin, the leader's son, drags me back before my first shift... a shift that will reveal my true mate. I never could have predicted who mine would be, but the moment my wolf looks upon him, I'm filled with hope for a brighter future.

Afterall, no one ever rejects their true mate, right?

Wrong. Very wrong.

When the wolves attack, my soul screams for vengeance, and somehow I touch the shadow world.

Somehow I bring him to our lands.

The Shadow Beast. Our shifter god. The devil himself.

Turns out being rejected by my mate was only the beginning.

*If you like sexy, dark paranormal romances, with humor, steam, action, a tough heroine and an antihero, this is for you. Rejected is full length (100k) words, is book one of three in Shadow Beast Shifters series, and ends on a cliffhanger. It's recommended for 18+ due to language and sexual situations.

ALSO BY JAYMIN EVE

Fallen Fae Gods (Dark Romantasy dragon shifter/fae 18+) (complete)

Book One: Gilded Wings

Book Two: Crimson Skies

Shadow Beast Shifters (Dark and Sexy wolf shifter/ god Romantasy 18+) (complete)

Book One: Rejected

Book Two: Reclaimed

Book Three: Reborn

Book Four: Deserted

Book Five: Compelled

Book Six: Glamoured

Bluebell House Duet

Book One: Forced Proximity

Book Two: Trauma Bonded (TBD)

Boys of Bellerose (Dark, RH rock star romance 18+)(complete)

Book One: Poison Roses

Book Two: Dirty Truths

Book Three: Shattered Dreams

Book Four: Beautiful Thorns

Demon Pack (PNR/Urban Fantasy 18+) (Complete)

Book One: Demon Pack

Book Two: Demon Pack Elimination

Book Three: Demon Pack Eternal

Supernatural Prison Trilogy (Complete UF series 17+)

Book One: Dragon Marked

Book Two: Dragon Mystics

Book Three: Dragon Mated

Book Four: Broken Compass

Book Five: Magical Compass

Book Six: Louis

Book Seven: Elemental Compass

Supernatural Academy (Complete Urban Fantasy/PNR 18+)

Year One

Year Two

Year Three

Royals of Arbon Academy (Dark, complete Contemporary Romance 18+)

Book One: Princess Ballot

Book Two: Playboy Princes

Book Three: Poison Throne

Titan's Saga (PNR/UF. Sexy and humorous 18+)

Book One: Releasing the Gods

Book Two: Wrath of the Gods

Book Three: Revenge of the Gods

Dark Legacy (Complete Dark Contemporary high school romance 18+)

Book One: Broken Wings

Book Two: Broken Trust

Book Three: Broken Legacy

Secret Keepers Series (Complete PNR/Urban Fantasy)

Book One: House of Darken

Book Two: House of Imperial

Book Three: House of Leights

Book Four: House of Royale

Storm Princess Saga (Complete High Fantasy 18+)

Book One: The Princess Must Die

Book Two: The Princess Must Strike

Book Three: The Princess Must Reign

Curse of the Gods Series (Complete Reverse Harem Fantasy 18+)

Book One: Trickery

Book Two: Persuasion

Book Three: Seduction

Book Four: Strength

Novella: Neutral

Book Five: Pain

NYC Mecca Series (Complete - UF series)

Book One: Queen Heir

Book Two: Queen Alpha

Book Three: Queen Fae

Book Four: Queen Mecca

A Walker Saga (Complete - YA Fantasy)

Book One: First World

Book Two: Spurn

Book Three: Crais

Book Four: Regali

Book Five: Nephilius

Book Six: Dronish

Book Seven: Earth

Hive Trilogy (Complete UF/PNR series)

Book One: Ash

Book Two: Anarchy

Book Three: Annihilate

Sinclair Stories (Standalone Contemporary Romance 18+)

Songbird

9 798988 115205